IN THIS RAIN

ALSO BY S. J. ROZAN

Absent Friends

IN THIS RAIN

S. J. ROZAN

Delacorte Press

IN THIS RAIN
A Delacorte Press Book / January 2007

Published by Bantam Dell
A Division of Random House, Inc.
New York, New York

Excerpt from "The Orphan of Zhao" by Stephin Merritt used by
permission of Gay and Loud Music.

Book design by Glen Edelstein

Delacorte Press is a registered trademark of Random House, Inc., and the
colophon is a trademark of Random House, Inc.

Library of Congress Cataloging-in-Publication Data

Rozan, S. J.
In this rain / S. J. Rozan.
p.   cm.
ISBN: 978-0-385-33804-2
1. New York (N.Y.)—Fiction. I. Title.
PS3568.O99 I6 2006
813.' 54 22   2006047405

Printed in the United States of America
Published simultaneously in Canada

www.bantamdell.com

BVG   10   9   8   7   6   5   4   3   2   1

To the memory of Jane Jacobs, who knew what cities are all about

For the support I can't do without: Steve Blier, Jim Russell, Hillary Brown, Max Rudin, Amy Schatz, Eve Rudin, Noah Rudin, Monty Freeman, Andrea Knutson, Susanna Bergtold, Jonathan Santlofer, Tom Savage, Reed Coleman, Jim Fusilli, Naomi Rand, and the great David Dubal.

For in-process critiques: Betsy Harding, Royal Huber, Jamie Scott, and Lawton Tootle.

For technical help: Nancy Ennis and her posse on law, language, and perfume. Pat Picciarelli on guns and ammo. T. Fleisher on plants and soil. The real Sandy Weiss on forensic engineering. And Grace Edwards, who, in the freezing cold and on a bad ankle, shared her Harlem with me.

For being always willing to listen, and able to see to the heart of the matter: Peter Blauner.

For reading and critiquing raggedy first drafts: Joe Wallace and, again, Nancy Ennis.

And Steve Axelrod, my agent, and Kate Miciak, my editor, for more reasons than I can count.

In this rain
I can't even see the garden.
—Stephin Merritt, *The Orphan of Zhao*

PROLOGUE

It surprised him, how light she was.

On reflection, he supposed he should have expected it. Doll-like delicacy had been one of her allures, along with silken skin and hair the color of sunshine. Though no child, she had a child's eagerness, a child's daring. She never balked, just giggled and plunged in. Her only request was not to be marked; she was vain about her beauty.

Though beauty like hers aged poorly. Sometimes, watching her sleep, he'd wondered what she'd do that dreadful morning when she woke withered and dry as an autumn leaf.

Now that day would never come.

Oh, he'd done her a favor, then? No, of course not. He'd done what he had to do, as always. That ability to see the necessary and carry it through was his singular gift. Though sometimes, particularly lately, particularly when hard choices leapt from nowhere as this one had, calling for decisive, irreversible action, he'd felt a wave of crushing weariness. He was exhausted by a lifetime of demands. Having to look ahead, outsmart, outmaneuver. Having to be better. Once, he'd been sure the view from the peak would be worth the climb. But slowly he'd come to know that the path he was on, littered with boulders, pitfalls, and traps, crept onward forever but never reached the top.

So he'd switched to a different route.

And it wasn't much longer until the climb would be behind him. What had happened tonight was an unforeseen stumble, and he'd done what he had to, to right himself. He regretted the need. But he couldn't risk her willful silliness endangering everything, not now.

He'd assumed she was asleep when the phone rang. He'd left the bedroom. But it should have occurred to him she might follow. It was her sport when he was on the phone to distract him with her tongue and her touch. He should have known.

Still, in the end, it was her fault. The flightiness he'd found so appealing was dangerous in the face of knowledge she never should have had.

"Ann Montgomery? She's a friend of mine!" she'd beamed, repeating a name she'd overheard him use. "I didn't know you knew her!" Then, pouting: "Wait. You're cheating on me with her, aren't you?"

He'd stroked her hair and whispered no, and she'd said, "You are! When do you see Ann? Daytime? Lunchtime?" It was a game to her, as everything was. "Oh, yes, you bad man! Okay, don't tell, see if I care. I'll ask Ann." He'd laughed with her and kissed her. And in his mind, run through his choices.

She might forget.

He might be able to buy her silence.

Or threaten her into it.

But only one choice could guarantee permanence. And way too much was at stake, now, for anything less than a guarantee.

Gently, he put her down. He gazed at her blanket-wrapped curves, then slammed the car's trunk. Rolling out into the pounding storm, he headed for a spot he knew where the river wrapped the island. He could ease her in and leave her there. No one would see, no one would take note, at this hour, in this rain.

CHAPTER 1

Sutton Place

Ann Montgomery sped up the Thruway thinking about Joe Cole's garden.

The old garden, the one at the house that wasn't Joe's anymore: she couldn't keep her mind off it. Its chaos of color and scent, shape and size. Its bright gleams and secret shadows.

How amazed she'd been, the first time she'd seen it. Joe had led her through the house, a shipshape sparseness that didn't surprise her, suiting well her new partner, so precise, methodical, soft-spoken, and civil. The wood floors and white walls stood in quiet contrast to the asphalt anarchy outside the front door; but outside the back she found a wild extravagance that stopped her, openmouthed. She'd turned to Joe to find out who the gardener was, himself or the thin-lipped Ellie who'd looked her up and down at the door. But Joe's eyes weren't on her. She followed his gaze to a vine loosed from its stake, a flower head faded but not yet cut, and she didn't have to ask.

Intense, powerful, this memory of Joe and his garden: but not enough to distract her from the highway or her location on it. She was coming up on the exit she'd never taken, that led to the college she'd never been near. There, the concert hall, to honor the man whose will endowed it, bore his name, which was the same as hers.

Ann added speed, pushing the car through curves. As she'd done for distraction and for buttressing since she was nine, she called Jen.

Not that Jen would answer. Sunday morning? Once, they'd been party animals together, dancing wherever the music was, drinking whatever was served, and though Ann these days preferred her own den, Jen was still joyfully on the prowl.

"Hey, get up," she said into the air, her cell phone on speaker in its car cradle. "The sun's shining. You remember the sun, I'm sure you've seen it. Guess where I'm going, win a prize. You have an hour till I'm there. Get on it, girl."

Brief, that phone message, but it took her past the college exit, this highway's only pitfall. The pounding storm that had started Friday night and hung stubbornly on through yesterday had left shiny roadside puddles and scrubbed the air clean. She loved to drive this road: her joy in it had led to guilt each time she'd taken it to the prison, to see Joe. She'd never told him how she'd looked forward to the wide sky (he could see a slice of sky from his cell), the rolling land (the prison's grounds sloped steeply), and the feel of soaring through it (he could go nowhere in the prison without permission). Odd, she thought, that though now he was out, she was heading up to see him along this same road.

It was her father who'd taught her to drive like this, fearlessly and fast, when she was too young to be legally behind any wheel, when, with her father beside her, she feared nothing. *Lean into it, Annie,* he'd say. *Be part of what's coming, not what is.* Her mother preferred the back seats of limos and cabs and to this day complained about Ann's driving.

"After what happened to your father I'd have thought you'd want to be more careful."

"Nothing 'happened' to him. You and that bastard, that's what happened to him," Ann always answered, because it was true and because it made her mother turn away, her lips pressed into a thin hard line.

Flying up the left lane, Ann was forced to slow behind a blue SUV cruising at sixty-five. She flashed the Boxster's lights, crept closer. Nothing. She gave the SUV the lights again and hit the horn.

He acted as though she weren't there.

Veering right, she moved alongside, held a moment, then shot ahead. As she swerved in front of him she slowed to sixty. His shiny bulk loomed in her mirrors. He blared his horn and flashed his lights.

She acted as though he weren't there.

Another blare, and he gunned the big engine; she had *Tosca* in the CD player but the blue SUV had so much power under that overgrown hood she could hear him anyway. He charged into the right lane; she sped up so he couldn't pass on her right. *Hell with you, you s.o.b.,* she thought, though she didn't know him, didn't know what was on his mind, any more than she knew what had been on her father's when he skidded his Ferrari through a curve and slammed into a stand of trees outside Zurich twenty years ago.

She was yanked back from that Swiss hillside by a cloud-splitting horn blast and a shriek of brakes. In her mirror a Toyota sprayed gravel as it peeled onto the shoulder. The blue SUV wove wildly back behind her, then steadied and slowed. The Toyota, which must have been tooling along in the right lane unseen by the SUV—God knew she hadn't seen it—squealed to a stop.

Ann held her breath and listened. Nothing: No scream of metal or crash of glass. She watched in the mirror as the Toyota edged back onto the road, its driver probably still cursing out the guy in the SUV. He had a right. Bastard almost killed him.

The bastard who'd been driving the legal limit in the proper lane until he'd pissed Ann Montgomery off.

Shit. Her hands pounded the steering wheel. She glanced back once more, then sped up and left them both behind.

The second act of *Tosca* came to an end. She tried to swallow away the sour taste in the back of her throat. No harm, no foul. And goddammit, maybe next time that SUV bastard would pull over when someone wanted to pass him.

No. He wouldn't. He'd never get it. The next time, he'd be the same jerk. People don't change.

Yes, they do, she argued with herself. A baby can distinguish between sounds that seem the same to adults, a skill that fades once a child starts talking and learns which sounds are useful. A person changes like that: by discarding pieces, littering the roadside with what he doesn't need.

If he's lucky, she thought, racing up the highway. Sometimes—a crumpled car, skid marks on slush—what a person throws away is something he really should have kept.

Harlem: 134th Street

T. D. Tilden leaned on the water tank steel and fired up a blunt. No way he was walking to the edge of the roof again, look down like some bitch wondering where her date got to. Not going to let this nigger get him stressed.

The first hit made him less jangly, like it always did. He looked at the clouds running across the sky. Truth was, sometimes he come up here just to hang. This roof, he could sit and draw, no one saying *Yo, lemme see that shit.* He drew the clouds, and the buildings, sometimes these right here or ones from his head, too, the ones he was going to build when he had his business. Sometimes he drew the flowers from the next-door backyard. He'd wave down at the old lady there and she'd always wave back.

No, not so bad up here. Just, this Kong fucker should have more respect. Making him wait every damn time, what was up with that? T.D., he liked to be on time. It showed you knew what business was and you wasn't scared of it.

T.D. watched the clouds some more and got lost in a movie in his head, him going off to his business. Setting his Kangol on, kissing Shamika goodbye. He could see her baby-don't-go smile, but he the man of the house. Got to take care of business.

Or maybe Shamika come with him. Shamika be his secretary at his office high up in some glass building, one of those buildings downtown he never been in yet but he been seeing them all his life past the roofs of Harlem. Shamika been working for Mr. Corrington for a year, so she knew all what secretaries got to know, typing, all that. Damn, he liked that idea. Shamika, sitting at a big desk, saying *Mr. Tilden too busy to talk to you now.*

That made him smile. Shamika wasn't like other girls T.D. knew. She didn't run around announcing his private business. He could talk to Shamika, like about this Kong asshole, he could brag on himself and he wouldn't find it coming back at him from the street.

Thinking about Kong messed up his mellow mood. The way Kong talked when he told T.D. what he wanted him to do next. Like T.D. was some retard, like what Kong wanted him to do was so hard. Even coming with those drawings that one time. Kong don't know about T.D., how he don't need drawings, how you tell T.D. something, he see the picture in his head. Well, how he gonna know? T.D. sure as hell ain't about to tell him, just like he ain't told Kong he know Kong wasn't the one drew those drawings. You could tell from how he explained them to T.D., someone else had to explain them to him.

Sure, job like this might be hard, if you was big and clumsy. That's why Kong didn't come with T.D. no more, T.D. knew that. Too busy, that was bullshit. The first job, Kong almost got their asses caught, all his noise clomping up that damn scaffold. Then taking out that drawing again, like T.D. wasn't about to remember? T.D. knew what the job was, he knew what to do. Truth was, he'd know which of them damn bolts to pull without ever seeing no drawing. It just worked that way with him. He knew what was holding what up, just by looking. But that was another thing he wasn't about to tell no one.

Anyhow, it was easier without Kong. T.D. was quick, he was quiet, he could slip in and out of places like a shadow. Sometimes, climbing on this water tank steel right here, he almost thought he could fly. Like if he let go the steel he'd swoop down close to the rooftops, for a second or two look like he was bound to hit something, but he'd soar back up again. Kong was lucky he found T.D., that was definite. Kong should be more grateful, not disrespect T.D. like he do.

The money wasn't that good, neither, now he thought about it. Maybe he'd tell Kong that. *These three jobs, they was*—what was it, when you was in the union? "Apprentice," that was the word—*they was apprentice jobs. Now you seen what I can do, you got to pay more.* Yeah, that's what he'd tell Kong. Serve the fucker right, always keep him waiting.

He jumped when the roof door creaked, but he made himself stay where he was. He watched Kong walk out onto the tar and look around. Big light-skinned fucker, head all shaved and shiny. Frowning around like this roof was his and better not be nothing on it he didn't like.

Kong found T.D., nodded, and said, "T.D., my man."

"I ain't your man." Fuck, this cocksucker was scratching on his last nerve.

Kong smiled. He didn't move, but it seemed like maybe he did. Like sometimes on the corner, you could feel the subway running uptown even if you couldn't hear it.

T.D. suddenly got cold. He blew out smoke and decided to quit. Didn't have to put up with this shit. There was lots of work out there for someone smart and quick as him. "You got what you owe me?"

"Sure, T.D." Kong walked toward him still smiling, like it was cool with him that T.D. was over by the tank and Kong had to do the work, walking over.

T.D. knew it wasn't cool but fuck if he was going to say anything. He finished off the blunt, ground out the fire, and pocketed the roach. "About the next job," he began. You got to give notice, he knew that. He wasn't in no union but he knew about being businesslike.

"No next job, T.D."

What shit was that? "The fuck you mean, no next job?" How could he give notice, walk out on this asshole, if there was no job to quit?

"There was a problem Friday, my man."

"I ain't your fucking man and there wasn't no fucking problem! Nobody saw me, heard me, nothing. The way that storm was pounding my ass, you lucky I ain't charged you double!"

"Guess you don't read the paper."

T.D.'s face heated up, like it always did when somebody talked about reading. His moms, always coming with *Reading is all that, you got to try, Thaddeus, you just got to try some.* He sneered, "Don't have no time for that shit."

Kong shrugged, like he knew it didn't have nothing to do with time but he didn't give a shit could T.D. read or not. "My people says there was a problem."

People? The asshole coming like he got people? He somebody else's people, no doubt about that. "Well, fuck," T.D. said. "Don't matter. Don't want no more of your shit, anyway."

"My shit? What shit is that?"

"I quit!" T.D. spoke too loud and too fast, like he seriously gave a damn. He told himself to chill. "I ain't working for you no more. I already decided that, before you come talking about *there was a problem.*" There, at least Kong would know T.D. got there first.

Kong nodded like T.D.'s moms did sometimes, like T.D. was right but it didn't matter. T.D.'s face went hot again.

"Just give me my fucking scratch," T.D. said.

"I don't think I got no more scratch for you, my man."

"The fuck? The fuck you mean, you don't think? You owe me!"

"You fucked up."

"Bullshit! Oh, bullshit, nigger! You pay me, or you be sorry."

"How you gonna make me sorry?" Kong asked this like he was just interested, like he was asking, *How you gonna light that blunt, you ain't got no matches?*

"How?" Damn, that was a good question. But from nowhere, T.D. had the answer. "Them drawings you give me. For the first job? The ones you say I better study, the ones you was so serious, I better give 'em back?"

"You gave 'em."

T.D. smiled big because Kong sounded confused. "I copied their asses."

"Say what?"

"I got copies. Zee-rocks."

Kong's face rippled into a grin. "Naw. You ain't got no copies. Why you gonna do that, make copies? I know you didn't."

"Did," said T.D. Damn, this was fun. "Because you was so serious. I thought, these things is so important, maybe I need to keep 'em." That wasn't the real answer. T.D. liked those drawings. They were like little pieces of blueprints. He was planning on studying them. Not the way Kong said, but to practice making lines like the ones in them. Maybe even work out the words. "You want them, you got to pay me. What you owe me, plus extra. For my trouble. I got to go get 'em for you."

"What, they far away?"

T.D. wasn't falling for that, no way. "Just show me the money, bro."

"Couldn't be no trouble, getting 'em. You just ask your moms, right? Nice lady, your moms. Got a skinny ass like you. Or Shamika. Bet Shamika got 'em. Hot bitch like that, I know I'd give her *my* copies."

"I ain't saying, cocksucker! You want 'em, you gotta pay me."

Kong nodded his huge head, up and down, up and down. "All I got to do? I pay you, you give me the copies? Awright." Kong smiled again. Because of the blunt, T.D. didn't see right away that this was a different kind of smile. He tipped to it just before Kong slammed him in the gut. As he crumpled, Kong's fist smashed his jaw. The clouds spun crazily. T.D. sucked in air, tried to stand himself up. Kong clamped onto his arm. T.D. tried to shake him off, to yell *What the fuck?* but he didn't have the breath and Kong didn't let go.

All this time Kong didn't say a word, even when he dragged T.D. to the edge of the roof, even when he picked him up, even when he tossed him off. *Whoa,* T.D. thought, tumbling through the air; and he tried to soar, swoop down near the rooftops and fly up again. For a second or two, he thought he had it.

Heart's Content

"Jesus, Joe. Say something."

But he could say nothing. Ann Montgomery stood at his door and he just stared.

A gust of wind streamed her unbuttoned coat and her hair behind her, giving her the look, against his dissolute front yard, of a stern Renaissance angel clipped from canvas and pasted on cheap pulp. She folded her arms as his silence stretched on. "Can I come in?"

"Ann," he said. Two steps behind as usual, Joe, he pointed out to himself with the smugness of self-disgust.

"No, Mother Cabrini." She swept past him as though he were not standing in the doorway, which he discovered he was not. As he always had done, he'd moved without thinking to accommodate Ann. "Joe." She faced him. "This is no way to live."

He looked around, trying to see the rented cabin with her eyes. Faded wallpaper, but fresh paint; battered furniture, but the scent of oil soap; vinegared-clean windows sheltered by pines, sunlight lying quietly on the grass beyond. He disagreed. It was a way to live.

Not a reason. But a way.

She plunked her bag onto his table and showed him his blank walls, his empty kitchen counter, his sofa, and the two kitchen chairs. Without asking, she turned and strode down the hall. He didn't follow and she briefly vanished; he imagined her leaning in the bedroom door, taking stock. Returning, she stood, hands on hips; clearly, to her mind, she'd made her point.

He asked, "How did you find me?"

"Find you?" She let her arms drop. "I called your parole officer. Earth to Joe Cole. Come in, Joe?"

Of course she had. It's what he'd have done if he were still on the job, and Ann was still on the job. She'd probably checked his employment status (a road crew with a contractor used to hiring men from the prison; they spread asphalt and crushed stone and he didn't give them keys to the office), his credit rating (it was still good), the status of his divorce (final), and the custody arrangements for Janet (Ellie had full custody; he could visit anytime but he had to call first).

Joe had to say something, so he said, "You want coffee?"

"You have two cups?"

"Just about." Actually he had three. The oddness of it had struck him when he'd taken the place: three coffee mugs, five plates, nine highball glasses, endless mismatched knives and forks, but just the two kitchen chairs.

All more than he needed.

He poured the coffee. Always, when he was here, he had coffee on. Even after he'd broken out the beer he'd leave the coffee cooking down and make a fresh pot when it thickened to sludge. In prison, coffee was strictly breakfast, lunch, and supper. Though if you behaved well and weren't locked down and had a few tokens in your pocket, and if the moody machine worked, and if the iron men weren't holding the day-room just to prove they could—if all these stars aligned for you, you could buy yourself a cup of cloudy muck that smelled like scorched newspaper and made even construction-trailer coffee taste good in memory.

Belatedly, handing Ann a mug, he recalled that she took cream and sugar, lots of both. He had neither. Then, as she lifted and sipped without comment, it also came back to him that she took great pride in her ability to improvise, and to adapt.

She said, "I need you."

Without an answer, Joe led her through the back door, out onto the porch.

Looking over the rail, Ann let her vision touch each part of the yard. "It's nice back here," she finally said, not in pleased surprise but grudging acknowledgment. Hearing her tone, watching her eyes, Joe could see her theories on who he'd become and how he lived now—suggested by his front yard, reinforced by his cabin—reeling from the blow of his garden.

City Hall

From a block away Charlie Barr spotted the news vans. He nudged Don Zalensky and pointed through the limo's darkened glass.

"Want to go in underneath?" asked Herb Washington, the mayor's bodyguard.

Charlie Barr ran his hand across his balding scalp. "No." He pressed the talk button, told the chauffeur—NYPD like the bodyguards—"The front, Frank."

The reporters on City Hall's cobbled drive engulfed the limo, shouting questions as the mayor and deputy mayor climbed out. Herb cleared a path up the steps, with the other bodyguard, Jimmy Ryan, behind.

"Anything to say to the victim's family, Mayor?"

"The DOI Commissioner and the IG for Buildings just went in—are they looking at someone in the Buildings Department?"

"What about it, Charlie? This a corruption problem?"

"Katz, *New York Times.* Could this be a result of your 'fewer rules and regs' program, Mayor?"

"Dolan Construction over again?"

The magic words. Charlie Barr stopped. He turned on the stairs and faced the reporters from mid-flight; he didn't want the above-it-all image he'd get at the top. Microphones strained toward him and the hubbub died down.

He looked the crowd over, nodding to some, making a point to acknowledge Hutchings from *The Amsterdam News.* "First," he said, "our deepest sympathy to Harriet Winston's family. In this terrible time, they're in our thoughts and prayers." He took a respectful pause. "But:

we have no reason to think that what happened at the Mott Haven development site was anything other than a tragic accident."

"Then why a Sunday morning meeting, Mayor?"

That was what-the-hell-was-his-name, the new guy from CBS. Charlie made eye contact. "Because I want to be *sure* we don't have a problem. And I want to be *damn* sure the city's doing everything we can."

"Denise Aday, NY1, Mayor. Three accidents in three weeks on that site, this last one fatal—you don't think that's a problem?"

"Of course it is. We're investigating the accident and the contractor. If there's any wrongdoing, we'll find it. We owe that to Harriet Winston. The question for this meeting is—and this is why the Department of Investigation is here—the question is, should the *city* have done anything differently?"

"Like more oversight?" Aday shot back. "Rules and regs?"

She never quit, Charlie would give her that.

"Edgar Westermann thinks something's not kosher," shouted someone at the back. "You want to say anything about that?"

Yeah, I'd say it's a funny choice of words, Charlie thought; but this was no time for smiling. "I saw his press conference," he said. "The Manhattan Borough President is entitled to think whatever he wants."

"Do you agree?"

"I'd rather have the facts before I make a statement like that. I'm about to meet with the Commissioners. I'll fill you in later. Come back at two."

He turned and double-timed the steps, Don hurrying beside him, Washington and Ryan keeping the shouting reporters at bay. Just before they hit the doors someone behind them yelled out, "Walter Glybenhall," but the mayor didn't turn around.

"You just set up a two o'clock press conference." Don, a heavy smoker, wheezed as they pushed into the City Hall lobby. "You want Sue Trowbridge here?"

"No, I'll handle it. But she might need to do a press release later. What's that new guy's name from CBS?"

"Bryon Quertermous."

"Spell it?"

Don shrugged. He stepped aside and waited for the mayor to walk before him into the metal detector.

Charlie swept through without a beep. He was the mayor; he could go around the thing and save the guards embarrassment every time he forgot to take off his watch and they had to wand him. But No Exceptions was his policy, and as long as he followed it none of the Commissioners or Councilmembers could get on their high horses. And No Exceptions also meant No Complaining about favoritism or its in-fashion flip side, racial profiling. Dodging that headache was well worth the inconvenience of repocketing his change.

They trotted up the stairs. Don hated the stairs and Charlie knew it, but not as much as he himself hated being squashed in the private elevator with Don and the bodyguards: too many people in too small a space, standing still.

As they hit the second floor, Don clamped his cell phone to one ear and stuck a finger in the other. At the door to Charlie's private office Don said, "I'll get back," and thumbed the phone off. The bodyguards gave the inner office a once-over, then retreated to the anteroom, closing the door.

"Sue's standing by," Don told Charlie.

"Good. Sorry about the stairs."

"Why should today be any different?" Don jacked a Camel, shoved the pack back in his pocket. "Is it going to be a problem?"

"Is what?"

"The press digging into Three Star."

"It's already a problem. I don't know what the hell Walter's thinking. I can't afford this. *He* can't afford this." Charlie pulled a contraband ashtray from a drawer—smoking was illegal in New York office buildings, an initiative the mayor, as a Councilmember, had co-sponsored—and clattered it to the desk.

"I don't think what Walter Glybenhall's thinking is the problem." Don pocketed his lighter and picked up the ashtray.

"Then he's not thinking. Walter wants to prove Three Star's a community-friendly developer, this is a hell of a way to go about it."

"Unless it's not his fault. Unless someone's doing these things to Three Star on purpose."

"Oh, Christ, Don, you too? Walter tried to sell me that. Buildings doesn't see it and DOI doesn't see it. Now NYPD's on it and they don't see it either." Charlie took off his jacket. "And you know I've got a meeting with Ford Corrington tomorrow that he set up two weeks ago? Christ, what timing. I think you'd better be here."

"I was planning on it."

"But no one else. You, me, them. Not Real Property, not Planning. We'll say it's too early for that. We'll say I wanted a chance to hear them out without political distractions."

"You that sure it's about Block A?"

"I don't know what it's about. I can't turn those people down, so what the hell's the difference what it's about?"

"You didn't ask?"

"They'd think I was deciding to see them or not based on the agenda."

"Because maybe Serita should be there."

Charlie smoothed his tie. "No. It's just a meeting. Might not be a race issue."

"It always is with Corrington."

"Well, yeah. But two deputy mayors, suddenly it's a big deal. And if I get Serita here without a specific agenda, it looks like I think I need a translator just to talk to them."

"Whatever it is, especially if it's Block A, they'll bring up Mott Haven and Three Star. White developers in minority neighborhoods. The city not doing enough to protect families. Promises made after Dolan Construction three years ago, now this."

"Stop, I get it."

"They might hold a press conference after the meeting, too. Edgar Westermann didn't let Corrington speak at his, yesterday."

"I was surprised Edgar let Ford in the room. You think they have a truce?"

"Maybe just temporary, for the cameras, for a united front on Mott Haven."

"To make up for Dolan Construction?"

"When Westermann was with you and Corrington couldn't stand it?"

"You blame him? I was suspicious of myself when I found out Edgar agreed with me. Do we get points for bringing them together now? 'Incompetence in City Administration Helps Black Leaders Bury the Hatchet'?"

Don blew out smoke, said nothing.

"I didn't think so," said Charlie. "Well, a press conference is Corrington's constitutional right. But he won't do it if we don't give him anything to say."

"How are you going to arrange that?"

"I'm going to pray to God for a miracle."

"That works for you?"

"God helps those who help themselves. I'm praying that whatever Ford Corrington wants, I can give him. Shit, Don, if they're coming to demand a piece of the Block A pie, what's the big deal? We'll make sure they get space, they'll do God's work in it, everyone'll be happy."

"Except Walter Glybenhall."

"Sounds like poetic justice to me, for Walter to have Corrington under his nose. Anyway, it's a small enough price for him to pay." The mayor looked at his watch. "But that's tomorrow. Right now, it's showtime. Go on in, give me a minute."

"Want me to go from the hall, so you can make an entrance from here?"

"Good idea. Don?"

"What?"

The mayor pointed to Don's cigarette. Don looked sadly at the half-unsmoked butt, took a long pull, and mashed it out.

Charlie rolled up his sleeves, gave Don time to make it to the conference room, greet the others, mix up his coffee, and sit. He timed another two minutes for small talk. Then he took a breath and yanked open his private connecting door.

Harlem: Frederick Douglass Boulevard

A siren started far off, swelled, and then cut out before Ford Corrington rounded the corner. But that didn't mean silence. Along this boulevard, street noises never stopped: airbrakes on the buses, thump of car stereos, rumbling subway. Kids shouting, laughing. And always the sirens: ambulance, police. Today, also, church bells collecting the flocks.

Ford was on his way to Tree of Life A.M.E., first time this month. He didn't always make it to church on Sunday. Sometimes he was needed at a retreat; in a conference; or on a park bench with some kid. Or else at a benefit breakfast, nibbling on croissants with silk-suited funders. Ford saw all that as the Lord's business. If it was important to Him for Ford to be in church, He'd arrange for it.

The wind blew hard this bright morning, snapping awnings and kicking up grit. It carried the hot-griddle smell of pork patties from Junior K's, on this block thirty years—long before Ford came to Harlem—and the scent of lattes from C'AFrica, open six weeks ago with its scrollwork sidewalk tables. Next to the coffeehouse, graceful hats of straw, silk, and feathers perched in the window of Morris John's shop. The store was closed but Ford would be seeing Morris—and some of his creations—in church.

Through the sharp sunlight the five-year-old Bowen twins ran toward him giggling, Avery chasing Averne. "You stop at the corner!" Ford called as they dashed past. The twins turned at the boom of his voice, laughed, and waved. Gloria Bowen, their grandmother, followed after them.

"Morning, Mr. Corrington."

"Miz Bowen. How's the hip today?"

She smiled ruefully. "Getting old quicker than the rest of me."

"Then it must still be younger than springtime."

"Mr. Corrington! You need to be ashamed, lying on the Lord's day."

"I never lie. Avery! Take hold of Averne's hand and wait for your grandma."

The boy recoiled as though his sister's hand were covered in slime, but then he grabbed it and the two of them started swinging their arms to the skies.

"Look how he listen to you!" Gloria Bowen said. "That boy don't never mind me."

"You don't scare him enough."

She gave him a sharp sideways look. "You ain't never scared a child in your life."

"That's the truth." Ford sighed, as though acknowledging a failing. "But I keep trying." He grinned, pressed her hand, and walked on.

At 134th he turned off the avenue and felt his grin fade. An ambulance — must be the siren he'd heard — was pulled half on the sidewalk. A double-parked police car squeezed traffic into a single inching lane. Behind yellow tape strung from light pole to tree to front stoop railing, a crowd milled uneasily. On the sidewalk a blanket covered an unmistakable form.

"Asher," Ford said to a man he knew. "What happened here?"

Asher Owen turned, his dreadlocks swaying. "Ford, mon." He shook Ford's hand. "Sad business surely." He gestured to the blanket. "This Thaddeus Tilden."

"T.D.?" A knot tensed in Ford's stomach.

"He fall from th' roof, or out window. Jump, some say."

"Oh, Lord."

"He a Garden Project kid?"

"Art classes, when he was little," Ford nodded. "And woodshop. He liked to build things." Ford remembered a foot-high, crooked skyscraper, blue squares for windows painted on the sides. "But he stopped coming around years ago. Had trouble in school, finally dropped out. His mother's been real worried for him."

"Knew him, too," Asher said. "Don't seem like jumpin' his style. Hard face and fearsomeness be more like."

Asher, who as far as Ford knew feared no one and so had no reason to act fearsome, spoke sadly.

"T.D. wanted to be a player," Ford said. "That's how he saw himself. A superstar of the street."

"He was that?"

"No, and never would have been. Not cold enough."

A police photographer ducked under the tape, spoke to the detective in charge, then pulled back the blanket. T. D. Tilden finally got his close-ups.

In the sunshine, lying motionless, the boy looked young and small. He'd never been handsome, T.D., but he'd had a light in his face. Ford remembered him at seven, at eight, waving his hands around to explain things. Even with his reading problem, they'd thought, for a while, they'd be able to reach him. But he'd slipped away. That was so many of them. So many slipped away. Ford closed his eyes and prayed: *Lord, here's another child you've called. Show him more love when he gets home than we were able to do while we had him with us here.*

He opened his eyes when he heard a stuttering: running footsteps in shoes not meant for speed. A thin form in springtime green pushed into the crowd, struggled to get past a policeman's navy blue. Ford slipped around Asher. "She's the mother. Let her through," he told the cop, though he had no authority here. The cop looked to the lead detective, a stocky black man, who saw Ford and nodded. His arm protectively around Sarah Andersen's shoulder, Ford lifted the tape and brought the boy's mother to where T.D.'s body lay. Sarah whimpered and sank to her knees, reaching for T.D.'s hand. "I'm sorry, ma'am," the photographer said. "I have to ask you not to touch anything."

"It's my baby." Sarah spoke in a tiny voice, looking up at the man as though an explanation would change his mind.

"Tom. A minute?" Ford, crouching beside Sarah, spoke to the detective, who motioned the photographer away. Sarah folded her son's hand in her own thin fingers. Ford kept his arm around her, feeling the tightening, waiting. Finally, as though a string were cut, she slumped against him and started to sob. He gave her a few minutes, then pulled her gently to her feet. She didn't resist. To the detective, he whispered, "Thanks."

The crowd rearranged itself to let them pass. A neighbor wordlessly held out Sarah's straw hat, lost in her frantic dash from church to home, found and returned by someone who could give her nothing else. Ford started with Sarah up her building's stoop. They'd reached the top when he was stopped by the slap of more hurrying footsteps, whose urgency rang with a different purpose. He looked over his shoulder, to see a portly Sunday-suited man quick-walking up the block.

To the neighbor with Sarah's hat, Ford said, "See her upstairs, will you?" The woman nodded quickly, glad of a task to do, and steered Sarah inside. Ford took the stoop steps fast, reached the sidewalk as Edgar Westermann came to a halt at the crime-scene tape.

Heart's Content

Joe had first seen this place in early March, three weeks and three days after he'd gotten out (counting the days still a habit with him then). The Realtor, praising expansively and stepping gingerly, led him along the overgrown path, past the mailbox where an amateurishly carved plank reading "Heart's Content" dangled from a single nail, to the warped front door. "Furnished, ready to go, coat of paint and it's a gem . . ." The front yard was a narrow, exhausted jangle; and in the musty interior everything sagged. But once on the back porch, Joe had blocked out the Realtor's babbling (a valuable skill to an investigator, an invaluable one to a convict). His eyes wandered the wide, hidden yard, encircled by a rocky wooded ridge on two sides, sloping on the third to a creek he could hear but not see. He'd paid attention to the angle of the sun, smelled the damp earth, felt the direction of the breeze. He'd signed the lease that afternoon.

The relieved Realtor asked nothing beyond a deposit and the first month's rent; not demanding, as he might have, character references or previous address. Joe was handed the keys five days later, after his check cleared. There was no problem with that. Ellie had been more than fair, splitting their joint bank account, giving him what was left from the sale of the house after she'd bought the condo: a new home in a different town in a different state, where as long as Janet's answer to "Where's your dad?" was a shrug and "They're divorced," no child would know enough to shriek, "He's in jail!" and no adult would smile with superior sympathy.

After his conviction, their bank accounts had been frozen as New

York State, in its outrage, tried to seize his ill-gotten gains. But their audit found none. The charges against him had been manslaughter, reckless endangerment, and criminal facilitation, with corruption suggested by the prosecution as an explanation but never proved.

And never true. Though sometimes Joe found himself wishing it had been. If venality and greed had led him to disaster, he would have understood. The path he'd followed was much more bewildering.

Waiting for the check to clear, he'd driven each day to the cabin in his rattling pickup. With a thermos of coffee he sat on the back porch in the thin light of waning winter. Trespassing; but who would notice him? The owner lived many states away, and the Realtor was clearly embarrassed to be connected with this disregarded place. The neighbors were kept from sight of the rear yard by the height of the ridge and the slope to the stream.

Sitting, he'd studied how the sun slid over the encircling trees, how the trees' black shadows traveled across the yard, how the broad, uncared-for yard swelled in some places and fell in others. He'd noted where rocks broke the earth, where water ponded, where soil looked good.

On the fifth day, after the Realtor's enthusiastic call ("Green light!"), he'd driven into town. He'd loaded the truck bed with shrubs and perennials—lilac, peony, privet, and calendula—and bulbs you could count on: allium, iris. In the usual course of things—a course that ran through his former life, though not through this one—he'd have waited out the first round of seasons, to understand the shape and substance of the land, of whatever garden was already in it. Watching as branches leafed and blossoms inched forth, he'd have incorporated the surprises, delights, and disappointments he'd inherited into the work he was planning. That's how he'd done it with the house he and Ellie bought when Janet was born, and he'd been rewarded with ragged masses of tulips in April, and a fragrant white wisteria that perfumed the air by the kitchen window all summer.

But he couldn't wait now. For two and a half years, he'd done nothing but wait.

It occurred to him as he sweated in the chill wind, digging and covering, staking and tamping, that he'd chosen plants that needed time. Some wouldn't bloom this year; it was too late. Some would, but tentatively, for practice. It would be next year, even the year after, before most of what he'd put in would feel comfortable enough to settle and unfurl. And some time after that until the colors, shapes, and scents would prove, or change, the pictures he'd woven in his mind of what this place could be.

Now it was early June. Leaves, stalks, buds, and blooms luxuriated, stretching up and out. Colors glowed and perfume swirled on a sun-warmed breeze. Sharp or soft, fragile or plump, everything was exuberant, boisterous with release.

And here was Ann, sitting beside him, telling him she needed him.

Harlem: State Office Building

"What happened here?" Edgar Westermann's chest rose and fell with his attempt to recover his breath, but his voice was loud and fierce. He scanned the scene. Tom Underhill seemed to be in charge. A good man, Underhill, even if he did buy into a system that remained way overbalanced in favor of white justice. Still, it had taken a lot of years and some real knuckle-busters to get black detectives promoted in numbers and stationed in the community, and having men like Underhill around was better than the alternative.

Edgar pushed through the usual New York disaster crowd, dressed incongruously well for rubbernecking because it was Sunday in Harlem. He'd almost reached the front when he heard a familiar voice: "Edgar, not now."

Ford Corrington. Should have known. Teeth instantly on edge, Edgar looked around for Corrington, and barked. "They tell me T. D. Tilden was killed! What the hell you mean, 'not now'?" He turned his back on Corrington. "Tom Underhill!"

"Yes, Mr. Westermann?" The detective faced Edgar across the yellow tape.

"What happened to this boy?"

"We don't know, sir."

"You don't *know*? Another black child lies dead on a city street and all the police can tell me is, you don't know?"

"He fell to his death. From the roof, probably. That's as much as we know."

"Was he alone? Was there foul play? Does the roof have railings?

What are conditions up there, did anyone think to check? Who's the landlord—this another city-owned slum?"

"We'll answer all those questions in good time, Mr. Westermann."

"*In good time?* Is that what you said to the family of the young woman whose body was found in the East River this morning? Or did you say 'Yessir, yessir, we're on it' because she was white?"

"With respect, sir, you're not this young man's family. And I'd ask how you know about that young woman—"

"And I'd tell you I keep track of what happens in Harlem!"

"—and I know that and that's why I'm not asking. That victim's still unidentified and yessir, we're working on it and yessir, we're working on this, too. Though occasionally we have to stop to respond to the questions of curious civilians."

"*Curious civilians?*"

"Yessir, and thank you for your concern. Now, if I could—"

Dismiss Edgar Westermann? I don't think so. "This boy's people—have they been notified? Have they been considered at all?"

"His mama's upstairs." From behind Edgar, Ford Corrington's voice came quietly. "I'd be obliged if you'd leave her be."

"*You'd be*—" Edgar stopped. Deliberately, he spoke again to Underhill. "Detective, Harlem is watching you. Harlem wants results!" He gave Underhill a glare, then faced Corrington. "Ford. I know you're showing good Christian concern, and I'm sure the boy's family appreciates it. Now I believe I'll go on up and offer my condolences, and any help the Borough President's Office can provide."

Corrington moved left a step or two, putting himself between Edgar and the building's stoop. "Not now," he repeated. "Sarah will be receiving later, I'm sure. Condition she's in now, she wouldn't be able to appreciate your visit anyhow."

Edgar eyed Corrington, not fooled but no fool, either. If he and Corrington got into a shoving match here, they'd both come out looking like natural-born halfwits. Which, he knew from experience, wouldn't bother Corrington at all.

It had been sixteen years since Ford Corrington had burst on the scene, the Harvard man ready to set the world on fire, to sweep prejudice, racism, and disrespect from the streets of Harlem. Edgar Westermann had been in public life nearly two decades by then, working his painstaking, compromising way from district leader to City Councilmember to Borough President, trading votes and influence for playground repairs, a reopened firehouse, a dental clinic. He'd been trying to tell himself for years now that Corrington was dancing the same dance, just with a different set of steps.

From the ambulance, the EMTs rattled out a gurney. The crowd's attention swiveled that way. While Edgar stood weighing his choices, the NY1 News van rocketed around the corner. A cameraman jumped out and a reporter followed. Edgar turned back to Corrington. "You give Ms. Andersen my sympathy, and tell her I'll be up as soon as she's receiving." Having discounted Corrington into a messenger, he spun on his heel and pushed back through the crowd to go meet the media.

City Hall

The mayor swept a glance over the conference room. "Where's Virginia?" he barked.

"She's aware of the meeting, Charlie." Lena L'Nore, Charlie's personal assistant since his Council days, spoke calmly. Lena was efficient, fiercely loyal, smooth with the press, and a hell of a looker. In fact, unless you counted as silly the faux-African spelling of her name, which the mayor would never be caught doing, she had no flaws.

The mayor was a flawed man himself and the first to admit it. Lena's perfection could get on his nerves. He snapped, "That wasn't the question."

Lena did no more than raise an eyebrow. The mayor walked around her, poured himself coffee, and dropped into his chair. He always got his own coffee. He didn't want to be accused of demeaning Lena's professionalism. Not that she'd ever said a word, but years ago he'd overheard other Councilmembers' secretaries muttering about their bosses. So he'd told Lena to knock off the coffee, she had better things to do. And for the price of a trip to the kitchenette, Councilmember Charlie Barr got known as a guy who respected women and the working class.

Now, from the head of the table, Mayor Charlie Barr moved his glare around the room.

Police Commissioner John Finn, large and ruddy, sat beside Lena, with another red-faced Irishman next to him: Ted O'Hare, the Chief of—what? Detectives? Department? Operations? Oh, hell, what did it matter? Everybody here had brought backup, and O'Hare was the guy Finn had chosen to hold his coat.

Les Farrell, Buildings Department Borough Superintendent for the Bronx, sat between O'Hare and Virginia McFee's empty chair. Heavy and shaggily balding, Farrell was career Buildings Department. He'd come up through inspector, plan examiner, and all the ranks of Deputy Superintendent, and clearly wasn't used to meetings where you had to wear a tie. The mayor impaled Farrell on his stare. Farrell swallowed and watched his own meaty hands play with a pen. "Said she'd be here."

Down at the end of the table, Greg Lowry from DOI ripped a sugar packet open and said reasonably, "She's got five minutes, Charlie."

The clock ticked off another minute. "Four," Charlie said. That was a damn technicality, though. All his people knew he wanted them in the room well before meeting time, so the jawing and coffee stirring would be done with when he got there. For him to beat one of them here was a problem, Sunday be damned.

The mayor swung his glare down to Greg Lowry but it bounced right off. Lowry's reasonableness, like Lena's perfection, could be irritating as hell. Clearly it grated on Lowry's boss, DOI Commissioner Mark Shapiro. Shapiro sat to Lowry's right, one chair closer to the mayor, wearing his usual frown.

Three years ago, when Charlie cleaned house after the Dolan Construction disaster, a half-dozen hats had been tossed in the ring for the Commissioner's job at the Department of Investigation. Lowry, then DOI's Inspector General for Sanitation, had thrown his first. Charlie had tapped Shapiro because putting a Jew in that job at that moment, like putting a black woman in Virginia's spot, had been politically critical. But under other circumstances he'd have chosen Greg Lowry. Lowry was Charlie's type, a quick thinker not afraid to take chances. Charlie told Shapiro to move Lowry from Sanitation to Buildings, make him Inspector General there. He knew Shapiro didn't like it and Lowry wasn't thrilled: to him it was a consolation prize. But Charlie also knew there'd be a spotlight on that job and Lowry could handle heat. After all, he'd spent pretty much his whole DOI career at Sanitation and come up smelling like a rose.

That was funny, and another time, Charlie would have snickered. Right now he was too pissed off.

The door opened and Virginia McFee strode into the room. "Sorry," she said. "Bad traffic." *On Sunday?* Charlie thought. Virginia had the smarts not to smile, but he caught her swapping a look with Lena. They made allies of each other, black women, or tried to. But everyone did the same, especially in New York. Jews, Latinos, Italians, Irish. No matter which side of an issue people were on, that connection could override logic and loyalty. If Charlie and Virginia were on a sinking ship and Lena had just one life preserver, she might very well toss it to Virginia.

And he didn't suppose he'd blame her. It was natural, sticking to your own kind. *Home is where, when you have to go there, they have to take you in.* Who the hell said that? Mark Twain? Robert Frost? Didn't matter: It was just a good thing to remember, about your own people and everyone else's.

Sitting, Virginia McFee took a Mont Blanc from her purse and held it poised. She looked expectantly at Charlie. The room was silent. Charlie, one eye on her and one on the clock, sat motionless until precisely ten.

Then he pounced: "Virginia, what the hell is going on?"

"I don't know that anything's going on, Charlie."

"Don't tell me you don't know. If nothing's going on, prove it. If there is something, you'd better stop it. We can't afford to go through this again."

"Nothing is a hard thing to prove."

"You expect me to say that to the press? Or do you want to?"

No answer.

Charlie spoke to them all. "You people were put in place after Dolan Construction so we could look New Yorkers in the eye and tell them that wouldn't happen again. That it's safe to walk past a construction site because we have departments and agencies whose job is to *keep* it safe. Then all of a sudden a scaffold collapses and five men are laid up. We got spontaneous combustion in a trailer and I'm visiting a firefighter in the hospital. Now we get a goddamn storm, bricks fly off a roof and suddenly three little kids are orphans! *What the hell happened?*"

He backed off slightly, a strategic moderation. "I hope and pray these were unrelated accidents, Virginia, of a type your inspectors couldn't have prevented. Everyone hopes that. But you *have to* be able to prove it."

"Exactly how, Charlie?"

If she were a white man, he'd have reamed her out for her tone alone. Instead, in a voice of immense forbearance, he said, "For one thing, you can prove your people went to the site. And if they found anything, they'd damn well better have gone back and reinspected. I want a mile-long paper trail."

McFee looked pointedly at Farrell. Farrell's eyes widened, as though it hadn't occurred to him he'd be asked to speak.

"Since . . ." Farrell cleared his throat and started again. "Since the scaffold collapse two weeks ago, we've had inspectors on the Three Star site every day."

"Why? You spot something wrong?"

"No," Virginia McFee interposed. "That collapse looks like just an accident to us. But we know how seriously you take construction site safety, Mayor."

"Go on, Mr. Farrell," Charlie snapped.

"We sent three different guys," Farrell said. "Rotating, so in case, you know? Found a couple things, routine. Point is, nothing related to the accidents."

"Or nothing they reported." That was Mark Shapiro, scowling.

Farrell shrugged. "Could be. But that trailer fire, we don't inspect the trailers anyway, so who knows? And this brick thing . . ." He wiped his mouth with his thick fingers. "Storm came up Friday night. Some idiot might have put those loose bricks on the tarp as just, like, insurance, before they left. The inspector who saw that tarp earlier in the week swears it was weighed down with strapped bricks."

"Strapped?" asked Charlie for the record, though he knew what it meant.

Farrell's hand made a circle. "Steel straps around the pallet. If those bricks was piled on a pallet, even without a strap, they'd never have flown off like that."

Charlie blew out a breath. "So what you're telling us, Mr. Farrell, is that your men went there, you have reports, there was nothing wrong?"

Farrell nodded.

Virginia McFee said, "Well, Charlie, that's what you wanted: nothing."

Charlie looked deliberately away, down the table to his DOI Commissioner. "Mark?"

Grimly, as though it were a matter of life and death—and it had been for Harriet Winston, Charlie reminded himself, and could be politically for him—Mark Shapiro said, "We're doing new background checks on the inspectors."

"Please tell me those were done *when* these guys were hired."

"Of course they were. And they checked out. But people change."

Charlie had his own theory about that but this wasn't the time. "What angles are you looking at?"

"A number," said Shapiro. "One possibility, and the best, would be if these were three unrelated, unpreventable, purely coincidental accidents. Nothing the inspectors should have found."

Out of the corner of his eye the mayor saw a tiny triumphant smile flicker on Virginia McFee's lips, as though by stating this possibility Shapiro had proved it.

"Or?" he pressed.

"Accidents, but preventable if the inspectors had been doing their jobs. Or," Shapiro said, "not accidents, but preventable: sabotage the inspectors missed, because they were born stupid or because they were paid to be."

"That's the theory the developer's pushing," Charlie said.

"Of course."

"But who?" Charlie demanded. "Why? A union beef?"

"I don't know. And frankly that theory's least likely. But it's one of those nothings I'd like to be able to prove."

Virginia McFee shot daggers at Shapiro when he said that. The mayor wondered if she knew that the filler pump on her Mont Blanc could, if pressed right, squirt ink across the table and all over Shapiro's white shirt.

Charlie turned to the NYPD guys. "From your point of view?"

Police Commissioner John Finn's voice was the kind of soft rumble that can be heard over every other sound on a crowded street. "Well, of course," he said, "if it turns out they're just accidents—preventable or otherwise—it won't be NYPD's territory. Right now, because the Winston woman died and foul play's still a possibility, we're investigating. Luis Perez from Bronx Homicide is the lead. He can liaise with DOI's people."

Shapiro nodded. He didn't offer the name of DOI's lead investigator in return. Why? Charlie wondered, hoping he wasn't seeing the beginning of a pissing match between Shapiro and Finn.

"Mayor?"

That was Greg Lowry. Charlie turned to him. "Mr. Lowry?"

"Just one thing, Mayor. I'd like DOI to look into the site crews, too."

"Three Star's people? It's a little outside DOI's jurisdiction. What are you thinking?"

"I'm thinking, if there's anything to find, it would be good if everyone saw DOI in on finding it."

Charlie nodded. "John? You have any objections?"

"No, of course not," said Finn, though of course he did and of course Charlie knew it. There'd be pissing and moaning at One Police Plaza when Finn sent the order down the line.

"Okay, do it," Charlie told Lowry. "Stop frowning, Mark. Think outside the box. Your IG just had a good idea and your mandate is whatever I say it is. All right, people." He stood and peered down the table. The possibilities Shapiro had articulated—three accidents, preventable or otherwise; or sabotage—weren't new. Charlie had thought of them all, and doubtless so had everyone else. But they'd had to be spoken aloud. They'd had to be on the record.

Now they were.

"This is it," he said. "We went through bullshit like this three years ago and it almost brought us down. That's not going to happen again. I have a press conference in four hours and I want to have something to say. I can tell them we're looking into this tragic death but we'd damn well better be. If there's anything to find and the *Post* finds it first, every single one of you can kiss his—or *her*—ass goodbye."

Turning his back on the meeting, he strode through the door to his office and pulled it closed behind him.

If there was anything Charlie Barr had down, it was how to make an entrance and an exit.

Heart's Content

Ann's voice flared: "Why the hell didn't you tell me when you were getting out?"

Joe turned to her. The blue of Ann's eyes was unequal, right a shade darker than left; but unless you were bold enough to stare straight into them—as not many men were—you'd think you'd imagined it. You'd think the oddness was in you, not Ann.

"Shit, Ann," he said. He sipped his coffee, strong and bitter. "Maybe because I didn't want you to know?"

"You think that's okay? After all this?"

All what?

Did she mean the icy moment, three years ago, when—from her—he'd learned about the shoring collapse on the Dolan Construction site and the death of little Ashley Moss: the moment that instantly and forever cut his life into *before* and *after*?

Or did she mean the shock of his arrest, the surreality of his trial, the sinking certainty of his conviction?

Or his divorce, uncontested but never for an instant unregretted? The ceaseless edginess, the round-the-clock clamor of the cellblock? The calendar days crossed off, each with a slow, identical line?

Of all that, what could she mean?

Joe Cole wasn't the Buildings Department inspector who'd taken cash to overlook bad shoring, or the Dolan Construction site super who'd paid that bribe. Those men, Larry Manelli and Sonny O'Doul, were also arrested. They were charged and convicted in hasty plea bargains: their lawyers saw the planets aligning. Both were headed for prison as Joe's trial began.

But they weren't enough. The public was outraged and the mayor was out for blood. He held a press conference to prove it. Surrounded by Commissioners and introduced, in a rare moment of civic unity, by Manhattan Borough President Edgar Westermann, the mayor spoke.

"City agencies will *not* continue to show citizens this kind of deadly disrespect! Hard-working" — (read: *blue-collar*) — "New Yorkers like Antwan Moss" — (read: *black*) — "have a right to expect their children to be safe walking down the streets! We demand accountability from the private sector — why not from government? Everyone responsible for the criminal tragedy that took the life of little Ashley Moss — whether they work for Dolan Construction, or for a city agency — will be brought to justice. We *owe* that to New Yorkers, and I promise you, we will *deliver*."

Oh, the mayor. Everyone loved the mayor. Joe had watched his rise; he'd even voted for him. A brash, glad-handing former City Council Speaker with a Jackie Gleason accent and an endearingly receding hairline, Charlie Barr gave it to you straight. He ate street food, spoke plain English, showed up at ribbon-cuttings and funerals in the outer boroughs (where his support was high), and aggressively courted skeptical Latinos and blacks, attending innumerable testimonial dinners, awards ceremonies, and church services. He joked with reporters and made great copy. Running on a platform of disgust with slack and sloppiness, Charlie Barr had declared that New Yorkers deserved better: higher efficiency, lower taxes. Cleaner, safer streets. Fewer rules and regs. He'd promised to cut through the b.s. if they'd just vote for him. Sick of unresponsive, incomprehensible, and self-protective city agencies, New Yorkers did. The newspapers, reviving a tradition that had faded in the reign of Giuliani and died in the days of Bloomberg, called Charlie Barr "Hizzoner."

And on the subject of the Dolan Construction disaster Hizzoner was furious. "People being what they are, you can't help but run up against corruption sometimes. That's why we have the Department of Investigation: so when the system breaks, we can fix it." He glared into the TV cameras. "People who work at DOI have a heavy responsibility. Am I saying they have to be better than the rest of us? Yes, I am. Is that unfair? You tell me. But *I* can tell *you* this: when it looks like DOI's where the corruption *is*, I'm shocked and quite frankly outraged.

"We're pursuing this situation aggressively. We'll find out just how and why little Ashley Moss died and we will punish those responsible. You'll see."

They saw.

Joe Cole had had Buildings Department inspector Larry Manelli in his sights for months. Joe Cole knew Manelli was taking bribes from Sonny O'Doul, site super for Dolan Construction. Joe Cole had been to the Dolan jobsite many times. Joe Cole was a licensed engineer and an experienced investigator; surely he recognized bad shoring when he saw it. Yet Joe Cole had done nothing. "Mr. Cole's defense?" asked the prosecutor rhetorically at Joe's trial (though the real trial had been in the newspapers and the verdict was long in). The rhetorical answer: "He was gathering more evidence! Making a stronger case! Mr. Cole claims he was going to present his evidence to his Inspector General 'very soon.' Well, you have in front of you the case file Mr. Cole developed. Ladies and gentlemen, it's two inches thick! How much more evidence would an *honest* man have to gather? How much stronger would the case have to be before a *conscientious* investigator blew the whistle on a situation this dangerous?

"Ladies and gentlemen, the defense has thrown a lot of engineering jargon at you. But I think we can agree it comes down to this: the job of shoring is to support the structures and the very earth around a construction site. To protect buildings, sidewalks, and roadways from being undermined and destroyed. Just as the job of a Department of Investigation Buildings Department investigator is to protect innocent *people*—protect them from corrupt and uncaring contractors! Dolan Construction's shoring failed at its job. And Joe Cole failed at his.

"I submit to you that Mr. Cole wasn't waiting for more evidence. Mr. Cole was waiting for *different* evidence. Evidence with which he could prove Larry Manelli was taking bribes from contractors without implicating *this particular* contractor. As we've shown, Mr. Cole had encountered Sonny O'Doul and Dolan Construction on three previous construction projects in the course of his work. I submit that Mr. Cole and Dolan Construction had a *relationship*, ladies and gentlemen. An arrangement!"

Pause for effect; the Manhattan DA had assigned an experienced and talented prosecutor to this high-profile case.

"And this *arrangement*, ladies and gentlemen, caused the death of little Ashley Moss.

"We ask you to consider carefully what you'll be saying to the people of New York, and especially to the employees of your government—*your* city government—about what is and is not acceptable, when you render your verdict. Consider, as you deliberate, what message you're sending."

The jury returned in under two hours.

The message was sent.

"Go on, Joe, say it. You're trying to start a new life, to put all this behind you." Ann combed fingers through her wayward hair. "You remember what you said when Ellie talked about 'starting over'?"

"Leave Ellie out of this."

"You said it was bullshit."

"It is. Ann, what do you want?"

"Help, Joe. I need help."

He shook his head, drank his coffee. Look at that: Ann, asking him for help right here on his back porch. After all this.

"We had an accident," she said.

In the way of speakers of arcane technical languages, he understood this to mean not that Ann and others had been involved in a mishap—say a car crash, or spilled soup—but that a construction accident had occurred on a site in which the Department of Investigation was taking an interest.

And that it must have been serious.

"A multi-use development in the Bronx," she said. "Mott Haven Park. Heard of it?" She wasn't asking if he'd heard of the neighborhood—of course he had, he'd grown up in New York—but of the project itself. She turned to him again; he noted this but stared steadily ahead.

"Huge," she said, when he didn't answer. "Two residential rental towers, commercial on the lower floors; between the towers, townhouses for sale. Both rentals and townhouses will go half at market rate, half affordable." Affordable: such a New York euphemism. What wasn't affordable, to someone? "A percentage of each type is reserved for current neighborhood residents. The developer's called Three Star. The city gave them a few tax credits but no big concessions."

"In Mott Haven? Things must have changed over there." Joe was startled to hear himself. He didn't care about Mott Haven, about the Bronx, about the city, not anymore. But talking with Ann, listening to a problem Ann brought him, was like hearing the opening drumbeats of a familiar though long unheard march; he fell into step automatically. And she would know that, she'd expect it. Angrily, he gulped his coffee and leaned forward over the rickety rail.

"It was starting to change before," Ann said. "In the last two years, the pace sped up. A lot."

Anyone else would have denied it, to be polite.

To deny, really, that he had missed the changes because he'd been away.

Away. Locked up. Held off to the side, voiceless and invisible.

When you were *away*, the world could change. Your wife could leave you, wars could start and end, development could come to Mott Haven.

"It's changed a lot," Ann repeated. She was not polite and denied nothing.

And he had never been invisible to her.

chapter 10

Harlem: Frederick Douglass Boulevard

Ford Corrington looked over the paper in his hand for the hundredth time, then let it slide onto his desk. Taking his tea to the window, he stared down through the unruly foliage of potted plants.

In cars and buses, on foot, on bikes, standing on street corners and sitting on stoops, Harlem was going about its Sunday afternoon business. Directly below Ford's window, laughing kids came and went through the Garden Project's front doors. On the sidewalk three girls jumped rope in a complicated rhythm, and two boys pored over a comic book in the garden Ford and the kids had wrestled, years ago, from a rubble-strewn lot.

"You receiving, son?" Ford turned to see Ray Holdsclaw, hand on doorknob. Ray's white hair and starched clerical collar framed his ebony-dark face.

"Sure, Ray. Come on in."

"Missed you in church."

"I know. You want some tea?"

"That? Son, where I come from, anything smelled like that, we fed it to the chickens."

"It's rooibos. From Botswana. African tea."

"Then feed it to African chickens. Don't suppose you have coffee?"

"Sorry."

Ray settled into an armchair. Ford skirted his desk, stopping to pinch a brown leaf off a windowsill ivy. "I was up with Sarah Andersen," he told Ray as he took the other armchair. "T. D. Tilden's mother."

Ray nodded. "Heard about that. The boy one of yours?"

"Once. Not for years now. When he was little, he'd come by for some basketball, woodshop. T.D. could draw and paint, we tried to reach him that way, but he never stayed. His girlfriend, Shamika Arthur, she came through some of our programs. Sweet kid. She works here now. You know her."

"Of course. Her mama sings in our choir. Didn't know Shamika was seeing the Tilden boy, though. How's the girl taking it?"

"Haven't seen her. Called, no answer. Thought she'd be at Sarah's but I hear they don't get along." Ford stared into his tea. From downstairs soared the enthusiastic, if not skillful, voices of the children's chorus. "Ray, we tried with T.D. He just slipped through."

"Not your fault, son. You tried."

"Doesn't matter whose fault it is. Seventeen, and he's gone. He had . . . a sweetness, a joy, when he was young. Big talk, big dreams. Even now, last time I saw him. Something the street hadn't killed off yet."

Ray waited a few moments, then asked, "Anyone say what happened?"

"He stank of weed, had a roach and some blunts in his pocket. Could have fallen. Cops are looking into it."

Ray snorted and said nothing. They both knew how that would go.

"Edgar was there," Ford said. "Showed up even before they got the boy in the ambulance."

"I feel a press conference coming on."

Ford nodded. "Edgar zeroed right in on the NY1 van. Kept him from buzzing around Sarah, though, so it's not all bad. Sarah, she's just staring out the window. Polite, thanks folks for their sympathy, then just sits there staring."

"Sounds like she's in shock."

"She tried so hard, Ray."

"We all do."

"Is it worth it?"

Ray's eyebrows rose. "Say what?"

"Trying so hard. Is it worth it?"

"Ford, son, I *know* I didn't just hear you ask that."

"The nights, the weekends, the meetings. Begging for money, begging for space. New programs, new ideas, new beginnings, new chances. And kids still go flying off roofs."

"You can't be the one to save all of them, Ford. That's vanity, son."

"But what's the *point*, Ray? What's the damn point? We've been bailing for years and the boat's still sinking."

"What are you going to do?" Ray asked evenly. "Just sit back and let it go down?"

"Of course not. I just—sometimes it's hard to see how it's worth the cost."

"Cost?"

Ray waited. Ford didn't answer.

"The Lord gave you work to do here, son," Ray said. "You took it on and now you got to keep doing it until the Lord tells you to stop. Yes, all right, you lost T. D. Tilden. He wasn't a child you could reach. But you've got kids here, now, today."

Ray spoke quietly but he was a preacher: his words filled every corner of the room. As their echo faded, the out-of-tune sound of the chorus swelled from downstairs, children singing a joyous, unintelligible song.

Ford shook his head. "How did you do that?"

Ray grinned the grin that was as sunny as his white hair and the scar on his cheek was fierce. "That, son, was the Lord moving in a mysterious way. Now come on, we got work to do. We need to talk about this meeting tomorrow. You want me to be your moral mouthpiece, I got to have some idea what's going on."

CHAPTER 11

Heart's Content

Regularly, Ann had come to the prison to see him. She didn't give a damn about the COs' smirks, the lewd stares of the prisoners. Only when she heard them needling Joe—"Hey, Cole, too bad you don't get conjugals. Must be hard, just sitting there with all that. Yeah, must be *hard*." High-fiving each other for their wit—did her face blaze, and that was anger.

"I'm sorry," she'd said to Joe, neither of them sure what she was apologizing for or what to do about it. And they'd done nothing, changed nothing. Until the morning, six months into his sentence, when he walked into the visiting room with his eye blackened, his cheek bandaged.

When she asked, "What happened?" he didn't answer; when, sitting straighter, she said, "It was about me, wasn't it?" he felt himself smile.

"It always is," he said, and he'd bought them each a cup of poisonous coffee and they'd gone on to other things. But that day she'd left early. The next time she came she wore flat shoes, no makeup; her hair was braided and pinned.

But she'd kept coming. He'd told her she should stop. It had to look bad, he said; and she said she didn't care how it looked or who was looking. "Everyone already knows whose side I'm on." With a twist of her hand she dismissed the visiting room's glazed tile walls and the bored guards in each corner, the convicts on molded plastic chairs knee-to-knee with desperately upbeat wives and girlfriends. "You think if I stopped now, they'd think I finally realized what a louse you are? Bull. They'd think I'm the type who turns my back on my friends."

"You think they're watching that closely?"

"If they're not, why should I stop coming?"

He grinned. "Well, hell. You win. As usual."

She hadn't stopped coming. But her visits got rarer. (Among the population and COs this was noted and wisecracked on.) It was a mixed blessing, seeing Ann less often. That was because it had been a mixed blessing from the beginning, seeing her at all.

Any day, in policy, was visiting day; New York State would not be accused of keeping its prisoners from the civilizing effects of friends and family. But because the prison population was largely drawn from the city's streets, and the prison was three hours north, most men had visitors only on weekends. And for most men, only one day counted: the second Saturday of the month, when their women (sometimes their parents, sometimes their friends, but it was the women who mattered, and it was the kids) scuffed off the bus the Department of Corrections ran up from the city. The women headed first to the washroom in the double-wide outside the gates. They changed diapers and scrubbed kids' faces and repaired their own makeup, trying to hide the puffiness and dark circles that would betray them: how hard it was at the end of the workweek to wake before dawn to get the six a.m. bus, how hard it was to keep the four-year-old occupied and the baby quiet the whole trip. How hard it was to talk the sullen twelve-year-old into coming one more time to see the father he'd been dragged up here to visit half his life. How hard it was.

Joe, because he worked the grounds, often saw the women's arrival. On the second Saturday he'd try to arrange his duties to be near the lot when the bus pulled in. One by one the women would step down, blinking. They'd peer around, getting their bearings. At first he'd thought it was the sunlight disorienting them, but soon he realized it was far more. Clasping the children's hands, the women would head for the trailer with, it seemed to Joe, more determination than desire; but they'd emerge softer, in a different rhythm. Lips reddened, hair brushed and braided, they'd chat with each other. Old hands took first-timers under their wings: a lot of kindness there. They shuffled inside, to the lines where, though he couldn't see it, Joe knew they were searched (clothing, mouth, and handbag, even the babies' diapers) and then to the gates that opened and slammed over and over, as each woman with her children stepped from the other world into the men's.

The men inside waited for the second Saturday; they called it family day. Aloud, no man expressed anything but indifference or a resigned indulgence. As though it were for the women and the kids; as though, inconvenient though it was, the men would let it go on. To admit to more would have been to show a weakness no one could afford. But you could tell: men who shaved only irregularly choosing that morning to demand a new razor; a shoving match in the breakfast line; envious eyes in the dayroom lifting from the droning TV to follow those men the COs came to fetch.

Things were tough for a day or two after the second Saturday; the COs hated those shifts. It wasn't just the loneliness that crashed down after the gates slammed and the bus drove away. It wasn't only the uselessness that some men felt, to see the changes in their kids just once a month, or once every three, or only in photographs because the kids had stopped coming. It wasn't the awakened and unsatisfied lust that hung in the air like a storm waiting to break. Family day cracked the illusion they lived by. They were their world, all actors on the same stage performing for no audience. Family day parted a curtain they'd agreed to call a wall. It showed them the other world, the one they'd once been part of, and then closed again, leaving them to try to believe their own lies instead of remember.

Ann, of course, didn't come on the bus. She'd drive up Friday night after work and stay at a bed-and-breakfast with a view of the river. She'd have a good dinner and sleep under down comforters and wheel the Boxster into the gravel lot on the stroke of eight. By her third visit the guards at the gate all knew who was coming and whom she was coming to see.

At first, Joe, like the other men, looked forward to these days. Except for his lawyer, he had few visitors. He discouraged everyone who offered, the way his mother had refused to see anyone at the hospital when she was dying.

He would have permitted Ellie, even after she divorced him, but Ellie wouldn't come.

She did only once, early on. Out of what? Guilt, worry, some understanding that when roots are so entangled a true separation is never clean, is always painful, could be impossible? Whatever her reasons, he'd been eager to see her. He was still new, then, still trying to live as though prison were just another place in the world. Ellie's brave face that day, her determined smile, the half-second pause before she spoke each time — each time! — were the tools that smashed to rubble the delicate structure of lies he'd built.

She hadn't come back. There was no question of bringing Janet; Ellie said, "I'm sure you understand." He wondered, if it had been Ellie where he was, he on the outside, would he have kept her daughter from her? But he did understand.

Janet sent him letters sometimes, and cards on his birthday, and she wrote that she missed him and in the beginning she probably did. Because she was so young her letters were short, and because she was living somewhere new they were soon filled with people and places he didn't know. His throat would tighten at the way she wrote about friends and teachers without explanation, sure as only a child can be that, though he was away, he was nevertheless familiar with everything important in her world.

Ellie asked him to call not more often than once a month, to permit her to "build a new life" and "put this behind me." Conscientiously she sent him photos: Janet in a party dress, or playing peewee soccer, or smiling with thirty other children in her class picture (in the back row, a boy looking the wrong way, his attention caught by something more compelling than the photographer; in his own class photos, that boy had been Joe). Ellie never sent pictures of herself and never spoke about anything in their phone calls except Janet, or some rational, resolvable issue related to the sale of the house, the division of the savings account; she presented these emotionlessly, and he was careful to respond in kind.

Though when, in November, Ellie told him she'd found a buyer for the house, he lost the thread of her words in thoughts of the plum tree he'd planted too near the door. Every winter, as its branches scraped the roof, Ellie was after him to take it down; he always agreed, but it blossomed so early that by the time the weather was good enough for cutting, the tree was too beautiful, and he let it stay. Would anyone tell the new owners not to decide about that tree until after they'd seen it flower?

So on family day he watched the other prisoners' women arrive, bringing their children, and as the last of them passed through the gate he turned back to his work, stabbing his shovel hard into the rocky ground.

He'd tried to discourage Ann, too. He could have refused to see her. But she'd have stayed all day in the waiting room, talking with the women, giggling with the children, drinking coffee from the clunking machine. She'd wait him out, and if he didn't break down she'd come back the next week, and the one after. She'd play chicken; he'd seen her do it. She'd make a fool of herself, challenging him to rescue her.

So he gave in. And though, like the other men, he wouldn't have admitted it, at first he was like the other men, counting the days. But three things happened.

Ann's visits began to loom like jagged rocks in the sluggish stream of his days. They interrupted the hypnotic flow, created eddies and undertow to disturb his dark slow progress. The unchanging boredom of prison days, often called a curse, was to him—to many—a secret salvation. Lose yourself in its seductive drone, stop tugging and straining to make the minutes move, and time passed more easily. It was the struggle that wore men out.

And though (or because?) his days didn't change, he was changing. Or not changing: early on, one of the iron men told him that men in prison never change, they just grow more like themselves. That might be true; either way, it meant some things mattered more to him, and some less, some things were getting easier, and some harder.

The third problem with Ann's visits was this: over the months the visits themselves seemed to fade, the way flowers soften and pale after they're cut.

As the first year grew old, Ann would arrive, fresh and smiling, and then sometimes after "How've you been?" neither of them seemed able to think of much to say. Ann would tell him about places she'd traveled, things she'd seen. "The only white person besides me and Jen, in all of Matsumoto, was a sushi chef." When she'd bought the new apartment she'd told him about that—"Unbelievable view. Small, but who cares?"—and he'd had to smile: her last place, where she'd lived barely three years, had no view. "But it's huge, so who cares?" she'd said then.

"I give it three years," he said, and she smiled with him.

But then what? What could they talk about? Office gossip? Everyone at DOI was keeping so clean you could probably eat off them. And a lot of Ann's colleagues were people Joe didn't know anyway: after his conviction, many people had retired at the new Commissioner's strong suggestion, or left for the private world, where Hizzoner didn't expect them to be better than the rest of us. Could he and Ann discuss films? He'd seen only what came to the prison, none of it less than a decade old. News? News stories came to Joe like moral-free fables from a mythical land. At first he tried, following national stories: hurricanes, blizzards; the Mideast war, surreal in itself; and local ones: the West Side stadium; the mayoral election; the Harlem 9/11 memorial, thwarted by schoolkids with "Save Our Park" signs. Ann got a great kick out of that one, a developer she hated, stopped in his tracks. "He couldn't get in at Ground Zero where the big boys are playing," she reported with glee. "So he wants to plant this thing in the middle of Morningside Park and Harlem's supposed to fall on its knees in gratitude. Pompous bastard!" Joe wasn't nearly as interested in the story as in the way it made Ann's eyes glow and her cheeks redden.

Nor could they discuss cases. Scooping lo mein out of take-out containers, they used to argue, brainstorm, and decide: whom to talk to, whose books and files to examine, how to handle what delicate political situation. Like any branch of city government, the Department of Investigation was a small craft driven by political winds. Not that they were ever steered away from a truth they'd gotten close to, he couldn't say that. But which truths were important to look for, and which questions didn't need answers, was decided from above.

That had never bothered him. "One rat's as good as another," he'd said the day Ann had stormed in fuming about being assigned to a small-time union kickback scheme when she'd asked to be let loose on a nest of double-dipping concrete inspectors in Queens. "Calm down," Joe had uselessly told her. "It's not like there's not enough lying, cheating, and stealing to go around." He felt permitted to speak this way to Ann; he was six years her senior in this business, though only three in age.

She'd thrown him a glare, told him he was a cheery bastard, and stalked out. And done both investigations, juggling the one she was assigned and the one she'd assigned herself. And gotten, simultaneously, a rap on the knuckles from their boss and a commendation from the grateful Queens Borough Superintendent.

What she had not done was calm down.

Now Ann, though exiled to the outer boroughs, continued in defiant, ceaseless motion, and Joe was shipwrecked.

And so each visit grew more difficult, she dropping anchor from time to time at his dry and featureless island. With no trees or grasses, hills or streams, no change in light or weather, what was it they could comment on? What did they have to say?

City Hall

The mayor walked to his window. City Hall Park was in lush bloom. Charlie Barr, a Red Hook kid, could only pick out the maples, oaks, and lindens, but he knew he was looking at a dozen other varieties, too, some of them important specimen trees dear to the hearts of the Parks Department. On the paths, between banks of pink and purple flowers, tourists consulted maps and teenagers flirted and families with strollers ambled along.

Charlie was gratified by the whole thing. He might not know one tree from another but he knew a city with well-kept parks looked prosperous and confident. Two years ago, after hearing the Hamptons crowd lament how they missed their gardens once they'd closed their beach houses for the season, he'd started a program for citizens to plant and maintain certain areas in certain parks, and turn into parks what were once weedy traffic islands and roadway shoulders. At the start this meant turf battles—ha, he thought, turf battles: he should remember to use that—between Parks and Transportation. Twice he had to bring both Commissioners in and bang their heads together. But finally they saw reason, or maybe, as Don had said, predestination, and Charlie got his program. A program that gave citizens a way to participate, added amenities, and cut costs: who could ask for more?

He watched the wind push the fountain's water around. At the height of last summer's drought, Environmental Conservation had ordered all the fountains off. Charlie had personally thrown the switch on the City Hall one at a press conference where he'd talked about public-spirited sacrifice, praised DEC's Commissioner for making tough decisions, and expressed the hope that the drought would be short. He'd looked into the suddenly still bowl and said, "Boy, I'll miss that fountain."

"You just said all citizens have to make sacrifices, Mayor," some press wiseass had cracked.

"Yeah," he'd snapped back, "but they don't have to enjoy them!"

Then he'd stalked off. It was one of the things the polls said New Yorkers liked about Charlie Barr, that he wasn't goddamn cheerful all the time.

The drought hadn't been short; summer stretched into fall and the fountains stayed dry. But this year New York could have its fountains, its grass, its gardens. Parks could stop fretting about their specimen trees (which they'd watered anyway last summer, legally but, by Charlie's order, in the middle of the night). This year there was plenty of rain.

The doorknob clicked. Charlie turned from the window. Lena was holding the door wide to admit Mark Shapiro and Greg Lowry.

"Thanks, Lena. What about Don?"

"Here." Don Zalensky, probably fresh off a Camel break, eased around Lena. She smiled at him. Don and Lena, so different in all ways, had always gotten along, seeming to share some private source of amusement. Charlie suspected it was him, but what the hell.

"You need me?" Lena stood in the doorway.

"No, go on home," Charlie told her. This meant, *This meeting's private and off the record*, but these days no one winked at a secretary and said, *Sweetheart, get lost*. "Thanks for coming in," he added.

"Anytime, Charlie," she said drily, and pulled the door shut as she left.

Don sat in the wooden straight-backed chair he favored, shifting it to face the leather armchairs Shapiro and Lowry were settling into. Don's gray suit, fresh from the cleaner (Charlie had had to suggest, after the limo picked Don up, that he pull the tag off the sleeve), was already looking rumpled. Greg Lowry had on a white shirt, brown jacket, maroon tie, gray slacks. Even if Charlie didn't know Lowry wasn't married, he'd know he wasn't married. No woman would let a man out of the house looking like that. Mark Shapiro, of course, was in full dark-suit-and-tie regalia, down to spit-shined shoes and NYPD twenty-year pin.

Charlie's own jacket was hanging in the closet where it wouldn't wrinkle, and his shirt was blue, for the TV cameras. He perched on the edge of his desk and folded his arms. "Well?"

Lowry and Shapiro exchanged glances. Shapiro cleared his throat. "Well, of course you can't guarantee anything based only on observation."

"Fine, disclaimer accepted. But?"

Shapiro shrugged. "But I can't say anything suggests either of them knows something they're not saying."

"Greg?"

"No, me either. Nothing raised a red flag for me about those two."

Charlie breathed out a long breath. "Thank God for that."

"Those two" were Virginia McFee and Les Farrell.

The stated agenda for the first Sunday morning meeting, just ended, was a briefing on the investigation into the fatal construction site accident late Friday night: falling bricks that had left Harriet Winston, single mother of three small children, dead on an inner-city sidewalk.

The agenda for the second meeting, just starting, was a discussion of the other reason for the first meeting.

"And nothing else, either?" Charlie asked. "New cars? Vacations? Either of them suddenly pay off a mortgage?"

"No," said Lowry. "Matches what we found at the lower levels at Buildings, over the last week or so. If anything's going on there, they're doing it for free."

In the chair beside Charlie, Don recrossed his legs for the fourth time. "Don, for chrissake, light up if you want to!"

Don, after a moment's hesitation, slipped a Camel from the pack. As he lit it, Shapiro frowned and shifted his chair away. Don went to the window, holding the cigarette outside between puffs. Shapiro didn't look any happier, but too bad.

"And it goes without saying," Charlie said, because it didn't, "that you've been absolutely quiet about it?" Looking at Shapiro's starched face, he couldn't help adding, "Like little church mice?"

Shapiro, probably never before compared to anything less ponderous than a bull moose, frowned again and looked to Lowry.

"I did it myself, Mayor," Lowry said. "On tiptoe."

"But they've got to know," said Shapiro. "McFee and Farrell. Everyone expects to be investigated in a situation like this."

"I don't care if *they* know. But I don't want to read in the *Post* that the city's investigating the mayor's appointees, unless and until one of them's arrested. And if that happens I want to announce the arrest myself."

Silence from the DOI men, which the mayor decided to interpret as accord.

"Okay. So—"

"Mayor?" That was Shapiro. "What would you have done if we'd found something?"

"Burn 'em," Charlie shot back. "Anyone I trust who fucks me up, they're on their own."

"No matter how it makes you look?"

"Makes me look a lot worse to slap their wrist and send them on their way. Why? Who're you thinking about?"

"I'm not. Just wanted to know how far you really wanted us to take this, if we did find something."

"All the way. If I end up eating crow, it won't be the first time and it won't kill me. Looking like I'm covering up for a friend, that's what'll kill me."

Shapiro nodded thoughtfully, the worry folds between his eyebrows minutely easing.

"Look at that, Don," the mayor said. "I made Mark happy."

Heart's Content

"The pressure's gotten so high in Manhattan"—Ann's brisk voice, Joe's back porch: she was talking about real estate; he wondered how much he'd missed—"developers are taking to the boroughs. These guys, Three Star Partners—you can tell what they think of themselves by the name, huh?" Interrupting herself, she turned to him. He continued to stare over the rail to the far bright corner of the garden. In the lee of a granite boulder, white peonies were unfurling from tight, waxy buds.

"Three Star," Ann continued. "They assembled a site in Mott Haven and got it cheap. Who wouldn't sell, up there? Near the subway, police station a block north, school two blocks south. Three Star says they can make it go."

He shook his head. He meant, *That area can't have changed* that *much in two and a half years.* And he meant, *Three Star Partners, whoever they are, are up to something.* And he meant, *I live in a different world now and none of this matters to me anymore.*

He shoved his chair back, strode across the grass to where the yellow irises glowed hard against the pines. From here you could hear the stream. He listened to the water racing south as though it had a place it had to be.

Ann crossed the yard and came to stand beside him.

She might have remarked, at that moment, on the beauty of his garden, the rush of the water, the sun's warmth. That was an interrogator's trick Ann knew well: say something that will suggest to the subject the connection of common ground. But this was not an interrogation and Joe was not a subject and the connection—even now, even after all this, even to his dismay—did not have to be suggested. Ann said nothing about the landscape or the weather.

She said, "It's why I need you."

"Go home, Ann."

She paused; when she spoke her voice held a new tone, part triumph, part wonder. "Oh! Wait. You think—Joe? You think I'm trying to do you a favor? That that's what this is about? I tracked you down and drove three hours to East Jesus on a Sunday to, what, save you from yourself?"

He didn't speak. The breeze shifted and he could smell her perfume. Hanae Mori, a fresh, green scent, the only perfume she ever wore. He didn't turn to her.

"For God's sake, Joe. Someone died."

CHAPTER

14

Harlem: Frederick Douglass Boulevard

Ford brewed more tea and brought it back to the armchair as Ray flipped through a spiral-bound booklet.

"Looks good," Ray told him. "Lot of work here already. Lot of time."

"Sixteen years," said Ford. "One way or another."

Pages dense with print alternated with tables, pie charts, and sheet after sheet of architect's renderings: gleaming glass and steel buildings, high and low, from a distance and in close-up detail, inside and out. Sunlight streamed. Store windows beckoned. A basketball player lifted off for a dunk. Dogs sniffed, cats stretched. People shopped, strolled, sat. Plants and kids were everywhere.

"All right, then," said Ray. "Take me through it."

"Start with the rendering on the fourth page."

Ray flicked the pages. His forehead creased. "Doesn't look like the same place, does it?"

"That's what was in the paper eight, nine months ago, remember? It's what got me going. It's what the city's proposing."

The page faced Ray; from where Ford sat the image was upside down but he knew it too well for that to matter. Reproduced from an architect's drawing in the real estate section of the Sunday *Times*, this bird's-eye view pictured the same site as the other renderings: a city-owned half-block in the center of Harlem. Ford walked by that site every day now; he'd deliberately changed his route from home to pass it. Most of it was a rubble-strewn empty lot, littered with rusting bedsprings, leaking batteries, ripe bags of garbage. Four buildings still stood, two half-full of squatters, two concrete-blocked and empty. The city had put up a chain-link fence well over a year ago; the neighborhood had torn holes in it within a week.

It was known as Block A, this neglected plot of land. It was the last large city-owned site in Harlem. The city had plans for it and Ray was looking at them now.

No sparkling glass, no shining steel. No streaming sunlight. No: nighttime brownstones with bow fronts, and back alleys for service and parking. Jazz clubs with neon signs. Not many kids, no jumbled foliage. Carefully trimmed, well-spaced trees alternated with cast-iron street-lights in a promenade up the avenue. A hip, multiethnic crowd with a subtle Roaring Twenties air lounged in sidewalk cafés, emerged from yellow taxis, and passed energetically in and out of the bars and restaurants.

"Remember seeing it?" Ford asked Ray again.

"Sure do."

"Harlemland."

Ray looked up. "That's what they're calling it?"

"No, of course not. The *Times* used fifty-cent phrases like 'contextual design' and 'harmonizing with the surrounding architectural fabric.' It said, 'The city's proposal recalls the glory days of the Harlem Renaissance.' "

"Did it make mention that those particular glory days were eighty years ago?"

"Look at it! Single-family townhouses. Private parking. Nightclubs, speakeasies—"

"Speakeasies?"

"You know what it is? It's a *theme park*!" Ford jumped up, calling like a carnival barker. "C'mon up to Harlem, see them black folks swing! Get your collard greens and hooch, your hams, your yams! Go to church on Sunday, hear that ole time gospel sound. Then turn and leave while the sermon's being preached."

At that, Ray laughed.

"Like it uptown?" Ford plowed on. "You can live here too! Like Disney World? You can live in Celebration. Like South Street Seaport? Battery Park City. And if you like slumming, here's: Harlemland!"

Ray smiled and nodded. "Tell it."

"Step right up! Meet a gangbanger! See a junkie nodding out! View the exotic colored folk from the safety of your Beemer. Drive right to the door of your own brownstone—period-detailed, with all the amenities, and so much more affordable than downtown! Park securely in your own garage. Harlem, USA! It's clean, it's new, it's sanitized. Dope deal-ers and welfare moms, the homeless and the jobless been swept clear out to the Bronx. Harlem, the final frontier! To boldly go where no white man has gone before. Harlemland! Sho' nuff."

Ford held his arms open a few seconds longer, then dropped them.

"You want my pulpit next week, you can have it," said Ray. "Now sit down."

Ford did.

"Go ahead. Tell me just who it is we're seeing tomorrow," Ray said, "what you think is gonna happen and what you want from me. And be succinct, son. We got a lot of work to do here, and neither of us got all day. I got parishioners to see. And you got a building full of children you got to keep off the roof."

Heart's Content

Someone died, Ann had said. But someone's always dying.

Joe had never had an arrangement with Dolan Construction, that tie of callousness and greed the prosecutor painted for the jury.

A relationship, that was true. Joe had run across Dolan three times before. Before what became known as the Moss case, though the case Joe was working was about nailing Larry Manelli, had nothing to do with seven-year-old Ashley Moss until she'd gone skipping down the sidewalk on a rainy day.

The guys at Dolan Construction had been a dirty little bunch. But they were small-time; they were punks. They hired nonunion, they built with shoddy materials, their night security was one ancient wino snoring in a shed. Dolan Construction paid off everybody they could find so they could avoid doing anything they were supposed to do. Joe knew all that but it wasn't his problem.

Larry Manelli was his problem.

Manelli was a Buildings Department inspector. Since the world began, bums like the Dolan crowd had infested the construction industry like roaches in the walls. In New York, it was the job of Buildings Department inspectors to keep them under control. Like the roaches, you could never completely eliminate them. But you could make their lives difficult, you could prevent them from flourishing. And if a roach colony lost all fear and all caution, if they began operating brazenly in the light, you could stamp them out.

Or you could become one of them. A giant swollen cockroach king, growing fat on bribes and kickbacks deposited at your feet by all the other busy little bugs.

Three years ago Larry Manelli had been on his way to becoming that kind of vermin royalty, and Joe Cole had been out to stomp him.

Joe knew the Dolan Construction site was a station along Larry Manelli's route, and he knew it wasn't a major one. Manelli had his everyday circuit, a bottle of whiskey here, Knicks tickets there, grease so small it didn't matter because what the giver got in return was sure to be small, too. Joe wasn't interested in nailing Manelli on penny-ante stuff. The biggest dance on Manelli's card was a huge commercial project near the Brooklyn Bridge. Joe knew Manelli was raking it in down there, trading big favors, sticking out both hands and squeezing his eyes shut. That site was Joe's target.

Knew how?

From hours, days, weeks of meticulous investigation.

And because Sonny O'Doul, one of the roaches at Dolan, had told him.

Not out of the blue. Joe had backed Sonny into a carefully built corner. But once he'd seen the trap he was in, Sonny hadn't fought it. A smart man, Sonny, and he'd done the quick calculus: maximize profit, minimize loss, save your own ass, and stick someone else to the flypaper as fast as you can.

Joe had known he would. So predictable, the insect world.

One blustery November morning, his facts, figures, and hidden-camera photos in a folder in his backpack (you can't climb a scaffold with a briefcase), Joe strolled unhurriedly onto the Dolan site, watched by the cold, appraising stares of men who didn't know him and the tight-lipped hostility of the ones who, from this job or some other, did. Sonny O'Doul double-timed out of his trailer. He hustled Joe inside before word of his arrival could spread.

"The fuck you trying to do to me, Cole?" Sonny banged the door shut, dropped himself behind the paper-drifts that engulfed his desk.

"How're things, Sonny?" Uninvited, Joe sat in the opposite chair.

"Like you give a fuck. Every time you show your ugly Yid face on a jobsite, six guys disappear in case you catch them at shit I don't even know they're doing. Last job you cost me my bonus, asshole."

"Come on, Sonny, it's not like you needed it. On kickbacks alone, you ought to be getting rich."

"Cocksucker. You have a warrant, show me. Otherwise, get off my job."

"I don't know. I thought I'd take a look around."

"Listen, Cole: I'm three days behind from the rain last week. I can't afford this shit."

Meaning: *How much will it cost me to get you to leave?*

"I'm tired of being indoors. All this rain, you know? Seems like this might be a good day to hang around outside, shoot the shit with your men."

Meaning: *Trying to buy me, that was a mistake, Sonny.*

"This is fucking harassment, Cole. I'm gonna call my lawyer."

"That might be a good idea."

Joe reached for his pack, pulled out a thick folder labeled "Dolan/ Manelli," and flipped it to Sonny. He left Sonny and the folder alone together while he ambled to the other end of the trailer, poured a cup of coffee, and took it outside. He stood beside a puddle, gazing at geometric lines of scaffolding against gray sky.

"Your coffee stinks," he told Sonny when he returned.

"What do you want? Shut the door." Sonny slapped the folder down.

"A decaf latte?"

"Oh, fuck your mother, Cole, don't play—"

"I want Larry Manelli."

Sonny glared at the folder as though his smoldering hate could ignite it, then raised that look to Joe. "Seems to me you've already got his ass in a sling."

"I do. You. You're the sling, Sonny."

"So why are you here? This your victory lap?"

"No. Your chance."

"To do what?"

Joe gave Sonny time to see if he could figure a way out. But the folder was a roach motel; there was no way out.

Sonny asked, "How?"

"This crap"—Joe cocked a finger at the file folder—"is so small-time, I don't know why you bother." He held up a hand to fend off Sonny's answer. "And I don't care. Don't get me confused with someone who gives a shit about you, Sonny, or this won't play out well."

"So what the—"

"If I give this amateur-hour junk to the DA, you and Manelli will do sixteen months apiece. For a double-dipping shit like Manelli, that's not nearly enough. For you, Sonny—well, like I said, I don't really care. You following me?"

With obvious effort Sonny kept his mouth shut.

"If Manelli got more," Joe said, "that would be better. If Manelli got a long time, and you got a slap on the wrist, wouldn't that be the best?"

————

Sonny O'Doul knew everything there was to know about the Brooklyn Bridge site and he gave it all to Joe. Joe took it in notes, not on tape: that was part of the deal. If he could bag Larry Manelli by squeezing the people Sonny was pointing him to, he'd leave Sonny and his low-grade crap alone.

"As long as you clean up your act, Sonny. Because the next time your name shows up on my desk—you know I can smell it before I see it, your name?—you're toast."

"Fuck you."

"Uh-huh. Go back to the stuff about the property line."

A couple of hours, that was all it took. Joe kept his eyes on Sonny, asked short questions to clarify points. Eventually Sonny slowed and stopped, like an out-of-gas car coasting into a stall. Joe closed his notebook, slung his pack over his shoulder. "You can keep the file," he said, knowing that Sonny would now have to spend the day worrying about where to hide it and the drive home searching for a place to ditch it. "I have a copy."

And then, standing in the open doorway, just before he left, he said, "And do something about that for-shit shoring, Sonny. I know you hate to waste the good money you're paying Manelli to not see it. But fix it. All this rain, more coming tomorrow, something's bound to give. Someone could get killed."

chapter 16

Heart's Content

During the trial Joe's lawyer had told him he didn't look sorry enough.

"But it wasn't his fault. Why should he look sorry?" Ellie had defended Joe stoutly, a loyal wife, a believer to the end. Past the end, or so she claimed: a believer still. Though she'd divorced him and was "moving on."

"Because when a child dies everyone's supposed to be sorry," Joe's lawyer told her. "Whether it's your fault or not."

There wasn't much Joe could do about it, though. He couldn't manufacture tears, or a look of public sadness, not even the agitated position-shifting of anguish and regret. Through the trial's four days he sat, his body still (not calm, but looking calm, he knew), his shadowed eyes darting from speaker to speaker (prosecutor, witness, judge) with an intensity he couldn't control, a sharpness that made people flinch.

"It's a Manhattan jury, Joe, *look* at them! Everyone who isn't black is some kind of white liberal, except the Irish guy who's probably pissed off at you about O'Doul and the Korean woman who probably doesn't give a shit. Ashley was a cute little black kid, you're a college-boy Jew. Her father's a bus driver, you own a house, in Riverdale yet. Joe, you gotta give me something to work with."

If that's the way it is, Joe thought, *maybe I should have hired a black lawyer instead of you, Feinberg.*

But he still said nothing, because he knew what his lawyer meant.

He didn't look sorry.

But he was sorry.

Sorrow was a part of him now, a stone in his gut, poison in his veins.

Not guilty of the crime of which he stood accused—taking graft from Sonny O'Doul—he was unmistakably guilty of something else: an arrogance that had said the crusade he was on, the capture of the archvillain Larry Manelli, was of overriding importance. Other problems could be tossed away, left littering the roadside like debris from a glorious parade for others to clean up after he, in victory, was gone.

Like the blood-spattered debris littering a downtown sidewalk after a shoring collapse. Shoring he'd cavalierly told Sonny O'Doul to repair, and then put out of his mind, gave not one further thought to, until the evening news reports and the ring of his phone.

Manelli and O'Doul, in separate deals, had both pled guilty to bribery, Manelli for demanding bribes, O'Doul for paying them. The pair also pled to reckless endangerment, and Manelli additionally to misuse of public funds (he solicited his payoffs while on the clock), harassment (once, when O'Doul's horse at Belmont beat Manelli's by a length, Manelli had said, "You fucking mick bastard, I'll cut your balls off"), and theft (Buildings Department markers, pads, pens, and tape were found at his Long Island home). Manelli was sentenced to varying lengths of prison time on the various counts, to be served, because of the bargain, simultaneously instead of consecutively. O'Doul was sentenced to far less time because, though no one but he himself denied he was a slimy sleazeball, O'Doul, as a private citizen, hadn't violated the public trust.

And because he was willing to roll over. Talking freely and fast, he provided as much evidence as the prosecutor could have hoped for against Larry Manelli. In return, he got a sentence shaved as close to the minimum as his lawyer could contrive.

And also because he offered as a bonus and without being asked, evidence against that other accused violator of the public trust, Joe Cole.

"Is any of O'Doul's shit true?" Feinberg, at one of the endless meetings in his office before the trial began, jabbed his thumb toward the box of tapes and transcripts his discovery motion had produced.

"No."

Feinberg chewed on his lip. "Then why is he saying it, Joe?"

Kenneth Feinberg was a fat, sloppy man, as careless and disorganized in appearance as he was meticulous and assiduous in process. He'd requested tapes of O'Doul's statements in addition to transcripts so the stutters, pauses, and throat-clearing of mendacity might reveal themselves. His strategy would be to pounce on these tiny knots in the thread and, by worrying them with the razor-sharp teeth of punctiliousness (for which his targets were never prepared, coming as it did from a man whose tie was perpetually crooked, his suit unkempt, his aspect preoccupied), try to unravel the fabric.

Joe said, "O'Doul hates me."

"Why does he hate you?"

"I was a son of a bitch to him."

"Why were you a son of a bitch?"

"Because he's a lying shit."

"And you liked to see him squirm."

"Standard investigative technique."

"Being a son of a bitch?"

"Squeezing people close to your target until they give him up."

"You enjoyed it?"

Joe wanted to be able to deny that, but what would be the point of lying to his lawyer? "So what?"

"Just asking." Feinberg rapped his knuckles on the transcript box. "So it's payback time. Okay, you never took a bribe. But O'Doul offered?"

"He tried to buy me off every time he saw me."

"Over, what, eight years you knew him, right?"

"It pissed him off that I turned him down. Called me a self-righteous kike."

"I don't suppose you have that on tape? Wrote it down, made a note?"

"Come on, Ken. My department is IAD for the whole city. If I made a note every time someone called me a name—"

"Yeah, okay." Feinberg waved that away. "You never took anything from him?"

"After he said that, I wouldn't have taken anything from him if I *had* been in the market."

"O'Doul says you did."

"No."

"You sure?"

"For God's sake! Does that sound like something I'd forget?"

"I gotta ask. A beer, Yankee tickets, nothing? If there ever was anything, *anything,* Joe, you better tell me. It'll come back and bite us in the ass."

"Coffee. I used to drink a cup of coffee in his trailer."

"That's it?"

"Tasted like shit, too."

"Oh, well, if it tasted like shit. We can get around that, then."

But they got around nothing. Sonny O'Doul perjured himself, lied with great abandon, bore false witness with ease. He repeated on the stand the same fictions he'd offered up around the DA's conference table, and if the jury saw the loathing and the triumph in his eyes each time he regarded Joe Cole across the courtroom, they listened intently to his words nonetheless.

Feinberg, not able to get around O'Doul, fought to tear him apart, like a terrier with a rat. He challenged every word O'Doul spoke, every pause between spoken words, every word not spoken. He fought the DA's arguments head-on in court, objecting, rephrasing, ripping huge ragged holes from tiny openings. On the courthouse steps, he fought the mayor, asking the public to rise above the easy, age-old answer—finding a scapegoat—and to resist any attempt to manipulate this tragedy for crass political gain. No one said "Jew" and no one said "black" and certainly no one said "voter," but New Yorkers, accustomed to translating, understood what each party was accusing the other of.

And the jury, to its credit (and led by the Korean woman who followed every argument with minute attention), refused to convict Joe Cole of corruption, having seen no evidence to sustain that charge but O'Doul's. The charges on which they did convict, manslaughter and reckless endangerment resulting from disregard for the public welfare, was, Joe thought, a stunning example of the way things could come full circle and emerge as their own opposites. The force of his determination to rid the public of that undeniable threat to its welfare, Larry Manelli, had disrupted Joe's compass as surely as a magnetic field. Fixed blindly on his destination, he'd passed right by the same danger Manelli had been paid not to see, and had disregarded his responsibility to correct it as thoroughly as Manelli had, and for free.

chapter 17

City Hall

"All right, so now what can we do to help you guys out?" The mayor addressed his DOI Commissioner and his DOI Buildings Department Inspector General.

"Well, like I said, Mayor," Greg Lowry answered, "I want to look into Three Star's people. If the Buildings Department is clean, then what's left is accidents or sabotage."

"Find accidents," the mayor retorted.

"If we can. I don't think sabotage is likely, but it wouldn't be a thorough job unless we looked for it, and if it was going on it would most likely be from inside."

"Three Star's already contacted us," Shapiro put in. "Offering to cooperate."

Really? Charlie thought. *Good going, Walter, that was a smooth move.* He said, "You know Walter Glybenhall's a big supporter of mine?"

"Yes," Shapiro said.

Lowry said, "That's why I brought it up."

Of course they knew. Anyone who read the papers had seen Charlie Barr and Walter Glybenhall, wearing the tuxedos they both looked so good in, squiring their elegant wives to testimonial dinners and exhibit openings and benefit galas and fundraisers for Charlie's first and second mayoral campaigns. If this thing didn't screw either of them over too badly, there'd soon be photos at Charlie's gubernatorial fundraisers, too.

And of course that was why Lowry had brought it up.

Charlie nodded. "I appreciate the heads-up."

"Just professional courtesy," said Lowry.

"Bullshit. You don't want to get a screaming phone call from me in the middle of the night after I get one from Walter."

"If you think this will be a problem—" Shapiro began stiffly.

"Of course it'll be a problem. But tiptoeing around Walter would be a much worse problem. Whoever the hell Walter is shouldn't matter to what you guys do. Even if I wanted it to matter, I can't afford it. Understood?"

"Yes. But Mayor?" said Shapiro. "There's another thing to consider."

"That would be?"

"If McFee and Farrell are clean, and their inspectors are, too, maybe we should back out. NYPD is running its own investigation—"

"No. No, no. Greg was right, what he said before. DOI needs to be *visible*. Front and center. This is the first serious building site problem since Dolan Construction. I want citizens to *see* DOI on the case."

"Even if we're out of our jurisdiction?"

"Yes. Try not to step on NYPD's toes, but yes. But fellas, do something for me. This is a damn explosive situation, and I cannot afford to get fucked over by this right now. If there *is* anything—if anyone at Buildings or at Three Star is dirty *in any way*—I want to know about it long before anyone else finds out. Can you do that?"

Shapiro paused. Formally, he said, "We'll do our best to extend you every consideration, Mayor."

Charlie said, "You know I'm planning a run for governor?"

Shapiro shifted in his chair. "I'd heard rumors."

"I haven't announced yet but it's not much of a secret. And Edgar Westermann wants to be mayor. You saw his press conference yesterday?"

Both men nodded.

"He'll play this up," Charlie told them. "So will the press and everyone else who thinks there's something in it for them. The press was already yelling 'fewer rules and regs' this morning like they were dirty words. We can't, *can't*, have anything like last time. The men you have on the case—they're clean? Squeaky clean?"

Shapiro looked to Lowry. Lowry kept his steady gaze on the mayor. Don, on his windowsill perch, rubbed his chin. "I took off the guy I'd had on it," Lowry said. "Reassigned him. He's one of my best but I want fresh eyes. I'm giving the case to Ann Montgomery."

"What? Oh, tell me that's not true." This must be why the DOI men hadn't offered their investigator's name to the Police Commissioner when he'd given them the NYPD's. They'd wanted Charlie to hear it first.

Shapiro said, "She's smart. Her record is spotless. It was Greg's idea and it's a good one."

"Ann Montgomery's a showboater! This calls for a certain amount of subtlety, for God's sake."

"Or not," Lowry said.

"What the hell does that mean?"

"You just said you want DOI front and center. If there's anything to find, I guarantee Montgomery will find it. But if there's not? Like Virginia McFee said, that'll be hard to prove. You want to be in a position where no one can say DOI was soft on Buildings *or* on Three Star."

"And using Montgomery puts us in that position how?"

"Because Ann Montgomery hates you. She'd do anything she could to jam you up. If she can't find it, it's not there to find."

Charlie looked at Shapiro. "You buy this?"

"I do."

The mayor threw a glance at Don. Don rocked one hand, maybe-yes-maybe-no.

"How do we know she's not bent herself?" Charlie demanded.

"I looked at her personally," Lowry said. "When I couldn't pry her loose when I first came in. I just wanted to be sure."

"And you are?"

"I am. She's clean."

"Charlie," said Shapiro, "what could buy Ann Montgomery? She's richer than God."

CHAPTER

18

Heart's Content

"There've been three," Ann said.

Three what? Bears? Kings? Wishes?

"Accidents."

Oh. Right. Joe listened to the rush of water in the creek, but it was not loud enough to drown Ann out.

"The first was a scaffold collapse. Five bricklayers hurt, two seriously. Then a fire in a contractor's trailer. A lot of damage, but no one was inside, and the Fire Department got there before it spread. One fire-fighter injured when the floor gave way. You're about to ask if the fire was day or night, and whether there was an accelerant. It was night. And it was an electrical fire, no evidence of anything suspicious."

The sun lay like a blanket on the egg-yolk lilies and glowed in the quartz veins of the granite boulder. Joe hadn't planted those lilies, just found them, pulled up the grasses and milkweed to give them a chance.

"You're also wondering about the scaffolding." Ann's voice continued from behind him. "Bolts sheared off in a section of the frame. Inadequate engineering, not suited to a reasonable load, says the contractor. He's suing the scaffolding sub." She pointed into the woods. "Can I see the stream from there?"

He looked at her, silent a moment, then said, "Stick to the path. The boulder's covered with moss."

The breeze played in her hair, danced the tails of her coat around as though pleased to accompany her. She strode over the leaves, between the lilies of the valley and the crocuses and, as he knew she would, left the path and leapt onto the boulder the moment she reached it. She stood, surveying the woods from her new height.

He followed, jumping onto the rock beside her. "It's just water."

She smiled, walked forward across the rock, and slipped.

His heart pounded. Too far away, he lunged anyway; she threw out an arm, grabbed a tree branch, and righted herself before he reached her.

"Shit," he breathed. "Dammit, Ann!"

"I knew it was there." Her eyes were shining. "The branch."

"It might have broken."

"I didn't think it would."

And she'd been right.

Sitting on the porch again, Ann told him what, if he'd been concerned with any of this, he'd have been wondering: What had brought the Department of Investigation into the Three Star case.

Construction accidents—or jail riots, or phony taxi medallions, or the theft of garbage trucks—never interested DOI just because they happened. Trouble and crime on a department's turf were its own lookout, handled by the department backed by the NYPD and the full force and majesty of the law. DOI was called in—or sent in by the mayor's office—only when the lowlifes suspected of being behind the trouble were employees of the department where the trouble was.

"The Buildings Department looked into the first accident—the scaffold collapse—but they didn't find anything. After the second, the trailer fire, they assigned extra inspectors to the site. All routine."

"Wait," Joe said. "Please, allow me. The inspectors showed up on the site a couple of times a week. Maybe even every day, if this is a project the mayor cares about?"

Ann lifted her eyebrows, nodded silently.

"Why, by the way? Big contributors, Three Star?"

"Walter Glybenhall," Ann said.

"Glybenhall?" Joe turned to look at Ann; this time it was she who stared resolutely across the garden. "He managed to muscle his way in, finally?"

Ann ran her hand through her hair. "To Charlie's heart, long since. To the New York real estate stratosphere, absolutely not. But he still desperately wants to be a player."

"And he thinks a development in Mott Haven will make him one?"

"Even Walter Glybenhall can't be that delusional. He probably just thinks it will make him money. But it's a toehold."

"I'm surprised he can even find the place."

"His helicopter can. He was at the groundbreaking. Big media event."

No doubt, then, the mayor had been there, too. A big media event in Mott Haven. A developer who'd made his fortune veneering theme parks onto swampland and spreading condos like mushrooms across mountainside and beachfront, now trying to use a godforsaken corner of the Bronx as a springboard. Would wonders never cease? But Joe didn't stop and try to sort it out. He had no intention of giving a damn.

Ann was waiting for him to speak, though, so he said the next line. "So Charlie Barr cares, and Buildings is on the case. But the third accident, the falling bricks, happened anyway. How am I doing?"

"Just this Friday, the bricks." Ann said. "You're doing fine."

Of course he was. New York City real estate was like riding a bike. You couldn't forget how it went even when you wanted to. "So now someone's been killed"—unbidden, his mind flashed back three years, to Ellie's surprised look as he rushed in from the garden, switched on the TV; she'd snapped at him to wipe the mud off his boots—"someone's been killed," he repeated, "and Charlie's livid. He's afraid the Buildings Department inspectors are being paid to look the other way while Three Star cuts corners. Either that, or they're useless jerk-offs who couldn't find their own butts with both hands and a map. Personally I'd go with that theory, but you're not asking me."

"Yes, I am."

"No, you're not."

Ann passed that by, but he knew she'd come back to it. She said, "Hizzoner wants that to be the problem—that the inspectors and Three Star's site personnel are all idiots—but he's worried that Three Star are crooks and the inspectors are bent. Both the city and Three Star look bad either way, but there's bad and there's worse. Three Star's offered to open their books. They claim to be clean."

"Cutting corners doesn't show in books."

"They've already fired the site super."

"So they can pin it on him."

"Maybe it is him."

Joe shrugged. "Sure. Fine."

"Hizzoner called Mark Shapiro and Greg Lowry to an emergency meeting this morning. Charlie wants this problem solved soonest."

"Because Charlie's in bed with Three Star. Incidentally, besides Glybenhall, who are the other two stars?" *And why, Joe, why are you asking?*

"I don't know," Ann said. "It may be more than two. Or the name may mean nothing; Walter's big on hyperbole. If they exist, they're bound to be the moneymen. Walter never risks anything of his own if he can avoid it."

And more power to him, Joe thought, if he's found a way to avoid it.

"Anyway, the mayor's in a hurry to make all this go away," Ann said. "If it gets any bigger it could mess up his chances of becoming governor."

"That bastard is running for governor?"

"You can't really be surprised."

"He was just reelected mayor."

"And he can't run again, so now's the time to think about the future. Word is Louise is already redecorating the governor's mansion. And guess who else is thinking about the future?" She gave him no time to guess; she must have known he wouldn't. "Edgar Westermann. He wants to be mayor, next time around."

"Come on. Borough President's half a dozen steps above Westermann's level already."

"He's feeling cramped in Manhattan. He wants the whole show."

"Bet that gives Charlie a swift pain." Joe shook his head. "Shit. Edgar Westermann running the city, Charlie Barr running the state. Makes me almost sorry I can't vote."

"A released felon can petition to get his vote back."

Heat flooded Joe's face. "After his sentence is served. I'm on parole for the next four years, by which time this election will be long over. Ann, leave me alone. Go back to your city and your department and leave me the hell alone!"

He threw back his chair and crossed the garden again, started snapping out weeds between the hollyhocks' stalks. Hollyhocks didn't care what grew around them and before Ann had suckered him into listening to her construction site problems he hadn't been planning to weed here, but here he was, yanking out dandelions and clover and littering the lawn with them.

Ann came up behind him. "Don't you want to know why I'm here?"

"No."

"Yes, Joe. You do."

"I can't leave the county."

"You could for a job."

"I have a job. Seven to three, five days a week."

"Digging ditches."

"I've had practice. Ann, goddammit, I didn't want to hear any of this and I don't want to hear the rest."

"Hear it?" A note in her voice made him turn toward her; she was smiling. "Joe, were you listening? You were the one who *said* it."

He stretched for a clump of clover that was already flowering. It came up easily (clover always did) but he had to untangle it from a young hollyhock's leaves before he could toss it away.

Ann said, "We started by looking at the Buildings Department."

"*You* started? I thought you were being rehabilitated in the country-side."

Though never accused of anything, she'd been his partner. At his conviction she'd been expected to resign. Above her, the Inspector General and the Commissioner had already been replaced. The suggestion came down from the new Commissioner's office that she clean out her desk; the new IG made it clear he was sorry to have to lose her and he'd recommend her anywhere she wanted to go.

You should have seen their faces, she told Joe on her first prison visit, *Shapiro and Lowry both, when I said I wasn't going.*

She was civil service; she couldn't be fired without cause, and no one could pretend to find any. From that day, she was reassigned to the outer boroughs, to low-level, off-radar cases. They couldn't make her disappear, but they arranged things so she was rarely seen.

"Three Star started as Dennis Graham's case. I just followed the gossip. From the rice paddies." The excitement in Ann's voice was unmistakable; when she sounded like that, her eyes would be shining. Joe didn't look to see. "But that was then. Now that everyone's watching, Shapiro and Lowry had a high-level meeting, and everything's suddenly reshuffled. Dennis got promoted to some high-profile joint-FDNY thing in Brooklyn. And Shapiro and Lowry gave this case to me."

"You?" Now Joe did turn. Ann flashed the fire-eater's grin that would have warmed him, would have sparked a matching grin from him, years ago. Seeing it today, her eagerness and her excitement, sent ice up his spine. "Ann—you're being set up."

"Of course. If I nail Three Star, the Commissioner will call a press conference. He'll put his arm around me and tell everyone I was always one of DOI's top people, lately working highly sensitive cases in the outer boroughs."

Joe moved hollyhock stems, searching for hidden weeds. He said, "Then they'll send you back to Siberia for busting the mayor's pal. They'll keep you on the payroll but you won't get another case, ever. Or another job. That's why they moved Dennis. To keep him safe. In case there's something to find and the finder has to be sacrificed, they don't want it to be him. But they don't think it'll come to that, do they? They're counting on you filing a clean report. What's the carrot?"

"There's a corruption task force forming. Building-industry-wide, open-ended. FBI, State Police, NYPD. Even the Port Authority and the MTA. They haven't picked the DOI people yet."

"Nice. And all it takes is a clean report." His voice was bitter and he was surprised to hear it.

At the time of his trial the department had hung him out to dry. Early assertions from the then Inspector General that Joe Cole was an out-standing investigator with a spotless record had been squelched by the Commissioner, who modulated them through a reasoned insistence on withholding judgment until the process was complete to, finally, a sad-dened gratitude that our great American system of jurisprudence could be counted on to get at the truth even when the truth was painful.

Joe hadn't expected anything different. Ellie, for her part, was shocked, as though the department Christmas parties and outings to Shea, the commendations, press conferences, and public shows of appreciation meant something. But Ellie had never worked in city government.

It would have been gratifying to have had the support of the depart-ment he worked for, but Joe knew the drill. The Commissioner's dis-tancing was predictable, it hadn't gotten Joe convicted, and he had bigger things to worry about. It hadn't saved the Commissioner's ass, either, or IG's. A week after the verdict, Hizzoner vowed to the citizenry they'd never again find DOI asleep at the wheel, and gave them both the boot. Reading in the *Post* in the prison dayroom that the Commissioner had been replaced by that SCA stiff, Mark Shapiro, and the Inspector General for Buildings by a Sanitation lifer named Lowry, had given Joe a cold glimmer of satisfaction. Beyond that, up until this moment in this garden when he heard the venom in his own voice, he'd thought he didn't care.

Ann smiled and straightened up, brushing dirt that wasn't there from her gabardine slacks. "Doesn't that kill your knees?"

"You get used to it."

He started for the shed at the back of the property, for some stakes and ties to help out the heavy peonies.

"Joe? The third accident. A woman. Killed by falling bricks."

"I don't want to hear this."

"She left three kids."

"Let the police handle it."

"The police don't have a crime."

"Yet." *Oh, Joe, if that's the best you can do, you're in trouble.*

"The bricks were on a roof tarp. High wind caught the tarp, bricks got tossed over the side. They fell five floors and smashed the skull of a woman named Harriet Winston, a nurse's aide just off a double shift. On her way to pick up her three little kids at her mom's. The contractor—Three Star, Joe, Walter Glybenhall!—says tragic conflu-ence of circumstances, site super's been fired, sorry, see you around."

Joe plunged into the shadows of the shed. Through the open door behind him he heard the birds and the wind and the creek; he saw blurred green forms beyond the cracked, unwashed window.

Finally, because he had to, he emerged into the sun. Beside a white peony, he pushed a stake into the ground; as usual, the whites were unfurling first, while the reds, always a few days behind, were still round, waxy fists. Now open, heads too heavy for stalks, the whites were starting to lean, threatening to fall.

Ann said, "I want Three Star."

"The FBI," Joe said. "Port Authority, the MTA. On the other side: Siberia. It's cold out there."

"I can't be bought that cheap."

"You can't bust Walter Glybenhall."

" 'Can't'? You'd never have said that before."

The breeze wound itself around them. He looked away from Ann, let his gaze wander. Except for the larkspur, nothing yet blooming was blue; and it came out early and was going by already. Its fading color was no match for Ann's eyes.

Still he turned to her and said, "No, Ann." Looking into those beautiful, mismatched eyes, he said, "Go home."

CHAPTER

19

City Hall

Charlie Barr closed the door behind Mark Shapiro and Greg Lowry. He turned to his deputy mayor, who was fumbling with a cigarette. "Well?" Charlie demanded. "What?"

"What, what?"

Charlie flopped on the sofa and stretched out. "Those things'll kill you, you know."

"Not faster than working for you will."

"Okay, you're fired."

"Fine." Don Zalensky puffed out smoke. He held his cigarette between straight fingers and smoked it from the center of his mouth, like a clueless nerd trying to impress the cool crowd. Probably, Charlie thought, Don's pack-a-day habit had started from just that situation. Don was a New York City first deputy mayor now. Charlie wondered what the cool kids had become.

"So?"

Don began tentatively, "I don't know . . ."

"Yes, you do. That tells you have. The thing you do with your chin." Charlie rubbed his jaw. "This thing."

"I did that?"

"Umm-hmm."

"Damn. I've been trying to stop."

"You'd be better off stopping smoking."

"The universe would unravel."

"Your altruism is noted. Now: the meeting?"

"Well, just . . . when Lowry looked at you."

"He looked at me funny?"

"No, he looked at *you*. When you asked whether their people were squeaky clean."

"Why shouldn't he look at me? I was talking. And I'm the friggin' mayor."

"Yes, I know, but . . . Shapiro was looking at *him*. Every other time you asked something, they looked at each other before they answered. It's kind of normal, people at different levels. Like when you and some staff are at a meeting, and they have the data."

"We look at each other?"

The deputy mayor nodded. "They'll wait a second to see if you want them to answer. You're the boss, so in case you want it yourself. All the Deps do it."

"Really?" Interesting; Charlie would have to watch for that. "Except, of course, for you."

"Except for me," Zalensky agreed. Don never spoke in meetings, at press conferences, in public forums of any kind. Charlie had gotten used to that years ago; in their business it was refreshing.

"But Shapiro and Lowry didn't do that?" Charlie asked. "And you think it matters?"

"They did it except when you asked about their people. Then Lowry just kept looking right at you. As though . . ." Zalensky sucked on his cigarette, frowning. "As though he wanted to look like this wasn't a problem he'd thought about."

"Meaning it was?"

"Not necessarily. It's just, I think the reason they moved those people out and brought in someone new might not only be because they wanted 'new eyes.' "

"What? Oh, Don, say it ain't so. Not again. You're telling me someone at DOI is bent?"

"I'm not saying that. I'm saying, there may be some other reason they wanted to use Montgomery on this, besides what they said."

"Like what?"

"I don't know."

"I have to know. They have to tell me. If there's shit between Three Star and Buildings, that's bad enough. If this is going to blow up, if it's DOI again . . . Shit. Ah, shit." He ran his hand across his head. "I'm calling Shapiro. What? I shouldn't call? Or there's something else? Shit. What else?"

"Ann Montgomery."

"You're worried about that?"

"I don't know. You think she still hates you, from back then?"

"She thought I should've kept my mouth shut. That my public state-ments poisoned the jury."

"How do you know she thought that?"

"She told me."

"Just walked up to you on the street and said that?"

"Our paths sometimes cross. Benefits, openings."

"Oh, the nightlife." Don, who spoke nine languages and read ten-pound books in all of them, wasn't much for the social whirl.

"Don't knock it. They vote, they contribute, and the food's good. She's your type, by the way. A blonde shiksa. I could introduce you. Could mend your broken heart from that Eliot girl you used to date."

"I didn't date her long enough to get one."

"Hey, come to think of it, they know each other. You could date Montgomery, keep an eye on her, piss Jen Eliot off at the same time—"

"I already pissed Jen off when I broke up with her, Charlie. She for-gave me, though, as soon as she found a new guy. So Montgomery: do we have to worry about her?"

Charlie pondered. "Maybe not."

"You said she was a showboater."

"What it really is with her . . . If you sing louder than everyone else, your voice'll get heard. It may not be because you want to drown every-one out, just that you like to sing loud. Jesus Christ, Don, you're actu-ally smiling."

"I never heard you do that before. A metaphor like that."

"I'm a man of undiscovered talents. Pass me the phone."

CHAPTER 20

Harlem: the Riverbank

"The job," the Boss said. "It went all right?"

"Ain't no thing." Kong squinted against the sun-gleam on the river.

"Glad to hear it." The Boss smiled. Guy could always be counted on for a smile. Kong smiled back. Wasn't that something was funny, but he had a secret: he knew who this guy was. "Just call me Boss," guy said on the phone, first time he called. Seriously? Fuck that shit. Kong wasn't about to work for no man he didn't even know his name. When they met first time, Kong had the bike hid. Easy to follow the Boss's car: ain't no one in New York gonna notice some crazy bike messenger. Kong watched the car slide down into a garage, saw the Boss come out, watched what building he went in. Then all he had to do was wait until lunchtime next day, and here come the Boss, going to some important appointment for lunch. Kong got next to a few pretty things coming out to sit in the sun. "Hey, baby, 'scuse me. Don't mean to bother you. That dude over there, I used to work for him. Can't recall his name, you know who it is?" Got the guy's name, and the cell phone digits of two hot bitches, too. That was the difference between him and that loser, T. D. Tilden. T. D. never even ask Kong who they working for, why they doing all this. Just took his pay and rolled a blunt, every time. Kong, he was different: he got game.

Not that he was about to let on what he knew, not yet. Just, someday when he needed it, there it'd be.

"You do good work," the Boss said. He was wearing Ray-Bans but Kong could tell his eyes were jumping around like he was nervous.

"Hey, chill, man. You see anyone else here?" Of course he didn't.

Even the old guy sometimes fished from the broken concrete wasn't there today. He never came on Sundays, that guy. The Boss told him, *As soon as it's done, somewhere no one's gonna see us,* and Kong knew what he was doing when he picked this place. That's what this guy didn't appreciate about him, the way he knew what he was doing.

"Well," the Boss started, but now was time for Kong to say his other piece.

"Was one thing, though."

"What thing?" The Boss pushed his hands deeper into his jacket pockets like some worried kid at school. Well, good. More worried he was, more likely to keep Kong on the payroll.

"Thought you ought to know," Kong said. "T.D. say he got copies."

"Copies? Of what?"

Kong grinned. Of course, he could have said what the copies was of, right off, but he wanted to make the guy ask.

"The drawing you give me. For the first job? What to take out from where? Of the—"

"Shit. The kid made copies?"

"Don't know if it's true. T.D. say so."

"Did T.D. say where they are?"

"Nah."

"Do you have any idea?"

"Maybe. I been checking on it for you, already. Got someone to see, later on."

"Do you? Where?"

"What you care? You gonna walk up and ring the doorbell, ask for 'em? You want 'em, you gonna need me to get 'em for you."

"You may not be the best man for the job. Not so soon after this."

"Then I do it later."

"Are they at his place?"

"Don't worry, I find out."

The guy smiled again. A weird smile, different from usual. "No, Kong, I don't think so. Sorry about this; you do good work."

"About what?"

But he didn't need to ask that. The Boss pulled his hand, that nervous hand, from his pocket. Kong saw the sun gleam off the .45, heard the crash of the bullet busting out, felt the slam in his chest all at the exact same time. The second one, too. And he thought maybe a third. But he never did know.

CHAPTER 21

Sutton Place

"Oh, what great good luck, a visit from the Ice Queen."

"Quite the pose, leaning casually on a mantel full of trophies, Walter," said Ann. "But the smoking jacket's pretentious."

The maid who'd glanced nervously at the badge clipped to Ann's coat retreated hastily down the carpeted hall of the Park Avenue penthouse, leaving them alone.

Glybenhall smiled. "I'll take your word for it, Ann; you're the expert on flamboyance. Though I seem to recall you liking my smoking jackets, long ago."

"I never liked anything about you."

"I fear that's not true, but if it's what you tell yourself, I shan't argue. So, am I to understand this is an official call? That the minions of the law work tirelessly, even on Sundays? Or perhaps that was just a ploy to get into my sanctum. Are you hoping to get lucky, Ann?"

"If I were, I wouldn't have come here."

Ann navigated the huge room, edging around an overstuffed sofa and a thick-legged coffee table. A niche beside the fireplace held a grandfather clock.

Once, long ago, Ann had walked into the apartment Glybenhall maintained in Zurich. Every detail of what she'd seen that morning was burned into her memory. She'd loathed heavy furniture and grandfather clocks ever since.

"Have a seat, my dear."

"I'll stand. Walter, I'm here because I'm investigating you."

"Is that a fact?" He sat in a studded leather armchair and smoothed the maroon silk of his jacket. "Well, Charlie Barr did say that the city would be forced to go through the motions of looking at me with concern, because of that unfortunate situation in the Bronx." He paused, which Ann assumed was to allow the echoes of "Charlie Barr" to die down. "But he didn't advise me that when someone did come barging in here, it would be on a Sunday and it would be you. Nor that being 'looked at' would include the privilege of being near enough to sniff your perfume. Hanae Mori, isn't it?"

"No."

"Oh. I could have sworn . . ." Walter shrugged. "That vulgar badge aside, you're looking quite decorative, I must say."

"Drop it, Walter. I'm here on business."

"I wouldn't be quite so quick to turn down a compliment if I were you. Your mother never has been."

"My mother's mistakes in judgment are legendary. What's going on in Mott Haven?"

"Investigating Walter Glybenhall." He eyed her speculatively. "What a plum this must be, in your world. Did you have to sleep with very many people to get it?"

Ann stood perfectly still, feeling the hot blood surge into her face, knowing Glybenhall could see it. In a voice of ice she said, "Mott Haven?"

"I beg your pardon, Ann. I don't doubt you're doing God's work, as ever, but on whose authority? I find I can't keep up with your rapid-fire changes of situation. However hard I try."

She unclipped the badge from her coat's lapel and dropped it on the coffee table.

He leaned forward to view it. "DOI? Isn't the mandate of that agency corruption within the municipal ranks?"

"And the corrupters."

He smiled. "And it would so please you if that were I! Well, I'm sorry I can't provide you with that thrill, especially as you won't allow me to offer you any other. Nevertheless, I shall try to help." The smile abruptly disappeared. "At Mott Haven, work on my site is being deliberately disrupted in an attempt to cost me both time and money."

"God, you really are the center of your own universe, aren't you, Walter? Five bricklayers were hurt, and a firefighter, and a woman by the name of Harriet Winston was killed. Does that ring a bell?"

"Those unfortunate outcomes are what I believe is called collateral damage. I and my finances were clearly the intended target."

"That's one interpretation. Another is that these men's injuries and Mrs. Winston's death are the result of sloppiness, corner-cutting, and rushed work that you're paying people not to see. In other words, you and your finances are not the victim, you're the cause."

"My dear girl, I've been in this business for many years. Accidents are rare on my sites, and I have never had a fatality before this."

A Vivaldi theme playing too fast on an electronic chip pierced the air. Glybenhall reached for the phone on the side table, his eyes still on Ann. "Is he really?" he said into it, then, "No, I can't right now, I'm having too much fun. Tell him fifteen minutes. Oh, will he? Well, it can't be helped. Yes, all right, tell the mayor I'll meet him at six. Thank you."

"Walter, if that was to impress me, it didn't work," Ann said as Glybenhall hung up.

"Good grief, why would I bother? Where were we?"

"You were about to give me your theory on why someone would disrupt your work."

"Ah, yes. To cause me to lose money?"

"As I understand it, you're already losing money at Mott Haven."

"Who told you that?"

"The grapevine. I've subpoenaed your records but the pattern's clear."

"There was no need for a subpoena, you know. We've offered to open our books."

"So I heard. But I wanted to go by the rules."

"How unlike you."

"And offering to open your books seemed unlike you. So tell me, is it true?"

He shrugged. "Losing money and losing a lot of money are quite different."

"It is true, then."

"Yes, it is. That's real estate development: some days you eat the bear, some days the bear eats you. As long as everyone's fed."

"There's no way you're that complacent about losing a fortune, Walter."

"Sit down, Ann. This is unpleasant, to have you looming this way."

She waited a long moment, then sat across from him, on the sofa.

"And you'll take off your coat?"

"Don't get greedy."

"Well, then. Listen closely, my child, while I explain real estate development to you. Projects such as Mott Haven are complicated. Because of the inclusion of the low-income component, the tax structure is complex. Certain advantages will offset losses in other areas, et cetera. As long as one doesn't lose *a lot* of money, one can lose and actually come out ahead."

"As I understand it, this is the first time you've done a low-income development. You don't usually even bother with residential except when it's attached to a resort or a mall."

"I do not build malls," he said flatly. "I create retail experiences. But I'm pleased to find you so current with my work, and I apologize for not being so with yours."

"Oh, mine wouldn't interest you, it's all about law and justice. Tell me, what made you decide to do something as out of character as Mott Haven?"

"I suppose I was looking for a challenge."

"Baloney. You never take risks, Walter."

"And nor do you, for all your physical daring. What's in Mott Haven for me, darling Ann, is the possibility of accomplishing something I'd been told could not be done: building a profitable development in a marginal neighborhood. Trump's never done it, nor that goon Kalikow, nor Silverstein: they've never even tried. Glybenhall will do it, and I'll end up with a handsome New York City project for my ever-growing portfolio."

"Ah. This is your chance to play with the big boys."

"Is the aim of that remark to make me so angry that I lose control and immediately confess to whatever malfeasance you're accusing me of? Which would be exactly what, by the way?"

"That your claim of sabotage is a smoke screen. That the three accidents at Mott Haven are the result of corners you're cutting that you're bribing city inspectors not to see."

"You disappoint me, but then you always have. Why would I do that?"

"To keep from losing *a lot* of money."

"Allow me to point out that on a job such as this, time *is* money. Since these accidents began, my schedule has been thrown into disarray by inspectors and police officers crawling all over my site."

"A plan gone awry."

"My plans do not go awry. But, if it relieves your mind, be assured all my employees have been given a severe talking-to, in which the limits of acceptable behavior were clearly laid out."

"And those limits are?"

"Their dealings with public officials must be unimpeachable. All forms are to be filled out, all permits applied for, and all approvals received."

" 'Public officials.' Lying, cheating, and stealing in the private realm are acceptable?"

"Whatever the case in the private realm, my darling, that's none of DOI's business."

"Is that so?"

"Am I wrong?"

"Technically, no. But if I—"

"If you overstep, my dear Ann, you'll be putting me in a very awkward position."

"Walter! That wouldn't be a threat, would it?"

"Of course not. Unless the prospect of discomfiting me fills you with dread."

"On the contrary."

"As I suspected. In fact, like the others of your kind who've been badgering me since these accidents began, you find me quite an attractive villain."

"Actually, I find very little about you attractive."

"So you've always maintained, though more stridently than convincingly. In any case, as to villainy, I'm a wealthy white man, irritatingly educated, not discernibly ethnic. I'm the perfect public enemy in this rainbow-coalition city."

"You think that's what this is about? Looking for a scapegoat?"

"What else?"

"Finding the truth?"

"You may be naive enough to believe that, but your superiors certainly aren't."

"No one's out to get you, Walter."

"Except possibly yourself, with your unhealthy inability to separate me from your sad father's fate."

Ann's stomach twisted. She fought a sudden need to jump up off the sofa, to move. "Walter, it's been years since you could get a rise out of me by mentioning my father."

"Oh, I don't think so. I think that's precisely why this assignment is so gratifying to you. You know, if it weren't such a terrible cliché, I'd tell you how lovely you are when you're angry. Your cheeks and your eyes are positively glowing; you're nearly as lovely as your mother once was. Now, if there's nothing else I can do for you . . . ?"

Ann stood. "You haven't done anything for me yet. But I didn't come here thinking you would."

"Then why come?"

"To let you know I'm watching you."

"O lucky man, to be watched over by you. Now, adieu. Until we meet again."

"Count on it, Walter." Ann strode across the priceless carpet, turned at the door. "Count on it."

Heart's Content

Joe spent the hours of the late afternoon ripping poison ivy off the slope to the creek. Snowdrops had sprinkled that hill when he'd first seen it, and he'd discovered crocuses and glory-of-the-snow nestled between tree roots. Beautiful, but small and low. He had an idea of a hillside of jonquils and anemones, planted in clumps this fall and blooming next spring, naturalizing through the years, popping up in places he hadn't put them, going wherever they wanted to be. And he thought he might try a new white forsythia he'd read about, for the edge of the wood. It was said to be a very early bloomer, pale pearl flowers on red stems bursting open on a cold gray day in March, one of those days when you're afraid that this is finally the year spring will not come.

He'd bundled the poison ivy stems, the roots and runners, and stuffed them into plastic bags and hauled them to the roadside for the county to pick up. He usually burned garden debris but you can't burn poison ivy; in some people, the smoke hits lungs as the sap does skin. He'd labeled each bag. Some people were so allergic they shouldn't even handle the bags, in case sap from the gardener's hands had coated them already. Ellie and Janet were both sensitive like that. He wasn't, himself; poison ivy had never even given him a rash. At one point, the hillside behind him cleared of vines but twice as much in front of him, he'd paused to wipe sweat from his eyes and asked himself why he was doing this at all. He could plant around, beside, and under the stuff without a problem. But still, it had to go. Someone sensitive to it might come here to wander this hillside, among the narcissus.

He stripped off his gloves and left them in the shed. He started to rinse his hands and arms at the outdoor spigot, so as not to bring sap into the house. As the icy water hit his skin he shook his head at his own foolishness. Every day, he discovered yet another thread tying him to nothing.

He had more to do, but he was hungry. A quick dinner, and then back out. He slit open a package of salami, cut a tomato, spread mustard on bread. Sandwich made, beer in hand, now he had a problem.

Ann's papers still covered the table.

In a last attempt to ensnare him she'd dumped photos and papers out and spread them. He'd refused to look at them; she'd refused to stick them back in the envelope and take them away. She'd walked out, leaving the cabin silent and empty but leaving her evidence behind.

For a moment he stood uneasily in the middle of the floor, as if the space between the counter and the table were a crossroads. But what turning could this pretend to be? What choice?

He walked to the table, put down the beer, reached toward a photo but pulled his hand back as though heat emanated from it. Was he afraid? Of what? He who could tear out poison ivy with no effect, did he think Ann's papers were going to burn his fingers?

No.

That they would cling to him like burrs. Stick like pine sap. That if he touched them they would not let him go.

Damn! Damn Ann, and damn her photos. He clattered his plate onto the table, swept the papers into a pile. He could shove them into the envelope himself, put her address on it and a couple of stamps, and stick it in the mailbox, flip up the flag that would tell the postman here was something to be taken away. Then Ann would understand he'd meant it when he said "Go home."

Or better: he'd burn them. Shove them into a crackling fire and let them keep him warm. She wouldn't have brought originals, just copies; she didn't need them back. He'd send her nothing. He'd let his silence speak.

At the last minute, instead of either, he slammed them into a drawer.

CHAPTER

23

City Hall

Brogan's. Hudson River landscapes on paneled walls; soft light on people in calm poses of power. Heavy silver clinking on delicate china; the murmur of off-the-record dealmaking. The aroma of single malt from Charlie's glass mingling with the filtered-air scent of money and success.

Brogan's went back to the days when the Carnegies drank with the Vanderbilts. A moss-green canopy curved over the sidewalk and a brass handle opened the door. No sign, no number: if you needed those things to find Brogan's, you weren't going to get in anyway.

With each seismic convulsion in American life, Brogan's had shuddered. The first Jew, the first black, the first woman to walk through the door had stopped all movement and sound within. Then, each time, Brogan's squared its shoulders and started up again, resuming its mission to serve the elect.

Or elected. Charlie, first brought here by a judge as an up-and-coming City Councilmember, was soon welcome on his own. The manager, Frank, had gradually promoted Charlie from the left-wall banquette through the center tables. When Charlie was chosen Speaker, he got to the booths on the right.

Charlie was halfway through his Glenfiddich when he spotted Louise breezing through the door. His wife's face was half hidden by the graceful brim of what Charlie thought might have once been called a picture hat. Her figure was not hidden at all by her black linen skirt or her cream silk blouse, and her calves were positively shown off by her strapback heels. As Charlie watched, she kissed Frank's cheek, then started across the room with graceful, unhurried steps, stopping to greet a banker here, a state senator there. She waved to Herb Washington, the mayor's bodyguard, sitting with his ginger ale at the bar. Charlie's eyes followed her, filled with her the way they had been since the day they met, the brash first-term Councilmember and the judge's daughter.

He stood; she kissed him lightly and slid into the booth.

"Saw your press conference." She smiled, took off her hat, and fluffed her dark hair. "You were great."

"Why, thank you, ma'am." He could smell her perfume, the rich floral scent she wore in the evenings. He never remembered its name. But Lena had it written down.

"Very direct, very angry," Louise went on. "Very much in charge."

A waiter appeared and asked if she'd like a glass of dry champagne. She smiled her thanks. Career waiters, they were at Brogan's, not actors between gigs. They made it their business to remember things.

"You handled the new CBS guy particularly well," she told Charlie. "I'm not sure I'm going to like him."

"I'll tell him; he'll be flattered."

She sighed. "You're probably right." She fell silent, her attention on the room, who was here, who was coming and going. She turned back to Charlie. "But honey?"

"Uh-oh. The 'but.' "

"Well, I just didn't think you were fair to Walter."

"All I said was we were looking into every possibility."

"You said it too fast. There should have been some 'Walter Glybenhall's a pillar of the community' statement first. You should have looked indignant at the very thought."

Charlie mugged indignant as the waiter set down Louise's champagne. She laughed. "You know what I mean."

"Seemed to me the problem was the opposite. I didn't think it was a good time to emphasize my relationship to Walter."

"I just don't want to see you alienating him."

"Or his friends?"

"Of course 'or his friends.' We're going to need them."

"We're also going to need credibility in the black community."

Louise looked pensively across the room. "We can win the state without that. But not without Walter and his friends."

"Win it, maybe. But not govern it."

Her brow furrowed and she shook her head slightly, as though she didn't understand something he'd said. But she didn't answer, just sipped her champagne.

A new OMB Deputy Commissioner came over to greet the mayor,

an exuberant young guy still at left-banquette rank but obviously pleased as punch to be here. He shook Charlie's hand, was introduced to Louise, exchanged small talk for the ritually prescribed forty-five seconds, and scrammed cheerfully back to his table.

"I wish I weren't getting old," Louise mused. "I've forgotten his name already."

"If you'd been paying attention instead of running your toes up my pants leg, you'd remember."

"If my toes had done their job, you'd have forgotten his name yourself."

"Sweetie, your toes could make me forget *my* name." Charlie gave her the OMB Deputy's pertinent facts again, adding, "Came over from Citibank. We think he's a guy to watch."

"Who does? Don?"

"For one."

Louise gave her usual skeptical eyebrow-raise to an opinion of Don's, but Charlie didn't respond; this had been going on for years. Nevertheless, he saw, she gazed across the carpeted expanse to the young man's table. Her eyes held the steady look they always had when she was filing information away in her mental database.

"What did you do this afternoon?" Charlie asked her.

"I thought, since we were in town, I'd have lunch with Edith. To talk about that Riverkeepers project."

Charlie nodded, though he was fuzzy on the details of the program: something about high school students cleaning up the Bronx River. Sipping her champagne, Louise expanded on the benefits of the idea, educationally, environmentally, and public-relations-wise. "So really, they're using me," she finished. "It's valuable for them to have the mayor's wife involved. And I'm using them. This will play well upstate."

"A beautiful relationship."

"Actually, I do kind of like Edith. A little too earnest, but she's very sweet. And Helene Aldrich was there, too. You know we're going out to Southampton with them Saturday? Why are you making that face? You forgot, didn't you?"

"No, just tried to. Lex is such a bore."

"I know, honey, but he's a real power in the center of the state. Lex owns half of Rochester."

"No way out?"

Louise shook her head. "The Aldriches aren't a good cancel."

Charlie had a sudden vision of Helene and Lex Aldrich, mouths open in surprise as a giant hand stamped "cancel" on their foreheads. "You think we need to spend the whole weekend?"

She considered. "I don't think that's necessary. If we go out late morning and sit around the pool a little, we can come back after dinner. Will you survive?"

"The pool." Charlie snorted. "They serve those chartreuse drinks with umbrellas in them."

"Don't exaggerate, it was plastic monkeys on the rim. Anyway, we can sneak out and walk on the beach. They have a lot of beachfront." She patted his hand, then glanced at her Cartier watch, the one he'd given her last Christmas. "When's Walter coming?"

"We said six. He'll probably keep me waiting just to prove he can."

"It's come to that?"

"With Walter it always was that."

"Fifteen minutes?"

"Oh, God, no. Under ten."

"Then I'd better finish up and go."

"You don't have to leave before he gets here."

"Oh, yes, I do. Otherwise how will you have time to miss me?"

She took another sip, then put the flute down, leaving an inch of liquid in the bottom as she always did.

Knowing how she loved champange, he'd asked her once, long ago, why she did that.

Newlyweds at a senator's Christmas party, they'd stepped out briefly to be alone on the penthouse terrace. Behind them people laughed and mingled beyond glass doors obscured by frost; on the terrace the air was cold and still. New York's streetlights and stoplights shone brightly below and the stars did the same above. Charlie's arm around Louise kept them both warm. She didn't answer his question, but, gazing over the city, slipped the strap from the shoulder of her velvet dress, guiding his hand to where she wanted it. Charlie heard her gasp at the first cold brush of his fingertips, then saw the dreamy smile start as her nipple rose to meet his touch. He nuzzled her ear, and was about to suggest they go home, when Louise laughed, pulled away, and straightened her straps again. She took a sip of champagne. "You need to talk to the senator," she said. "About the water resource bill."

"I'll call him tomorrow."

"Now is better." She smiled and put the champagne flute down on a glass-topped table. As she walked back into the party, leaving him and her champagne unfinished, Charlie could see the outline of her still-hard nipples under her velvet dress.

Now, as she slid out of the booth at Brogan's and kissed his cheek, say-ing, "See you at home. Dinner's at eight," he searched the folds of her blouse, but the fabric was rippling and loose and he wasn't sure what he saw.

CHAPTER

24

City Hall

Louise left at ten to six. Charlie was alone at Brogan's for another nineteen minutes before Walter Glybenhall arrived, Walter clearly pushing his under-ten as far as he dared. Given the mess in the Bronx, Charlie might have been surprised, but Walter had always believed in the good offense, the preemptive strike.

And it wasn't like Charlie had a chance to get lonely. Spotted alone with a Scotch, he was fair game. Herb raised his ginger ale as Louise left, wordlessly offering to come shoo people away until Walter showed, but Charlie waved him off. You don't want to be in public demand, he thought, don't run for public office.

So he'd shaken two dozen hands, been part of a dozen quick conversations where the words were nothing and the subtext everything (and a couple of them he'd made a note to himself to remember to report to Don, to get his take), by the time Walter turned up.

Silver-haired and broad-shouldered, his Nordic ancestry glowing from his handsome profile, Walter Glybenhall was right-side-booth material, too, and a discreetly gorgeous hostess stood ready to guide him across the room. (Women might be welcome to drink at Brogan's now, but Brogan's understood where the power still resided and what made the powerful feel the effort had been worth it.) But Walter murmured something to the hostess that made her giggle, and crossed the carpet alone. The United Fund vice president who'd been chatting with Charlie greeted Walter, asking jovially whether any of his end-of-the-fiscal-year audits had discovered unexpected surpluses, because if so he could suggest a use for them. Walter gravely promised to look under the mattress and the vice president, chuckling appreciatively, returned to his table.

"She's married," Charlie remarked as Walter slid into the booth. "And you're late."

"Pardon?" The faintest hints of a vague mid-European accent inflected Walter's speech. It summoned up ski slopes, vast hotel lobbies, boardrooms with unfamiliar skylines beyond tall windows.

"Alyssa." Charlie nodded toward the hostess. "Mei-lin, too. It's the redhead who's single. Carmen."

"Carmen's not working today. I adapted. Rum and Coke," Walter told the waiter. Walter was mercurial, his choices unpredictable. There was nothing for the waiters to memorize, except that whatever he ordered, he expected it to be mixed from the top shelf.

"So, Charlie. I apologize if I've kept you waiting. Especially when I assume you've called me here to chastise me?"

"Partly."

Walter's smile was impressive against his golden tan. "I didn't have the opportunity to see your press conference earlier, but I was given quite a detailed report. I understand you're investigating me."

"Three Star, yes."

"Of course, Three Star. Good, good. It would be a shame to waste all the time and money it's costing me to do this project on the complete up-and-up."

"The up-and-up was the deal, Walter."

"Well, no. The deal was that I would create a project the community would adore."

"A project that would stand up to scrutiny. And killing people makes the community adore you exactly how?"

"Not 'people.' One unfortunate woman. One tragic accident."

"Three accidents, if you want to be accurate."

"Only one serious, that affected your beloved 'community.' For which I assure you we'll pay. Our insurance company has already made quite a generous offer to Harriet Winston's family."

"That's not the point."

"Whatever the point, sufficient money will blunt it. And Charlie, if you *really* want to be accurate, you'll have to stop saying 'accidents.' "

"Don't start that again, Walter, because I'm not buying it."

"I see. You'd rather believe in coincidence."

"No, I'd rather believe you're cutting corners and paying people off."

"Charlie!" The waiter set down Walter's rum and Coke; both men were silent until he was gone. "Would I do that? On this job? After I promised?"

"I didn't think you would. But as I told you on the phone, I have a problem."

"Which is?"

"Oh, for Christ's sake, Walter!"

"Charlie. Outside of Ford Corrington, who wants my scalp, and Edgar Westermann, whose animosity is not quite as rabid but who can surely tell a sound bite when he sees one, no one will care about any of this by the middle of next week."

"Harriet Winston's kids?"

"Now that's a low blow, unworthy of you."

"Walter? Are you paying off anyone to get anything done up there? Anyone, anything at all?"

Walter's eyes sparkled with amusement. "No, Charlie. I am not."

"Because if you are, you and I are both dead. Dead, Walter. Like Marley's ghost. Dead, dead, dead."

"Charlie, you've always had a tendency to melodrama. But—" Walter held up a hand while he sipped his drink, "one thing I certainly don't want to be is dead. Which is why Three Star is the straight-shootin'est developer you ever saw. From the start, everyone up there has been instructed to conduct their business with city personnel as though the nuns were watching. As I told you they would be."

"You guarantee that?"

Another sip, and Walter looked Charlie straight in the eye. "As I told you they would be," he repeated. "I keep my promises, Charlie."

Charlie nodded and sat back. "Good. Because I'm counting on you."

"And I on you. Although . . ."

"Although what?"

"Although if you really loved me, you'd consider seriously the possibility that these aren't accidents and they're not my fault. Not Three Star's fault. That their cause is sabotage."

"Talk about melodrama, Walter."

"I know, I know. It sounds that way. But barring any corner-cutting on my part—which you've just granted me—three accidents in two weeks does become painfully coincidental."

"I didn't agree you hadn't been cutting corners. I bought your promise you haven't paid my people to look the other way while you did it."

"What you're saying, Charlie, is that you trust me to keep to our arrangement, but not much farther than that."

"Consider it a tribute to our friendship that I trust you that far."

"You're seriously irritated, aren't you? Beyond what's required for public consumption?"

"You're damn right I am. The whole point of Mott Haven was to look good under a microscope. Right now it would look rotten in a fog on a dark night. You need to clean up your act, fast."

"But if it's sabotage—"

"Then hire better security! Get more supervision! Sabotage doesn't make you innocent, Walter, just cheap."

"More supervision? Why, Charlie, I thought you were opposed to excessive supervision. Hinders efficiency, creativity, productivity. I've heard you give that speech."

"For God's sake, Walter! Someone died."

"And I'm very sorry about that, but I didn't kill her."

"Your project did." Charlie drank the remains of his Scotch. "I'm beginning to wonder if this whole deal was a mistake."

"Are you?" Walter gave Charlie a speculative look. "Are you really? Well, I assure you it was not." He put down his glass. "I'm sorry if I appear insensitive. I do understand how serious this is, both for the unfortunate woman's family, for the project, and politically for you."

Charlie didn't point out that wasn't "both," it was three. He waved the waiter over, asked Walter, "You want another?"

"Why not?" As the waiter glided away, Walter said, "I'll tighten up. I'll have people watching everybody and I'll have people watching them. But, Charlie, I do wish I could persuade you to explore the sabotage angle."

Charlie sighed. "We are. Shapiro and Lowry want to, so we are."

Walter beamed. "Why didn't you tell me? Instead of letting me hector you?"

"For the same reason I still lift weights."

"May I ask at whom you're looking?"

"No."

"Because Ford Corrington—"

"Don't even whisper that, Walter, not even here."

"Oh, come, Charlie."

"He's—"

"—not the type. Ford Corrington's a saint, Ford Corrington's the Great Black Hope. I've heard it all. The man hates me."

"Christ, Walter. He fought you, you lost. Get over it."

"I don't enjoy losing."

"Does anyone? But every time you sneeze you accuse Corrington of giving you pneumonia. You got your damn memorial built, what are you still sore about?"

"In Riverside Park! I made a legitimate, generous offer to honor the sacrifices made by the uptown communities on that horrendous day, and Corrington—"

"—didn't see it that way."

"He accused me of colonizing! In the press!"

"And personally I thought a lawsuit was an overreaction," Charlie said.

"Yes, you mentioned that at the time. I did rather hope to enjoy your support, as one comes to expect of a friend. However, I understood when the exigencies of political life intervened."

"No, I just thought you were wrong."

"Then you must have been overjoyed when my lawsuit was dismissed."

"I didn't care enough to be overjoyed. But I got a kick out of the grounds."

"It was not a 'vague allegorical reference'! It was a deliberate slur, damaging to my good name—"

"Walter, drop it. You told it to the judge already, and you *lost*."

"Yes, well, I'd like to see what a white judge would have said."

"To Corrington that whole thing was just a way to get his name in the papers, fighting the good fight. It wasn't personal. You made it personal with the lawsuit."

"What choice did I have?" Walter protested. "Corrington would ban white people north of Ninety-sixth Street."

"That's crap and you know it."

"Charlie, please calm down, I'm speaking metaphorically. And *you* know it."

"Let me suggest you lower the level of anti-Corrington rhetoric over these next few months."

"Damn it, Charlie, this is a man who gives press conferences and won't talk to white reporters."

"To help black reporters get their faces on TV. And what do you care? You're not a reporter."

Walter's pale blue gaze held Charlie. Charlie returned it steadily. "Whatever my reasoning, and whatever its merit," Walter said, "I think we can agree that Ford Corrington hates me. I really think it would be a good idea to have a look in that direction."

"How would I justify that, Walter? A pillar of the Harlem community suspected of sabotaging your job up in the Bronx? Why?"

"To stop me successfully completing—"

"—a deal he doesn't know you and I have."

Walter shrugged. "Maybe he does."

"How would he?"

"I don't know. But—"

"Trust me, he doesn't. If he did he'd have gone running to the press the moment he found out. Which you can count on him doing if we start investigating him. It's a good thing this is just a paranoid fantasy."

The waiter returned, setting down fresh drinks and removing their drained glasses.

"And," said Charlie, tasting his Scotch.

"There's more, beyond 'paranoid'?"

"If it *were* sabotage, it's much more likely to be someone who works for you and feels like he got screwed over at some point, than Corrington. An inside job, so it would come back to you again. Sabotage, incompetence, graft, whatever. It keeps coming straight back to Three Star, Walter. To you."

Walter sighed. "In other words, I can expect you and the luscious Louise to send your regrets and not attend my Fourth of July festivities after all?"

"Looks that way."

"Alas. Well, in that case, my friend, bottoms up."

Walter smiled. Charlie didn't, but kept his eyes locked on Walter's while they lifted their glasses to each other and drank.

CHAPTER 25

Heart's Content

A week after he walked through the last gate, as soon as he'd found a job and a room and so could convince his parole officer that he was likely to come back, Joe turned in a detailed description of his proposed trip out of state (what the long-timer two cells over used to call "filing a flight plan") and headed the rattling truck south down the Thruway. Though if he had told no one and filed nothing, just gassed up the truck and, after his visit, kept going, how long would it take them to notice, he wondered, and how much would anyone care? But while he had no reason to return, other than the state's insistence—he had not yet found the cabin and the derelict acre behind it—he also had no reason to go any other place.

Following Ellie's precise directions, he'd arrived at the new condo in Teaneck with chocolates and flowers for her and gummy bears and a large wooden-boxed watercolor set to give to Janet. Things were wrong from the moment he walked in the door.

Janet wore a yellow party dress and a band in her hair. "She wanted to dress up for you," Ellie explained. Joe smiled, but remembered: when his daughter was younger, when he was home, Janet had hated dressing up; dresses got in the way of roller-skating and mudpie making. Ellie took the flowers, kissed his cheek quickly, stepped away. Ellie's lips smiled but her eyes didn't, and Janet didn't smile at all.

"Hi," he said to Janet, squatting down as he used to so he could look her in the eye. She was taller now, his position awkward. Janet gave her mother a swift, confused glance. Ellie said nothing.

"Hi," Janet finally said, polite child civilly greeting a stranger.

Joe held out the candy in one hand and the gift-wrapped paints in the other. Janet looked to her mother again: *Is it okay, can I take them?* Ellie nodded and now Janet smiled. "Thank you," she said. She flicked a glance at the gummy bears, then put them on the coffee table: the gift-wrapped box was more interesting. She untied the ribbon patiently but, when the tape proved recalcitrant, flashed Joe the cockeyed, conspiratorial grin he remembered—she looked like his daughter then—and ripped the paper off.

She was a well-mannered child. When she'd opened the box, examined the contents, and shut it once more, she thanked him again, and smiled. Not, this time, the crooked grin, but a smile startlingly like one he used to get from Ellie, a smile that charitably forgave him for things he never knew he'd done.

"You like to draw," Joe said, still smiling himself, still trying. "And paint."

Janet shrugged and looked at Ellie again, and Ellie said, "Come on, let's have cookies." They sat at the table in the breakfast nook. Beyond the picture window late-season ice floated at the center of a cattail-bordered pond. Joe had noticed as he parked that unlike many in the complex, Ellie's condo had no flower beds, no trees or shrubs: no landscaping but the lawn.

"Janet sings," Ellie told him, pouring coffee. "In the chorus at school. She's gotten very interested in music. Isn't that right, honey?"

Janet shrugged, embarrassed. Joe recalled, now, reading about a music teacher, lessons, a chorus, in a penciled, misspelled letter; and she was learning to play the piano, too, was he remembering that right? But he'd read that in prison, in a metal cell. In his mind, everything from those years lay at the bottom of a steep-sided, shadowed ravine. He had hoped to build a bridge from one cliff's-edge to the other, to step from the terrain of his old life to the new as though he never had set foot in that dark valley; and so everything he acquired during that changeless stay he'd tried to leave behind. But now he sat over coffee in Ellie's bright, new kitchen. The sweet sounds of children's voices rose and fell from the tape Janet put on for him of last year's chorus performance. He stared at a refrigerator whose magnets held photos and a list and a calendar and not a single crayon sketch or Magic Marker drawing. He saw his foundationless bridge crumbling, teetering, crashing through tree branches to the valley floor, and he understood he'd been a fool again.

Heart's Content

It was full dark when Joe came in from the garden.

The planting beds were free of rose-of-Sharon runners. He'd pruned the buddleia, the deep purple one that would make small fragrant blooms and the white one whose blooms would be much larger and more showy, striking against their dark foliage though the bees and hummingbirds would like them less. He'd weeded and watered and staked and now he could no longer see and finally he had to give it up.

Inside, he washed up. He opened a can of soup and made a sandwich, Swiss on rye. He brought his dinner to the chair by the window. On moonlit nights the garden, viewed from here, appeared sharp and fresh, a crisp black-and-white snapshot of itself; but tonight low clouds blocked the moon, and the garden's forms, framed in the squares of the window, looked soft edged, drained of color. He knew every inch of this ground but still tonight's murky shadows seemed to hide secrets. Until, finally, he switched on the light, and all he saw in the glass was himself.

He ate slowly, did his dishes, made new coffee. A fresh pot, coffee just brewing: to him, the smell of beginning, like the feel of a clean shirt, like a song's opening notes. That last moment before you knew the promise would not come true. That the cloth and the music and the scent (that the man wearing and hearing and breathing in) were not, not quite, good enough.

He poured the coffee and he drank. It was disappointing as it always was and he savored it, loved it. As he always did.

When the coffee was gone he turned on the lamp above the table. A warm yellow light, comforting to read by. Not good for the forensic deconstruction of photographs, but it was what he had.

It took over two hours.

As always, he absorbed the photos first, seeing not the pictures but the patterns. Contours, swirls and shapes, sharp lines and small specks: abstracted of meaning, surface only. It always worked like that for him.

Next, the reports. Trying in his mind to invent images, illustrating the words as though narrative were all he had. What should it look like, the thing described?

Finally, the photos again, this time as pictures, compared to the words and their imaginary illustrations. But always also as patterns. Like the garden: at some times mass, form, blocks of color; at others, individual stems reaching or leaning, particular blooms swelling or fading; always, both.

He opened a beer and he drank it slowly down. He called Ann.

"I found it."

Sutton Place

An animated crowd at the bar, a Latin beat to the music. A laughing, catching-up, everyone-at-once conversation among four law school friends while they waited for another. A glance at a wristwatch, raised eyebrows.

"Anyone hear from Jen?"

"It's only half an hour. For Jen, that's on time."

"It would be," Ann said, "if she were here."

"You know," said Beth, "she never confirmed."

"You mean we don't even know if she's coming? I'm *starving!*" Irene wailed. "We just going to sit here and wait? I don't *think* so!" She unholstered her cell phone and hit speed-dial.

Beth sipped her martini. "I haven't seen Jen in months."

"She's got some new guy," Ann said. "But she won't tell me who."

"Not even you?" Shondi asked. "You and Jen go back to, like, kindergarten, don't you?"

"More or less. They moved a lot, like we did, on the Americans-in-Europe circuit. Our mothers both believed in sticking their daughters in the snottiest school available. So our paths kept crossing."

Beth grinned. "Oh, I can just see the two of you terrorizing Miss-Nose-In-The-Air."

"No, wherever did you get that idea?" asked Ann innocently.

Shondi reached for a taco chip. "But she won't tell you who her new guy is?"

"She's being discreet." Ann shrugged. "Maybe he's married. Or he's famous."

"Okay, voice mail." Irene snapped her phone shut. "I told her to get her diamond-draped micro-butt over here right away."

"Diamond-draped?" Beth lifted her eyebrows.

"Twenty-four-karat chain." Irene's ebony fingers circled her own waist. "Tiny hanging, uh, baubles. No catch," she added. "Doesn't come off."

"Oooh! Well, whoever this new guy is, he's kinky!"

"Not this one," said Ann. "That was from a guy three or four back."

"Tell me it was that geeky deputy mayor!" Shondi's eyes sparkled with the hope of scandal.

"Who, Don Zalensky? God, no. The whole problem with him was, he was no fun. She'd be ready to go out dancing and he'd be reading a water-quality report."

"No wonder she dropped him."

"Actually, he dropped her. She was kind of smitten. She wanted to see if she could loosen his tie."

"If she couldn't, it can't be done."

"It can't. Getting Charlie Barr to Albany is his religion. Everything else is just a distraction."

"Distraction!" Irene stood. "Hunger is *driving* me to distraction! Come on, girls, let's eat."

They wove through the bar to a table in the garden. Sliding her chair in, Ann almost missed her own cell phone's ring. She dug fast, to grab it before it stopped. "Ann Montgomery."

"I found it."

It took Ann a minute. "Joe?" She leaned down to block out more sound. "Joe? Found what?"

"Can you hear me?"

"Hold on. Be right back." She stood. "A call from work," she told her friends.

"You should have stayed at the DA's office, girl," Irene said. "You remember how no one ever calls us after hours."

"Liar. Get extra guacamole."

Sympathetic smiles, a bye-bye wave. Ann zigzagged through the crowd, stepped into the cool of the night. Second Avenue was a comparative zone of silence.

"Joe? You still there? Joe?"

"I'm here."

A breath of relief. Why? If she lost him, she knew how to reach him. He said, "I wasn't sure this cell number would still be good."

"Why wouldn't it be? It hasn't been that long." For her. For her it had only been time. For him, she suddenly knew, it must have been something else, something so alien she did not understand how to begin to understand it. "Joe? What do you mean, 'found it'?"

"I looked at your photos. Read the reports. I think you were right. It looks deliberate."

A bus pulled into the stop in front of her, its engine rumbling. Ann turned away, finger in her open ear. "You did? You looked at them? You saw something?"

"It looks deliberate," he repeated.

A thrill ran over her skin. "You mean sabotage?"

"Looks that way."

"Wow. Tell me. And talk loud. I'm on the street."

He raised his voice. "Nothing I can tell about the fire, though an arson investigator might get something. But I guess they looked?"

"Sorta-kinda. No one's buying the sabotage angle."

"Well, there might be nothing on that one, or anyway nothing you could find. I didn't get to the bricks yet. But the scaffolding, I'm pretty sure."

"Why?"

"The bolt holes."

"How?"

He paused. She could almost see him, his eyes' distant look as he considered what words to use, how best to explain the technical to the untrained. Never, with Joe, impatience; no pained condescension. Just the attempt to be clear, as though translating from his mother tongue.

"When a scaffold collapses," he said, "especially if it's overloaded—I mean, say, not from wind—the overloaded bolts shear off from the force of the collapsing sections. Before they shear, they bend. They deform the bolt holes as they're bending."

"Okay."

"The place was littered with sheared bolts, right? Bent and sheared?"

"Right. They're in the photos."

"But I can see three bolt holes that aren't deformed."

"Meaning?"

"Those had no bolts."

"The bolts couldn't have just come loose? Fallen out as the scaffold was collapsing?"

"Unlikely. One, maybe. Not three in the same place. And three is all I can see in the photos. There might have been more."

"Well, Three Star swears the scaffold was inadequately engineered. Maybe it was installed badly, too. Maybe they just left some bolts out."

"Scaffold's inspected before it's used. The inspector wou.
seen it."

"The inspector could have been bought. Just signed off without goi.
up there. To speed up the schedule."

"The laborers would have seen it as they were laying plank. The masons might even have checked it out as they went up the first time."

"The first time? Not every time?"

"You do it the first time, you figure it doesn't change. And once the
planks are down, some of the bolts are hard to see. And anyway, you
know construction workers. They don't like to get caught looking nervous. They don't even wear hardhats when they can get away with it.
They're cowboys." *Like me*, Ann thought; and laughed with delight when
Joe added, "Like you."

"How kind of you to notice."

"Who could miss it? How long was that scaffold up?"

"I don't know. I could find out."

"But it wasn't new? Under a week, say?"

"No, more like six weeks, two months."

"Then I don't buy a bad installation. And I don't buy bad engineering, either. This is the kind of routine design an engineer could do in
his sleep."

"Maybe one did."

"Then it would have been done right. No, I'm telling you, someone
took those bolts out after the scaffold went up."

"You're totally sure."

"I'd stake my reputation on it," Joe said, and paused. "If I had one."

CHAPTER 28

Sutton Place

Ann stood on Second Avenue watching the flowing traffic alternate: downtown, across town, down, across. She thought about a hand easing bolts from steel. She saw the scene at night, a shadow slipping along the scaffolding. She watched the shadow pocketing the bolts, heard them jingle as each bolt was added. She saw the five bricklayers coming to work in the bright morning sun, joking with each other, maybe one lighting a cigarette as they climbed onto planking they'd stood and walked on all day yesterday and the day before.

How things can change in an instant.

How she could drive up the river to see Joe, as so many times over the last three years, but now take a different turn and it was just the two of them alone, in a garden surrounded by trees, arched over by sky, no gates clanging, no walls pressing in.

How Joe, though without bars or doors, could still lock her and her world out of his, just by turning his back.

And how her phone could ring and Joe was there, telling her the door was unlocked once more.

She wanted to call him back and ask him why he'd looked at the photos. But she wouldn't get an answer. When talk around the water cooler had drifted toward the personal, Joe could always be found at his desk, comparing charts, checking printouts. *"I'm a boring guy, Ann. I'm an engineer."* Except about his garden. Once he was convinced she was interested—and she was, though not in flowers and soil, but in Joe's eyes and voice when he talked about them—he'd begun to paint pictures in the air for her with his hands and his words and his smile.

She pulled her phone out of her purse again, but it wasn't Joe she called. She speed-dialed the cell phone of Luis Perez, her police liaison, whom she'd met briefly first thing that morning. He was a cop from Bronx Homicide; the death of the Winston woman was his case.

"Perez." He sounded irritated. In the background she could hear a child crying. Perez must be at home. Well, why not? He was a family man, three kids, lived in Brooklyn if her background check was accurate. He was also a smart-ass, a straight arrow, and sometimes sloppy in his paperwork, or so ran the book on Luis Perez.

"It's Ann Montgomery," she told him.

"Ah, the Princess! Jesus, you still at the office?"

"No, I'm outside a bar on Second Avenue."

"Oh, gee, I'd love to but I can't."

"I can hear. And you're not invited, it's girls' night out."

"Oh, man, I always wanted to be in on one of those! You talk about nail polish, nylons, things like that, right?"

"Those things interest you?"

"Is there a good answer to that?"

"No. Luis, listen. What would happen if one of the accidents at Mott Haven were for sure sabotage?"

Perez paused. "Which one?"

"The scaffold collapse."

"You know who did it?"

"No."

"You sure it was?"

"I had—I had a forensic engineer look at the reports and the photos. He's pretty sure."

"Well, if we were convinced, I guess we'd treat it as property crime resulting in injury."

"High priority?"

"Property crime?"

"Five men were hurt."

"Not seriously."

"Two of those bricklayers will be laid up for weeks!"

"They'll recover. They'll probably sue and never have to go to work again. Their wives'll sue for loss of services. You know what that is?"

"Yes, Luis, I do. And one guy just has a broken ankle."

"So he can't take out the garbage. That's a service. Listen, your engineer—does he have anything to say about the bricks?"

"He's going to get back to me."

"Because *that* would be manslaughter, at least."

"I'm not sure we can prove that."

Perez was silent; Ann watched the traffic. "Listen," the cop finally said. "I'm homicide. You have a suspect on the scaffold, I'll see if he looks good for the bricks. If you don't, but you convince us on the scaffold, the squad guys'll see what they can scare up. Might be able to make first-degree assault—injury in the course of committing a crime. Best I can do."

"Can't we call the scaffold attempted murder?"

"It's a stretch."

"Not a big one. Those five guys were lucky they weren't killed."

"So are you, every time you cross Broadway. And what if we did call it that? I still need a suspect. You gonna bother me at home on a Sunday night, least you can do is give me a suspect."

"I'll find you one," she promised. "And I apologize for calling you at home."

"Hey, I'm just yankin' your chain. Do princesses have chains?"

"I don't."

"I bet you do and I bet I can find it. Anyway, call me tomorrow, I got that list you wanted in the office. I'd've brought it home, I'd known you worked 24/7."

"I thought everyone knew that, Luis. Okay, thanks. You'll hear from me."

"Can't wait. I want to talk about nail polish and nylons."

"Pantyhose. These days we call them pantyhose."

"No kidding? Wait till I tell my wife."

"I guarantee you, Luis, she knows."

She clicked off, dropped the phone in her purse, and headed back into the bar to rejoin her friends.

"Did we hear from Jen?" she asked, sitting down.

"Miss Flaky? Girl is lucky she's rich, or she'd be dead by now." Irene lifted her margarita. "What *I* want to know is what *you're* so happy about."

"I'm happy?"

"Oh, come on, girl, you're lit up like a Christmas tree! Give. Who was on the phone?"

"I told you, it was work."

The three others exchanged grins as Irene said, "Wish my work made me all shivery, gave me reason to lie to my friends."

"Now come on, you guys know I'd never lie to you."

"Yeah, you just don't tell us nothin'. All right, well, I'm going to drown my sorrows in guacamole."

Ann scooped some salsa on a chip. She savored in her mind once more the astounding thought that had brought the visible heat to her face.

Joe had looked at her papers.

CHAPTER 29

Harlem: Frederick Douglass Boulevard

Ford Corrington and Ray Holdsclaw swept briskly up the City Hall steps. Yesterday's winds had died down to gentle June breezes. Here in lower Manhattan, where the island was narrower than uptown, the wind brought the scent of water. Ford had noticed that before.

They identified themselves to the cop at the desk in the cool, echoing lobby. While he phoned upstairs they entered through the metal detector, waited with arms spread while another cop drew their outlines in the air with wands. They both got wanded, even though only Ford's watch set the beeper off, and even though Ray was wearing his clerical collar.

"You suppose Donald Trump and Walter Glybenhall get security checks like this when they drop in?" Ford asked Ray as the cop pawed through his briefcase.

"Everyone gets the same treatment, sir," the cop deadpanned, though the sergeant at the desk, who was black, met Ford's eyes with a brief, eloquent look. Ray grinned his sunny grin.

The cop snapped Ford's rummaged briefcase shut as Don Zalensky came clipping down the stairs. Sending the deputy mayor to greet them, Ford thought: Charlie Barr's way of letting them know he was taking them seriously. Or at least, letting them know it was important to him that they think so.

Zalensky shook everyone's hand and led the way to the elevator. Ford could smell the tobacco smoke on the deputy mayor's jacket; he could hear his faint wheeze. The man probably used the elevator even to come down, when he was alone, Ford decided. The grand stairs routine had been to impress them.

And Ford was impressed. He always was, here; and in cathedrals, concert halls, museums, and endowed universities. Impressed with the power of buildings to speak, in a language as clear as words: *My grandeur surrounds the grand. My beauty houses the beautiful. My wealth shelters the wealthy. My importance contains the important.* And Ford was impressed by what was said, also, by the paint-flaking walls of public schools, the dingy stairwells of subway stations, the urine-scented entryways beyond housing projects' broken doors.

Who mattered and who didn't. What the world thought about you. What your place was: you learned that young from the language of the buildings you lived in, walked through, and saw in the distance.

Upstairs, they were shown into the mayor's private conference room by a self-possessed black woman whose name Ford couldn't quite bring to mind. The mayor stood when they entered. He shook their hands, saying, "Ford, good to see you again. And Reverend Holdsclaw. A surprise, but always a pleasure."

Ray spread his gleaming smile. "You're welcome at Tree of Life anytime, Mayor."

Charlie Barr grinned back. "Seems to me my presence takes your parishioners' minds from the sacred straight to the profane."

"The world offers faith many challenges."

"Hear that, Don? I'm a challenge to faith. Come on, folks, sit down. Ford, I know it's tea for you. Reverend, you want some coffee?"

Carafes of coffee, both high-test and decaf, and hot water sat among tea bags, sugar, sweeteners, milk pitchers, and two plates of cookies on a sideboard. Ford fixed himself mint tea in a mug with the New York City seal on the side. He took a couple of cookies, too, on a china dish. The mayor always had good cookies.

With mugs and plates they arranged themselves around the table. The mayor's mug, Ford noticed, was no different from the others. Charlie Barr, man of the people.

"Okay," the mayor said. "So what can I do for you two? Do we want to have minutes, by the way? Should I ask Lena to come in?"

Leaving it up to them whether this meeting was on the record; nice touch. Ford smiled. "Personally, I have a very good memory."

That didn't mean there'd be no record of what they said here. Ford didn't know it for a fact but he always assumed that above a certain level all public officials taped their meetings. He hadn't practiced law as such except for the two years right after Harvard, a decade and a half ago; but if he were advising the City of New York, that would be his advice.

But keeping the meeting off the official record was a way for Ford to let the mayor know that they valued candor and they trusted him to keep any verbal promises he made.

Or at least, to let him know it was important to them that he think so.

"Whatever you want." The mayor sipped his coffee. "I can't remember what day it is, myself, but that's why Don's here."

Zalensky scowled and, as always, said nothing.

"We'll get right to the point, Mayor," Ford said. "I appreciate your seeing us and I don't want to waste your time."

"We've had our differences, Ford, but you've never wasted my time. What's up?"

Ford reached into his briefcase. He pulled out a pile of spiral-bound booklets and handed them around. The mayor and deputy mayor glanced at the covers, with their map of Harlem, a half-block rectangle in the center colored red. Zalensky opened the booklet and thumbed through it, but Charlie Barr looked up at Ford.

"This is about Block A."

"Are you surprised?"

"No. But we're not ready to make decisions on that site yet. It's too early. Housing tells me two of the buildings aren't even emptied."

"You can make decisions at any time."

"Real Property won't even start the final legal steps for a month or two. Then there's the Community Board, all the rest."

"You can make decisions at any time," Ford repeated. "All we're talking about is an informal commitment. From the mayor's office. Once we have that, we can wait on the Community Board and the other pro forma steps."

"Pro forma? The Community Board wouldn't like that."

"I won't tell them."

The mayor smiled. "Well, we'll be happy to hear what you have to say. You're representing the Garden Project?"

"Among others."

"And you want to make sure you're included? You want space in the development that ends up there?"

"No," Ford said. "We want the site."

The mayor stared.

Ray grinned, shaking his head. "Ford, son, I believe you've nonplussed the Mayor of the City of New York."

Charlie Barr said, "You sure as hell have. What do you mean, you want the site? Who does?"

"Garden Walls. It's all in there." Ford pointed to the booklet. "Our prospectus. 'Garden Walls' is the name of our consortium. Our members are a number of community groups and churches, and we have the support of a variety of other churches, faith-based groups, cultural institutions, social-service organizations—"

"Financial support?"

Charlie Barr, cutting to the chase.

"We have a group of investors prepared to purchase the site from the city, and also to finance the project outlined in the prospectus."

"Who are they, your investors?"

"We have bank commitments, and the commitments of three equity investors for the first phase."

"The first phase?"

"It's in the prospectus. The first phase will be one hundred and ten units of housing and some commercial property."

The mayor still made no move to open the booklet in his hands. "And the other phases?"

"More housing, low- and mid-rise. An arts center with a museum, studios, a theater. Athletic facilities. A school. A rooftop park."

"Rooftop park," the mayor echoed. "You have plans for all this? You have an architect on board already?"

"An architect, yes. And preliminary plans."

"Who would head this project?"

"Hilda Daniels. From Second Federal Bank."

Charlie Barr nodded. "She was on that Business Initiative Review Commission we set up three years ago. Very impressive. But unless I'm wrong, she's not a developer?"

"She's a banker. In Second Federal's mortgage and lending unit. In that capacity she's worked on a number of large projects."

"Is Second Federal behind this?"

"They've given us a commitment."

"But this isn't a project of the bank's?"

"No."

"Has Ms. Daniels ever developed a project this size on her own?"

"On her own, no."

"Are any of your consortium members developers?"

"One. Cruz Brothers. They'd be the builders."

"I know Cruz. Ramon and Paquito," the mayor said, and nodded. "Have they successfully completed anything this size?"

"Their projects are all financially successful and very well liked by their residents."

"But none of them are this big."

"Not yet."

"Ford," Charlie Barr said, "we'll read your proposal, but I can tell you, I don't think this is likely to happen. I can't see that site going to an inexperienced developer."

"The Garden Project would take a lead role," said Ford. "We've been successfully developing city properties for sixteen years."

"All of them renovations, though. Small buildings and parts of buildings. Nothing the size of Block A. Unless I'm missing something?" The mayor looked to Don Zalensky, who shook his head.

"No, that's true," Ford said. "Those are what we've been offered."

"They're what you've proposed on."

"We've proposed on whatever we've been invited to."

"And I haven't noticed you've been invited on this. Come on, Ford, be realistic. This property's huge. Projects this size are tough enough. The city's job is to boost the chances of success as high as possible by at least picking a developer who's done this kind of thing before."

"This kind of thing?" Ford lifted the booklet.

"What do you mean?"

"What Garden Walls is proposing for Block A is far different from what the city's thinking seems to be. With all due respect, Mayor, that nonsense in the paper was an insult to Harlem." He spread the booklet open, swiveling it so the *Times* rendering faced Charlie Barr.

The mayor glanced down and up again. "What's wrong with it?"

"It's about *yesterday*! It tells the children of Harlem their glory days are behind them, the best they can do is go *backwards*. Do you know how offensive that is? And it's destructive. What we need to be talking about is the future!" Ford flipped to the next page. "Harlem needs buildings that look like *tomorrow*. That let in the light and the air and say they're part of the world. And that the people in them are welcome to be part of the world. Not part of someone's nostalgic daydream of what Harlem used to be!"

"Contextual design. Isn't that what they call it?" Charlie Barr looked to Don Zalensky, got a nod, and looked back at Ford. "Appropriate to the neighborhood. Same materials, same heights, same basic shapes. They tell me that's what we're supposed to do now. Evoke the surroundings. Blend in. 'Reknit the urban fabric,' an architect said that to me. Landmarks likes it. The Art Commission likes it."

"If it's too early for a decision," Ford asked, sitting back, "why have you been to Landmarks and the Art Commission already?"

"Oh, Ford, relax! No one's trying to put anything over on you. Those guys read the *Times* just like you do. They *like* it. They haven't *reviewed* it. I promise you, Block A will go through the usual approval processes." Charlie Barr tapped the blank white back of the *Times* rendering. "But chances are what gets built on Block A will be along these general lines. And it will be built by an experienced commercial developer."

"A commercial developer may not have the best interests of the Harlem community at heart."

"The city will require the developer to provide both residential and commercial property on the site and to guarantee commercial tenants for the first two years. I can't see how new housing, new jobs, and an increase in tourism and the tax base wouldn't be in Harlem's best interests."

"Mr. Mayor, Harlem's not for sale!" For the first time since they'd sat down, Ray's voice thundered. "Harlem is a *community*. Harlem is people's home. It's filled with poor folks who struggled and are struggling and now they're being *dis*placed and *re*placed by rich folks from downtown who've suddenly discovered our beautiful buildings. Buildings that are only still standing because no one's spent any money in the last fifty years to wipe 'em away. And now you're proposing to build more just like 'em, so those rich folks can have bow windows and back gardens! Block A"—slapping a brochure down on the table—"is the last city-owned developable site in Harlem and *Harlem wants it!* Housing and jobs and a new tax base are wonderful things. But who lives in the housing? Who works at the jobs and who pays the taxes? People who've gone without decent apartments, gone without heat, and gone without jobs for years in the *community* where they were born? Or people who need a map to go to Rucker Park? And tourists? Harlem loves tourists! Harlem welcomes tourists! But to *Harlem*. Harlem, Mr. Mayor! Not Harlemland, USA!"

The mayor sipped his coffee. "You deliver that sermon yesterday, Reverend?"

Ray smiled. "I've been preaching on these lines for years, Mayor." His smile dropped away. "Years. Long before another black person was killed in a construction accident in a black neighborhood on a white developer's site."

The mayor shot a glance at the deputy mayor. "Okay, you brought up Mott Haven. Point made. If you bring up Dolan Construction, I'll throw you out of the room."

"There's a clear parallel," said Ray.

"Maybe. Maybe not. But it's not anything you can use to leverage this."

"Mayor," said Ford, "you'd rack up a lot of moral points in Harlem if a black-run community group were chosen to develop Block A."

"And moral points vote, is that what you're saying?"

"People watch what you do, Mayor. Word on the street is, you're thinking of running for governor."

"That so? I'm also thinking of retiring to Tahiti."

"Well, Harlem's got some great travel agents. I could hook you up with one. All I meant, Mayor, is that people appreciate being treated with respect. They give consideration to folks who treat them that way."

"So do I, Ford. And Harlem's not the only thing that's not for sale."

"Touché. If I've offended I apologize. We're just trying to make our position clear."

"It's clear." The mayor wrapped his hands around his coffee mug. "Listen, folks. Whatever developer's chosen for Block A will be required to involve the community in whatever they do. As usual in these projects. A percentage of the housing will be set aside for local residents at both affordable and market rates. As usual. And community groups will get space. I think you people ought to be coming up with proposals to get yourselves a piece of the pie. Instead of pipe dreams."

"Edgar Westermann's behind us," Ford said.

The mayor raised his eyebrows. "You're kidding me. You went to Edgar?"

"In the interests of Harlem, yes, we did."

"He knows you're behind this and he still supports it?"

"He can see it's the right thing for Harlem."

"Edgar Westermann and Ford Corrington shoulder to shoulder, now that's front-page news."

"He'd hoped to be able to join us this morning—"

"But you told him hell'd freeze over first." The mayor glanced over as Don shifted in his chair. "I think Don's telling me not to run Edgar down to you. But my opinion of Edgar's no secret. I didn't think yours was, either."

"In this case Edgar and I are both putting Harlem's interests before our own."

"You'll excuse a little political cynicism, Ford, but it seems to me that getting your hands on a project this size would be very much in the Garden Project's interests." The mayor shrugged. "Well, Edgar has a right to his opinion. It doesn't change mine." He lifted the booklet on his palm and moved it up and down as though weighing it. "Look, I'll read this. I'll have Real Property take a look. But I don't think it's going to happen and I'd hate to see you lose out by putting all your eggs in this basket. The Garden Project's a valuable resource. I've been assuming you'd want a piece of Block A and I've been assuming the city would be favorably disposed toward your proposal. My advice would be, don't bite off more than you can chew."

"Thanks, Mayor. But we didn't come here for advice."

Charlie Barr sighed. "No, I guess you didn't. You came for a promise you're not going to get. Except that I promise to read this. But that's it."

"Well," Ford grinned, "that's better than a poke in the eye."

"You'll never find that here, Ford. I hope you know that. Now, is there anything else I can do for you?"

"No, we've taken up enough of your time." Ford stood. "Thank you for seeing us. If you have any questions you know where to find me. And I'm sure once you've studied our proposal you'll see the viability of it. And the moral righteousness, too."

The mayor eyed him for a moment, then also stood, and also grinned. "I'm sure," Charlie Barr said, "that you're sure. I just hope you have a fallback."

"Faith. That's always been my fallback."

"Well, I've heard it moves mountains. Thank you for coming."

They all shook hands again. The mayor saw them to the door and the deputy mayor escorted them down just as he'd brought them up. On their way back to the lobby, at Ford's suggestion, they took the grand, curving stair.

CHAPTER 30

Sutton Place

On her way to the office Ann speed-dialed Jen's number and left a where-the-hell-were-you-last-night message. Not that she was angry—if you were a friend of Jen's this was just how it went—but, it being Jen, there was probably a funny story behind her no-show, and if so, Ann wanted to hear it. She was in the mood for a funny story.

In the open DOI bullpen, the morning sun cut glaring squares on the vinyl floor. Ann slung her bag over her chair, sat, and slid open her file drawer. The Pendaflex she lifted out was labeled "Three Star" and it was so far pretty thin but it wasn't going to stay that way.

Ann worked alone. Since Joe's arrest she hadn't had a partner. At first she didn't see the point of getting used to someone new; Joe would be back as soon as the stupidity of this whole thing became as obvious to everyone as it was to her. Later, after his conviction and her exile to Siberia, she'd refused every partner Greg Lowry tried to assign her. She didn't have the seniority to take that stand but Greg must have sensed what would happen if he didn't back off. And no one was clamoring to work with Joe Cole's partner anyway.

Three years ago, on an overcast morning after days of rain, Joe had stopped by her desk. From the sparkle in his eye she could see he was about to go out in the field. Before he spoke she'd shrugged, pointed to the six-inch pile of affidavits, reports, and notes in front of her, and said, "I can't."

"Damn," Joe had said. "Well, no big deal."

"What's up?"

"That Buildings Department inspector. Manelli."

"You've been chasing him for months."

"I think I found a guy who can lock him up for me."

"Who?"

"Site super named O'Doul, Dolan Construction. I'm going to go sniff around."

"I hate to make you do it alone."

"No problem," Joe had said. "I know these guys."

Ann fingered the Three Star file. From nowhere it occurred to her how beautiful the morning light would look glowing off a bowl of flowers on her desk. Peonies, maybe, like the ones just opening in Joe's new garden.

She peeled back the lid of the latte she'd brought up from the lobby—no reason in the world she'd ever seen to drink DOI coffee—and sipped while she punched in a phone number.

A ring and a half, then "Bronx Homicide. Sergeant Perez."

"Hi, Luis, it's Ann."

"Hey, my favorite bureaucrat. How are you? Recovered from girls' night out?"

"Completely. You? Recovered from your weekend?"

"Hey, I'm a real cop. Peewee soccer, sixth-grade graduation, mother-in-law's birthday—bring it on, I can handle it."

"NYPD's lucky to have tough guys like you, Luis. You have that list for me?"

"Looking at it. Go stand by your fax machine in a minute or two."

"I'm standing there now."

"It'll still be a minute or two. I gotta walk all the way to the other end of the room to fax it, so I'd have to hang up on you, which I don't want to do, you being the bright spot in my morning and all."

"If that's your best stuff, it needs work."

"Yeah, that's what my wife says." Perez sighed. "But listen, this list: we checked them out, and there's nothing juicy."

"How many on it?"

"Eight."

"And none of them looked good to you?"

"Couple of people not so happy, but didn't look like anyone had a grudge against Three Star that would be big enough for something like this."

"You never know what sets people off."

"Ain't that the truth. But to keep going back again and again . . . And you gotta know what you're doing, pull off this kind of accidents, make them look like accidents. Couldn't find anyone who fit. So the thinking here is, probably they *were* accidents." He paused. "Unless you can prove what you were saying last night."

"You better believe I'll try. But even if my engineer's wrong, there could be contributory negligence on Three Star's part."

"Could be, but not from the people on this list. They don't work there no more, that's why they're on it."

"Well, my investigation's a little different from yours. I'd still like a look."

"Whatever. Like usual, us real cops are happy to cooperate with DOI. You find something, though, I'll be the first to know?"

"Absolutely. DOI's always happy to cooperate with real cops."

"Great. Hey, when are you and me going to go out?"

"When pigs fly?"

"Yeah." Luis sighed again. "That's what my wife says."

The fax came through a few minutes later. Eight names, employees who'd been terminated by Three Star in the weeks before the scaffold gave way. Terminated employees were always a good bet for trouble-making, and she and Joe had gotten far focusing on them. Though Joe had laughed at "terminated," preferring "fired." *If someone had gone ahead and terminated them, they wouldn't be here making trouble,* he said.

In the corner by the window, at the desk that used to be Joe's, Eve Rudin leaned over two sheets of paper, comparing them. She'd had the most seniority when Joe went to prison, so she'd gotten that desk. Ann liked Eve well enough, but she'd found herself moving her file cabinet and reorganizing her things so that her chair faced the other way.

Ann carried the fax back to her desk. The room was filling up. Beefy ex-cops loosened their ties, reached across steel desks for their phones. Two young guys, recent John Jay grads, came out of the kitchenette arguing about the Knicks. They were all good investigators, but she couldn't come up with a single one who'd give her more than a blank stare if she asked whether they thought the word "terminated" was funny.

She sipped her cooling latte while she studied the list. Perez was meticulous and thorough. Though his handwriting, which she'd never seen before, was interestingly illegible. Below each typed name was the last date of employment, current address, and official reason for termination, all also typed. In the margins, Perez had scrawled the name of the current employer, as well as whatever off-the-record comments he'd been able to worm out of Three Star's personnel department. He hadn't found what he was looking for. But Ann was looking for something different.

She checked the reasons for termination. For the six office personnel, it was department restructuring or downsizing. For the two construction workers, one had obviously had some appeal for Perez—drinking on the job—but that guy had been in jail in Riverhead for disorderly conduct (Perez's scribble read "pissing in public") when the scaffold collapsed, and when the fire started. The other had been let go for clocking in late way too often. The week after his layoff he'd moved to Las Vegas.

She scanned Perez's scratchy comments on the six desk jockeys, looking for people with bad attitudes. She found two. One was a man from Accounting with what the HR director called a "negative personality." Now, what was that? Like matter-antimatter, contact between him and normal people made the office explode? Or was he some kind of black hole, a gravity well of personableness, into which anything pleasant and easygoing was sucked and crushed?

Ann was tempted to call the HR director just to find out. But it was a random tangent, the kind of thought that, when she spoke it out loud, used to make Joe stare and then burst out laughing.

The other employee the HR director had allowed, off the record, was "difficult" seemed more promising. Margaret Mary Tiemeyer was in the construction management department. Not just a desk jockey, Tiemeyer was responsible for certain kinds of paperwork and also jobsite supervision. Putative reason for being let go: "department reorganization." But in reorganizations some people stay and some are shown the door, and there's always a reason. In Tiemeyer's case, her supervisor had found her "insubordinate" and "inappropriately confrontational."

Now, that was just what Ann needed: a woman who didn't know her place.

She was lifting her bag out of her desk drawer when her phone buzzed. She stuck it between ear and shoulder. "Montgomery," she said, shrugging into her coat.

"You have a few minutes?" Ann looked over to Greg Lowry's office in the corner of the room. He was leaning out from behind his desk, angled so he could see through the door. She nodded rather than answering, took off her coat, and hung it over her chair. When she got to his office, Lowry was on the phone again. "How's right now?" he said, and hung up. "Sit down," he told Ann. She waited for the sound of footfalls crossing the room. Quick, light. And leather soled: a John Jay guy, then, not an ex-cop. Dennis Graham, whippet thin and, as usual, in a gray suit more or less the color of a whippet's coat, trotted through the doorway. Dennis was young, ambitious, and smart, and if he sometimes reminded Ann of the student manager of her college track team in his eagerness, that probably wasn't his fault.

"I wanted to do a little information sharing here," Lowry began. "Make sure Ann's up to speed on everything you had, Dennis. How's Brooklyn, by the way? Going okay so far?"

"So far, great," Dennis said. "Was out there over the weekend just to scope it, going to go on out and set myself up there this morning. Looks like it's going to be fun."

"Great," said Lowry. "So, Ann, this is your chance. Any questions for Dennis? About Three Star, the site, anything?"

"Not really," said Ann. "I spent the weekend going through Dennis's files. They seem very thorough. Just one thing: How seriously did you take the sabotage idea?"

"Not very," Dennis Graham said. "I expected Three Star to claim it—gets them off the hook. But I couldn't find any evidence. Or any reason—union problems, insurance, pay disputes, no reason I could see for anyone to do that."

"Why sabotage?" Lowry asked Ann. "You have something?"

"I might. About the scaffolding. But if Dennis didn't find anything . . ."

Dennis shook his head again.

"Were you looking beyond Three Star?" Lowry asked Dennis. "A guy like Glybenhall's bound to have enemies."

"I started down that road. I didn't find anything that looked promising. The only thing I was thinking, if it were true, maybe it would have something to do with the other site."

"What other site?" Lowry asked.

"There's a persistent rumor the only reason Glybenhall's doing this project at all is because he's been promised another site if he succeeds," Dennis said. "I was thinking, maybe someone doesn't want him to have that site."

"Where did you hear that?" Ann asked. "It's not in your files."

"Seems to be floating around. Didn't write it down because I couldn't verify it. I don't know if it's true. Or where that site is. Or even what 'succeed' on this one would mean."

Lowry snorted. "At this point, 'finish the job without anyone else getting killed.' "

Ann and Dennis exchanged a glance. "Mayor's meeting yesterday didn't go well?" Ann asked Lowry.

"Oh, it went fine. Sort of. Mark and I told the mayor we didn't see Virginia McFee or Les Farrell as bent."

"Is that bad?"

"No, it's good, except we didn't offer him anyone else."

"Seems like what he'd be hoping is that no one's bent."

"What Charlie Barr's hoping is that someone can make this whole thing go away before he starts to fundraise for his next race. Look, Ann, if you think there's something in this sabotage thing, get someone to look at it. A forensic engineer."

"I already—I was planning to. I'm sending it to Sandy Weiss, at Packer."

"Good."

In the old, pre–Dolan Construction days, DOI used in-house engineers for forensic work. When you had people like Joe Cole on staff, you didn't need outside experts. The shift to outsourcing had been Lowry's first major procedural edict as the post-Dolan IG.

"And see if you can find that other site and who's involved," Lowry went on. "It would be nice." He sounded almost wistful.

"If the sabotage were real?"

"It would make Hizzoner very happy if Glybenhall turns out to be a victim, not a snake."

"He may turn out to be a victim," Ann said. "He's still a snake."

Harlem: Frederick Douglass Boulevard

Ford and Ray rode the subway back uptown. Don Zalensky had offered them the use of the mayor's limo. "He's here all day," Zalensky said, lighting a cigarette. "He won't need it."

"Thank the mayor for us," Ford answered. "But we'll take the train."

Zalensky nodded, shook their hands again, and watched them down the wide stone steps.

"You ever know him to say a word in a meeting?" Ford asked Ray.

"Not everyone loves a soapbox," Ray answered. "Or a pulpit."

The subway was too crowded for conversation and too hot for words. They lurched, swayed, and sweated for twenty minutes until finally they escaped up the stairs into what was, by contrast, a cool breeze. Standing in the sunlight, Ray retrieved a handkerchief and wiped his brow. "Maybe we should have taken the mayor's ride."

" 'Neither a borrower nor a lender be,' " Ford said.

"That's Shakespeare, not scripture."

"I don't want to owe Charlie Barr anything. Especially now. Besides, how would you explain stepping out of the mayor's limo at high noon on 125th Street?"

"To who?"

"Edgar Westermann, for one."

Ray chuckled. "Well, that would sure burn that boy up, wouldn't it?"

"Now that Edgar's on our side I want to keep him there. And he's only with us because he knew Charlie would oppose us. If he thinks we're buddying up to the mayor, he'll cut us loose."

"What's he getting out of this?"

"Who, Edgar? Points in the community for running against the mayor."

"I guess. Surprised me, though. I was him, thinking about running for mayor, I believe I'd side with the money."

"If you were him, you'd do no such thing. You mean, you'd have expected *Edgar* to side with the money."

"Well, yeah. Might be some nice contributions to be had for a Harlem politician who favors the city's plan for Block A."

"From the developer they pick, you mean?"

"Sure as the Lord made little apples. Wouldn't matter who, he'd owe Edgar big. He needs it, too."

"Needs what?"

"Money," Ray retorted. "Election's barely two years away and he hasn't got his war chest going. Edgar's a rich man, but not enough to fund his run himself."

"Well, but in this case," said Ford, "siding with the money would be siding with the mayor. Edgar would lose credibility with his base. Black candidate's bound to have trouble in the boroughs. He can't afford to alienate Harlem."

"Yeah," said Ray, "but siding against the mayor puts him next to you. I imagine the dilemma gave him some sleepless nights."

"Probably did." Ford grinned. "Ain't that a crying shame?"

Sutton Place

Ann pulled the DOI car—a Cavalier: four-door, automatic, black, a big yawn—up to a hydrant and stuck a "City of New York Official Business" card in the window. She badged herself past the guard's station at the construction site gate and flashed the badge again to a gum-snapping young woman at the first desk in the GC's trailer. She asked to speak to Margaret Mary Tiemeyer.

The young woman hesitated and half-turned toward the back of the room, where a burly man looked up suspiciously from a set of drawings.

"Not Tiemeyer's problem." Ann raised her voice before the man could speak. She looked past the woman and spoke directly to him. "Guy in an investigation named her as a witness. I need her to confirm his whereabouts."

"This that Bronx thing? Where she used to work?"

"Related."

The man's glance slid over Ann's unbuttoned coat and her long blonde hair. A tiny, smug smile pulled at the corner of his mouth. She knew what that meant. In his head he'd already taken her to bed, satisfied her in every possible way, and left her begging for more. Which, however unlikely in real life, made her in his mind a conquest, and so not a threat.

He nodded to the young woman and, the little smile still on his lips, went back to his drawings. The woman met Ann's eyes briefly. She picked up a walkie-talkie and spoke Margaret Tiemeyer's name into it. The response was a crackle Ann could make nothing out of. The young woman told the crackle to report to the trailer, got another crackle, and lowered the walkie-talkie. "She's on the scaffold. She'll be right down."

At the back desk, the man lit a cigarette. *Oh, so you smoke afterwards?* Ann thought. But it was handy. "I'll wait outside," she said, wrinkling her nose as though smoke-filled rooms bothered her, which they never had.

"Hardhat site. Don't leave the trailer yard." The man spoke around his cigarette without looking up. "And don't keep Maggie long. She's got work to do."

Ann threw the young woman a look of sympathy and stepped out into the sun.

This was a small project, a low-rise office building in Queens on what had been a parking lot. Real estate in New York these days, even in the boroughs, was too valuable to waste on cars. Though it was worth wondering where all the cars were going to park when all the lots were buildings.

Squinting into the sun, she made out a thin figure clattering down the scaffold stair. In hardhat, overalls, and heavy boots, the figure headed in an unswerving line from the stair to the trailer, jumping a mud puddle, climbing up and over a pile of two-by-fours, covering the remaining distance in a dozen strides, and coming to a halt in front of Ann. "Tiemeyer. You looking for me? You from the waterproofer?"

Tiemeyer's tan face was lined around the eyes and mouth. Wisps of bottle-blonde hair curled from under the hardhat. She was a few years older than Ann, almost a foot shorter, and if she broke a hundred pounds it was the hardhat and boots.

"I'm looking for you, but that's not why." Ann dredged her badge from her pocket.

"Oh, crap!" Tiemeyer shot a glance at the trailer. "What do you want?"

"Relax. I told him it's not about you. I said I just needed you to corroborate some guy's story."

"You said. But that was bullshit? It is about me?"

"It was, but it's not. I need your help."

"If it's not me, gotta be Mott Haven, right? I told that other cop, I been off that job eight weeks now. I got no idea what's going on there."

"What did you do there?"

"Mott Haven? Same thing I do here. Construction management. Check the work, answer questions, fill out forms." She turned in the direction of a shout from the steel frame, and yelled, "Oh, sit on it, Bernie! I'll be up in a minute!" Back to Ann: "Look, I got no time. I got steel going in up there."

"Maggie—can I call you Maggie?—I'll try to keep it short, but this is serious. I need your help."

"Maggie?" Tiemeyer snorted. "You must've got that from Pete. He's the only one ever calls me Maggie. Most people call me Em."

"Em. Sorry. I'm Ann." She smiled. "No one calls me Annie, either, not for years now. Can you just tell me, what was your impression of Three Star when you worked there?"

"This is still about the accidents? Those masons, and the firefighter? That woman that got killed?"

"Yes, and more than that. I'm interested in Three Star themselves. I know they laid you off recently—"

"Back off! I told that other guy—"

Ann held up her hand. "I'm not saying you have a grudge. This truly isn't about you. I'm just thinking people who still work there might not feel as free to talk."

Tiemeyer nodded as though that made sense, but she said, "Nothing to talk about, really. Those guys are pretty much the same as everybody. Better than some."

"Meaning what?"

"Nothing. They get the job done."

"There are a lot of ways to get the job done."

"Listen, just tell me what you're looking for, okay? I got work to do."

Tiemeyer's tone said, *Get lost.* But she stuck her hands in her pockets, shifted her weight to face Ann squarely.

Ann said, "Evidence of illegal activity."

"Like?"

"Graft. Payoffs. Bribes."

"A little grease, sure. Nothing huge."

"Who do they grease? The Buildings Department, people like that?"

"Oh, Christ, no, not on that site. No, just the regular shit. Teamsters. Local 3. This one galvanizer, his backlog suddenly clears when he sees a case of Dewar's. Crap like that."

"But nobody official? Why did you say it like that?"

"Like what?"

" 'Christ, not on that site.' They usually do that, on other sites?"

"Whatever. I wouldn't know."

"But not there. Is there a special reason?"

Tiemeyer cocked her head at Ann. "Hon, say you're a pitcher. Triple A, pretty good. You got a fastball, slider, all that shit. Now say your secret weapon's a spitball. You gonna throw it with a Yankee scout in the stands? You'd be outta your mind."

"You're saying, even if I generally used an illegal practice, I'd skip it when someone was watching and something big was at stake?"

Tiemeyer frowned, as though downgrading her assessment of Ann's intelligence. "That's what I said."

"So what's at stake for Three Star?"

"Ha. The sixty-four-million-dollar question. No one knows."

"Any rumors, thoughts, ideas?"

"Lots. Mostly, everybody figures there's another job waiting someplace. Something Three Star can make a lot of money on, if they can pull this Mott Haven thing off."

"How would that translate, 'pull it off'? Make a lot of money here, too?"

"Hope not, because if that's it, they're screwed. No, Mott Haven is some kinda loss leader for Three Star. Don't know what the point is but they sure as shit aren't making money there."

"No?"

"They were losing their shirts when I left. For one thing, schedule's way behind. Though I hear the new guy's catching them up. That would take lots of grease, which they say is what he does best."

"How so?"

"Lot of work in New York right now. That means lots of sites to deliver to, labor shortages, materials shortages, suppliers calling the shots. This guy, they say he knows who to call. How to stroke 'em so his shit moves to the top of the list."

"Payoffs? Kickbacks?"

"He just knows who likes Knicks tickets and who likes a night at Hooters. That's not graft, hon, that's business."

"He sounds like a valuable resource."

"Bet your ass. Otherwise why would they hire a guy like him?"

"What's wrong with him?"

"One, I hear he's an asshole. But so's Pete, right?" Tiemeyer looked toward the trailer and shrugged. "This one, he's an ex-con, too."

In her mind, Ann saw the afternoon sun lying on Joe's garden. "Ex-cons have a right to work."

"Yeah, well, from what I hear, that's what they wanted this guy for."

"For being an ex-con?"

"Because this is the shit he went to jail for. So they figure he knows it real well."

Ann felt a sudden chill that wasn't weather. *Forget it*, she told herself. *That would be too good.* Nevertheless, she asked, "Can you tell me who he is? This new guy?"

"His name? Fuck if I remember. I was gone by then. But you want to know what gives over there, you could try talking to him. Listen, is that it? I gotta get back to work. I'm hoping to last at least until Christmas around here, before I rot Pete's socks so bad he cans me."

"You think he will?"

"You think he won't? Gal like me? I get to them all, sooner or later."

"Sorry to hear that."

"Bullshit. It's part of the fun."

"I know the feeling. But take another shot at the new guy's name at Mott Haven?"

"Shit. Something Irish. O'Dell, McDougal, I don't know."

Carefully, Ann said, "O'Doul? Sonny O'Doul?"

"Son of a bitch, yeah, that's him! You know him?"

"Yes," Ann said. "I know him. Son of a bitch."

Harlem: Frederick Douglass Boulevard

Ford glanced through the message slips Yvonnia handed him on his way in. "Westermann's office called twice?"

"So far." She smiled. Yvonnia St. James was lighter than he, and round in all her parts: round face, round figure, round hands and eyes. She kept her hair close-cropped and dyed a glorious golden yellow.

"Good," Ford said. "Did Shamika Arthur come in?"

"No. I hope she's okay. Poor kid." Yvonnia shook her head. "If I lost my boyfriend like she lost T.D., young as she is . . ."

"Did she call?"

"No. I tried her mama's place and her cell, but no answer."

"Well, keep trying. Just so she knows we're here."

Ford plugged in the teakettle and sorted the messages, setting them in the order in which he'd like to take care of them. He studied them for a minute and then re-sorted them into the order he actually would. That moved Edgar Westermann from the end to the beginning. The kettle steamed; he poured hot water into his cup, left his tea to steep, and walked to the open window.

Midday sun on long-shuttered storefronts; neon being hoisted into place over the new Delta Lounge. Rumbling traffic, boom-box rap, and the singing of a jackhammer; but still, in their pauses, the rustle of leaves in the garden beside the building. Diesel fumes and fried chicken, and the fragrance of the tea brewing on his desk.

He sat down and called Edgar Westermann.

"Ford Corrington," he said calmly, three separate times: at Westermann's office you had to fight your way past a receptionist and two secretaries.

"Ford! Glad you called!"

At Westermann's boom Ford yanked the phone away from his ear, replacing it gingerly. "Good morning, Edgar. I'm returning your calls."

"My—? Oh, yeah, yeah! LaTasha's calling just about everyone about the Studio Museum benefit, see who we can count in. Must have been that."

"The benefit, yes, I'm planning on it." Ford had a strong urge to continue, *Well, thanks then, see you there, goodbye,* just to see what excuse Westermann would come up with to call back—or have LaTasha call back—but that would be petty, and self-destructive besides.

There was no hint in Westermann's voice of yesterday's standoff, but to clear the air before they got to the real business, Ford said, "Anyway, I'm glad you called. I wanted to apologize if I came on too strong at Sarah Andersen's yesterday."

"Oh, no harm done. I could see you were trying to protect the poor woman, best way you knew how. I went up later, offer my sympathy, see if there's anything we can do."

"Later" was an elastic term: According to T. D. Tilden's cousin Lemuel, Westermann had gone up to speak to T. D.'s grieving mother so soon after Ford left that an uncharitable person might have thought he'd been watching.

"I would have gotten back with you first thing this morning," Ford said, switching over to what he knew was the real point of this conversation, "but I had that meeting with the mayor."

"The mayor . . ." Westermann's distracted tone implied he'd not only forgotten about Ford's meeting with the mayor, he'd forgotten exactly who the mayor was, so many and weighty were his concerns. "Oh, of course, right, right! You wanted to talk to him about getting your hands on that building site, wasn't that today?"

"Yes, that was today."

"How'd he do you?"

"He said it was unlikely."

"Ain't that just like Charlie?" Westermann chortled. "Not about to come out and tell you no, keep you from pitching a fit in his office. But you didn't really expect him to say yes, now did you? Can't tell me you're still that naive."

Ford sipped his tea. "I didn't expect that, no."

"Good, good. You always were a smart fella. Wrongheaded half the time, but smart, can't deny it. So what's your next move?"

"To wait. He's reading our prospectus."

"Your prospectus?"

"He said he'd read it and get back to us."

"You really think Charlie's going to *read* it?"

"He said Real Property and Planning would look at it, too."

"Ford, Ford, Ford. Charlie Barr's not about to waste his time like that. He has plans for Block A and you ain't in 'em. He doesn't care what's in your prospectus."

"Maybe not. But I have to give him the chance to do what he said he would before I take the next step."

"Which would be what?"

"Haven't decided."

"Was I you, I'd hold a press conference."

"I know you would. And I might, but not yet."

"That's a mistake. You gotta put some pressure on ol' Charlie, use the power of public opinion. Get the people on your side now, before Hizzoner dazzles 'em with that pie in the sky."

Ford had to admit to himself Westermann's point was a good one. Once the mayor started talking about tax revenue and jobs—and once white folks started hearing, in the subtext, that Harlem's well-located, once-elegant streets weren't going to be scary and unwelcoming anymore—Garden Walls would be shouting into the wind.

Had to admit it to himself, but not to Westermann. Westermann's points were often good. The Borough President had been fighting this fight much longer than Ford. The cynicism of his aims and his tactics might, Ford suspected on bad days, reflect reality better than Ford's own optimistic approach.

"I'll think about it, Edgar. Just wanted to bring you up to speed. And to thank you for your support."

"No need to thank me! That's my job, do what I can for the community! You and me, we don't always see eye to eye, but I know we both want the best for Harlem. After all, I was born here, and you been living here, what, fifteen years now?"

"Sixteen. But I get your point."

"You just keep it up. And you need any help from me on this project of yours, you let me know. LaTasha has standing instructions to put Ford Corrington through anytime."

"I appreciate that, Edgar. I'll talk to you later."

Ford dropped the receiver in the cradle and leaned back. He wondered why, though Westermann had gone to the trouble of pointing out which of them was the native here and which the carpetbagger, and though the Borough President was in the habit of taking credit for every beam of sunshine that fell on Harlem, he nevertheless referred to the Garden Walls project as "yours."

Heart's Content

Joe heard the phone ringing as he jumped down from the truck. Heart pounding, he fumbled with the cabin key. This might be someone trying to sell him satellite TV. But it might be Ellie, calling about Janet; it might be something bad.

He threw the door open and grabbed for the phone. "Hello?"

"It's me."

Not Ellie's voice. His pulse slowed, though under the relief he felt a small, surprising stab of loneliness. But "me"? Who the hell was "me"?

Oh. "Ann?"

"God, Joe, you make it sound like it's been months. I'm beginning to think it really is Rip Van Winkleville up there. I was there yesterday, remember?"

"I just . . ." Joe tossed the keys on the counter, flicked on the kitchen light. Sink, table, mug in the dish drainer, everything the same. The same as yesterday. The same as the day before yesterday, and the day before that. "I . . . Ann, why are you calling?"

"Look at the roof bricks yet?"

"No."

"I have news."

News. "I just got off work, Ann. I'm sweaty and tired. The light's going and I have things to do in the garden."

"That all of your excuses, or you have more? I'll wait."

"Ann, what do you want?"

Silence. Ann, with no answer? Especially to that question?

"Ann?"

"Joe, listen to me: Sonny O'Doul works for Three Star."

Outside the window a wide triangle of honey light lay on the grass; the rest was shadow.

"Joe? You still there?"

"What are you talking about?"

"Three Star hired Sonny O'Doul as an assistant site super for Mott Haven a little over a month ago. Logistics, deliveries, scheduling. O'Doul's keeping a low profile but I'm willing to bet he's in charge of graft and corruption."

Phone propped on his shoulder, Joe spooned grounds into the coffee filter. He ran water in the pot, poured it through, reached for a mug, all without putting the phone down, but also without a word to Ann.

"Ha! Like old times," Ann said.

Joe remembered those times: Ann on the phone, passing along something she'd come up with. Something he'd hear, assess, evaluate, all in silence, while Ann waited. For his question. His comment. His suggested course of action.

But not now. Not now.

Sonny O'Doul. Joe wished the man were dead. He wanted him in hell, writhing in flames, screaming for mercy.

But more than he wanted that, he wanted to be out in his garden in the afternoon sunlight, pulling up rogue roses of Sharon before they took hold and became almost impossible to remove.

"They hired him because he knows the ropes," Ann said. "He's laying kickbacks on suppliers and cash on union reps. I don't have him yet for paying off anyone in the city, but it's got to be."

"Then go get him."

"Oh, I will. But he's got to have enemies, Joe. You can't be the only person O'Doul ever screwed. Maybe they're behind the accidents."

Behind the accidents. Why did she still think people were behind things, that things happened as people planned them? "No. It's too oblique. Especially if he's doing logistics and deliveries. You want to mess up the guy who does that, you slash the tires on a Teamster truck." And why, oh why, was *he* talking at all?

"Okay, so maybe he's causing the accidents himself."

"Why?"

"I don't know! Maybe he's being paid by someone. Or maybe he's trying extortion. If Three Star doesn't pay, the accidents go on and their schedule's blown."

"That's a dangerous game for an ex-con." As anything is. He gazed through the glass between him and the garden.

"Also," Ann hurried on, "there's another thing. Word is Three Star's losing money on Mott Haven and they're only doing it because there's something else they want. Pulling this off is the price of getting it. And it's something big, Joe. Another site, maybe. And maybe someone doesn't want them to have it."

"What site? Who?"

"I don't know yet. I don't know, Joe, but please? Look at the paperwork on the bricks. Tell me it wasn't an accident. With Sonny O'Doul there, it can't be coincidence. This is our chance, Joe."

Saying nothing, Joe drank coffee. The triangle of sun had narrowed to a long sliver, pointing to the creek.

"I'm going to go up and talk to him," Ann said. "But I want to know what's going on before I do."

What's going on. Always, always what drove Ann: as though what was going on could be known. As though knowing what was going on would do you any good.

"Joe?"

"Ann." If he went outside right now, he could still get in a few hours' work before the light was gone. "I'll call you," he told her, and hung up the phone.

Harlem: State Office Building

Edgar Westermann hung up the phone, creaked his desk chair way back, and sighed at the ceiling. This must be his day for talking to fools. At least it was easier to get rid of them on the phone than if they were here in all their physical flesh. He checked his watch. He'd been planning to head down to the Centre Street office for the rest of the afternoon. Showing his face in the corridors of power a couple of times a week was something he'd made sure to do since he'd been a Council member and had to find excuses. Now he went downtown just often enough to remind everyone that if they had anything to say to him they'd find him up in Harlem.

But if this particular fool he'd just called was correct, he'd best stay up in Harlem and call a press conference. Well, that was all right. He enjoyed press conferences. This one would irritate that other fool, Ford Corrington, but that couldn't be helped. He buzzed LaTasha, telling her to get out her press list. If they were quick enough, the trucks and microphones could be set up by five. He could be outraged but succinct, the press would have time for some quick Q and A, and he could still make the six o'clock news.

City Hall

The mayor watched the six o'clock news and thought, *Oh, shit.*

He was dressing for dinner, some black-tie function at a temple in Brooklyn—synagogue, you called this one a synagogue, though what the difference was, Charlie was never sure—and he had the news on in the background out of habit. Buttoning his shirt, he saw Edgar Westermann's indignant face on the teaser and shook his head, wondering what poor chump was Edgar's target today. Tying his tie, he heard the anchor announce the segment so he turned to find out. Fastening his cuff links, he discovered it was him.

CHAPTER 37

Harlem: Frederick Douglass Boulevard

Ford Corrington didn't watch the six o'clock news because he was still in the office. TVs were banned from the Garden Project Building. Kids spent too much time in front of the screen; it was one of the things they preached on hard, here, that getting out and doing was better than sitting back and watching. Radio, though, was different. Music—live and broadcast, rap, hip-hop, reggae and ska, but also Afro-pop, world beat, jazz, and even the classical music of all those dead white European men—was everywhere. It competed with the percussion in the wood and metal shops and wailed above the basketball court, wove through the gardening class, and was the very point of the orchestra, choir, and chorus.

In Ford's own office, end-of-the-day catching up went better with WBGO, the jazz station out of Newark. It was on their six o'clock newscast that Ford heard Edgar Westermann screwing things up for him again.

City Hall

Charlie was shrugging into his tux jacket when Louise strolled through his office door. She looked stunning in something blue and slithery.

"You're gorgeous, Mrs. Barr."

"You're not so bad yourself, Mr. Mayor. Ready to go? Limo's waiting."

"It's a UJA dinner. Jewish events always start late. I have to make two quick calls."

"Do you have your speech?"

Charlie touched his pocket to make sure, though he was sure. Before he could answer, his cell phone rang. He checked the readout. "Walter," he said. Louise raised her eyebrows, waiting for him to answer, as though there were no possibility of just letting it ring. He sighed; there probably wasn't. He flipped the phone open and said, "Walter."

"Charlie. Now really, was that necessary?"

"If you mean Westermann's press conference, give me a break. Obviously I'm as surprised as you are." Charlie exchanged glances with Louise, then perched on the edge of his desk.

"And no doubt even more dismayed," Glybenhall said. "Did you have any idea he was going to go public like that?"

"I think I'd have mentioned it to you if I had. Until this morning, I didn't even know there was a consortium put together up there to go after that site."

"Well, that's unfortunate, isn't it? Your intelligence apparatus is clearly faulty."

"My apparatus? You have to be kidding. I'm the mayor, not the

Homeland Security Director. You think I have spies in the Borough President's offices?"

"Don't you? You should."

"That's not how it works."

"Maybe you should have served a term in business rather than going directly into government, Charlie. You'd have a better sense of how it does work. Now, this consortium: Have you any idea who its members are?"

"Yes, and if you think you're unhappy now, wait until you hear this: it's Ford Corrington."

"Oh, my Lord! Not seriously."

"Of course seriously."

"That *bastard*. He knows it's me. He knows I want it—"

"Oh, for Christ's sake! No, of course he doesn't know. Come on, Walter, it's his neighborhood. Except that they seem to have actually put together a viable financing and development package, there's nothing surprising in this. You and I had talked about Corrington wanting a piece of Block A."

"A *piece*. Which, for the sake of community relations and at *your* insistence, I was planning to hold my nose and give him. But for God's sake, Ford Corrington's not competent to develop a project that large."

"That large? You don't even know what he's proposing."

"What he's— Does that matter? Do you think I'd feel more charitably inclined if I did?"

"I doubt it."

"He must know. He must have found out what I'm planning—"

"Of course he knows what you're planning, it was in the paper! What he doesn't know is that it's you. He would've said something when we met, you can bank on it."

"When did you meet?"

"Like I said: this morning."

"Why?"

"What kind of question is that? He's a powerful constituent and he wanted a meeting. We must have sat down together twenty times over the years."

"You didn't tell me this last night. That you planned to meet with Corrington today."

"I didn't know what the agenda was. The fact that he was coming in to talk to me, no, I didn't tell you that. There was no reason to."

"It didn't occur to you the *agenda* might have been my site?"

"Walter, I'm sure this comes as a surprise to you, but unlike the press and your own PR people, I don't automatically assume everything that happens in this city is about you."

"Your sarcasm is unnecessary."

"So's your wounded innocence. We got sandbagged: shit happens."

"Not in my world. I keep a close eye on what's going on around me and I arrange things as I prefer them. So tell me, what did Corrington want when you met with him? For you to just hand the site over? No review process, nothing?"

"He wanted a promise that when the smoke clears Block A will be his. You know: sort of like what you have."

"Ah," said Walter. "Yes. Well, what did you tell him?"

"I said I'd look at it."

"According to Westermann, you said it would be a cold day in hell."

"Actually, that phrase came up in the meeting, but that wasn't the context. But I have to tell you, Walter, this complicates things."

"How so?"

"It's not a bad package. I read the prospectus. None of them have any experience with anything this big, but otherwise it looks pretty good. I don't think they'd be the best choice to develop the site, but it's not impossible that if they tried, they'd succeed."

"Oh, Charlie, please."

"It's not just Corrington. It's also Ray Holdsclaw, some other church people, other nonprofits. A construction company. A couple of banks. Maybe not the best choice, but they'd be a hell of a popular one."

Louise tapped her watch. Charlie stood up and headed with her to the door.

"Charlie?" came Walter's calm voice. "You wouldn't be considering . . . renegotiating?"

Charlie took Louise's hand as they walked down the carpeted hallway. "No, I'm not. But I can't say I like your tone, Walter."

"Well, I'm very sorry about that. I suppose I'm distressed at any suggestion that our friendship might not be as close as I thought."

"Oh, cut the crap. The real problem is, if we're not careful we could both find ourselves in positions we're not going to enjoy. One, no, we hadn't planned on Corrington and his crowd making a play for the site, but two—"

"We should have seen it coming."

"Let me finish! Two is the mess you made up at Mott Haven."

"*I?* I didn't—"

"One way or another, you did, and everything I said last night goes double now. Six people got hurt and a woman died. You'd better be able to stand up to scrutiny, because you're sure as hell going to get scrutinized."

Walter chuckled, surprising the mayor. "I suppose that's better than screwed. But Charlie, did I really have to hear about Corrington's consortium on the evening news?"

"Goddammit, Walter, I tried to tell you but you ducked my calls twice today! What the hell did you think I was calling about?"

"Charlie, I had no idea. I was . . . otherwise engaged."

"I don't give a shit what you were doing. I expect you to talk to me when I call you."

"I don't work for you, Mr. Mayor."

"And I don't work for you!"

A pause. "Good, now that's out of the way. There's really no need for this level of rancor, you know. Tell me, are you embarking upon a pleasant evening?"

Charlie and Louise stopped at the private elevator. Charlie couldn't ask her to walk down the grand stair in heels like those. In answer to Walter, he sighed. "I don't think so."

"Oh. I'm sorry to hear that. In my case, quite the opposite. Carmen," Walter said.

"From Brogan's?"

"Indeed."

"Walter, she's half your age."

"Nearly two-thirds, Charlie. And impressively pneumatic."

"Where's Helene?"

"In Southampton for the season. Probably enjoying the company of the pool boy even as we speak. Do you at least have the delectable Louise by your side?"

"Yes, I do."

"Then your evening should be bearable. For myself, I shall put all this unpleasantness out of my head, lavish caviar and affection on Carmen, and worry about the Bronx, Harlem, and other unsavory places when the new day dawns. Good night, Charlie."

The elevator doors glided open. Charlie thumbed his phone off and waited for Louise to go first. "He's getting on my nerves," he said.

"That's okay, honey, but you can't let it show."

"Who the hell does he think he is? If he were going out of his way to piss me off on purpose these days, he couldn't do a much better job of it."

"Sweetie, calm down."

"I thought that was part of my charm. How I wear my emotions on my sleeve."

"It's only charming when it's the good ones."

"Really? Like how crazy I am about every inch of you?"

"Yes, that's very appealing. What did Walter want?"

"To piss me off."

"That's more likely a by-product. Why did he call?"

"If I tell you will you kiss me?"

She smiled. "Maybe."

Charlie ran down Walter's complaint for Louise. By the time he was done, his leather soles and her stilettos were clicking down the first floor's marble hall. "He's getting too damn big for his britches," Charlie said. "And he's got this personal feud going with Ford Corrington that I sure as hell don't want to be in the middle of."

"Over the memorial? Still?"

"Over a lot of things. Walter feels dissed."

"By a black man."

"That's part of it, yes."

"Is it a big deal to Corrington, too?"

"I doubt it. I don't think Walter looms nearly as large in Corrington's mind as he does in his own. Besides, Corrington's the one who won. Damn! Who does he think he is?"

"Corrington? No, you mean Walter, don't you?"

"I don't like it that he thinks he can not take my calls, and I don't like the way he refers to Block A as 'my site.' "

"Well, it is. You promised it to him."

"No. I promised him I'd do everything I could to throw it his way, but he had to provide me with ammunition by how he handled Mott Haven. What's happening over there isn't ammunition, it's a goddamn land mine." He pulled her into an alcove just before the rotunda. "Now kiss me."

"Didn't you have calls to make? Before Walter called?"

"Corrington. And Edgar. To put my unhappiness about Edgar's press conference on record."

"Do you think Ford Corrington had anything to do with that?"

"I bet he was as blindsided as we were. But he must have been the one who told Edgar about our meeting. He should know better than that."

"So go ahead and call."

"No hurry. Their offices will be closed. It's just pro forma. Kiss me first." Louise cocked her head, made a show of weighing the pros and cons. "Why not?" Their kiss didn't last long, just long enough to make Charlie wish B'nai Barak were way out in Bay Ridge instead of in Boerum Hill. Or even better, in Kankakee.

"Now you have lipstick all over your face," Louise said. She took out her mirror and checked her own damage. "Why call Edgar's office? Don't you have his cell number?"

"I don't want him to think I give that much of a damn." Charlie wiped his mouth and stuffed his handkerchief back in his pocket. They walked through the rotunda, Louise smiling at the guard who held the door.

Heart's Content

Joe Cole didn't watch the six o'clock news, or the eleven o'clock news, or listen to the radio, either. Never, ever, in prison, had he found quiet, except in the stolen moments when, far enough from the rest of the grounds crew that their talk was inaudible, he paused in his work, silenced his shears or his shovel to hear, however briefly, nothing. Now, after a day of rumbling traffic overlaid with frantic DJs and numbing Top 40 beats belting from the asphalt truck, after the trash talk and joshing necessary to keep the social wheels greased on a four-man road crew, after a supper of fried chicken and Frank Sinatra in the diner up the road, he sat drinking beer in the silence of the cabin.

He let his ears react to the quiet the way his eyes did to the darkness. He heard the patient sawing of cicadas, and the busy rushing creek. A bird, startled from a nest, squawked into the air and complained. Stars sprinkled the black sky behind blacker trees. When the moon rose behind the house, its cracked reflection rippled in the windows of the shed. All these pieces amounted to nothing: no multi-strand melody, no woven tapestry. Just pieces, scattered over time. The last few years had taught Joe the laughable futility of searching for patterns, for help in predicting what was coming by studying what was. The biggest joke of all, he thought, was how he kept looking.

He was half asleep when the phone's ring ripped the emptiness. Joe stumbled to the counter and croaked a hoarse "Hello?" He pulled the light chain, blinded by the sudden brightness.

"It's me," said Ann. "Did I wake you?"

"Jesus Christ!" he said, and after a pause, "It's the middle of the night." And wondered why, now that he knew it was only Ann, his pulse still sped.

"I'm sorry. Were you asleep?"

"No."

"Were you thinking about my photos?"

"I—that's why you're calling me at midnight? About your photos?"

"No. Joe, I found it."

"Found what?"

"The other site."

"What other site?"

"I told you about that. Why Three Star's doing Mott Haven in the first place. To get their hands on another site. Where they could make some serious profit."

"Three Star? Ann, I don't—"

"Both sites are city owned," she pressed on. "Walter must have some secret deal with the mayor."

Joe opened the fridge to get a new beer, clicked the light off, and returned to the chair, phone in hand. "So what?"

"What do you—"

"So Glybenhall has a deal with the mayor. You call that news?"

"Of course not. But this could explain what's going on."

"What's going on?"

"The accidents. The sabotage, that you found."

"I might have found. In one case."

"You said you were sure. Are you backing down?"

Joe thought about the bolt holes in the scaffolding, smooth as the day they were made, perfect ovals blithely unaffected by violent catastrophe. He shook his head, though she couldn't see that. "No."

"Joe, listen to me. It's a site in Harlem. Huge. The city calls it Block A. There's a consortium of local groups that wants it, too."

"Who says?"

"Edgar Westermann. He held a press conference this afternoon. I just caught it on the news. It was like he was handing me the answer on a platter."

"Westermann? You believe—"

"However much baloney this was, the kernel's there. Westermann was in righteous indignation mode. 'The city's selling our homes to the highest bidder! They're putting our community and our people on the auction block!' "

"He called Charlie Barr a slave trader?"

"He came close. Apparently this consortium met with Hizzoner and got blown off. The city already has plans for Block A. It was in the *Times* months ago, labeled as 'proposed,' but Westermann thinks the site's signed, sealed, and delivered."

"To Glybenhall? Did he say that?"

"No. But—"

"Then how do you know?"

"I don't. But it's got to be. This is exactly the kind of thing that would make Walter drool."

"Or any other developer."

"Oh, but Joe! Glybenhall and Sonny O'Doul? It's like Christmas."

"So Glybenhall has a dirty deal with the mayor. What's that got to do with what you're looking at? Accidents, a fire, a woman killed—I can't see how that helps anyone out."

Ann paused. "Well, first of all, if Walter and Charlie do have a deal, there's a possibility of corruption right there."

"You're going to investigate the mayor?"

"If I have to. Besides, I've started to look at Walter's finances. I was right. As usual, his pockets aren't nearly as deep as they seem. And he's overinsured. These accidents generated a nice little cash flow for him."

"What are you saying? He's behind them himself?"

"I'm saying something smells, and Walter's never been innocent. I'm going to get him, Joe."

"So get him."

"I will," she said. "I will. I just wanted to . . ." Her voice trailed off. Joe stared through the glass to his dark garden; he should have spent the extra hour this evening, planting the dicentra whose white blooms he could see, waiting for him.

"Joe?"

"I'm still here."

"What were you doing when I called?"

Sleeping. Drinking. Painting the porch. I wasn't here. He finished his beer. "I was thinking about your photos."

CHAPTER
40

Sutton Place

"My photos? You were?"

"Isn't that what you wanted?"

"Yes, but I—"

"The roof tarp. The bricks."

Ann caught her breath. "This could be major, Joe. This is the one. If you found something."

"What you gave me," he said neutrally, as though this were merely a business discussion, something he was in a hurry to get out of the way; though when they'd worked together he'd never used that tone. "I did some calculations, in my head. Area covered, height, likely wind speed. There's a formula."

"For holding a tarp down?"

"Tarp, canvas, whatever. It's in knots and pounds, but you can translate it into miles per hour and bricks. Bricks weigh about three pounds each," he added. She didn't need to know that, but that was Joe, the old Joe, showing her the tools he'd used.

"Okay," she said, trying to make this sound normal, just the two of them going over a case. "And . . . ?"

"Looking at the roof area, the bricks left on the roof, the bricks on the ground. The site hadn't been tampered with?"

"In what way?"

"Bricks removed before the photographer got there?"

"Unlikely."

"Then there weren't enough."

"To hold the tarp?"

"Not nearly. Looks like a lot, but when you count them up, it's no more than half the bricks you'd need."

"Well, but couldn't that just be a mistake? They'd used the bricks from those pallets and hadn't brought up more?"

"If the site super went to the trouble of hoisting pallets onto the roof to hold down a tarp, it would've occurred to him to check his weight when a storm was due." Joe paused, that familiar pause. Ann knew better than to speak through it. "Sonny O'Doul's a lot of things," Joe finally said. "But he's not an idiot."

"Would O'Doul know it?" Ann asked. "The formula?"

"The formula, probably not. But he wouldn't need it. I didn't either, not really, but I ran it because I'm an engineer. But if I were up on that roof I could tell by eyeballing it. So could Sonny."

"What about the bricklayers?"

"What about them?"

"Wouldn't they have known there were too few bricks on the roof?"

"Not their job. They put in the bricks they need, wash up, and go home. The roof's not their problem. If they start sticking their noses in another trade's work, they'll only get told to butt out, anyway. If one was particularly bothered he might have mentioned it, but that's it."

"So you're saying . . ."

"All I'm saying is, chances are good Sonny O'Doul knew how much weight he needed on that tarp. And he knew he didn't have it."

"He's only the assistant super."

"In charge of scheduling and logistics, isn't that what you said? That includes moving bricks around."

"What about his boss, the guy who was fired? Wouldn't the responsibility have been his in the end?"

"In the end, yes."

"I'll talk to him," Ann said. "Before I go see Sonny. Anything else?"

"No," Joe said. "It's late, Ann. I have to work in the morning."

"Of course. I'm sorry. As soon as I find anything new I'll call you again."

"Great."

His sarcasm made her smile. She said, "Good night, Joe," but he was gone already.

CHAPTER

41

Sutton Place

Early Tuesday morning, Ann searched the files she'd inherited. She frowned over her latte and reached for the phone.

"This can't be you," Dennis Graham said, answering his cell. "Much too early."

"I'm turning over a new leaf. Did you see Edgar Westermann's press conference yesterday?"

"On the news. You lucked out, huh?"

"You think so too? Got to be."

"I agree. That why you're calling?"

"No, no. Though as long as I have you: you know anything about that Block A site?"

"In Harlem? Not a thing."

"No, I don't suppose anyone does, yet. Listen, Dennis, I'm looking for Three Star's site super. I'm reading your file here. He left the country? What do you mean, he left the country?"

"Mike Statius? Tried to talk to him myself, Saturday. My last official act," Dennis said cheerfully. "Before Greg moved me here and gave you that mess."

"The guy wasn't even fired until Saturday!"

"Morning. And escorted off the site. And apparently to the airport."

"Escorted to the *airport*?"

"I'm exaggerating. But by the time I called Saturday afternoon, he was on a plane to Curaçao. Where he's from."

"You didn't find that peculiar?"

"He goes back and forth a lot, they tell me. His family's there.

NYPD—Luis Perez?—talked to him. They cleared Statius to go because they had nothing to hold him on. But we alerted the authorities
down there. If we need him, they'll pick him up for us. If he tries to go
anywhere else, we'll know about it. Or," he added, "you will. Me, I don't
have to care anymore."

"Try not to be so depressed. Does Greg know?"

"That the guy's gone? He wasn't happy, but there's nothing he could
do. And like I say, you can get him if you need him."

"Is there a number in—" she looked at the file, "Fredrickstown?"

"I didn't find one. But you can call the cop down there I was dealing
with. Lieutenant van Drost."

Ann hung up and let Dennis get back to his task force. Call the cop
in Curaçao? Oh, well, why not? It had a nice ring to it.

"Lieutenant van Drost." He had a nice ring to him, too, Ann thought.
Clear tenor, slight Dutch accent, and friendly, for a cop. She explained
who she was and what she wanted.

"Yes, I was told someone from New York might be calling. Do you
want me to pick him up for you?"

"I just want to talk to him. Maybe you have a phone number?"

"I'm afraid he doesn't have a telephone. I've already checked."

"Very efficient, Lieutenant. Yes, then, please."

"It's possible to be as efficient here among our soft island breezes as
up there in the asphalt jungle. Though more difficult."

"Then you deserve even more credit. Call me anytime."

She gave him her phone numbers and hung up as Greg Lowry
walked into the office. He headed straight for her desk, grinning. "You're
here early," he said. "You catch Edgar Westermann's press conference
yesterday?"

"Sure did."

"Ever get the feeling a politician's speaking directly to you?"

"Rarely. But you think this is it, too?"

"The other site? How could it not be? Have you called Westermann
yet?"

"I was about to."

"Keep me in the loop. As soon as you talk to him."

"Yessir."

Still grinning, Lowry rapped her desk with his knuckles and strolled
to his corner office.

Ann called the Bronx Borough President's office, checked the
Cavalier out of the DOI garage, and headed uptown.

Harlem: Frederick Douglass Boulevard

"Wait!" Yvonnia stopped Ford as he strode past her desk on his way into his office.

"Don't stop me, I have to call Edgar and yell at him before I find a way to put it off."

"Later."

Yvonnia's tone made Ford halt. "What's up?"

"First of all, the mayor called last night. After hours."

"After Edgar was on the six o'clock news?"

"That's right. Hizzoner left a message. He's not happy."

"I don't blame him. Okay, what's second?"

"Shamika Arthur. She called three times."

"Is she coming in?"

"I don't think so. She's in Georgia."

"*Georgia?*"

"Crawford County, Georgia. She has people there, her mother's kin. But she wants you to call her. Said she'd stay by the phone." Yvonnia handed him the message slips.

Do you suppose it's a sign you're getting tired of public life, Ford asked himself, when making a long-distance call to a grieving teenager who's lost her first love is more appealing than speaking to the Borough President or the mayor? He plugged in his teakettle, sat down, and dialed the number in Georgia.

A "Hello?" came right after the second ring, but it was a man's voice.

"Shamika Arthur, please."

"Ain't no one here by that name."

Ford checked the message slip and the readout on his phone. They were the same. "I'm sorry. I was told she called me from this number."

"That so? And who would this be?"

If she's not there, Ford thought, *what do you care who this is?* He gave his name again. He heard it repeated into the room, and in answer, a girl's fainter voice. A moment later Shamika came on.

"Mr. Corrington! Hello."

"Hello, Shamika. What's going on? Are you all right?"

"I'm—I'm okay. I'm sorry I run out on you like I done."

"Where are you? Who was that? Are you all right?"

"I'm staying with my cousins. That was Ralphie you just spoke to. Don't mind him, he's just looking after me. I . . . I . . ."

"I understand, Shamika. Sometimes when tragedy happens we feel like distance will help."

"No! I mean, yeah. But it ain't just that."

"Not just what?"

"T.D., him—him dying like that. Yeah, I feel awful. He wasn't bad, you know, Mr. Corrington. He was just . . . sorta like a kid. He was sweet when he wanted to be. He had big plans."

"I know that. I liked T.D. I wish things had turned out differently."

"His mama—she okay?"

"I think she will be. She's a strong woman and her faith is strong. Right now she's suffering."

"You tell her—I mean, her and me, we didn't always see eye to eye, but I wouldn't of run out on her, leave her alone at a time like this. You tell her I'm sorry?"

"I will. Shamika—"

"Because, thing is, I, like, I had to go."

"Had to?"

"Yeah. Yeah, 'cause I was scared."

"Scared? Of what?"

"See, and that's why I'm calling you. 'Cause T.D., see . . ."

"Shamika?"

"One thing, like, most people don't know about T.D.? He's a very . . . like, he could dance, you know? But not just that. What I mean, he could climb, like in the playground, even up a tree . . ."

"He was athletic, you mean?"

"Mr. Corrington? Ain't no way, no matter how stoned he be, ain't no way T.D. gonna fall by accident off no roof!"

"Shamika," Ford began gently, but she didn't let him go on.

"No, see, and what he told me," she insisted, "what he told me, he was making good money, he was doing jobs, working for this guy Kong. You know Kong?"

"Huge man, light skinned, shaved head?"

"That him! I told T.D., that Kong, he a nasty fucker—oh, sorry!"

"Don't worry about that. What do you mean, doing jobs?"

"I told T.D., I said you don't want to be working for no one like Kong, wasn't gonna be nothing but trouble. But T.D., he just kept on. And he was—he was making accidents."

"He was what?"

"I knew it wasn't right! I told him he better stop. There was this place he would go, up to the Bronx. They was building a building. He'd just do little sh—little stuff, and make something go wrong. Just to cost them some money. I told him, that ain't right. But he say some rich white man building it, who cares, he got to spend more money? I ask him how come Kong give a—how come he care? And T.D., he say that ain't none of his business, he just do what he be told, he gonna come out with enough cash money for him and me to get our own place."

Ford suddenly realized he'd been hearing his kettle whistle for a while. He reached over and clicked it off. "Shamika? Are you sure about what you're saying?"

"Yeah. T.D. bragged on it. You gotta understand, he was, like, proud. He was sneaking around, climbing stuff couldn't nobody else climb, getting in and out without no one seeing him. Maybe I should of told someone, or made him stop. I mean, I know it was bad, what he done. But T.D., mostly he felt bad about himself. You know? He didn't have no self-respect. And it wasn't hurting no one, except some rich white man." She was silent for a moment. "I'm sorry," she blurted.

"Shamika, what did you mean when you said T.D. wouldn't fall off a roof?"

"Because he wouldn't! That morning. Sunday? Him and me was gonna go down to the park. Sort of like a picnic. He was gonna call me, soon as he went and did what he had to do."

"Up in the Bronx?"

"No, uh-uh. Somewhere close. He was hooking up with Kong."

"Did he call?"

"No. And after . . . what happened, I'm like all upset and nervous. I'm over to my girlfriend's house, fixing to go up to see T.D.'s moms, and my mama call. She say, this big shaved-head dude come over, he be asking where I was, and she take one look at him and tell him she don't know. He say he a friend of mine, name of Kong, and when I come home, maybe I can call him? He give her his cell phone number. He say he think I got something belong to him, he want me to give it back. My mama say he say please."

"What do you have?"

"Nothing! That belong to Kong? I ain't never had nothing of his!"

"So what did he mean?"

"I don't know!"

"All right, Shamika. Go on."

The girl sniffed. "He real polite, my mama say, got gold teeth when he smile. And my mama say to me, 'Girl, you know I don't never ask you your business. And I ain't asking now. But I'm telling you: Get your skinny ass out of town.' "

Ford hung up the phone and clicked the kettle back on, waited for it to whistle again, and poured. He went to the window, holding the mug in both hands as he would have on a winter morning. When the tea was brewed he sipped at it, but it didn't warm him.

CHAPTER

43

Sutton Place

The Manhattan Borough President didn't keep Ann waiting.

The minute his receptionist passed her name and business along, Edgar Westermann popped out and ushered her into his glass-walled office. Seeming not at all put out that she hadn't called for an appointment, he waved her grandly to a chair.

"I won't take up much of your time," she began, but Westermann cut her off.

"No, no! Whenever the city's crime fighters are on the job, I'm happy to help. Crime in Harlem's down eleven percent the last three years, did you know that? And that's despite how we don't get our fair share of city services." He looked at her severely, in silent reprimand. Then he smiled, giving her a second chance. "All right then. Tell me, what can the Borough President's Office do for DOI?"

"I saw your press conference on the news last night. I'd like to ask you some questions about some of the things you brought up."

"Go right ahead. About time the city looked into how development contracts get awarded. How it is that the same old boys' club of wealthy white men gets their hands on prime city-owned sites over and over, while community groups get left out in the cold. Whose pockets are being lined? That's the question you have to ask yourself, you see Donald Trump, Larry Silverstein, Walter Glybenhall, all walking off with contract after contract at the expense of the communities, the people who built those communities, the people who made them what they are! People who never—"

"Sir?" She held up a hand. "Can we keep to this specific issue? You said yesterday the city had turned down a community group's bid on the site known as Block A."

He gave her a pitying look. "You think this is an isolated issue, you're wrong. This is a problem with the system, can't be solved without a thorough investigation, a complete overhaul! But maybe I'm expecting too much, thinking the city's about to look at itself for real. No, most likely you're here to say you came here. Westermann's shooting off his mouth again, best look like we're taking him seriously. All right, let's get it over with."

"That's quite a set of assumptions."

"Years of experience, Inspector. I've seen it all before."

"Sometimes, Mr. Westermann, you see what you're looking for, not what's there."

"Oh, now, is that a fact? You come here to lecture me?"

"No. I'm sorry if that's how it sounded. But you're assuming I'm not taking you seriously, and I assure you, I am. Can you please answer my question? Did the city turn down a community group's bid on that site?"

Westermann snorted. "Charlie Barr didn't give them so much as a how-dee-do. Threw them right out."

"Who is this group?"

"Garden Walls. A consortium."

"Who are its members?"

"People and organizations who have a stake in this neighborhood, whose roots and families and businesses are here—"

"Can you give me some names? Are you a member?"

"Wouldn't be right for the Borough President to be involved. Block A's city-owned property. But my office supports Garden Walls. We'd like to keep the 'neighbor' in 'neighborhood'!"

"Who are they, the members? Who speaks for them?"

"It's a large group. You want to talk directly to someone, I suppose you could try Ford Corrington. Over to the Garden Project."

"Garden Project, Garden Walls. I get it."

"You ask Ford what his group plans for that site, and how the mayor treated him, as a representative of this community. And you tell Ford that Edgar Westermann sent you."

"That won't get me thrown out of his office?"

Westermann's eyebrows rose. "Was a time it would've. Surprised you know that."

"Actually, I was surprised to see Mr. Corrington at your press conference Saturday, when you spoke about the woman who was killed at the Mott Haven construction site. Anyone who reads the papers knows you two don't get along."

"Well, it's no secret Ford and me have had our differences of opinion. Ford's a headstrong young fella. Sometimes I guess he can be a little unorthodox. But let me tell you, sometimes in this world a man's got no choice! When Ford asked could he stand up with me Saturday, I thought, Yes! Let's show the world Harlem united!"

"When you say 'unorthodox' . . . ?"

Westermann's eyes narrowed. "See, now, there you go. You're looking at a black man don't toe the line, you're thinking all kinds of bad things. I've been telling that boy for years, you want to make a point or you want to be effective? You keep doing like you do, all that happens, you scare white folks off."

"Mr. Westermann, I'm not thinking anything. I'm an investigator with a job to do. I'm about to go see Mr. Corrington on your suggestion and I'd like to have as much background as I can."

"Background? You check me out before you come up here, get yourself some background?"

"I didn't have to. I've followed your career. You're a public figure."

"Well, I suppose I am." He nodded gravely. "Made it my life's work, to be visible, give the black community a voice. Now Ford, maybe he's a little hotheaded. But I think in his heart he wants the best for Harlem, too. Take that garden over by his building. Beautiful place, can't argue with that. And big. Lot used to be owned by the city. One spring, Ford took it over. Borrowed a bulldozer, cleared it, had all the little children plant flowers. After that, all that spring and summer, never a minute when there wasn't a dozen children in the garden, day and night. Put up a tent, had 'em sleeping there. They called it a 'sleep-in.' Pressuring the city to give it to him. Mayor had plans for that site, but who's gonna send marshals to evict little children? Too much like Selma. This here's the civilized North. Turned into a standoff."

"I remember reading about that. In the end Mr. Corrington won."

"In the end he got lucky. So did the mayor, you ask me. Not Charlie Barr, guy before him. Oh, this was years ago. Ford was out hustling while the kids were sleeping in. Found a wealthy white lady, lots of money, lots of guilt. Struck a deal with the city. She bought him the lot. Nice tax-deductible donation. Everybody comes out smelling like a rose."

"And that's typical of how Mr. Corrington operates?"

"Hundred and ten percent. I suppose you could call it civil disobedience, twenty-first-century-style."

Ann thought back. "As I say, I remember reading about it at the time. You were opposed. Or am I wrong?"

Westermann grunted. "Yeah, I thought it was a lot of hallelujah for not much rain."

"You liked the city's plan for the site better?"

"The city wanted to build a walk-in clinic. Not as flashy as a garden, but something Harlem sorely needs."

"That's right, now I remember. In a program the city used to have to decentralize that kind of service. Those programs were administered through the Borough President's offices, weren't they?"

"What's that mean?"

"It doesn't mean anything, Mr. Westermann. Just checking my memory."

"You saying my opposition came from—" He broke off. "No disrespect, but you look very familiar. Have we met?"

"Three years ago," Ann answered levelly. "Dolan Construction."

Westermann nodded. "Quite a tragedy. That little girl died. But how—?"

"More than one tragedy. My partner went to prison."

"Went to prison? That's right, that was a DOI man, wasn't it? The one who took bribes—"

"He didn't."

"He was convicted."

"Unfairly. Because of public pressure."

"Public pressure. Oh, oh, I see. I spoke out on that case, as I recall."

"Yes, you did."

"To demand justice for that poor child's family."

"You were pretty unrelenting, Mr. Westermann."

"Why should I relent in my demands for justice?"

"Another man might have waited until the facts were in."

"If he was black that other man would have done just what I did."

"Mr. Corrington didn't."

Westermann gave her a long look. She returned it.

"So that's what this is all about?" he asked. "You're looking to poke holes in what I said yesterday because of your partner? Make me look like a fool if you can?"

"No. You were the one who wondered if we'd met. We have. But that has nothing to do with why I'm here."

"I don't believe you told me yet why you're here."

"Yesterday, you made allegations at your press conference. I'm following up."

"About Charlie's dirty deal on Block A."

"If you're right, I'll investigate."

"Yeah. Only I get the feeling I'm not about to be right. Just ol' Westermann, don't pay him no mind, he's been going on like this for years and years. Now, I don't suppose there's anything else I can do for you?"

She regarded him steadily. "Not right now, thank you. If I need to speak to you again—"

"Oh, you just call me. I'll give LaTasha instructions, go ahead and put you through. Anytime."

CHAPTER

44

Harlem: Frederick Douglass Boulevard

It was a soft summer afternoon in Morningside Park, pale green grass a thin thatch over the damp black earth. And it was a hard-faced group of young men who, from the benches under the oaks, turned their eyes to Ford.

He was walking straight at them, something no one did. Most folk, if they had any reason to come this deep into this part of the park, cut a wide circle around these benches. The *Amsterdam News* regularly bemoaned the lawlessness of this path between glacial boulders as though it were a valley held by bandits. The *Times* joined in sometimes, usually when some oblivious Columbia student had been made to understand that the meaning of "public" had as many shades as skin had. Cops would make sweeps and politicians would make promises, but nothing changed. The area was governed by a social contract as powerful as any other. One of the contract's clauses was the inarguable truth that everybody has to be someplace. These young men, never offered anyplace worth going or anything positive to do when they got there, had staked out their own territory. For its part, Harlem seemed willing to cede them this path as not too bad a price, considering the alternatives.

It was one of the things Walter Glybenhall hadn't understood when he offered, as part of his rationale for sticking his 9/11 memorial here, the idea that it would bring visitors to this area of the park, making it safer. "Safer for the visitors," Ford had declared at the first of many press conferences, "at the expense of the people who walk along the streets, shop here, live here." Harlem wasn't interested in breaching a contract. Especially for a red-white-and-blue-blooded memorial that had nothing to say about the complex patriotism of people uprooted, first from tribal Africa, then from the rural South, and then, over and over, from New York neighborhoods disregarded by white people until the morning some white developer woke up and sniffed money in the ghetto air.

They'd won that round: Glybenhall's memorial had been built in Riverside Park, where the joggers and dog walkers had been, according to Charlie Barr, "pleased and proud to welcome it." And Ford had squeezed a new swing set and bench repairs out of the Parks Department, as guilt money.

You guys don't know it, Ford thought as he approached the young men along the bandit path, *but wasn't for me, your bad asses would have no place to sit.* It was a funny thought, but it would have been a mistake to smile. He slowed his stride as he came close, let his hands dangle open, held his shoulders loose and easy. He searched their faces, to see who was here. Three of them were young men he'd known when they were boys, still knew to talk to. Most of the others were familiar by face and reputation. When he reached the group, he stopped. He nodded but kept his expression carefully blank.

A short, tense silence; then, "Mr. Corrington." A dark-skinned boy, younger than the others, acknowledged him. His voice was sullen and his eyes narrowed, but he spoke. "What you doing here?" His name was Armand, this boy, and when he used to come around the Garden Project for tutoring, that's what they called him. But the tutoring didn't take and Armand stopped coming. One day his mother moved upstate with her boyfriend, taking Armand's younger sister, leaving Armand on the street at thirteen. If Ford remembered right, he called himself A-Dogg now.

"I'm looking for someone," Ford said.

"We ain't seen him." That came from a chubby guy. Ford searched his memory for the kid's street name. Something unexpected. Blowfish, that was it. Blowfish snickered and Armand's eyes took on a worried look.

"Kong," Ford said.

A ripple went through the group: backs straightened, a fist clenched. Blowfish shook his head, suppressing a smile. The rest of the group moved closer like a gathering storm.

"Fuck shit is that?" A handsome kid, a deep voice. "What you say that for?"

"Carlo, I'm looking for your brother," Ford said to the kid. "I know Kong hangs here."

"Yo, nigger, you think you funny? I show you funny!" Carlo's sneakers thudded to the earth. Blowfish shrugged, then stood, and another kid stood, too, one easing to each side of Ford as Carlo came and crowded him. Ford didn't move back, didn't move at all.

"Yo, Carlo, back off," said Armand. A request, this was, not a command, and from the look Carlo snapped him Ford could see Armand was overspending his currency even so.

"Shut the fuck up, A-Dogg," Carlo muttered, eyes locking again on Ford.

"Yo, nigger! Mr. Corrington ain't like that." Armand licked his lips nervously. "Y'all just better go," he said to Ford.

"I'm not trying to piss anyone off," Ford said. "Or get anyone in trouble. I just need to talk to Kong."

"Fuck that! Fuck that!" Something jumped in Carlo's hand: a box cutter, thin blade glittering.

"Carlo! Damn, Carlo, chill. He probably don't know." Armand looked at Ford with pleading eyes. Ford read: *That's all I can do for you, man.*

Ford forced his hands to stay open, his feet not to jump back. He'd have liked to wipe the sweat newly trickling down his temple, but he didn't move, didn't even look down at the hand gripping the blade. Carlo's face smoldered six inches from his. "If there's something I don't know," Ford said in an even tone, "and my not knowing has caused offense, I'm sorry. I mean no disrespect."

"Fuck you don't know," Carlo snarled, but his hand didn't move and the electrical charge in the air dropped a volt or two.

"He don't!" Armand grabbed his chance. "My man Kong," he said quickly to Ford, glancing at Carlo, "he passed."

"*Passed?* Oh, bitch, what you talking about, *passed?*" Contempt curled Carlo's lip. "He ain't *passed.* Some motherfucker blew him away! And when I find him, I make him the sorriest motherfucker was ever born!"

CHAPTER 45

Sutton Place

Ann stepped from the air-conditioning of the glass lobby onto the hot, bright plaza. She bought a package of honey-roasted nuts and stood in the sunlight at the sidewalk's edge.

People streamed into the State Office Building behind her and surged along 125th Street in front of her. Sellers of shea butter, foil-wrapped incense, and essential oils lined the curb. A man in a mud-cloth robe sat surrounded by posters of a dark-skinned Jesus floating above the African continent striped red, green, and black. Buses plowed by and pigeons swooped. Ann was eating peanuts and admiring some terracotta tracery across the street when her cell phone rang.

She wiped her hand on a napkin and checked the phone's readout. "Hello, Luis."

"Hey, I'm on her speed-dial! Is that like getting to first base these days?"

"No, it's so I know whom to avoid."

"But you answered! You can't lie to me, I'm getting to you."

"Yeah, but maybe not in the way you mean."

"Don't break my balloon. Listen, beautiful, I'm sitting here with someone I think you should talk to. Two guys, actually. Much as I hate to share you, any way you could come up here?"

"Funny, I was just wondering what to do now. It's important?"

"It's really just an excuse to get next to you, but please?"

"You know, Luis, they have laws against this stuff."

"Special exemption *para los Boriquas*. With us it's genetic."

Ann laughed. "Where's here? Your place?"

"My wife wouldn't like it."

"I meant—"

"Yeah, I know. But no, I'm in Manhattan. The two-eight."

"Harlem?"

"Yeah, 123rd and Frederick Douglass."

"What's that, Eighth Avenue?"

"To you honkies, yeah."

"Luis, you're as white as I am."

"Princess, no one's as white as you. How soon can you get here?"

"Ten minutes."

"Even you don't drive that fast. No, seriously, because—"

"Nine."

She clicked off, grinned, and slipped her sunglasses on.

Ann strode up the street past sneaker stores, discount clothing stores, a hair-braiding parlor, and three storefront churches. A sagging cross clung to the face of a brick rowhouse; through the open door Ann heard jackhammers and saw sunlight striping dust. On the next block stood the Apollo. When she and Jen had gone there a few years ago, to a Harlem Boys Choir benefit, the terracotta facade and plaster interior had both been shabby. Now a scrim draped from roof to sidewalk and the ruckus of construction was loud.

Ann was expecting a police station like the buildings around it: carved stone, tall windows, ornate doors. But apparently in the seventies the city had built the Twenty-eighth Precinct a new home. Raw concrete and polished stone stood frostily back from the sidewalk and then, in canted overhangs, loomed above it. Smoked glass ran high on the walls. The door was blank steel. On the front drooped the banner most precincts had carried since 9/11—*The NYPD thanks you for your support. The Police and the Community, working together*—but if one citizen in a hundred felt comfortable anywhere near this building, Ann would eat her hat.

Inside, the place was identically welcoming: scuffed vinyl tile, cold fluorescent lights, announcements and warnings Scotch-taped to block walls. Ann showed her badge to the sergeant behind the desk and asked for Luis Perez.

"Perez? There's no—oh, Bronx Homicide. Interview Room 2," the sergeant told her, copying her name and badge number into his log.

She clipped her badge to her lapel and took the stairs.

Interview Room 2 held a table, six chairs, a dozen empty coffee cups, and the smell of stale coffee. It also held Perez and two black men. One she'd never seen before. He was dark-skinned and wore the rumpled suit and weary eyes of a cop. The other, from newspaper photos and TV, was familiar: Ford Corrington.

"Jesus." Perez stood, voice full of wonder. "How the hell did you do that?"

"What?" she asked innocently.

"Get here so fast."

"DOI, on the spot." She looked at the other two men and inquiringly back to Perez. In other circumstances she'd have introduced herself, but this was a cop shop. Appearances aside, until she knew better she had to assume one or both of these men might be a mutt, someone Perez had in the bag. You didn't go around screwing things up by being all warm and fuzzy with another cop's suspects.

"Guys, this is Ann Montgomery, Inspector, DOI. This is Tom Underhill," Perez said. The rumpled man stood to shake Ann's hand. "Detective, here at the two-eight," Perez told her. "Tom and me used to work together years ago, at the one-one-six. And this is Ford Corrington."

"We haven't met, but I recognized you," Ann said to Corrington. "I've followed your career."

Corrington shook her hand silently.

"Pull up a chair," Perez said. "You want coffee?"

"No, thanks."

"Oh, yeah, you only drink lattes. We could send someone out. They got a Starbucks on 125th Street now."

"No coffee, Luis. So what's up?"

"Ooh, she's all business! Okay, Tom, why don't you start? Don't want to waste DOI's time with, like, friendliness."

Underhill turned to Ann. "We had three homicides in this precinct last couple days. Young blonde woman, two local gangbangers. Woman made the papers, gangbangers didn't, but no matter what Edgar Westermann said at his press conference about how the city works, it's them we're interested in."

"The suspense is killing me," Ann said.

"The one we found this morning, Shawann Little, went by the name of Kong," Underhill said. "Dead since Sunday. Three slugs, two to the chest, one to the head. The other was Thaddeus Tilden. T.D., they called him. Took a header from a building on 134th. Stoned to the gills. We figured he fell. But Ford has new information." He looked to Corrington, but the man stayed silent, so Underhill took it up again. "According to T.D.'s girlfriend, Shamika Arthur, T.D. was working for Kong. 'Making accidents' on a construction site in the Bronx."

"So Tom called me," Perez said. "Me being the guy who caught the Mott Haven case and all."

Ann, spine tingling, glanced from Underhill to Corrington. "It's that site?"

"Shamika doesn't know where." Corrington spoke for the first time.

"There are a lot of construction sites in the Bronx," Ann pointed out.

"Hey, I thought you'd be happy," Perez protested. "If this is our site, we might have a homicide. You were asking me for a homicide. Anyway, we're canvassing other sites, to see if anyone else's had trouble. So far, nada. That means 'nothing,' " he added. "To gringos."

"Can it, Luis." Ann was still holding Corrington's gaze. "Do you know what he was doing, the kid making accidents?"

"No," Corrington said. "His girlfriend described him as 'climbing' and 'sneaking in and out.' "

"This Kong—what was his interest?"

"I don't know that either."

"What do we know about him?" Ann turned to Underhill.

"Kong got his start with strong-arm work, mostly building sites. He'd bring his boys around, offer not to stop deliveries or bust up the work, for a few bucks. Lately he'd expanded his line. Had a reputation for getting things done."

"A contractor?"

"More of a go-to guy. We never had a homicide we could lay on him. But you wanted a weapon, drugs, a particular make and model of ride for your birthday, Kong was your man."

"So maybe he was working for someone?"

"I'd say likely."

"Or he had a grudge himself."

"Sending someone to 'sneak in and out' is a little subtle for Kong."

"Then who was he working for?"

Underhill shrugged and looked at Corrington, who said nothing.

Ann said, "I want to talk to the girlfriend."

"She's left the state."

"Still." Ann turned to Perez.

"Take a number," Perez told her. "Tom and me, we got a homicide. You're only corruption."

"I'm the Mayor's Office. Your boss works for my boss."

"Ay, she pulls rank on me! That's gotta hurt. Princess, have your boss call my boss. Until then, take a number."

"Shamika ran away because she was scared," Corrington said. "I'm not going to tell you where she is."

"Scared of Kong, you said." Underhill leaned forward. "Kong's dead. He's no threat anymore."

"Whoever put three bullets in him might be, though."

"You have a suspect?" Ann asked Underhill.

"Not yet."

"A weapon?"

"Not yet."

"Mr. Corrington," said Ann, "how did you come by this information?"

"The girl called me."

"Just to tell you this?"

"Yes."

"From out of state?"

"That's right."

"Why?"

"She works for me."

"Doing what?"

"An administrative assistant. Sometimes she helps out with the kids."

"I've never had a job where my boss was the first person I'd call if my boyfriend were committing crimes."

Corrington shrugged.

"Even," said Ann, "if my boyfriend were dead and I were scared."

Underhill said, "That's not so surprising here. A lot of kids in this neighborhood came up through Ford's programs, over at the Garden Project. Some've known him all their lives."

"I'm familiar with Mr. Corrington's position in the community. What about these two gangbangers? Did they?"

"Kong and T.D.?" Corrington shook his head. "Not Kong. T.D., when he was young, but not lately. Except he started coming around sometimes to see Shamika. I thought we might still get through to him, even if it had to be that way. Thought it might not be too late. But it was."

Ann sat back. "Walter Glybenhall's the developer of the Mott Haven site."

"We've never met."

"You've traded punches in the press, Mr. Corrington. More than once."

"Mostly, he's thrown them. I quit when I win."

"But he doesn't when he loses."

"What are you getting at?" Perez asked.

"According to Edgar Westermann's press conference yesterday," Ann said, "a group headed by Mr. Corrington was refused the chance to develop a city-owned site in Harlem."

"It wasn't Edgar's to make that meeting public," Corrington said. "And he's premature. We made a proposal. The mayor's studying it."

"So you still have a chance at that site?"

"I think so."

"Unless the city's already committed."

"That would be illegal. There's a required review process that hasn't even started yet. It takes a year just to get through that."

"Then why were you meeting with the mayor this early? What were you asking for?"

He gave her a long look. "Consideration."

"Ann?" Perez, again.

"The city can't commit on the site," she said. "But what if the mayor has? Informally? Under the table? What if Walter Glybenhall asked for 'consideration,' too?"

"Well, what if?" Perez demanded.

"How unpopular would that be in this neighborhood?" Ann asked Corrington.

"An under-the-table deal with Walter Glybenhall? Very."

"Why?"

"Because bloodsucking gentrification doesn't go down well here."

"But if Glybenhall could show off a project in some other neighborhood? Low-income housing, the whole package? Something that worked well and everyone loved it?"

"He'd be the Great White Hope. Harlem still wouldn't welcome him."

"But wouldn't it make the mayor's life a lot easier? He could say Glybenhall was an experienced developer, the right choice for the site, look how well he handled that marvelous development in Mott Haven. It would give a terrific out to anyone looking for an excuse not to oppose the mayor. And if you wanted that site, you'd be left to fight Glybenhall on your own."

"Then we'd fight him."

"You'd lose."

"You think Harlem couldn't win on our own?"

"Glybenhall would eat Harlem alive. If Mott Haven went well."

The three men were silent.

"But the playing field would be a lot more even," Ann said, "if Mott Haven ended up a disaster."

Corrington stared at her. Abruptly, he stood. "If you have an accusation to make, call my lawyer." He pulled the door open and strode from the room.

Underhill rose, too. "I don't know who the hell you think you are, lady," he said from the door, "or what that badge entitles you to, but you've got a helluva lot to learn." He looked from her to Perez. "Don't be here when I get back."

"Shit," Perez breathed after a minute, looking at the open doorway. "That that velvet steamroller thing they warned me about?"

"Who did?"

"Everybody and his monkey. You're famous, Princess. Did you have to come on like that?"

She nodded at the door. "He's kind of touchy."

"Corrington? You expected him not to mind, you just about accusing him of some pretty serious shit? Maybe you missed this part, but the guy's a *witness*, not a suspect. Came forward voluntarily with information."

"Or a smoke screen. Two gangbangers too dead to say who they were working for, and a girlfriend conveniently out of town who calls in to point the way. Very handy."

"Far-fetched. And hard to buy, you know anything about Corrington. And even if. If that's what's going down, we'd find it sooner or later. Us real cops, we're not that stupid, you know."

"Oh, put a sock in it Luis."

"What the hell is it to you? Why the attitude?"

She stood, slinging her bag onto her shoulder. "The idea that Corrington's mixed up in this makes me mad."

"Why? A guy in his position, should be a role model, owes the community, something like that?"

Ann looked at Perez. "Are you kidding?"

"Then what?"

"I wasn't looking for him to be the one," she said. "I want it to be Glybenhall."

Harlem: Frederick Douglass Boulevard

Ford stood just inside the garden fence. He'd had the short, fast walk from the police station to the Garden Project building to try to cool down. It would be lying to say he was now serene. But watching fourth-graders from PS 175 push trowels into the earth, tamp with childhood single-mindedness around young plants, and giggle at their muddy hands was going a long way toward slowing his heartbeat and draining the heat of anger from his skin.

It was late in the season for planting. But waiting made it more likely that the kids would still be interested when school let out next week. They'd come around to see how their tomatoes were doing, and it would be the job of the staff to find, in the gardens, workshops, and classrooms, reasons for them to stay. And the tomatoes would be tasty, anyhow, just smaller and fewer than if they'd gone in three weeks ago. It all depended, really, on what kind of crop you wanted.

"If I apologize, can I talk to you?"

He whirled to find the blonde DOI cop standing beside him. The wind stirred her hair; behind her sunglasses her eyes were unreadable.

"No. I told you, call my lawyer." He cut around her and out onto the sidewalk.

"I'm sorry anyway. And I'm not interested in your lawyer. Or in you, really." He listened for the sharp tap of footsteps behind him, ready to shrug her off again, but heard nothing. Turning, he saw her still inside the garden, facing him through the fence.

"What does that mean?"

"Ten minutes?"

"No."

As he spoke, a little boy, running along a stone path—against the rules in the garden—slipped on a slick of spilled water. The cop lunged to grab him. She was fast and sure and yanked him to his feet a moment before his left knee would have cracked on the stone it was headed for.

"Whoa," said the boy.

"If you're going to fall," the cop told him, letting go her grip, "turn like this." She demonstrated, twisting. "So this part hits the ground." She patted her own hip. "It'll hurt, but nothing'll break. Got it?"

The little boy looked at her like he was hearing English from a Martian. He nodded, then tore across the grass.

The cop took a napkin from her pocket and wiped the boy's mud off her hands. She looked up, stopped as she found Ford still watching her.

"Ten minutes?"

He paused, then nodded. "All right."

As she caught up with him on the sidewalk she asked, "Why?"

"Why what?"

"Why agree to talk to me? Because I did like Wonder Woman and saved a kid?"

He pulled open the door and stood aside to let her pass. "You move like an athlete," he said. "You play college sports?"

"Track. All events but relay. I'm not so good on teams."

"Basketball, Harvard, two seasons. Watched a lot of tapes of the competition. More time you spend with them, more you know about their strategy."

"If that's it, you'll be disappointed. I have no strategy. Strictly instinct. I jump at whatever looks good."

He glanced at her. "Maybe. But not without knowing how to fall."

He led her up the stairs and through the outer office, picking up his message slips from Yvonnia. Inside, he shut the door, started to head to the armchairs by the window, thought better of it, and went around to sit behind his desk. The cop took off her sunglasses and stayed standing.

"We got off on the wrong foot," she said. "My name's Ann, by the way."

Ford looked pointedly at the chair on her side of the desk and didn't answer until she was seated, too.

"Inspector," he said. "You accused me of being responsible for vandalism at least, and probably murder. In front of two cops, one of them a friend of mine."

"I was following the money."

"Really? You see a lot of that here?"

"I see a major site about to come into play, something someone could make a fortune developing."

"Commercially. The proposal we presented to the mayor was strictly not-for-profit."

It flashed on fast, her smile. "Don't be disingenuous. There's a lot of money in that world, too. You have quite a kingdom here in Harlem, Mr. Corrington, but its real estate is dispersed. The Block A site would give it a capital city."

"Inspector, what's the point of this conversation?"

"Like Luis Perez said, I'm corruption. My orders are to look into Walter Glybenhall. Or, to be exact, Three Star. To make sure whatever's behind these accidents in the Bronx, it's not the tip of some corruption iceberg."

"And . . . ?"

"Suppose I'm right, what I said before. Suppose Walter Glybenhall's only doing the Mott Haven site to give the mayor an excuse to hand Block A over to him."

"That would be an extraordinary length to go to."

"Not really. It's not as if he's going to lose money up there. If everything works out, Glybenhall will come out with a small profit. And have a large development in New York in his portfolio for the first time. Which, according to him, are reasons enough."

Ford shrugged. "Maybe they are."

"Sure, and maybe I really am Wonder Woman. Walter Glybenhall wouldn't bend down to pick up a small profit if it were lying on the sidewalk."

"All right, suppose he's got a deal with the mayor. Then what?"

"Then I find your consortium wants the site, too. But that's a harder sell. If Mott Haven works out and a lot of the people you might expect as allies—"

"White liberals, like yourself."

She arched her eyebrows. "—if white liberals could throw up their hands and say, *Gee, Mr. Glybenhall's proved he can operate in a community like this, he'll do a wonderful job in Harlem*, they could avoid getting Charlie Barr mad at them. And you and Harlem would be on your own. So, hypothetically and in spite of what you say, if you didn't think you could win on your own, maybe a little preemptive sabotage would be in order."

"If, hypothetically, all this were going on, why would I march into a police station and call attention to it?"

"Maybe some of what you said is true. T.D. was working for Kong, say. But maybe—hypothetically—Kong was working for you. And maybe it was about to come out some other way. No man looks as innocent as the one whose own words make him look guilty, only he opens his eyes wide and says, *I didn't think of that.*"

Ford gazed at her, registering the fact that she'd remembered, and used, the street names of the two dead boys. He turned away, toward the soft June breeze drifting in the window. Across the avenue, the shadows of wrought-iron railings zigzagged down the steps of five identical rowhouses. When those houses were built, they were six, and dazzling: twining vines carved into limestone door frames, granite medallions set on brick facades; mahogany mantels and pressed-tin ceilings behind high parlor windows. Now each house was eight apartments. Now the glass was cracked and the mahogany, where it hadn't been ripped out, had been painted so many times the edges were rounded, the hollows filled. Stone foliage choked on a century of smoke and dust. And now the five buildings stood three on the north, two on the south of a lot mounded with the ruins of the sixth. The city had knocked that down a decade ago after a fire left it wrecked and dangerous. Every year since, they'd slapped a violation on the absentee landlord for not clearing the debris. He never responded. In a front corner of the lot, an ailanthus tree—the dandelions of the city—had broken through and flourished, reaching, by now, nearly ten feet.

Ford turned back to Montgomery. "Inspector, everything you're suggesting is wrong, and, incidentally, offensive. I don't know who Kong was working for, but it wasn't me. And for the record, I had no idea Walter Glybenhall was interested in Block A until you mentioned it, and I still have no idea whether it's true and, again for the record, I'll bet you don't either."

"I said I was speaking hypothetically."

"I dislike your hypothesis."

"Occam's Razor. The idea that—"

"—the simplest solution's likely to be the truth. I have a BA and a JD from Harvard, Inspector."

"And I was kicked out of two boarding schools, ran away from another, and finished high school on a GED. I have a BA from Oberlin and a JD from NYU. And I think Occam's Razor can cut this another way."

She met his eyes and smiled; her cheeks were flushed pink.

He let her eyes hold his. Something about them was strange. Their color: not quite matched. One like water, one like sky. He reached to the windowsill and plugged the kettle in. "What way?"

She crossed one trousered leg over the other. "Do you remember me, Mr. Corrington?"

"Should I? Have we met?"

"No. But three years ago, Dolan Construction? That DOI inspector who went to prison? He was my partner."

Ford thought back: the news stories, the press conferences. The little girl's funeral. "You testified in court."

"My partner was innocent. But Edgar Westermann and Charlie Barr were both eager to burn him at the stake. So were a lot of people. You were the only voice of moderation coming out of your community. You stood up to the Borough President and the mayor."

"I hate to disappoint you, but what I said then had nothing to do with your partner. He might have been guilty. In fact I thought he was." He'd raised his voice on that last sentence to override her protest, but she sat wordless, watching him. "My point was, the DA, under what anyone could see was pressure from the mayor, had let the real criminal, the one who'd paid bribes to keep using the bad practices that actually killed that child—they'd let him grab a plea so the city could clean its own house. Whatever your partner did, he was the lesser criminal. But he was the one who was making Charlie Barr smell bad. Personally, I don't care how Charlie Barr smells. I care about little black girls dying."

"And I cared about a friend of mine being railroaded. You were a voice of sanity. It doesn't matter why. Maybe I feel like I owe you something."

That caught him off balance, and he laughed. "And that's why you accused me of sabotage and murder?"

"No. It's why I did some rethinking after you stormed out of the police station."

The kettle began to sing. He clicked it off. "Do you want some tea?"

"Coffee?"

"Oh, right, you only drink lattes. Sorry, just tea."

"Don't believe everything you hear. What kind?"

He pointed to the row of mismatched tins along the sill. She stood, walked over, picked up one, another, a third. "This." She held a silver box out to him.

"You like kukicha?"

"I don't know. I've never had it."

"It's made from twigs."

That didn't seem to deter her so he scooped some up, dumped it in the pot.

She didn't return to her chair, but stood looking out across the avenue. "I'm persona non grata in my own agency," she said. "I was supposed to resign when Joe went to prison. Protocol." A bus rumbled by; her eyes followed it. "But I was too angry. So I stayed. For three years now I've had nothing to do and they've made sure I'm in Far Rockaway and Tottenville doing it. Suddenly I'm hauled in from the ends of the earth and handed a delicate assignment. Look into Three Star, in other words Walter Glybenhall, a dear pal of our dear mayor. They promised me permanent reassignment back to Manhattan, and some nice juicy cases, if this 'works out.' "

Ford heard the quote marks in her voice. He poured deep brown tea into a lumpy mug made by some child in a long-ago ceramics class and handed it to her, wondering suddenly what child had made this mug and what had become of him, or her.

"And it would work out," he said, "if you came to the conclusion that Walter Glybenhall was pure as the driven snow."

"Walter would enjoy that image. It's so . . . white. Yes, that's what I assume is going on, from DOI's point of view." She gave her tea a tentative sip. "You don't know Glybenhall, so you say. But I do. I have since I was a child. He's greedy and cold-blooded."

"You don't have to know him to know that."

She nodded. "What made me angry earlier was the idea that you might be behind Three Star's accidents. Instead of Walter."

"Glybenhall? You think he's attacking his own project?"

"For the insurance. His finances are often shakier than you might think. I haven't got a full accounting report yet, but I'll bet his cash flow is off. There's an accident, he claims lost time, the insurance money makes the payments—salaries, suppliers—that he couldn't actually have made. It's the construction equivalent of burning down your own warehouse."

Ford watched her lift her mug in both hands and sip her tea.

"You like it?" he asked.

"The tea? Yes. Tastes like I always thought mud pies would when I was little."

"Did they?"

"Mud pies? They were awful. We lived in lots of places and I tried the mud everywhere, but they were always awful."

The breeze snaked in the window to ruffle the fronds of a fern.

"I'm getting an image of windmills," he said. "And knights with lances. These things never work out well for Sancho Panza."

"It's not the right metaphor. Those windmills weren't really dragons."

"You have a better one?"

Her grin flashed again. "Luke Skywalker and Princess Leia?"

"What do you want, Ms. Montgomery?"

She leaned forward. "Access. People here will talk to you in ways they'll never talk to me. T.D.'s girlfriend, Kong's homeboys: whomever I need."

"I have a lot at stake here. I can't afford to be left holding the bag."

"What would it take?"

In his mind he saw the mayor's glossy conference table, the pile of prospectuses. He heard Charlie Barr's furious voice: *Harlem's not the only thing that's not for sale.* "Minimally, to know you're right about Glybenhall and Block A."

She nodded and put down the mug. "You'll hear from me," she said, standing abruptly. She turned and left.

Harlem: Frederick Douglass Boulevard

Ford finished his tea, sipping slowly. He stared through the open office door, watching the business of the Garden Project go on. A cornrowed little girl waved to him as she dropped off a sheaf of papers with Yvonnia; he waved back and she ran off giggling. Two social workers passed in the hallway, heads bent together, one of them gesturing emphatically: some kid's future might be about to change.

A rooftop park. A gym, a theater. Safe, cheap apartments with heat in the winter, working elevators, and wide windows.

Or brownstones, bistros, and supper clubs, with tourist buses out front and private parking in the back.

Used to be, the black musicians who played the clubs had to come and go through the back, except in Harlem.

Of course, in his day so did Mozart.

Ford sighed and stood. He walked down the hall and stuck his head in the social workers' office.

"On a third-grade level," Peter Muller was saying from a chair in front of Kathy O'Loughlin's desk. Peter, dark and tall as Kathy was dark and small, never made a point without circling it in the air, and as he waved his huge hands around, Ford feared for Kathy's mounds of un-filed papers. "But his raps? In the internal rhyme there's a sophistication you can't—" He stopped and looked at Ford.

"Sorry to interrupt," Ford said.

"No problem." Peter seemed suddenly to notice his hands, still in the air. He pulled them down.

"Just a question. Either of you remember a kid named Armand Stubbs?"

"A-Dogg?" Kathy asked.

"That's right. Know where he's staying now?"

She shook her head. "Running the streets, is all I know. Took up with Kong, and Kong brought him into that hard crew."

"I know the crew. I need to talk to Armand alone. Oh, well. Thanks."

"Oh, wait! Try Wimp's."

Ford had turned to go, but he turned back.

"Wimp's? Boy has a weakness for sweet potato pie?"

"He's working there, unless I'm remembering this wrong. Condition of probation, from his last arrest."

"What was that for, you remember?"

"He and Kong boosted a dozen CD players from an electronics place. He got nailed, Kong walked. First offense, so they gave him a choice: Rikers or get a J-O-B. The day manager at Wimp's knew his mama, thought she did badly by the boy."

"We were involved?"

"No." Kathy's look was almost embarrassed, as though she'd been caught at something. "Some of them, I just keep track. No reason. Just in case . . . you know."

"Yeah," Ford said. "I know."

"You thinking, you could use Kong and T.D. for object lessons, this might be a good time to pry A-Dogg loose?"

"No, I wasn't," Ford replied. "But it's not a bad idea."

Wimp's, on the north side of 125th, had renovated just this last year. The cracked tile floor and the old thick-glass hanging lamps were gone. The show window ran sidewalk to ceiling now and a fluorescent-lit mezzanine perched over the counter floor, for folks who couldn't wait until they got home but didn't want to shovel down their massive slabs of cake directly in front of the bakery, out on the street.

What had not changed was the cake. Or the cupcakes, pies, or aluminum dishes of vanilla, banana, coconut pudding. In air swirling with allspice and chocolate, Ford stood at the counter, glad for the line: he needed the time to make his choice.

"Can I help the next customer?" a young woman with high, wide curls sang out. Ford let an older lady, leaning on a cane, go ahead of him. He smiled in answer to her thanks, wondering why the world couldn't be full of such win-win situations: he'd had time to make up his mind, and the next free counter boy was Armand Stubbs.

"Help you?" Armand's mouth beat his eyes by a half-second. His glance narrowed with suspicion as his customer's identity registered.

"Hi, A-Dogg. I'll take tea and a slice of that red velvet cake."

Armand nodded guardedly. "You gonna eat it here, or take it with you?" His hand hovered between a pile of paper plates and a stack of plastic containers.

"Here. And make the tea a large. And I'd appreciate it, you gave me five minutes."

"What? Aw, no, I could see that coming. Look, man, I ain't in no shit! And anyway, I already had my break."

"I believe you're clean, I'm not here to lecture you. I need your help. Straight up, A-Dogg."

"Whatever shit this is, I wanna stay out of it."

"Five minutes, upstairs, in the back. None of your boys'll see us. They'd never come up there, it's full of church ladies." He moved down the counter. "Vera?"

The day manager, a thin, quick woman with slanted eyes, looked up from the eight-inch-high coconut cake she was slicing. She smiled. "Well, Ford. You needing a fix of shoofly pie?"

"Red velvet cake, my serious weakness. Vera, I need to talk to Armand for five minutes. He's not in any sort of trouble, I just have to ask him something."

Vera met Ford's eyes, then glanced around the shop and nodded. "Grace be back off her break soon. When she come, you go ahead and take five, Armand."

"I already had my break, Miss Vera."

"So you saying you don't want another one? I ain't never seen you turn down no chance to sit. Grace come back, you go sit with Mr. Corrington. What's that?" she asked sharply, but whatever Armand had muttered under his breath, neither she nor Ford was going to hear it, because the boy just shook his head and ran his knife through the white-iced crimson mound of a red velvet cake.

It wasn't five more minutes, Ford working his way through what must have been a half pound of pastry, before Armand appeared, still in his white counter apron. The boy looked quickly around and slipped into the seat across from Ford. He kept his eyes on the staircase.

"What you want?" he asked sullenly. "I told you, I ain't in no shit."

"That crew you run with, that could change any minute."

"That your problem? I ain't a kid no more."

"No, you're not. A-Dogg, listen: you want out of that life, you come to me any time. And that's all I'm going to say about that because it's not why I'm here."

"Yeah, great. So why you here? What you want?"

"What's the word on who killed Kong?"

"Kong? How I'm supposed to know that shit?"

"He was a friend of yours."

"Yeah, so?"

"There must be talk."

"I ain't heard it."

"You don't know who Carlo's going after?"

"Carlo be going after any motherfucker he think it might be killed his brother. But I ain't heard nothing, who that is."

Ford nodded, took up a forkful of cake. Rich, heavy, spicy, Wimp's red velvet cake had always suggested to Ford what geraniums ought to taste like, but probably didn't. He didn't know; unlike the DOI cop and her mud pies, he'd never tried geraniums.

"That it?" Armand asked. "Can I go?"

"What? No, there's more." Ford drove mud pies from his mind and washed the cake down with tea. "Kong was into something. With T. D. Tilden, who died Sunday, too. Heard about T.D.?"

"Yeah."

"You knew him, right?"

"Guess so."

"Friend of yours?"

"Naw."

"Why?"

"Dunno. Him and me, we don't have nothing in common. You know, game recognize game? Don't nobody recognize T.D."

"He claimed to be a player."

"He wish. His mouth always writing checks his body can't cash."

"What do you mean?"

"Nigger always bragging on himself, gonna do this, gonna be that. He baaaad. Yeah, right. Ain't but talk. He gonna be a engineer, build bridges and shit. Learning how to make drawings. Last week he come waving 'em up in everybody's face. Tryin' to get us to think he all that."

Ford put his tea down. "What drawings, A-Dogg?"

"Wasn't but bullshit! You know, like blueprints? But dig, that shit, they ain't just pictures. They got words, tell you what the parts mean. What they made out of, what to do with 'em. Ain't no way T.D. made the ones he showed us."

"Why not?"

"'Cause of the words! Nigger can't read, know what I'm saying?

Gonna be a fucking engineer." Armand snorted. "Damn, dawg, he drop outta school."

"You dropped out yourself, A-Dogg."

"I ain't planning no three-piece-suit career! And you said you wasn't gonna lecture me, yo."

"Sorry." Ford scraped up the last of the vanilla frosting. "Wonder if I could get a job here myself?"

"See if I can set it up for you."

"Thanks." Ford nodded gravely. "Okay, you didn't like T.D. But someone murdered him and I'd like to know who it was."

The boy's eyes widened. "Somebody done him? I thought he fell."

"I don't think so. And I think it had to do with whatever T.D. was into with Kong. Could be the same person did them both. You know anything about it?"

"Naw."

"Nothing at all? Hanging with that crew?"

"Kong don't hang. Always got something going on. And plus, him and Blowfish don't get on."

"Okay, but it was Kong brought you into that crew. You were his homey. He never told you anything, about T.D., what he had going? Never mentioned him?"

Armand shifted in his seat, scratched the back of his head. "Kong be talking some shit. Not about T.D. Don't know nothing about that. But."

"What is it?"

Armand hesitated, glancing at the stairs. No one was moving up or down. He looked back at Ford. "Kong, he come around couple days ago, have some flash new bling. Look like Jacob the Jeweler, but Carlo, he say Kong ain't got that kind of paper, thing must be a fake. Kong say, yeah, okay, ain't no Jacob the Jeweler, he yesterday's news. This the real deal, though, platinum and ice, come from a guy so hot he *next* week's news. Levi something. You know, like the pants? Kong say, when you working for white bread, you be raking it in, so you could go ahead and get your bling from a Jew. Why they call it 'jewelry,' he say. He musta thought he saying something really funny, because he say it like a hunnert more times. Reason I remember, because he keep saying it. 'Taking so much off white bread, buy my jewelry from a Jew.' Then his phone ring, and he check it out, say, 'Yo, this him, I gotta go get paid.' Next thing . . ." A-Dogg shrugged. "Ain't no next thing, far as Kong go."

"White bread. You know who?"

"Ain't never said."

"And Kong didn't say anything about T.D.?"

"Naw. I didn't even know they was tight." Armand looked down over the railing again. The line at the counter stretched to the door. "Look, Mr. Corrington, I better get back. Miss Vera, she be pissed off, I hang around up here too long. They got customers."

"Okay, Armand, I appreciate the help. Now go on. Don't want Miss Vera to fire you, screw up your probation."

"Shit, that was up three months ago." Armand stood.

"It was? Why are you still working here?"

"I like it. Miss Vera, she teaching me to bake. That red velvet cake?" He pointed to Ford's empty plate. "I made it."

Ford, watching the boy trot down the stairs, asked himself if wonders would, in fact, ever cease.

Sutton Place

Ann retrieved the DOI Cavalier from the State Office Building garage and sat in traffic on 125th Street, trying to decide where exactly to go.

She was fighting her first choice: Walter Glybenhall's midtown building. She'd leave the car double-parked, storm up to his office. Eyes blazing, she'd demand he admit causing the accidents at Mott Haven in a nasty scheme to secure for himself a fabulously valuable city-owned Harlem site. She could see the color drain from Walter's face, hear him gasp and then, breaking down, admit all, sobbing. She'd raise a merci-less Ice Queen eyebrow and call Perez, who'd haul a broken shell of the once-arrogant bastard off to rot in prison for the rest of his life.

She inched another block. Three kids in the too-large baseball caps that were this year's fashion gave her predatory stares as they crossed in front of her. One tapped her hood and cocked a finger-gun, showing a malevolent smile. She gave him a second to think how clever he was, then she smacked the Cavalier's powerful cop-car horn and almost blasted his ass into the next block. Screeching the car into action as the light changed, she peeled hard out past a bus and down the avenue, leaving the kids standing in the crosswalk screaming curses.

She was six blocks on before she managed to wrestle the car east again. If any of her arresting-Walter fantasy after the storming-in part had a snowball's chance, she'd do it. But the real truth was, Walter would laugh. He'd pat her head, metaphorically or maybe even physi-cally, though he should know better than to touch her or she'd have him up on assault. With a pitying smile he'd point out that she had nothing except an active imagination. And he'd throw her out.

She turned the car onto the FDR and drove south, toward the office. She had nothing. But there had to be something. And whatever it was, she was going to find it.

Sparkling water, the white wake of a fast tug, the soaring arcs of bridges on her left; on her right, skyscrapers, car-clogged streets, and huge fenced holes where more skyscrapers were coming. As the road rose she could see, over one of the fences, men standing in mud fifty feet below. Yellow vehicles with massive tires crawled, coming and going on unfathomable errands. Unfathomable to her. Joe would understand. Joe would be able to explain all this equipment, all this activity. If she could call him now—if he weren't standing in the wake of some huge yellow rig himself, spreading asphalt on a dusty road—and describe the dance she was watching, he'd tell her what it meant. She could hear his patient voice theorizing, extrapolating from what she was seeing to what end result the architect must want that required this hole dug or that connection made now, a dozen steps back.

What end result the architect must want.

The architect.

Ann slapped the gumball on top of the car and switched the siren on.

Dumping her bag and coat on her desk, Ann slid into her chair and flicked the computer on. With impatient clicks she dug into the *Times* archives. She needed the piece on the city's plan for the Harlem site, the one Westermann had said ran months ago. She found it in a Sunday real estate section, three cheerleading paragraphs and two illustrations. One was a photo of an architect's model: gleaming wood, tiny metal people, and wire trees, shot from above. Next to it, a drawing: neon, jazz clubs, couples strolling night sidewalks. She scanned the article, didn't find the architect's name. Nor was it credited on the model or the rendering. Could this be a first, a self-effacing architect? She called the *Times* reporter and got no satisfaction: the photos had come from the press liaison in the mayor's office who'd sent out the release. The reporter had no idea who'd done the design work.

"You didn't ask? You weren't curious? A project this big?"

"Half the press packets I get are for projects that'll never get built. I don't have time to waste running them down. This one on Block A went right into my pie-in-the-sky file."

"Then why publish it?"

"To keep the conversation going."

Newspaperese, Ann assumed, for *Why piss off the mayor if you don't have to?*

Ann took the mayor's press liaison's name, thinking therein lay nothing. Staring at her monitor, she let her eyes wander from model to rendering. The model was too abstract to interest her, but she found herself getting absorbed in the picture. Her skin felt the sharp, exciting chill of an autumn night. She smelled fallen leaves, heard laughter and the soft wail of music floating from an open door. But as the music grew, a new sound rose over it: Joe's voice.

Not the picture.

It was what he used to say, when she'd ask him how he did it, read the photos and drawings, made them give up their secrets in a way she never could.

Not the picture. The pattern.

She grabbed the phone and called the *Times* reporter back. "Who took the photo?"

"Of the Harlem model?"

"Right. Can you check?"

"Don't have to. I remember, from the look of it. It's a Katherine Katz."

Ann Googled Katherine Katz and found her website. An architectural photographer, specializing in models, furniture, buildings, and interiors. Color or black-and-white, film or digital, large format or small. Well, that covered the waterfront. She scrolled through the sample photos. There were even three of the waterfront. The rest were rooms, chairs, intricate cabinetry. Many were sensuous close-ups: smooth curves, sharp edges, breathtakingly precise joinery, lit in a way so lush, so ambiguous, that they looked alive.

And then there were the straight-ahead architecture shots: buildings, and models of buildings. Though the buildings were the work of many different designers, the photographs had a family resemblance, the same unsettling living-thing quality of the close-up details.

And because a photographer's website is a selling tool and Katherine Katz clearly wanted visitors to know the A-list nature of her clients, each architect's name stood boldly beneath the photo of her, or his, building.

And her, or in this case his, model.

Another thing she'd learned from Joe: You don't call.

As a prosecutor her training was formality. Make appointments, give notice. A prosecutor, in court, was actually forbidden to surprise. Ann had become extremely good at it, the formality business, the way serious foreign-language students can learn to out-talk native speakers.

Then she'd come to DOI. "The less they know about what you're up to, the less likely it is they'll hide what *they're* up to," Joe had told her. "You seem to have a natural talent for throwing people off balance. Use it!"

She pulled the Cavalier into a midtown No Standing zone and stuck the Official Business card on the dashboard. This red granite building stood not three blocks from Walter Glybenhall's office. Probably one of Walter's criteria for choosing an architect, that he wouldn't have to travel far to go see him. Or, come to think of it, maybe not. Walter no doubt made his architect, like everyone else, come to him.

She waited in a polished-stone lobby and was carried up in a stainless-steel elevator that might as well have been a Star Fleet transporter. She imagined it disassembling her molecules, shooting them in a speed-of-light beam into an identical pod on the thirty-fourth floor for reassembly. Though she'd always had a suspicion that wasn't how those things would work: they wouldn't reassemble you, they'd record you and, using elements found at the place you wanted to be, they'd re-create you. It would be easier that way, and you'd be always new, always made of the place where you were.

And always destroyed, over and over, as you left the place you'd come from.

When the doors opened Ann's first thought was that the beam must have been aimed at the wrong planet. Or the wrong century. After the sleek stone lobby and silent steel elevator, what was this rich patterned carpet, this mahogany furniture, this crystal chandelier? But between oddly proportioned wood columns with fanciful capitals, gilded letters spelled out HENRY M. MARTIN AND PARTNERS LLP. So she must be in the right place. And the receptionist sat before a flat-screen monitor, so it must be the right time.

Ann stepped to the desk and said briskly, "Mr. Martin, please."

The receptionist lifted her eyes from the screen, took Ann's measure, and with blank, unhurried politeness, asked, "Do you have an appointment?"

"I'm with the Department of Investigation." Ann showed her badge. "I need to speak with Mr. Martin."

"You're a police officer?"

"We're an investigatory agency."

"I'm sorry, Mr. Martin doesn't see anyone without an appointment. If you could give me some idea what this is about, maybe I could find someone else who can help you."

"It's about a homicide, it has to be Mr. Martin, and it won't take long. Unless no one cooperates, in which case it could take days."

"I'm sorry—"

"No, but you will be."

"I'm—"

"You're supposed to protect him from gate-crashers. I'll tell him how hard you tried. But I guarantee you, *everyone* will be happier if he talks to me now than if I have to go all the way back downtown for a warrant."

A brief pause; then, "Just a minute." Pressing a button, the receptionist murmured into the headset of her phone. She busied herself with some papers: she didn't look at Ann again.

Moments later, a young Asian woman emerged from a molding-encrusted, brass-handled door to beckon Ann through.

On the other side of the door—here featureless and smooth, with a brushed-steel knob—Ann found the spot and moment her transporter beam had been aimed at.

Rows of large-screen monitors marched to a window wall, interrupted here and there by tables awash in unfurled drawings. Well-groomed young people sat behind the monitors or stood over the drawings, while men and women half a generation older sat in cubicles down both sides of the room. Nowhere did Ann see a drafting table, but paper was everywhere, pinned or taped to every vertical surface: computer drawings, hand sketches, correspondence and calendars, notes and memos, instructions and lists. File cabinets and binder-stuffed bookcases supported desks and separated spaces. Everything was white and gray, sleek and minimal: industrial carpet, plastic laminate, glass and steel. The air buzzed with low talk and the ringing of phones, and Ann could practically smell the midnight oil.

Her guide led Ann down a hall and deposited her in a conference room. She hadn't smiled once and she didn't smile now, just nodded distractedly and hurried to her next task.

Ann walked to the window. The East River, Roosevelt Island, and Queens straight ahead, Brooklyn in a haze to the right, parts of the Bronx to the left: the view here was vast.

She wasn't so much interested in the real world before her, though, as in the renderings and photos on the conference room walls. Brick, clapboard, cedar shingles; Dutch doors, mansard roofs, and, on one beach house, shutters clipped back to siding with wrought-iron scrollwork. The steel and glass of Modernism might never have happened, if you skipped the drafting room and went by the materials and elements in the work of Henry Martin.

And yet these buildings would never be mistaken for the products of a previous century. Like the columns at the receptionist's desk, they were subtly wrong. The shutter clips were too heavy, or the window mullions too thin. The overhang of a low roof ran the length of one hilltop residence like a single glowering eyebrow. Oddly proportioned and strangely shaped, their details inappropriately applied and dissonantly numbered, these buildings spoke so loudly of the architect's cleverness, education, and erudition that even Ann could hear it. They were showy, idiosyncratic, self-referential, and vain.

And three of them were Walter's.

The Glybenhall name appeared under photographs of a hypergenteel shopping mall with canopied wooden sidewalks; a seacoast spa built as steroid-pumped, porticoed cabins on a previously unspoiled stretch of shoreline; and a computer rendering of a Civil War theme park, proposed but as yet unbuilt due to vociferous local opposition. Ann remembered reading about that one. What would the rides be like, she'd wondered, and the dinner-theater shows?

"Are you the police officer who demanded to see me?" The man who spoke, closing the door behind him, was short, with heavy black-rimmed glasses, thick gray hair, and a withering glare. His nasal accent was New England prep school. He wore a white band-collared shirt. A worked-silver buckle set off his Armani jeans.

"Mr. Martin?"

"Of course. Who are you and what do you want?"

"Ann Montgomery, DOI." She unclipped the badge from her lapel and held it out to him. He didn't take it, just threw it a glance.

"DOI? Not the police? You threatened my receptionist. What kind of hysterical melodrama was that?"

"On the contrary, I complimented her on how well she did her job and promised to tell you about it. You should give her a raise."

"I'm letting her go. If she did her job you'd never have gotten in. I don't see people without appointments."

"Mr. Martin, this isn't a consultation, it's a homicide investigation."

"I don't care what it is. My people have instructions: I do *not* talk to people who walk in off the street. I'm only seeing you now to tell you to leave."

"As soon as you answer my questions, I'll go and you can fire anyone you want."

"You're treating this as if it were funny. My staff's obligation is to *me*."

"No, I don't think it's funny. But my obligation is to the law."

"And mine is to my clients and you're wasting my time. What exactly do you want?"

"To talk about those clients. Who was your client for the Block A site in Harlem?"

"For the— What kind of a question is that?"

"The *Times* article didn't list your name but the model and rendering were unmistakable." As she said that she wondered if it was true. Would Joe, more attuned to the visual world than she, have known from a glance at the drawing who the architect was?

Maybe so, because Martin accepted the tribute without question. Appearing slightly mollified, he sniffed, "That was done for the city. The article described it as a city project. You can't have missed that?"

"You're forgetting I work for the city. 'The city' never does anything. It's DDC, HPD, HRA, Real Property. And even then, it's always the Division of This or the Bureau of That. Someone had to give you the number of apartments, the amount of commercial space, the parking. Someone had to approve your design concept."

"No one 'approves' my design concepts. Clients come to me based on the way I approach design and then they stand back."

"In this instance, who came to you?"

"The city."

"Who paid your bill?"

He fixed his eyes on her. Unexpectedly, they were gray. With his coloring she'd have expected brown. Maybe they were contacts, to fit the office-and-clothing color scheme. "I did it pro bono."

She laughed. "*Pro bono?* Wait, I know—you want to hear me do my warrant routine, the one your receptionist found so moving."

"What's the point of this, exactly?"

"The point, Mr. Martin, is that three people are now dead in connection with Block A. Withholding information regarding that property is a really bad idea."

"Dead?" He hesitated. "What do you mean, dead?"

"Didn't I say 'homicide'? I know I meant to."

"That project's not built. It hasn't even reached working drawings; it's still in schematics. How can anyone be dead?"

"You're finding that a hard concept to wrap yourself around? Then try this: explaining to the state licensing board why you obstructed my investigation."

He paused, like a car at a crossroads, trying to choose a direction. "You're from DOI," he said, motoring on. "I don't believe you have the authority to investigate homicide."

"Technically, no. I could call Detective Perez from the NYPD if you'd like. He's my liaison." She took her cell phone from her pocket. "Of course, once the NYPD's involved—"

"Oh, don't be stupid." Martin waved an irritable hand. "I don't know what the big deal is and I'm certainly not going to be left holding the bag. I was asked not to discuss it and I was attempting to honor that request. But you're forcing me to break my word. I did that project for Walter Glybenhall."

Ann felt her skin tingle. "Glybenhall hired you?"

"I believe that's what that means."

"His requirements? His design ideas?"

"Of course not. *My* design ideas. Walter's a developer. He has a lot of money and a lot of ego, but a boringly pedestrian aesthetic sensibility."

"You do a lot of work for him."

"Why wouldn't I?"

"Because you don't like his aesthetic sensibility?"

"I don't have to. He likes mine."

"I see. But the approach to the Block A project was his idea?"

"Yes, though I modified it."

"Why?"

"As usual, he wanted too much."

That would be Walter. "What does that mean?"

"He was crowding the site. His program contained the same number of townhomes as the current design, and of course the entertainment-district atmosphere. But he wanted too many smaller rental units. They'd have to be shoehorned in. You need that in a place like Hidden Bay." Martin nodded at the photo of the seaside resort. "But not in Harlem."

"I'm not following."

"I'm not surprised. And I really don't have time to complete your education. But long story short, in an isolated setting the developer has to include housing for the waiters, gardeners, and maids. Something they can afford. Walter's used to thinking like that."

"Walter Glybenhall? To including things people can afford?"

"In those developments, it's necessary. Otherwise you get a trailer park springing up down the road. That will lower the price point of your units."

"Oh, the price point. For a second I thought I was hearing altruism."

"Cue the violins! No developer's ever been in business out of altruism. And no great project ever came from it, either. You think Andrew Carnegie built Carnegie Hall so New York could hear great music? He wanted to make certain that when New Yorkers went to a concert, they'd have to speak his name."

It was a spectacular building, Skidmore's Montgomery Hall, or so they said. Glass and concrete, austerely detailed, elegantly proportioned, quietly sited. Everything in the service of the music, the performers who made it, the audiences who came to hear. Ann had argued vehemently to her mother that her father, who did many good deeds without publicity, would not have wanted his name on the building. But her mother, focus of much publicity and author of few good deeds, decreed that was rubbish. She instructed the architect to use foot-high letters of bronze.

Ann swept her hair from her forehead. "Go back to Block A."

Martin's glittering eyes watched her through the heavy glasses. "In Harlem you don't need to build that kind of housing. The service class can live right in the neighborhood. They already do."

" 'The service class'? Do the people in Harlem know you call them that?"

"I doubt they know anything about me, I don't consult the public for input. In fact I've seen Block A exactly three times. Since what we make of it will have nothing to do with what it is now, I, unlike Walter, don't see any need to spend a lot of time there."

"Glybenhall does?"

"He visits the site in what I'd call an unhealthily obsessive way. He stands outside the fence and stares, smiling. I went with him once and felt like a chaperone on a date. Extraneous, only distracting him from his contemplation of his beloved. And I didn't care for the way people looked at us. I suggested, if he felt he had to keep going there, he stay in his car."

"Did he take your suggestion?"

"I doubt it. He said not to worry, he could take care of himself."

"Maybe he's been studying the martial arts."

Martin actually laughed. "And ruin his manicure? No, Walter's solution is more straightforward. He carries a gun."

Sutton Place

"Perez. Talk to me." The voice came from the car's speakers, hooked up to the cell phone.

"Luis, it's Ann." Steering the car through traffic, she spoke into the air.

"Oh, gee, Princess! What, you run out of punching bags?"

"And here I thought real cops were tough. Listen, Luis, one of our gangbanger victims, the one who was shot?"

"Ours? Those vics are Tom Underhill's. Harriet Winston's mine. And you don't have any."

"I'm starting to see why people say the NYPD's a pain in the butt. What was he shot with?"

"A gun. Yeah, I know, 'Put a cork in it, Luis.' I don't know if they have ballistics on that yet. I could ask Tom, but it'll cost you."

"Cost me what?"

"Dinner?"

"Won't your wife get mad if you come home with your arm in a sling?"

He sighed. "Okay, how about you talk me up to your boss in about a year and a half?"

She glanced at the phone. "Really?"

"Just hedging my bets, Princess. Every level you hit, the next level gets harder. You see a lot of *Boriquas* wearing brass in this department?"

"Mine either, Luis."

"Yeah, but where you are the girl cops are prettier and you don't get shot at. Why do you want the ballistics?"

"I want to play mix and match."

"You have a gun?"

"No, but I know someone who does."

"Who?"

"Later. When you call with the report."

"Hey—!"

Ann switched the phone off and cruised downtown.

Eve Rudin still sat at her desk in Joe's corner, leaning over paperwork. She looked as if she hadn't moved all day. That was her way: the phone, the computer, almost never the field. Ann had once expressed to Joe the hope that Eve at least had a wild after-hours life, stiletto heels and micro-dresses, clubs and raves and private parties in bar lounges with no street signs. Joe had shaken his head without looking up from the report he was reading. "Three ex-husbands," he'd said. "All cops."

Ann hung her coat up and peeled the top off her latte. She took out her directory, ran her finger down the NYPD page, found the number of the License Division. There'd be a rigamarole: her ID, their call back on her office phone to make sure she was legit. It was irritating, and Perez could get it done faster, but she didn't want Perez involved until she was sure she was right.

She was about to dial the number but her message light was blinking so she checked that first. Only one call, but interesting enough to move the NYPD License Bureau to the back burner.

"This is Lieutenant van Drost." The call had come in half an hour earlier, and the Curaçao cop sounded as relaxed as he had that morning. In New York, cops—and DOI inspectors—usually snarled and snapped as the day wound down, even if they'd started out upbeat. Maybe she should consider relocating. "I had Mike Statius picked up," van Drost's voice told her, "but he's gotten a cell phone so I let him go. He promised to answer if you call him. He says he has nothing to hide and he's happy to talk."

Van Drost recited the number twice. Ann took it down thinking, *Sure he doesn't, and of course he is.*

She punched in the country code and Statius's number, expecting a message telling her to call back sometime in the next century. Sipping her latte, she was taken by surprise when a live voice said, "Hello?" and waited for a response.

"Hello? Mike Statius?" Ann put the coffee down. "Can you hear me?"

"Very well. This is the police in New York?"

"Inspector Ann Montgomery, DOI. How do you know?"

"This is a brand-new phone, no one has the number. Lieutenant van

Drost said he would give it to you. And this call is from New York. The phone tells me that." His voice was deep and rich, his accent West Indies, not as Dutch as van Drost's but without the French overlay of, say, Trinidad.

"Mr. Statius," she said, "I want to talk about the accidents at Mott Haven."

"Yes, I know. Please believe me, I had nothing to do with them."

"If that's true, why did you leave the country the day after the last one? The fatal one?"

"I had not seen my family in nearly a year. I was given a ticket and a month's pay. And my conscience was clear."

"A ticket and a month's pay? From Three Star?"

"Yes, ma'am."

"Didn't that seem strange to you?"

"Strange?" He laughed, a hearty sound. "Ma'am, no, it did not. It seemed very clear they wanted you to have difficulty in getting in touch with me."

"Why?"

"Most likely, to imply those accidents were my fault."

"They've more or less stated as much. That you were incompetent, now you've been replaced, end of story."

"I am not surprised."

"And it doesn't bother you?"

"Yes, it does. I do not want it thought I am associated with these troubles. For that reason I acquired a cell phone, as there is no telephone at my family home."

"But you didn't call me."

"No, ma'am. I thought perhaps the authorities could clear the matter up without my involvement."

"Well, we haven't been able to."

"I am sorry about that. But you must see that when a large and powerful firm like Three Star orders me out of the country, and pays me handsomely for obeying orders, I must consider that there is more at stake than I am aware of. I have made it simple for you to find me. But I thought it not my place to come to you."

"You were afraid?"

"I have five children, Inspector Montgomery. Site super work in the U.S. pays quite well. In Curaçao, at this time, there is no such work."

"But you're speaking to me now."

"I would have been quite mad to turn down a ticket home and a month's salary. And what point would there have been to my remaining in New York? Certainly, I would not have gotten more work as a result;

the building world is a small place. But this island is also a small place. If Lieutenant van Drost suggests to a man that he make himself available to the New York police, everyone will know if he does or if he doesn't. Thus no one, not even a large New York firm, can fault him for answering his phone."

"I see," said Ann. "All right, tell me this: Why do you say these incidents aren't your responsibility? Isn't everything that happens on a job site the responsibility of the site super?"

"Of course. This is why I was fired. If you yourself, Inspector, made a serious error in your work—an error costing lives—or if you were to indulge in criminal behavior, would your supervisor not be forced to resign? And yet, who could say any fault was truly his?"

"Criminal behavior?"

"A possibility only. But I tell you this: our safety record at Mott Haven was quite good, until the day one of my assistant supers was replaced with Mr. Sonny O'Doul."

"You think O'Doul's responsible for what's been going on?"

"I don't like to accuse any man. But Mr. O'Doul caused me to wonder."

"To wonder what?"

"He is not a pleasant man. And he is greedy. The kind of man who will eat two doughnuts from the box someone else has brought, and then take the last one to his desk, in case he should want it later. I've worked with many men like this. Rarely do they offer to make your final inspection round on a Friday afternoon."

"And Mr. O'Doul did? That Friday? The night the storm came up and Harriet Winston died?"

"He said he was waiting for a late delivery, and that he would walk the site for me at the end of the day. Greedy and unpleasant, Inspector, but competent. I had strained my back and thought perhaps he had a talent for sympathy I had not seen before. I took his offer."

"So you never saw the bricks on the roof Friday?"

"No, I did not. I do not know if Mr. O'Doul did, either. Perhaps he never made the inspection."

"Perhaps not." *Why would you, if you knew a kid from Harlem was on his way uptown to remove half of them?* "Did O'Doul often work late?"

"It was necessary for the responsibilities of his position. For deliveries. Unless he has been fired also, I think you'll find he still does."

Ann finished her coffee, now cool, as she slogged through the NYPD License Division's process. After verifying her identity and legitimate need, it didn't take all that long, just a few minutes of bland Muzak before she learned that Ford Corrington had no gun license. And that Walter Glybenhall had, for a Wilson Combat custom-built .45 semiautomatic.

"Either you're surfing the Chippendales website or your case is going well." Greg Lowry, fresh from some meeting—he was wearing a jacket and tie—rapped her desk with his knuckles as he passed by. "Can I have a report?"

"Sure. They have a new blond hunk with a thong—"

"Ann?"

"Yes, boss. Your office?"

"Good idea."

Ann got up and followed Lowry across the room.

"You're grinning like a banshee because you've found irrefutable proof that some random madman is sabotaging the Mott Haven site and Walter Glybenhall is a choirboy." Lowry dropped into his chair and thudded his feet onto his battered metal desk. "Right?"

"Why would that make me happy?"

"Because it would make the mayor happy. Which should be enough to have all loyal municipal servants jumping for joy."

"So try me for treason."

Lowry asked, in the voice of a man who already knew the answer, "I'm not going to like this, am I?"

"No," she replied. "But I love it."

She gave Lowry a complete report. All during it he stared at the ceiling. "I so do not like it," he said when she was done. "And," he pointed out, "it's circumstantial. Even the case against Corrington would be circumstantial, but it would be better."

"It wouldn't be better. You'd just be happier if it were Corrington."

"It would be a hell of a political hot potato, if it was him. But it's far worse if Glybenhall had anything to do with it. Jesus, Ann, I can't believe this."

"For God's sake, Greg! You were IG at Sanitation eleven years. You never ran into rich guys with feet of shit?"

"In the garbage business, they wear pinky rings and their names end in vowels. And the mayor doesn't sail to Bimini on their yachts." He sat tapping a pencil on his desk. "If you're right, here's one way to look at it: it turns into a simple homicide. Civilian comes down from his penthouse, has business with a couple of civilians in the gutter. Things go bad, people die, but no one in city government's involved." He nodded, face brightening. "Not our problem. You can drop it all on Perez and—who was that other guy, at the two-eight?"

"Tom Underhill. And no way, Greg."

"Ann—"

"Corruption, Greg. That's our job. If Harriet Winston died because of a dirty deal Glybenhall has with the mayor—"

"No! Fuck, no, we are not going down that road."

"Greg? Perez is a good cop. A pain, but a real good cop." *There, Luis, an early installment.* "If you take me off this he'll be all over it. And the NYPD's a lot more heavy-handed than I am."

Lowry shook his head. "Mark Shapiro will have a cow."

"Look: if Charlie Barr's smart, nothing's on the record. I go in surgically, wrap up Glybenhall—if it's him, if it's him—and whatever Glybenhall says about Charlie during the froth-at-the-mouth stage, Hizzoner can deny. He can admit to being too trusting, to being taken advantage of by a snake in the grass. He can say how hurt he is to find he's been used that way. Voters love that teary stuff. He'll probably *gain* in the polls. But if it's Perez, the whole thing'll fly out of control. They can't control spin at the NYPD, you know they can't. Right now Perez isn't spending a lot of time on this because he's not convinced Harriet Winston's death is a homicide. Tom Underhill has no idea yet his dead gangbangers are even connected to this."

"You don't either. It's all conjecture."

"So let me find out! I'll be subtle. I'll keep them—Perez and Underhill—at arm's length. Until I really have something."

"And if you never do?"

"On Glybenhall? Then I'll find you your random madman and everyone'll be happy."

A long silence, Lowry staring at his pencil as though it might suddenly start to move, spirit-writing an answer for him.

"No," he finally said. "No. It's way beyond our mandate. If no one at Buildings is dirty, we wash our hands of this investigation."

"You told me the mayor said 'think outside the box.'"

"From where you want to go you can't even see the box."

"You can't just ignore this! A woman died!"

"I'm not ignoring it. I'm telling you to give it to the NYPD. From this moment. I'll instruct reception to direct all inquiries over there. Our jurisdiction—"

"Corruption in construction! This—"

"No, I said!" He swung his feet off the desk and faced her straight on. "Look: one of the reasons I put you on this was so you could prove yourself. I want you back, Ann, not out in Bay Ridge. You'd figured that out, right?"

"No. I thought it was because you saw this as a sacrificial position and you didn't want to lose Dennis."

"Dennis? You're kidding. Dennis is good but he's not half the investigator you are. Your exile was political and I thought it was a waste from the day I got here. This was my chance to get you back. We have work coming up—"

"The multiagency task force. Industry-wide. You told me."

"Damn right. There's going to be a lot of pressure on me behind that and I want top people. What you've already done on this proves I was right about you, but one slip when it's someone like Glybenhall and you're done, Ann. Finito forever. You screw up like that, I won't be able to help you. And I won't try." He gave her a long look. "Please. Just give it to Perez, let the NYPD see where they can take it. We have other things to do."

When Ann got home, she took the Boxster from the garage and told herself she just needed a little air to clear her head.

Why anyone looking for a little air would choose to sit in rush-hour traffic on the FDR, the Deegan, and the Tappan Zee was a question she wouldn't have been able to answer, but luckily she didn't hear herself ask it. Finally released to the soaring freedom of the Thruway, she lowered the top and raced north in the soft purple evening.

CHAPTER

50

Heart's Content

Headlights swept his wall, bounced to a stop, and cut off. Never before, a car in his driveway at this hour; never since he'd gotten out of prison, this once-familiar swell of adrenaline and dread.

And never anticipated, this surprise of shock and longing as Ann's tangled hair, unbuttoned coat, and long-legged stride neared his open door.

"Expecting someone? You didn't even give me a chance to knock." She stopped in the dust of the yard.

"No. No one. No one comes here."

"I do."

The breeze and the scent of pine needles wandered together through the silence.

He realized she'd made no move to enter. Ann, waiting for an invitation. "What do you want?"

When she didn't answer, he stood aside; when he stood aside, she stepped past him into the darkened room.

"I wanted to fill you in." She spoke without facing him. "Tell you what's happening."

"You could have called." He closed the door.

"Joe . . ."

This would be the time to snap on the light, open a beer, walk away. This would be the time to tell her to leave.

She turned and, knowing what he was about to say as he knew she did, she touched a finger to his lips. Her touch was impossibly soft, as though a petal, after dancing in a whirlwind, had come to rest on a stone.

Three times in the night he awoke. The warm silk of Ann's skin, the soft rise and fall of her breath, did not surprise him, so natural did it seem to have her next to him. That fact itself dismayed him. All his old reasons and all his new ones, his towering, impassable mountain range, nothing but a trick of mist, dissipated this easily.

He awoke a fourth time just before dawn. Ragged black branches snaked through gray sky in the squares of his windows. Beyond the ridge, an edge of burnt rose; he knew where to look for that. She wrapped an arm around him. In the first light her skin seemed to glow.

"Ann," he whispered.

She smiled and pulled him closer. "Yes, we can."

"No."

"Yes." She touched his face. "Yes. It was always you, Joe."

He wanted to say "No" again, but to what?

They sat with coffee on the porch while the climbing sun pointed out certain trees and blooms, until finally it burst from behind the rocks and flooded the yard with light.

"I can hear the creek," Ann said. "Can you climb down to it that way?"

"I don't go down there much," Joe told her.

"I'm this close," she said. "To taking up Walter Glybenhall."

He looked to where he'd planted violets at the edge of the wood; whether they would survive or not, he didn't know. "You can't."

"You're very negative this morning."

"Be serious. Whatever you have, it won't be enough. They'll stop you."

"They're already trying. Lowry ordered me to drop it."

"And you took that like a bull takes a red flag."

"What do you think? He should have known better."

"Ann—"

"He said to give it to Perez. So the NYPD could bury it."

"Perez doesn't sound like that kind of guy."

"He'll get orders too! No one wants to screw up his career over something like this."

"Except you." She stood. He twisted to watch her as she went inside, came out a moment later with the coffeepot, as though she did this every day.

"Joe?" she said as she sat. "I'm right. I *know* I am."

"Even if you are, you have nothing on him."

"I will. I'm waiting for ballistics on the bullets. That kid Kong."

"You have a gun?"

"Walter does. A Wilson Combat .45. A four-thousand-dollar handgun. Carry permit, too, on the basis of being an envied public figure. Bastard."

"You can't think Glybenhall shot Kong himself?"

"I'm hoping."

"Ann—"

"And if not, maybe a night in jail with people he wouldn't let clean his bathroom—"

"He won't spend the night. He won't spend an hour." Joe looked at the dicentra, patient in its pot. "It doesn't make sense."

"What doesn't?"

"If Walter Glybenhall has an under-the-table deal with the mayor, why endanger it this way?"

"Because he needs the money. Because he's greedy and arrogant. Because he thinks he can get away with it."

Joe shook his head. "It doesn't feel right."

"You've been away too long!"

That was true. He had been; too long, and too far, and too completely.

She turned to him and the texture of the silence changed. "I'm sorry," she said, sounding tentative. "I didn't mean—"

"You're right." He felt a surge of anger and wondered at its source. Because of what she'd said? No: because suddenly she didn't sound sure of herself. Certain things were expected to be dependable, like the seasons. "To me this sounds crazy. But I've been away."

"Everybody's always said it's crazy. Going up against Walter. That's why he gets away with things. Not anymore. This time, I'm going to shut him down."

Joe waited and watched: Ann in the early-morning sun. "You ever have a home?"

"What are you talking about?"

"All those places you lived as a kid. You ever feel like any of them was home?"

After a pause she said, "All of them."

"How can that be?"

"What do people mean when they use that word? A place where

you're safe? Where you don't need a back door out of, because you don't ever have to leave unless you want to? That's how it felt everywhere we lived when I was a kid. As long as my dad was there."

"And after he was gone?"

"Then it was different."

He let the silence flow, let the rustling leaves and the whisper of the creek fill it. After a while he said, "They planted a dozen pear trees in front of that theater. They're in bloom now. White flowers. Beautiful in the morning light."

Her eyes flared. "At Skidmore? How the hell do you know?"

"It's half an hour from here."

"You've been there?"

"A student orchestra concert. Pretty good."

A moment; he thought she was going to get up and storm away. Then her smile flashed and she shook her head. "A concert in the beautiful morning light?"

He smiled, too, and shrugged. "I wanted to see the building."

"I don't."

"You could stop on your way back to the city."

"You could mind your own business." She emptied her mug and stood. "I have to get back. It's a long drive. And you have work to do." She gestured out over the garden.

He stood also. "Be careful."

"Driving?"

"That too."

They kissed long and slow. The beat of his blood mixed with the racing of the creek, and the warmth of the sun on his back underlined the heat of Ann's arms around him.

He walked her to the driveway, stood and watched as she drove away, and for a while after. Before he went back to the garden he tried to straighten the "Heart's Content" sign on the mailbox, but it kept slipping and he gave it up.

Harlem: Frederick Douglass Boulevard

"You have a visitor." Yvonnia's call found Ford in the gym office, where he and Coach Fagan were going over the midnight basketball schedule.

"We're almost done here," Ford told her. "Who is it? Can they wait?"

"Probably. But I'd rather you came up."

"What's wrong?"

"Nothing. He says his name's Blowfish and he has information for you."

Blowfish. The park, Ford thought. Carlo's crew. Not surprising that Yvonnia, generally hard to rattle, sounded tense.

"Okay, I'll be right up."

As Ford stepped into the office Yvonnia's eyes flicked to a chubby young man in Knicks colors and a do-rag. He stood examining the photos on the wall: Ford with politicians, funders, and public figures. Those pictures were there to impress other politicians, funders, and public figures, and the fact that they worked always seemed to Ford both reassuring and ridiculous.

"You're looking for me?"

Without haste the young man turned to Ford and smiled, showing a row of gold-capped teeth. He tapped one of the photos. "Hey, man. You really know Tyra Banks?"

"She's given us some generous donations."

"I'd like to give her a donation. Be damn generous, too. You got her number?"

"No, sorry. That what you came to ask?"

"Didn't come to ask nothing. Came to give you the wire."

"On what? Come inside." Blowfish followed Ford into his office. He dropped into one of the armchairs by the window, swung his puffy, untied sneakers onto the coffee table.

Ford sat in the other chair, put his feet on the table, too. "You go by 'Blowfish'?"

"What my boys call me. It's a poison fish. You could eat it, but you don't know how to handle it right, it gonna kill you." Blowfish grinned. "Sometime, don't matter how you handle it, it kill you anyway. How about you?"

"I go by 'Mr. Corrington.' "

Blowfish laughed. "Damn! Well, listen here, *Mr. Corrington,* 'cause I got some shit you want."

"What's that?"

"Four-one-one. You was asking A-Dogg about Kong."

"Who said?"

"A-Dogg told me. We tight like that."

"All right, suppose I was. You know something A-Dogg didn't?"

"Got to, because my man A-Dogg, he don't know shit. Except about Kong's bling, and his bragging on the cracker he workin' for. Told me he told you that."

"You can do better?"

"I seen him. The cracker."

"You know who he is?"

"You mean, his name? Naw. But I could tell you some shit about him."

"You can describe him?"

"Ain't no thing." Blowfish shrugged, but he didn't go on.

"I see. What's it going to cost me?"

"Tyra Banks's phone number?"

Ford stood. "See you around, Blowfish."

"Yo, man, why you buggin'? I'm just messing with you. This one's free."

"How come?"

"Carlo, that's my main man. Kong's brother, dig? Carlo can't get no read, what happen to Kong. This vanilla fucker, I tell Carlo about him, but what he gonna do? How he gonna find out shit? Now you, *Mr. Corrington,* you a guy hang with white bread with money." He thumbed over his shoulder, toward the outer office and its photos.

"This guy has money?" Ford sat again.

"Got the ride, got the threads. Got to get 'em somehow."

"Tell me about him."

"S'pose I do, what you gonna do?"

"If he had anything to do with Kong's death, I'm going to find out about it, and he's going to pay."

"You mean, the po-lice? I got a better idea. You tell me who he is, where he hang, me and Carlo take care of it."

"No."

"You think nine-one-one gonna come down on him? He prob'ly own every cop he ever met."

"I have some people who listen to me, Blowfish. I promise you, if I find out this man was involved, he'll pay. But if he's not, I sure as hell don't want you and Carlo hunting him down."

"Hey, he guaranteed mixed up in some shit, with my man Kong. You could take that to the bank."

"Doesn't mean he had anything to do with killing him."

"Why you was askin' about him, then?"

"I wasn't. I was asking A-Dogg if he knew what Kong was mixed up in, and this white man was what he told me about. Look, you have something to say or not?"

Blowfish rubbed his mouth with a pudgy hand. "People listen to you, huh?"

"Some do."

After another few moments, the kid said, "Yeah, okay. That's dope." He nodded. "Tall guy, white hair, sharp nose. Always look like you smellin' bad to him."

"You saw this man with Kong?"

"Down to the river. Maybe last week. I'm gettin' next to my woman, I see this big slick limo pull up. White bread gets out, walks to the rail. Leans there next to a brother. I squint my eyes—it's just getting dark, you know?—and fuck if it ain't Kong. I'm thinking, damn, what business do he got going and how can I get him give me a piece of it?"

"Did you find out?"

"Naw. Ask Kong next day, he tell me the same shit he tell A-Dogg, 'bout how good he bein' paid, but he ain't never said for what or by who. My first idea, this cracker some new supplier in town and Kong movin' his product. But if a new operation start up, everyone hear about it, and no one ain't heard shit. And if Kong movin' product, why he cut me and A-Dogg out? He gonna need a army, come to that."

Blowfish grinned, but his eyes were ice, as though challenging Ford to pass judgment. Ford met his stare. "How long were they together, this man and Kong?"

"Quick. Five, maybe. Vanilla get back in the limo, drive away. Kong leave right after, over the bridge."

"Anyone else with them? T. D. Tilden?"

"T.D.? You shittin' me. My old daddy, rest his soul, he used to call suckers like T.D. 'no-account punks.' "

And mine used to use the same words for gangbangers like you, Ford thought. "T.D. was into something with Kong. You know anything about that?"

Blowfish shook his head. "A-Dogg tell me you say that. How come you think that?"

"I heard it."

"From where?"

"I heard it around, Blowfish. You know anything about it?"

"No, but can't be nothin'. T.D. strictly small-time."

"All right. Back to this white man: you know anything else about him? I don't suppose you got his license plate?"

"What I look like to you, five-oh? He ain't on your wall, neither. But I seen him around, before."

"Where?"

"Couple blocks from here. Seen him get out that damn limo over by that lot on 128th. Where them four buildings is standing in all that shit? He just look through the fence and smile, like them rats and alley cats better watch their asses because they ain't got much longer. Like he got some plan, and they just totally fucked. Tell you something."

"What?"

"I ain't never wanted to be no old alley cat. But I never been so glad I ain't one before, till I seen that smile."

CHAPTER 52

City Hall

"Edgar." Charlie Barr strode briskly into the conference room. "Good to see you."

"Charlie." Westermann didn't get up. He was dunking a cookie in his coffee and kept at it. "Glad you had time for me."

"For a Borough President? Always. Okay if Don sits with us?"

"Sure, you feel like you need someone to watch your back." Westermann grinned. "Morning, Don."

Don nodded his hello and took his usual seat at the end of the table.

"What can I do for you, Edgar?" Charlie asked.

"It ain't what you can do for me, Charlie. I'm here to do somethin' for you."

It was true Westermann had been born and raised in Harlem. But it was also true, according to both his official bio and Charlie's quiet digging, that his home had been and continued to be a brownstone his doctor parents had owned on Strivers Row; that he'd spent his high school years at Fieldston; and that he had both a BA and a master's in public administration from SUNY Albany. And true, too, that like fat in milk, the percentage of street in Edgar's conversation varied wildly. His talk could range from completely skimmed to full, rich cream, depending what, or whom, he was pouring it on.

"I'm all ears," Charlie told him.

"It's come to my attention, you got DOI investigatin' this construction site situation up to the Bronx."

Half-and-half, Charlie thought. Could mean trouble. "That's DOI's job. And from your press conference Saturday—not to mention yesterday's—I'd have thought you'd be pleased."

"Any time the system takes a black community seriously, I'm pleased. The investigator on the case, though. Ann Montgomery."

"What about her?"

"Not a good choice, I don't believe."

"Oh? Why's that?"

"One thing, she's hotheaded."

"You know." Charlie smiled. "I've heard that about you, too. Never stopped me from appreciating your work."

Westermann grunted. "You'd stop appreciating me damn fast, I stopped delivering Harlem for you. Anyway, we ain't talking about me. You aware Montgomery got a hate on for Walter Glybenhall? She finds a way to fry his fat, she's gonna do it."

"If there's a reason to, then I have no problem with that."

"Really? You're talking about a friend, Charlie."

"Friend's a fluid concept in politics, Edgar."

"For some people, so I hear." Westermann popped the last of his cookie in his mouth. "You know much about her?"

"Montgomery? I know she was the partner of that DOI guy from the Dolan Construction case, which means she hates *me*. But I don't think that's a problem, if that's what you mean."

"What I mean got nothin' to do with that. Word is, she's known Walter Glybenhall since she was a kid."

"The circles she travels in, I'm not surprised. Are you telling me they're particularly close?"

"I'm saying the opposite. I don't know the details, but something happened, lot of years ago. What I hear, she'd be happy if she could nail his hide to the barn door."

"I'd think that would make you happy, too."

"Would, if she could make it stick. But you beat the bushes before the shotgun's loaded, turkey gets away every time."

Charlie had to grin. "Edgar, when you talk like that I could listen to you all day. But I know you're a busy man. What are you saying?"

"Just trying to make sure DOI builds a case. Solid, know what I mean? No shortcuts that'll jump up and bite 'em in the ass. My constituents don't want to see another rich white man get away with the murder of a black woman—"

"Stop right there, Edgar! Your down-home metaphors are charming but you will *not* sit here and say Walter Glybenhall murdered Harriet Winston. That accident—"

"Whoa! Couldn't let that go unchallenged on your tape, could you, Mr. Mayor?"

Charlie sat back. "Everything that happens in this room is on the record, Edgar. You know that."

"Yes, I surely do. And I want this on the record, too: If DOI makes a case against Walter Glybenhall, which I imagine they won't, him being such a good friend of such a good judge of character as yourself, but if the Lord is passin' out miracles and they do, I want it to be a good case. Some screwball with her beady eyes drawing down on Glybenhall from the get-go, she might not be the right person to make that case. All I'm saying."

"Your objection is noted," Charlie replied evenly. "And thank you for your advice. Anything else?"

"No, no. I best be getting on." Westermann hefted his bulk from the chair. "And no need to thank me, Charlie. Any time I can help, you just call me. Any time at all."

With the door safely shut behind Westermann, Charlie pressed the hidden button that stopped the tape. He turned to Don. "What the hell was that?"

Don shrugged. "He's running for mayor. He wants to be on record defending his community."

"Anything in it, you think? You know anything about Montgomery and Walter from 'a lot of years ago'?"

"Can't hurt to check it out."

"Or maybe I should just have Mark Shapiro pull her. To be safe."

"You can't."

"Why?"

"Because she hates you, and Glybenhall's your bud."

"Well, when you put it that way . . ."

"It would look that way. Now that it's on the record."

"Damn. Boy, that's like Edgar, isn't it?"

"How do you mean?"

"If he'd gone quietly to Shapiro, he might have gotten Montgomery pulled. As long as I didn't know anything about it."

"Yeah, but this is Westermann. He's not about to talk to a Commissioner when he can make the mayor sit down with him."

"That's what I mean. He made me listen, but now he won't get what he wanted. Now she's *got* to stay. All we can do is hope to hell there's nothing for her to find."

Sutton Place

For the first hour flying south down the highway, it was just Ann and the sunshine and *The Barber of Seville*. Then, as she neared the Tappan Zee, her cell phone rang. She wiggled the hands-free earpiece in and glanced at the readout.

"Good morning, Luis." NYPD shifts started at seven a.m., a good reason, if you needed one, not to be a cop.

"Hey there, Princess, you sound cheerful. *Que pasa?*"

"*Nada, papi. Y contigo?*"

"Oh, shit! I didn't know you could do that!"

"It means you can't have any secrets from me, Luis."

"Why, you read minds, too?"

"Yours is an open book, I'm afraid."

"Yeah, well, if you're so smart tell me why I'm calling."

"You have my ballistics report."

"Happens to be *my* ballistics report. Now tell me what's in it."

"I don't know, but I hope it's good."

"Depends what you call good. You'll probably like this, because it's cold and cruel."

"I'm flattered. Go ahead."

"What blew Kong away was an ExtremeShock 'Explosive Entry' load. Three of them, actually. You know anything about that?"

"No, go on and tell me."

"High-class hollowpoint. Way more destructive than you need, rips flesh to shreds. ExtremeShock calls it 'Fang Face.' NYPD won't let us use it."

"Gee, that's too bad. What kind of weapon is it good in?"

"Forty-five auto or semi."

"Easy to come by?"

"Got to be special-ordered, but any supply shop'll do that for you. Or you can get it off the web."

"You can?"

"You surprised?"

"Not really. Any way you can trace this load?"

"You mean, serial numbers on the bullets? Take it up with the NRA."

"But if we had a gun?"

"Then we could compare. One is too mangled, but the other two may be in good enough condition."

"Keep them that way," Ann said, and clicked off.

Morning traffic was beginning to build. Still, she made good time. A few minutes after Perez's call she swept onto the Tappan Zee Bridge. The wide curve of the roadway ran just twenty feet above the water, giving drivers a man-against-nature thrill until finally the bridge arched and soared, over and down. With some regret she slowed to pay the toll and melded with the Thruway traffic pouring toward the city.

Walter Glybenhall's Wilson was a .45 semiautomatic.

But so were half the licensed handguns in New York. You couldn't pick up a guy, and especially not Glybenhall, on that basis alone. You couldn't even get a warrant for the gun.

In her mind she saw Walter in his overstuffed penthouse, leaning against the fireplace. A smoking jacket, for God's sake!

In Zurich, twenty years ago, a maroon smoking jacket had hung over a chair the morning she'd blundered into Walter's apartment. Her mother had been invited there for coffee, and Ann had gone to say goodbye, on her way up to the ski lodge to join her father. It had been Walter's suggestion that Ann drop by.

She clenched her jaw. Shifting and shooting around a van, she wove into the right lane and out again. Driving like this required concentration; Walter's image began to fade. Clock and trophies and Walter's cold smile dimmed in the sun.

Trophies.

Abruptly, Ann slowed. She focused on Walter's Manhattan living room again, zeroing in on the mantelpiece: A silver yacht. Assorted gold-plated golfers. A damn polo player.

And a marksman.

She pulled off the next exit and speed-dialed the phone.

"Luis?"

"Back so soon?"

"Find out where Walter Glybenhall shoots."

"Walter Glybenhall? What the hell are you talking about?"

"I'm in the car. Find his gun club and give me a call, okay?"

New York City had only two licensed civilian firing ranges. Glybenhall wasn't likely to belong to either of them; the idea that he'd shoot beside bus drivers and off-duty security guards was laughable. It was likely he took his four-thousand-dollar gun to Westchester or the fox-hunt hills of New Jersey, and she was near both. Or maybe he shot somewhere near his Southampton palace. She could be there in under three hours.

She drove into Tarrytown, because it was near the exit, and parked. She was window-shopping without seeing whatever was there when her phone finally rang.

"Took you long enough!"

"Ann?" Not Perez. A woman's voice, both familiar and oddly tentative.

"Irene!" Ann laughed. "I'm sorry. I didn't even look. I was expecting someone else."

"Girl, I have bad news. Brace yourself."

"What's wrong?"

"It's Jen. I just got a call. Ann, honey . . . Jen's dead."

Everything froze, nothing moved in the bright morning. "What? Irene?"

A short pause. "She was killed."

"Killed? I . . . In an accident?" From the depth of Irene's silence Ann knew that was wrong.

"Someone killed her."

"Oh, no." A car drove by, the whoosh of its tires impossibly loud. Ann turned, but couldn't get away from the sound.

"I'm so sorry," Irene said. "The call I got, it was to an NYPD briefing. I was on the rotation. When I found out it was Jen, I bowed out, of course."

"Do they know who?"

"No. It was Friday night. They found her Saturday afternoon, but she wasn't identified until this morning."

"Why?"

"Oh, honey," Irene said, voice wavering, "she was naked. No bag, nothing to ID her."

"No jewelry? That ring with the grape leaves, she never took that off. And my God, that welded chain?"

"The chain wasn't there. I told the detectives about it. No abrasions, so it must have been cut, not pulled off. She was wearing the ring, but there's nothing identifying about it."

"I guess not . . ." Ann said it reluctantly. She felt like arguing, disputing every word Irene was saying, disproving every fact until the conclusion they pointed at—Jen was dead—was revealed for the sham it was.

"No one reported her missing," Irene went on, "until she didn't show up at some benefit committee meeting for something last night. You know her, half the time she doesn't show up for stuff anyway. . . ." Ann's mind went back three days: the restaurant, the laughter, the empty chair. "But it turned out no one had seen her for days, so her mother finally called Missing Persons. They put it together."

"Damn." Ann's vision blurred. Savagely, she wiped her tears away. "Damn! Oh, damn."

"Honey—"

"Do they have a theory? Where did they find her?"

"In the East River. She was—"

"Oh, my God."

"Ann? What?"

"She's the unidentified white woman in the East River?"

"Yes, how—?"

"I'm working a case connected with two homicides in Harlem and the cop mentioned it. I blew right by it. Oh, *hell*."

"Why wouldn't you? How would you know?"

"Oh, but . . . *Goddammit!* How was—what killed her?"

"She was strangled."

"Attacked?"

"Someone dragging her into an alley? It doesn't look like that. She had some old bruises but except for the marks on her neck, no new ones, nothing on her hands or face. And you know, she was into that stuff . . ."

"I know. I was thinking that. It got out of hand?"

"It does."

"Do they know who that new man was, that she was seeing?"

"Not yet. She kept it a big secret. We were the people she'd be most likely to tell, and she never told us."

"The men she didn't tell us about," Ann said, thinking of Jen's shimmering hair, her conspiratorial giggle, "were the ones she thought we'd disapprove of."

"When did we ever disapprove?"

"I did, when they were married. You all know how I feel about that."

"You have a right," Irene said loyally.

"That's not the point. I was really hard on her a couple of times, once especially when it was a man I knew."

"I wonder if any of us knew this one?"

"If we did, he was keeping it a secret, too. What about that deputy mayor? Zalensky? Did they talk to him yet? Maybe he knows."

"I don't know but I'll suggest it. And I'm sure they'll find whoever the guy is. They'll find who did this, honey. And I'm so sorry to be the one who had to tell you."

Ann, swallowing tears, heard a small sound and realized Irene was weeping, too. Nothing remained to be said, but neither cut the connection. It was a big, bright morning to be alone in.

CHAPTER 54

Sutton Place

When her phone rang again Ann realized she'd been standing blankly on the street corner, for how long she couldn't have said. She checked the readout. "Hello, Luis."

A brief pause. "Hey, *mami*, you okay? You sound down. And you're not yelling that I took too long."

"I just got some bad news."

"Sorry to hear that. Any way I can help?"

"I don't think so, but thanks. Did you find where Glybenhall shoots?"

"Listen, I think maybe you better take a breath. I don't like where you're going with this."

"What, Glybenhall? He has a license for a Wilson Combat .45. It can take that ExtremeShock load, right?"

"Anyone's .45 can. And I thought you were looking at Ford Corrington for these homicides and I thought you were crazy *then*."

"Dammit, Luis! Did you find the gun club, or not?"

"Princess? Even taking into account your bad news you just got, you're pushing it."

The wind blew a sheet of paper against Ann's leg. She shook it off. Turning away from a dog walker's inquisitive stare, she said, "I'm sorry, Luis. You're right."

"*De nada.* Now fill me in. Why do I care where Glybenhall shoots?"

"Because I think he's behind it."

"Behind what? Behind his own accidents?"

"And the killings."

"The Winston lady, you mean? The brick accident?"

"And Kong and that other kid, too. T. D. Tilden."

"You better explain."

She did, as she had for Joe. Though Perez asked questions, didn't follow her leaps. "I don't get that," he said more than once, and she tamped down a surge of impatience and went over whatever it was again. Maybe he was just being cautious. Or maybe, she thought as she heard him ask, "Princess? You still there?" and realized she'd lost her thread and fallen silent, maybe it was she who was being unclear. A part of her kept wanting to get Perez off the phone so she could call Jen. When Jen answered, the two of them would have a big laugh, and then call Irene, trying to be properly respectful and sad about whatever poor girl had really been found in the East River—

"Princess? Where are you? Is there a landline? I think this connection's bad."

"Luis? No, no, it's not the connection. I . . . where was I?"

"You were about to tell me why you and me should stick our necks out to prove all this crazy shit."

"Because it's *true*, Luis!"

"Maybe they got a bunch of cowboys over at DOI, but the NYPD is gonna crap its pants, I tell them I want to look at Glybenhall."

"Here, too. My boss already told me to back off. He wants me to turn it all over to you."

"Oh, shit."

"But I want to follow this up first. Luis, the more we have, the harder it'll be for the brass to stop us."

"I like the way she says 'us.' " Perez paused. "All right, here's what we'll do. I'll give you what I found. Then I'm gonna go work on some nice bodega robbery or something. Unless you can make a case so airtight even Walter Glybenhall can't breathe in it, you're not gonna mention this crazy shit again. How does that sound?"

"Thanks, Luis."

"Forest and Stream Hunt and Fish Club, 77 Hughes Road, Golden's Bridge. And in case you're interested?"

"Yes?"

"Ford Corrington has no gun license."

"I know."

"You know?"

"I checked yesterday. I'm surprised you did, though. You said thinking bad thoughts about Corrington was crazy."

"Just because you're crazy, Princess," Perez sighed, "doesn't mean you're wrong."

Ann called the Forest and Stream Club for directions. She took *The Barber of Seville* out of the CD player and slipped in La Bohème. She blasted it, drove fast, worked hard on thinking of nothing but the music and the road. Twenty-five minutes after she climbed back in the car in Tarrytown, she was pulling into Forest and Stream's gravel lot.

The half-dozen cars scattered around were high-end: two BMWs, a Jag; near the walkway, a black Lexus SUV and a white Hummer. Well, she thought as she pulled in beside the Lexus, the Boxster would feel right at home.

For a place whose mission, one way or another, was slaughter, the clubhouse at Forest and Stream exuded a jarring refinement. The wicker groupings on the stone porch were reflected in the upholstered arrangements inside. A glass counter displayed holsters, straps, and cleaning kits. The young man behind the counter had thick arms and shoulders.

"Yes, can I help you?"

She showed her badge. "The manager, please."

"Can I ask what this is about?"

"No."

"I'm sorry—"

"You'll be sorrier if you don't get the manager out here. You look like a nice kid. This looks like a nice job. You probably want to keep it."

That got her a scowl, but also a request into the intercom for Mr. Onito to come to the front. Onito, thought Ann: Japanese? Latino? Irish, if you allowed for an apostrophe? A round, balding man appeared from a door at the end of the room. Ah: Italian, and ex-cop besides, if the mustache and wary eyes were anything to go by. "Tony Onito," he said, as he neared. "Can I help you, ma'am?"

"Ann Montgomery, New York City DOI. I have a few questions about one of your members."

He took her badge and peered at it, ran a thumb over its surface as though reading it in Braille, and handed it back. "You have—"

"—no jurisdiction here. I could go get one of your locals and come back and he could ask the questions. But your members might prefer discretion to hair-splitting."

Onito glanced at the only two members in evidence, an elderly couple zipping up matching leather gun bags. The woman's plucked brows furrowed.

"Come inside." Onito led Ann to his office. When they got there he shut the door. "All right, what is it?"

"Walter Glybenhall's a member here."

"Is that a question?"

"No. I need to know what weapons he shoots and what bullets he buys."

"The club owns shotguns and rifles and I think Mr. Glybenhall's used both, though he generally brings his own guns. Most members do."

"And handguns?"

"You know the law, I assume? In this state you can't shoot a handgun you don't own."

"What guns does Glybenhall own?"

"I don't keep track of the members' guns, Inspector Montgomery. He'll have a permit for whatever he owns. Why don't you check that?"

"I have. He has a permit for a Wilson Combat .45."

"Then that's your answer. Why are you asking me?"

"You ever see him with another handgun?"

"Like I said—"

"You don't keep track. What ammunition does he use?"

"It depends on the conditions he's shooting in. Range, size and mobility of target, indoors or out—"

"You ever know Walter Glybenhall to buy hollowpoints?"

"I don't—"

"—keep track. But you have records?"

"You have a subpoena?"

"You want me to get one? It's a long trip back to the city. I might think of more things I need to know. What's in his locker, maybe other members' lockers, maybe your safe. If I don't find the gun I'm looking for, I might have to drag your streams. You could be closed for days."

For such a swarthy man, and with an outdoor tan besides, Onito darkened a surprising number of shades. "Is that a goddamn threat?"

"All I want is a look at your sales records."

"My members—"

"Look, Mr. Onito, one of your members may have been involved in a crime. That has nothing to do with you and it's no reflection on this club unless you were involved, too. If you keep stonewalling me I'm going to start to wonder if you were. In fact, let me ask you: Is something going on here that you're trying to hide? Double set of books, sloppy record-keeping, money unaccounted for? *Guns* unaccounted for?"

"Of course not!"

"Then what's the problem? Let me take a quick look at what loads Walter Glybenhall's been buying and I'll be on my way."

He gave her a long stare. Abruptly, he pivoted and walked behind his desk. "Shit. You know, I liked it better on your side of the line."

"Pardon me?"

"Croton PD, retired eleven years. Used to be me throwing my weight around. Worked with a few NYPD guys, joint cases sometimes. Never worked with DOI, though."

"You would have liked us. We're fun."

Onito snorted. He clicked on his computer and typed his way through a set of passwords. "Here we go. Give it a minute to sort by buyer." They waited while the computer hummed. "Walter Glybenhall. Usually buys Winchesters. A month ago, ordered two twenty-round boxes of Explosive Entry from ExtremeShock. That what you're looking for?"

"You bet. When did they come in?"

"The next week."

"Did he shoot any of them here?"

"That I can't tell you. Really. If he did, that brass is long gone. We keep the range clean. You wanted one out of his gun, huh?"

"Can't win 'em all. Didn't it surprise you, ring any warning bells, a member ordering lethal loads like that?"

"Why would it? They do that all the time, all kinds of twisted brass. 'Just want to practice handling it, Tony. In case I ever need it, you know.' "

"Are they that different, in the gun?"

"You don't shoot, huh? At DOI?"

"Only as much as I need to to keep my license. I've never shot a load like that."

"Different-size loads have different kicks, but no, a flesh-cutter like that isn't any different than anything else the same size. They just like to shoot 'em. Makes them feel like Dirty Harry. When the hell do they think they'd need a load like that? When the Apaches overrun the ranch?"

"Okay," Ann said. "Thanks. This helps a lot. But tell me something else: Why the stonewall? You don't sound like you're crazy about the members here. Are you always this protective?"

"My members expect discretion."

"There's discretion, and there's throwing yourself on the grenade."

"I suppose I might've backed down a little sooner. But Glybenhall asked."

"Asked what?"

"He said someone, New York cops, might be sniffing around. He said if they did, if there was any way to keep his private affairs private, he'd be grateful."

"Did he really? And did he give an advance expression of his gratitude?"

"Of course he did. A C-note. Patronizing s.o.b." Onito pulled a copy of the ExtremeShock purchase record from his printer and handed it to her. "My advice? Enjoy that badge while you got it. Nothing lives up to that once it's gone."

CHAPTER 55

Sutton Place

Racing down the Thruway again, Ann speed-dialed Perez and had just slid the cell phone into its cradle when his voice mail picked up.

"Luis?" she said into the air. "It's Ann. I have Glybenhall buying two boxes of those ExtremeShock hollowpoints, the ones that killed Kong. And bribing his range manager not to mention it. Call me."

She tried Lowry next, but got his voice mail, too. This time she left no message. What she had was hot, but Lowry had ordered her to drop Three Star on Perez and walk away. This would need to be handled.

She wished she could call Joe. Maybe she'd buy him a cell phone. There couldn't be any regulation against ditch diggers carrying cell phones. Or ex-cons having them, either.

Thinking about cell phones brought her face-to-face with what she'd been squirming all morning to avoid: the image of Jen, bloated, ashen, her hair snarled and dark with river water. Ann had never worked a homicide: it's not what they did, at DOI. The only bodies she'd seen were falsified ones in funeral homes. But the scene that had burst into her mind with Irene's call included flashing red lights, a body bag, even the scratching sound of a zipper closing.

Her eyes grew hot, threatened to spill tears. *Think! Call the office. Get back to work.* Someone, some cop, was working Jen's murder and if Ann focused now, busted and sweated for answers, for *justice*, in the case she was working, maybe that cop would, too, in Jen's.

She called her own voice mail. One message. She played it, hit re-play, and listened again. Though it was short and unambiguous and she knew perfectly well she'd gotten it right the first time. A man's voice, belligerent, unpleasant, and familiar. "I can tell you some things you'll want to know. Come up to the Mott Haven site and ask for Sonny O'Doul."

So this was it.

Ann pulled the Boxster to the curb and let it idle while she stared at Mott Haven's steel frame, the bricks and concrete and pipes and wires rising behind the fence across the street.

Walter Glybenhall's generous gift to the people of the Bronx.

Clearly not a Henry Martin. Now that she knew what to look for, she could tell. Too straightforward. No irony, no architectural jokes: nothing out of proportion, no elements missing, twisted, repeated too often.

Not that the lack of snideness made these buildings admirable. Two tall corner towers flanked a lower central section; flat roofs, neat white trim, square windows neither big nor small. Everything where and what you'd expect. The architectural equivalent of the Cavalier. Did its job. But no fun.

There was no way she was leaving the Boxster on the street, so she eased back into gear and drove to the gate. She answered the guard's "Can't park here, miss" with her badge. He shrugged, and thumbed her to a muddy expanse near a half-dozen trailers. She parked near the biggest trailer, a triple-wide, took the four steps and pushed through the dented steel door.

Right inside, no need to go farther: three men in hardhats stopped a loud argument abruptly, turned to stare at her. Two she didn't know; her eyes swept and dismissed them. The third man looked older, more worn than the last time she'd seen him, but his lined face and defeated shoulders got no sympathy from her. No: a flash of anger. Sonny O'Doul had spent eight months in jail, right here in New York, close to home and family. Now he was back in the world he knew. His sentence was short because of his lies; and because of his lies Joe had lost two and a half years, lost so much more than that. What the hell entitled Sonny O'Doul to a tragic air?

"Help you?" one of the men said.

"Ann Montgomery. To see Sonny O'Doul." She said this staring at O'Doul.

He stared back. To the others he said, "Just get that fucking pipe up there, I don't care how." He turned and crossed the trailer to an office at the far end. The other two started to exchange smirks; Ann gave them each a long, deliberate look. Their grins faded and they stepped aside to let her pass.

O'Doul's office was a paper-piled wreck. Ann tossed a handful of files off a chair and sat.

"Remember me, Sonny?"

He stared with disgust at the papers she'd strewn. "I knew it was you, I wouldn't of called." He shut the door behind her.

"I was wondering about that. But it is me, Sonny. So this had better be good."

"Look," he said, sitting. "Reason I called, I don't want to be messed up in no shit."

"Spare me. You have no idea how little I care. You said you had information. I'm waiting."

He gave a sour smile. "Always thought you were a hard-ass. From when I first saw you in court."

"I am. And I'm still waiting."

"How's your boyfriend? He out yet?"

Ann stood, slammed the door open, and was halfway across the trailer when she heard O'Doul yell, "Oh, Jesus Christ! Why the hell is it women got no sense of humor? Come on, get back here. You want to see this."

She stopped and turned. O'Doul stood in his doorway. A man stuck his head out of a file alcove to look from her to O'Doul. "Forget it, Sal," O'Doul snapped, and the head disappeared.

"Sonny," Ann said, raising her voice for the benefit of Sal and anyone else who might be in the trailer, "I'm a cop. You're on parole. I can make you no end of trouble."

"Christ's sake, that's why I called." He hurried over, speaking low. "Quiet down! That parole shit. Like I say, I'm clean and I want to stay that way. Come on back inside."

She gave it a few moments, to make him worry, before cutting in front of him and leading the way back to his office.

"I just want to do my damn job and have a beer at night. Is that such a big deal?" O'Doul dropped into his desk chair again. "I don't know what crap's going on around here but I don't want it to come down on my head."

"Didn't like it inside, Sonny?"

"Sucks."

She said nothing, letting the silence stretch.

"Fuck this job," he said. "Fuck it all. I tried to quit."

"What do you mean, 'tried'? How hard is quitting?"

"Word came down. 'Guy on parole, don't look so good, he quits a steady job. His case officer might not understand. We need you, Sonny. Stick around.' "

"Word from where?"

"Came through the new site super, guy they moved over from some other project after Statius got canned. But he says, from the top."

"The top?"

"Fucking blackmail, making me stay. Cocksucker's setting me up, I swear to God."

"Who are we talking about, Sonny?" Ann kept her voice steady.

"Who the fuck you think we're talking about? Fucking Walter Glybenhall! You believe that shit?"

"No, not really. Why would a man like Glybenhall bother with a litle worm like you?"

"Fuck!" O'Doul yanked open a desk drawer, spilling a landslide of papers. He rummaged, pulled something out and tossed it to her.

She caught it in the air and held it up to look: a gold chain dangling a diamond-studded *K*. "If this is a bribe, Sonny, it's not really my taste. And the catch is broken."

"You're doing your goddamndest to make me sorry I called, aren't you?"

"I'd like to make you sorry you ever lived. Right now I'll settle for knowing what this is and why you think I care."

"I found it."

"Good for you. Where?"

"On the roof. Saturday morning. After the accident, where the bricks killed that lady."

Ann lifted the chain. The *K* twirled slowly. "Go on."

"Security has a whole list of emergency numbers, something goes wrong. I'm number two. I got here before Statius. It was me took the cops up to the roof, to show them where the bricks was supposed to be. They're looking at this and that, I spot this thing in a corner, partly under some crap. I grabbed it up when no one was watching."

"You thought it might be worth something."

"If those are fucking diamonds, you bet it is."

"I think they are," Ann said, and smiled. "I think it's extremely valuable. So why the change of heart?"

O'Doul threw the chain a sorrowful glance.

"Sonny?"

He shook his head. "Like I said, I tried to quit. Asshole Glybenhall won't let me. Why the hell not? I start to wonder. I'm so important around here, Walter fucking Glybenhall can't live without me? Like hell."

"And?"

"You stupid, or you playing stupid? What, you think some one of these masons wears shit like that on the job, maybe he *forgot* it? I walked that roof the end of the day. Bricks up there should have held that tarp down through a fucking *tornado*."

"Gee, Sonny, I'm still not getting it. Tell it to me in small words."

"Jesus Christ! Someone was up there *after I left!*" He pointed at the chain. "Them hip-hop assholes wear this shit."

"So do guys from Howard Beach."

"Yeah, whatever. All I'm saying, someone went up and moved those fucking bricks. It's night, it's dark, wind's blowing, you're trying to get out of there before the rain starts, maybe you don't notice you lost nothing. Maybe when you get home and figure it out, you think you'll come back for it, say like the next night. Except the next morning you find out some lady got killed because of the damn bricks you moved, and suddenly, forget it."

"I suppose it's possible you're right, Sonny. But even if you are, *K* doesn't stand for 'Glybenhall.' "

"Not him personally! Jesus, asshole probably never picked up a brick his whole life. I'm saying, these accidents are no goddamn accidents. Look, this is a clean job, union job, no trouble anywhere. Everyone's happy as pigs in shit. I been at it from all angles, I can't see anybody who'd be coming out ahead on crap like this. Except one guy. Fucking Walter Glybenhall. Because insurance pays off for accidents."

"Very clear analysis of a complex situation, Sonny. But now explain why you called me? Instead of going to Glybenhall and trying to get yourself a piece of the action?"

"What, me blackmail Glybenhall? That's a joke, right?"

"You're right. He's way out of your league."

"Oh, for Christ's sake! That's got nothing to do with it. What I'm saying, if you're playing your insurance company, you need insurance, too. In case somebody tips to you. So you hire an ex-con out of the blue, and then don't let him quit. Fuck, lady, *you* do the math."

CHAPTER 56

Sutton Place

"Ann Montgomery."

"Inspector, this is Ford Corrington."

"Mr. Corrington. I was about to call you. I think I can show you what you wanted to see."

"And I'd like to talk to you. I'd appreciate your time this afternoon, you have an hour to spare."

"How's now? I'm in the car, I'll head right down. Fifteen minutes?"

"I'll be waiting, Inspector."

"Hi, Luis."

"Hey, Princess. I'm calling you back against my better judgment."

"Luis, I have two boxes of ExtremeShock hollowpoints on Walter Glybenhall's American Express Card."

"Yeah, your message said. It's legal ammo."

"I have a forensic engineer who says the scaffold collapse and the falling bricks were both deliberate. Sabotage, Luis."

"I'm losing you."

"You wish. I have a gold chain with a *K* on it. *K* like 'Kong.' "

"You do?"

"And I have a long conversation I just had with Ford Corrington to tell you about. I'm in Harlem. You want me to come up there, or you want to come down to me?"

"Greg? It's Ann. I'm glad I caught you. I'm up in the Bronx with Luis Perez."

"What the hell are you doing up there? I hope you're dropping off your files and saying goodbye."

"Luis and I need to meet with you, Greg. And I think Mark Shapiro ought to be there."

"What the hell are you talking about? What's going on?"

"The Three Star thing."

"I told you to drop Three Star. You didn't hear me? I can say it again."

"It's too big, Greg. It's about to hit the fan. If we don't take charge, we'll be the ones covered in it."

chapter 57

City Hall

Charlie Barr stared around his office, holding each pair of eyes before moving on. This was a trick he often used. It let people know he was serious. And it bought time.

This morning he was using it to do both, and also hoping that, with sufficient concentration, he could get one of these men to sprout horns or turn into a duck or do something else surreal enough for his theory and prayer—that this was a bad dream—to be borne out.

It wasn't working, though. They just sat there and looked back at him. Shapiro and Lowry at least seemed sorry, Lowry even nervous, as though he was worried Charlie might forget they were just messengers. Don sat glowering as usual, but his heart wasn't in it. Jen Eliot's death was eating him. Well, Charlie could understand that. Don and the Eliot girl hadn't dated very long, but it still had to be tough when a body you'd held in your arms gets raised from the river. When the cops brought the news yesterday, Charlie had suggested Don take a few days off. Or a day. Or ten minutes. But of course he hadn't. And Charlie, sitting in this unthinkable meeting, was damn glad of it.

Briefly, Charlie entertained the notion that what they were discussing was so preposterous that the fact Shapiro had even brought it up *proved* this meeting was just a nightmare.

That didn't work either.

So, with a sigh, he took one of the most bizarre steps of his political career. He began a rational discussion of arresting Walter Glybenhall for murder.

"You looked at it from all angles?" he asked Mark Shapiro. "You tried every possible way to make it mean something else?"

Shapiro nodded slowly. "Which doesn't mean it's true."

"Or, if it is, that we can prove it," Greg Lowry said. "There are a couple of huge gaps. The gun, for one."

"Mark?" said the mayor.

"That's true. We don't have the gun. But to look for it we'll need a warrant. Once we get that I don't think we can keep this out of the news."

"No, you're right," Charlie agreed. "But that's why your case had better be airtight."

"It isn't," said Lowry. "It can't be, without the gun."

Shapiro said, "We may never get the gun."

"Then what?" asked Charlie.

"Everything Montgomery has is circumstantial," Lowry said. "We have no physical evidence. No paper trail."

"Then why do we have to do this?"

"Mayor," said Shapiro, "the point is, it may be circumstantial but it's as strong as we have in ninety percent of the arrests we make. Either way, it's a powder keg. If it was anybody else, we'd already have gotten a warrant for the gun. If we don't at least go that far, if we don't at least question Glybenhall, sooner or later the press will pick up on *that*."

"What if you're wrong?"

"We'll apologize. That'll be easier than apologizing to the citizens for sweeping this under the rug."

"You can't," Charlie said. "You can't even think you can. Ah, shit. I don't suppose we could call Walter off the record and ask him to turn over his gun for testing? If it's not the one . . ."

Shapiro frowned and Lowry looked embarrassed. "Yeah," said Charlie. "Dumb idea. Okay, run it down for me. What we have."

"We have the forensic engineer's statement on the scaffold bolts and on the bricks."

"One of DOI's people?"

"No, a guy named Sandy Weiss, at Packer Engineering. In Chicago. No axe to grind here."

The mayor nodded and Shapiro went on. "We have statements from the two kids in Harlem—Armand Stubbs and Leonard Fisher: A-Dogg and Blowfish. And from the jeweler, about the chain found at the jobsite, that it was Kong's. We have Glybenhall buying ExtremeShocks, and the range manager's statement that they're not Glybenhall's usual load, and that he was paid to stonewall if anyone asked about them. And Corrington's evidence on T. D. Tilden's girlfriend's statement. That's hearsay but we can make Corrington produce her later if we need to. I thought you'd rather we didn't lean on him now."

"Good call." Charlie nodded wearily.

"We have a doubling in the insurance coverage for Mott Haven four months ago, for no reason we can see."

"It's a dicey neighborhood?"

"The neighborhood's the same as the day Three Star broke ground. If they need this level of coverage now, they needed it then. And they had no trouble out there until after they got it. Also, without being obvious about it, we've been looking at Glybenhall's finances."

"What's 'without being obvious'?"

"We've stuck to Mott Haven, which he offered us, and to the public record. But from what we can see, he looks to be short. A few bad decisions in the last few months. We can't tell how deep it goes, but it fits together. Guy needs money, hires people to put together some accidents, scams his insurance company. Things go way bad. He has to get rid of anyone who knows it's him."

A breeze caught the blossoms on the chestnut tree outside the window. They bobbed and wove, like fighters sizing each other up. *I know how you feel*, Charlie thought.

"We're just talking about a warrant, Mayor," Shapiro said. "If we can't find anything, that's that. But if there is something and it comes out later that we never acted—"

"No, you're right. You're right. I don't want the press to say we dragged our feet. You talked to the DAs' offices?"

"We haven't talked to anyone yet. We wanted you to hear it first."

"This would involve Manhattan and the Bronx both. Jesus, they'll be fighting over it."

"The crime we're focusing on, because the case is potentially strongest, is the shooting of the gangbanger, Kong. That's Manhattan."

"Hal Levine's a hundred and three. He was planning to retire when his term's up," the mayor said. "Lucky bastard, what a way to go out. Listen, don't talk to Levine without the Bronx DA's office there, too. Go for whichever case you think you can make, but keep Levine and Hernandez both in the loop. And make sure they know I told you to."

"Whatever you say."

"And the NYPD? Are they going to let you do it? Isn't this a collar they want for themselves?"

"Oh, it is. And because it's homicide it should by rights be theirs. But I figured if it had to be done you'd be happier if DOI did it. So you could salvage something in terms of public relations. I talked to the Chief of Department."

"You named names?"

"No, sir. Gave him a hypothetical. NYPD's willing to put it in the 'owed' column, pending the actual facts, of course, and if our spokespeople use language like 'joint operation.' "

Charlie sat peering into his long-empty coffee cup. "All right. Do what you have to do."

"I'm going to ask for simultaneous warrants in all jurisdictions. Glybenhall's office, home, summer home—"

"Do what you have to do," Charlie repeated. "Do what you'd *normally* do. But do it quietly. If you need an official statement, ask Walter to come down at his convenience. Bring him in the back door."

"We'll do that, Mayor."

Charlie gave up and stood. "All right. I'm going to keep my hands off. Christ, maybe I should consider a trip. Mongolia. Or Zanzibar. But obviously, keep in touch minute by minute."

"Will do."

"And Mark?"

"Sir?"

"Thanks for the heads-up."

Shapiro nodded, rising. "Part of our job."

After Shapiro and Lowry left, Charlie turned to Don. "We're fucked."

"It's bad," Don agreed. He lit the cigarette he'd been rolling around in his fingers. "But it may not be fatal."

"How can it not be?"

"You'll distance."

"Zanzibar, great."

"You'll deny having promised Glybenhall anything. In fact"—he waved the cigarette—"we'll put it out that that's why he did it. Because you *wouldn't* promise him anything. So he had to find a way to make sure he got his hands on Block A however he could. We can even hint you were leaning toward Corrington. I'll call Sue. That's what we'll have her say when the press starts calling for statements."

"Off the record," Charlie said.

"Naturally off the record. As though she shouldn't be saying it, except whoever she's talking to is her best buddy. Sue knows the drill. You'll have to do a lot of repair work with Glybenhall's friends. But on the plus side, we can spin this well in the black community. Corrington's people will love it. This could work out all right. You can replace the Upper East Side money with Upper West Side money."

"When the hell did you get to be Pollyanna?" The mayor threw open the door to Lena's office. "Get me Ford Corrington. Don't stop until you find him." He dropped into the chair behind his desk, swiveled it around, and stared up at the bright morning sky through the branches of the chestnut tree.

CHAPTER

58

Heart's Content

Again, Joe heard the ringing as he jumped down from the truck. He unlocked the door and grabbed for the phone, surprised to find that he was worrying, not that it was trouble, but that the ringing would stop before he reached it.

"Joe? It's me. Did you see the news?"

He paused, somewhere between relief and fear. Ann, calling with news. The last time he'd spoken to her was two days ago; she'd told him her friend Jen was dead, had been murdered.

"How are you? Are you okay?"

"I'm fine." She brushed that away with a single-minded briskness he knew well, and knew better than to contradict. "Well, have you? Seen the news?"

"No."

Silence. She was waiting for him to ask. Why didn't he? To confound her? No. Because he didn't care? Not that, either.

Because he did.

"We searched Walter Glybenhall's office," Ann said. "And his apartment, and the Southampton house, and the goddamn yacht. And his safe-deposit box. He can't produce the gun."

"You got a warrant for all that?"

"There are things you don't know. Things that happened since I was up there."

Joe looked out the window to the porch, where vines spiraled up the posts. The clematis had opened, perfect six-point burgundy stars. That's what had happened since she'd been up here.

"I talked to Greg, and to Mark Shapiro," Ann went on. "They talked to Charlie Barr."

"What did he say?"

"Summit meeting; I wasn't there. But next thing I knew, we had our warrants."

Joe tried to keep his attention on the sea-swell motion of the breeze moving through the grass. Still, he heard himself ask, "But you didn't find the gun?"

"Walter says it's gone from the bedside table where he keeps it and he doesn't know what happened to it."

"That's it?"

"He obviously hoped it would be. He expected us to say, 'Oh, well, in that case sorry to have bothered you.' When we didn't leave he called Charlie Barr to back us off. Charlie wouldn't take his call."

"But you still don't have the gun."

"We have something better."

The triumph in her voice glittered through the phone wire. Down the center of each clematis petal ran a thin, glowing line of white.

"Bling," she told him. "A god-awful gaudy platinum-and-diamond chain. And a ring."

"You think they're that kid's."

"Kong's."

"Are you sure?"

"No. We're checking it out. But it's so Walter: shoot the guy, and take his diamonds. Walter takes trophies. So he can prove who won."

"What does he say?"

"He says they were a gift, too ugly to wear but too valuable not to lock up."

"Any chance—"

"No! No no no! Who would give Walter Glybenhall anything like that? Joe, this is for real! We've got him. It's all over the news already. And wait until tomorrow."

"What's happening then?"

"Assuming the bling checks out, we're arresting him. Me and Luis Perez. Luis so NYPD can get in on the publicity, but it's a DOI collar. Do you get the New York papers up there?"

"No."

"I'll bring them up."

"Ann . . ."

"What?"

In the evening's cool some flowers had closed, waiting for daylight to show themselves again. Not the clematis, though. Once open, those blooms remained, through night, chill winds, clouds, and rain.

"See you later," Ann said, and was gone.

CHAPTER

59

Harlem: State Office Building

Edgar Westermann shook out the *Post* and folded it to the inside page to read every word of the story. Of course, there weren't all that many words, the *Post* being a paper for the workingman. But for that selfsame reason the pictures were much better than the ones in the *Times*. The best the *Times* had were the police crawling all over Glybenhall's yacht and mansion yesterday afternoon, and except for the grin on that blonde from DOI none of those was really worth spit. But this photo right here? Walter Glybenhall in handcuffs, being led away by some Puerto Rican cop and that same blonde?

Now *that* was worth a million bucks.

City Hall

"My God, Charlie! How could you let this happen?" Louise's eyes, blazing from her dressing-room mirror, walloped Charlie as he walked through the door. When she swung around to face him the impact was even worse.

"What did you expect me to do?"

"He's your friend!"

"Not if he killed someone, he's not."

"A gangbanger. Who was probably threatening him."

"What the hell makes you think that? And that would make it all right?"

"Don't get all holy with me, Charlie! You know what I mean! For Christ's sake, do you really believe Walter could have done this?"

"I don't know. I hope not. But I told you yesterday: there was enough evidence for a warrant. I might as well blow my political brains out as screw around with this."

"Are you sure you have any political brains? Did you have to arrest him?"

"*I* didn't arrest him. DOI and NYPD determined—"

"DOI doesn't determine *anything* without talking to you."

"All right, that's true. But what was I going to say? 'Leave him alone, he's a pal of mine'?"

"And what are you going to say now? 'Sorry you're in jail, Walter, but about that campaign contribution . . . '?"

"Don thinks we can make the money up."

"Oh, Don! Don's an idiot!" Louise spun to the mirror to fasten her earrings. Her eyes in the glass held his. When she turned to him again her voice was quiet, disappointed. "All this work, Charlie. We were this close."

"We could still be all right."

"Is that what Don says?"

"Yes."

She stood, her eyes softer now. She smoothed his lapels, leaned forward, and kissed him. Her perfume brought him a lazy velvet evening, a tropical garden, banks of flowers whose names he didn't know rolling away into the purple twilight.

He folded her in his arms and stroked her hair.

Holding him, she whispered, "Don's wrong."

Heart's Content

It was morning again; again, Joe woke beside Ann.

When she'd come north last night, arms full of the New York City late editions, he'd tried to tell her she couldn't stay. "Joe," she'd said, "if you didn't want me to stay you would've told me not to come."

And that was true.

So again in the pale dawn he searched the ridge for the glow announcing the sun, and he felt Ann stir. The blanket rippled and shifted as she slid a hand across his hip and nuzzled his neck.

"See?" she whispered. "I was right."

He found himself laughing. "You're always right."

"Only about some things. You were right about Walter. He didn't spend ten minutes in jail." Her fingers wandered him both tentatively and surely, an amazing mismatch, like her eyes. "Listen. I need to be in the office today. Dotting and crossing. So I have to leave soon."

"It's Sunday," he said, as if she didn't know that, as if he hadn't once spent Sundays in the office himself, as if he'd rather she didn't leave.

"Yes, well, duty calls. But before I go, do you think . . . ?"

"With that? All men do."

This time it was she who laughed.

Harlem: Frederick Douglass Boulevard

"You taken to corralling the congregation to make sure folks get to church, Ray?"

Ford sauntered up the avenue, hands in the pockets of his Sunday slacks. A stickiness waited in the warm, hazy air, about to blossom into full-blown, shirt-wrinkling damp.

Ray fell into step beside him. "Only when I want a private word with them."

"I'd listen to you anytime. Right now I'm feeling especially benevolent."

"I know that, son. That's why I wanted to speak to you."

"Ray! You about to put the bite on me? I told you I'd put your Activist's Library pitch in our newsletter—"

"Nothing like that. Though you find yourself with cash got no home, we've got shelves full of Audubon Ballroom papers could use a curator."

"How about I lend you an intern?"

"You got one you can spare?"

"A volunteer from Columbia. I had a full schedule for her, but truth is, I just picked up three more volunteers, behind this Glybenhall thing. Can't beat those rare times when you look like the underdog *and* the winner."

"I'd be appreciative. But it's those rare times I want to talk to you about, Ford. You've been a hard man to get to, last day or so."

"Sorry about that. A lot of reporters calling, to get my point of view on Walter Glybenhall."

"I can see that every time I pick up a paper or turn on the TV. Ford Corrington's face, Ford Corrington's name."

"Uh-oh. Do I hear a sermon? Am I rejoicing too much in my enemy's downfall?"

"If I had your immortal soul on my mind, I suppose I might make mention of it. I intend to preach on Proverbs 16:18 later, anyway."

"I'll be sure to pay attention."

"See that you do. But that's not it. Just strikes me, son, there's some danger in all this."

"Danger of Ford Corrington getting too big for his britches?"

"Besides that. Way the headlines read this morning, Charlie Barr gave you the key to the candy store, left Glybenhall outside with his nose against the glass."

"You can see why Charlie wants it to look that way. Get as much distance between himself and Glybenhall as he can."

"Sure, but it don't sit right."

"Because it's not true?"

"That's between Charlie and the Lord. It's just, it stands you worrisomely close to Hizzoner."

"In this case, I think the trade-off's worth it. Charlie's just about publicly promised us Block A now."

"Only if nothing goes wrong. Mud starts flying, you could get hit."

"You don't mean 'mud,' do you?" Ford grinned.

"In the Bible, they call it 'dung.' "

"I'll keep it in mind, Ray. But I don't know exactly what to do about it. I didn't plant the leaks the reporters are writing from."

"He told you it was coming, though? Charlie did? Asked if you'd go along, help him out?"

"Yes."

"Well, son," Ray said, "I just hope there's no snake hiding in this high cotton."

Sutton Place

With the Boxster's top down, Ann raced south through crayon colors: daffodil sun in an azure sky, crimson flowers dotting emerald hills. She'd tied her hair back but the wind pulled tendrils loose and whipped them around her face.

On the Autobahn at thirteen, with her dad beside her, she'd opened his Ferrari to 105. Her mother had been horrified when they told her. Jen had been wildly jealous; she'd begged Ann to swipe the keys and take her for a ride. Ann's dad's only comment was that if Ann planned to drive like that she might consider short hair. Less than a year later he'd plowed the Ferrari into a stand of pines. Ann had never stopped driving like this, and she wore her hair long.

In the noise of the wind, she almost missed the phone ringing. By the time she pressed the button it had gone to voice mail: Greg Lowry. She raised the Boxster's top, casting the interior into shadow, and hit speed-dial.

"Greg? It's Ann. Good morning."

"I just left you a message."

"I know, but I didn't hear it yet. Tell me."

"Where are you?"

"Just south of the Tappan Zee. Heading in."

A pause. "What are you doing there?"

"Visiting a friend. What's up?"

"Glybenhall's lawyer called. He has the gun."

"What? Say again?"

"Glybenhall found the gun. The lawyer's bringing it in."

"The Wilson? What do you mean, he found it?"

"In the back of a closet."

"We searched the closets."

"As soon as it gets here I'm sending it over to the NYPD for testing."

"I'll meet you there."

When Ann pushed through the door of the NYPD lab she found Perez there, too. The cop was leaning on the wall while Greg Lowry scowled in an orange molded chair.

"We're running it again," Lowry said, skipping any greeting. "To be sure. But it looks like it's not the one."

It took her a second, and even then all she could manage was "What?"

"The rifling's clear," Perez said. "We don't need a second test. It's not our gun."

"Hell," Ann breathed. "But it's Glybenhall's? The one the permit's for?"

Lowry nodded. Perez shrugged.

"And tell me again where he said he found it all of a sudden?"

"In a guest bedroom closet in the Hamptons house," Lowry said.

"Greg, that's absurd! We had a guy out there and NYPD had two! They searched every inch—"

"Were you there?"

"Me? No, I did his office."

"Then you don't know. They may have goofed off. Maybe it was lunchtime. Maybe Glybenhall's French maid distracted them with margaritas by the pool."

"Not my guys," Perez growled.

"You weren't there either." Lowry stood. "There's no way around it: this is a mighty fuckup. If we'd tested the gun two days ago we wouldn't have arrested him."

"If he'd produced it two days ago we would have tested it!" Ann objected. "And even without it—"

She stopped as the door opened. A plump lab tech gave them an abashed smile and handed Lowry a printout. "Sorry," he said.

Lowry stared at the paper. "Shit," he muttered. Stuffing the sheet into Ann's hand, he stalked out.

Sutton Place

"Princess," said Perez, "what the hell happened?"

"What happened? For God's sake, he didn't use this gun. He shot Kong with some other gun—"

"This is the one on his license."

"So he has one that's contraband! How surprising would that be? He gave us this to throw us off."

"Why wait? If he gave it to us two days ago, like your boss says, it would've saved him a lot of embarrassment. If we have it, we stop searching, we don't find the bling."

"Maybe he forgot where he put it. Maybe the French maid moved it. Who the hell knows? But we *do* have the bling. It was him and everything else still points to him. We've got him, Luis, and I'm not letting him go. We've *got* him."

Perez shook his head. "Princess, I hope to hell you're right."

She was wrong.

The first to recant, early Monday morning, was the jeweler, Levi Morgenstern.

"I told you I *thought* so," he said. "I said I needed a few days to make sure."

Ann, in answer to Morgenstern's call, had gone up to the cluttered third-floor warren on Forty-seventh Street that served as the jeweler's office, showroom, and workspace. She stood before his desk as he said,

"Those pieces, the chain and the ring, plus also the pendant with the *K* on it, they did look like the ones I made for the gentleman."

"Gentleman?" Ann snorted.

The jeweler blinked. He was shorter than she, his white shirt tieless and buttoned to the neck, his black yarmulke bobby-pinned to his thinning hair. "Here, my customers are all gentlemen," he reproved mildly. He gestured to a wall crowded with photos of lesser-known rappers and minor NBA players.

"And now you've looked more closely at the pieces?"

"The pieces, you didn't leave. I looked at the photographs you gave me. I compared carefully. The authorities say it's important, who wants to make a mistake? I'm telling you, these are three good copies but they're not my pieces."

"You mean they're fake?"

"The stones? For that I would have to examine the real thing. From the pictures, I suppose they could be diamonds, the chains could be platinum and gold. But I didn't make them."

"But Kong did come here?"

"Yes, of course. And I made him some fine pieces. Which someone must have seen, to copy like this. But the pieces you have, these are not the ones that belonged to Mr. Kong."

"You're sure?"

"From the pictures—"

"I'll bring back the pieces themselves. So you can look again."

He shrugged. "Bring, if you want. I'll look. But if you're asking me, I have to tell you: this is what it is."

"Ann—"

"He got to him, Greg."

"Sit down."

"What's the difference if I sit or stand? Walter Glybenhall—"

"Sit down!"

She met his glare and abruptly sat.

"Sure," he said, and his voice seemed to have weight, actual tonnage in each word. "Got to him. It's possible."

"For God's sake! Even if they are fake! What are the chances of Walter Glybenhall having *copies* of Kong's bling? A diamond-crusted chain and a ring big enough to choke a goddamn horse, just happening to be in his safe? And the *K* O'Doul found at the Mott Haven site—"

"Dammit, Ann, there's no connection between that *K* and Glybenhall except in your mind! And Glybenhall doesn't have to explain why he has copies of Kong's bling. If those pieces aren't actually Kong's we lose a big link between the two of them."

"How about this: Kong sold the real stuff off, had these copies made, and was wearing them when Walter shot him. It's possible."

"Oh, sure. And it's also possible we arrested one of the most powerful men in New York and we have *no goddamn case!*"

"No, it's not! Dammit, Greg! We were careful. We checked and cross-checked. Everything fit. If it were anyone but Glybenhall we'd have gone to the DA with *half* of what we had!"

"And if it were anyone but Glybenhall nobody would give a damn that the case is falling apart."

"That's pretty cynical."

"Your ass is on the line, Ann. Your buddy Perez's, too. And Mark Shapiro's. And *mine.*" He stood and began pacing. Ann almost sprang up to join him, but he hit her with a look that spoke very loudly about whose office it was. Chafing, she stayed in her seat. "I thought going after Glybenhall was crazy from the start," Lowry said. "But you got to me. What you had sounded solid. I went out on a limb to talk Shapiro and the mayor into it and now—! *If it were anybody else.* Well, it's not anybody else! You may think you've seen trouble in your life but I'm telling you, none of it comes near what you'll see if this blows up in our faces."

"We had a case," she insisted. "We still have one."

"Then get the hell out of here!" He backhanded the air as though chasing a fly. "Get to work. Double-check and triple-check and make damn sure there are no more surprises. If we—" His phone rang. He mashed the speakerphone button. "What?"

"It's Detective Perez," said the receptionist defensively. "He's looking for Ann. I told him to leave a message, but he says it's urgent. He says there's a problem."

Harlem: Frederick Douglass Boulevard

Blowfish came strolling into Ford's office fifteen minutes late, like any powerful executive who'd called a meeting. "Nice of ya'll to come." He flashed his gold-capped smile around the room.

"Skip the bullshit," Luis Perez snapped. "I'm this close to taking you in."

"And I'm closer," said Ann Montgomery, beside Perez. Tom Underhill said nothing, but he didn't look any happier than the other two.

"Fuck you say, taking me in? I ain't done nothing and I ain't gotta be here." Blowfish spun and headed for the door.

"All right, that's enough!" Ford stood. "Blowfish, these people are here because you wanted them here. You have something to say, say it."

"Fuck that! This asshole—"

"Skip it, Blowfish," Ford told him calmly. "Or I'll swear you were trespassing, and someone will arrest you."

"*Trespassing?* You are fucking shitting me."

"It would get you a few nights in jail. Nothing you couldn't handle, I'm sure, but you probably have better things to do. So go ahead and say whatever you made everyone come here to hear."

Blowfish rubbed his chin, appearing to consider this. "Well," he drawled. "Like I already told *Mr. Corrington.* It ain't him."

"Not who?" Perez's question came through clenched teeth.

"That guy. White bread with the fucked-up name."

"Walter Glybenhall?"

"Yeah, him. The dude I saw with my man Kong, it ain't him."

"You identified his picture, Blowfish. You picked him out of a lineup!"

"Yeah, well, must've been a bad picture. And that lineup—shit, all them tall, pointy-nose white dudes look alike. Know what I'm saying? Now I seen him on TV couple times. I'm telling you, it ain't him."

"You're lying," Montgomery said. "Perjury's a bad crime, Blowfish. It could get you some serious time."

"Shit. This what a citizen get, trying to help out?"

"How much did he pay you to change your story?"

"No one ain't paid me nothing. Shit, guy like me get nervous in a cop shop. Them pictures, I thought they was the dude I saw. Then one of them fuckers in the lineup look like the picture. So I pick him. 'Cause that's what you wanted." Blowfish grinned. "But now I been seein' Glyben-what-the-fuck on TV, like 24/7. And word: he ain't the guy. It just ain't him."

CHAPTER

66

Harlem: State Office Building

Edgar Westermann was enjoying himself. Long time since he'd stood in the back row at anybody's press event, and longer—maybe since never— that he'd stood up with a white man like this. Something to be said, he had to admit, for being able to just watch the reporters' faces, not have to decide what to say next or how to play anyone. All he needed to do was look sorrowful, determined, and outraged all at once, which in all humility he could say he had down. After that it would be up to Walter Glybenhall, and damn, he had a feeling the boy was going to be giving it his all.

City Hall

Don Zalensky blew into the mayor's private office.

"Where's the fire?" Charlie, reading a briefing on an upcoming union negotiation, looked up.

"Glybenhall's holding a press conference." Don yanked open the armoire doors and clicked the TV on. Walter Glybenhall flashed into view, standing at a podium in front of his midtown office building.

Out of nowhere, Charlie had the election-night jitters. "Jesus Christ. Is that Edgar with him? What the fuck's that?"

Don slipped a cigarette from his pocket. "The bald guy on the other side's his lawyer. George Bradhurst."

"—my recent arrest," Glybenhall was saying. "It saddens me to be forced into this. But what choice did I have? To permit the vast power of the City of New York to be used in a witch hunt, without vigorous protest, would be irresponsible. If accountability is demanded of the private sector, how much more must that be true of government?"

"The son of a bitch is quoting me!"

Glybenhall looked straight into the camera, as though he'd heard Charlie. "You all know me. You know how deeply I care about this, my adopted city, my home, and how hard I've worked—and the resources I've expended—for civic improvement. The Mott Haven project, in one of the city's most blighted neighborhoods, is a private development. I've taken no city money, and frankly spared no expense, in an effort to afford poor New Yorkers what rich New Yorkers have always had: safe, functional housing.

"As work proceeded on that site, a series of mishaps occurred which, anyone could see, were not accidents. The Department of Investigation, which reports to Mayor Barr, assigned an investigator to examine this series of crimes. Of which my project was the *target*. Unfortunately, this young woman has an irrational hatred of me stemming from an incident in her youth in which I was in no way involved but for which she has always held me to blame. Whether the Department of Investigation knew about her obsession when the assignment was made, I can't say. They do seem to have had some idea of how difficult she can be. Her career there had a promising beginning, but in recent years she's been assigned unimportant cases, where, presumably, her headstrong behavior could create little trouble. And then, out of nowhere, she was handed the—I would think—somewhat delicate assignment of investigating me. Why DOI made this assignment I don't know, but I want to assure you I'm not among those who believe it was in the support of any sinister agenda.

"In any case"—Glybenhall peered around, taking obvious care to find each camera—"whatever DOI knew or didn't know, it's certain the mayor himself was informed of this young woman's problem." Behind Glybenhall, Edgar Westermann nodded somberly. "Still she remained on the case, with the sorry result all New York has watched over these past few days. There is, of course, the damage to my good name. But much worse, five workingmen and a firefighter were injured; a woman is, tragically, dead; as are two young men in Harlem, one of whom *I* was accused of killing! The workers on my jobsite continue in peril until the madman behind these acts is apprehended—and the city has squandered the taxpayers' time and resources persecuting *me*.

"This administration took office with promises of candor and accountability. Those promises seem to have been less than truthful. On a personal level, I thought I had reason to consider the mayor my friend. It's distressing to find my friendship has meant so little.

"For all these reasons, I feel I must take action. At the very least, perhaps I can prevent this sort of governmental abuse from victimizing other innocent citizens."

Glybenhall gave the cameras one more look, then stepped aside to let Westermann take the podium.

"As you all know," Westermann declared, "Walter Glybenhall and I don't have much we agree on. Our visions for New York"—he turned to look at Glybenhall—"aren't the same." Back to the camera: "But we're talking here about a serious miscarriage of justice. Now normally I wouldn't get involved, something like this. No offense, Walter, but I have more pressing concerns than what happens to society people. The kind of resources Mr. Glybenhall has, he doesn't need my help. New

York's poor, New York's minorities—communities that don't *have* much in the way of their own resources and don't *get* much from the city they work so hard to support—that's where I concentrate.

"But here, you see, I'm involved already. I was the one went to the mayor, told him about Ann Montgomery, the problem she had with Walter Glybenhall. Just seemed so wrong to me. Once you have knowledge, you've got to act, can't just sit back. And black or white, wrong's wrong. I thought, if Mayor Barr knew, he'd want to hurry to fix things up.

"Well, Hizzoner didn't hurry, and he didn't move slow to do it, neither. He just sat back.

"Now, Mr. Glybenhall's mentioned a 'sinister agenda.' I don't like to hear that kind of talk. I don't like to think anything the city calls 'evidence' is anything else. But black people been railroaded like this for hundreds of years. Might say we're sensitive to it. So when I saw what was happening, I stepped up, offered to help Mr. Glybenhall out. The outrage perpetrated on Walter Glybenhall is identical to that perpetrated on young black men every day. If Mr. Glybenhall's *vis*-ibility is what it takes to force the city into *account*-ability and *response*-ibility, then so be it!"

Keeping his distance from Glybenhall and his eye on the crowd, Westermann stepped away.

Glybenhall's attorney adjusted the microphone. "On Mr. Glybenhall's instructions I have filed multiple lawsuits. We're seeking aggregate damages in the amount of fifty million dollars: forty from the city—specifically, NYPD and DOI—and five each from the investigator in question and from Mayor Barr."

There was more—details, a brief Q & A—and Charlie watched the whole thing, though he kept getting the odd feeling he might be hearing another language, where the sounds seemed like English words but had completely different meanings. When the new CBS guy asked what "sinister agenda" the city might have had, though, Charlie needed no translator for Walter's answer.

"All I can do is speculate, of course." Glybenhall sounded restrained and reasonable. "There were reports in the press soon after my arrest that my motive was insurance fraud. As even the most cursory of looks would show, my financial position is as strong as ever. I am, and remain, a very wealthy man. Other rumors circulated that the situation somehow involved a city-owned building site in Harlem that I've been interested in, but which the mayor has apparently, quite improperly, promised to another developer. Perhaps, if anything more than ignorance is operating here, it might be a wish to ensure that developer's control over this valuable property. Although as I say, this is pure speculation."

Lena had come into the room. She'd stood and watched with Charlie and Don, calm, efficient, waiting for instructions. A great comfort, Lena was, during a crisis. Why didn't Charlie feel comforted now?

Don switched the set off. "Lena, get Sue Trowbridge in here."

"And the Corporation Counsel." Charlie had to shake himself into action and was a second late with that, but no one seemed to notice. "Otherwise hold my calls." The phone was ringing already. "That son of a bitch. Son of a bitch! Who does he think he is? No notification? No phone call? Just slapped it on us, and I hear about it from a *press conference?*"

"Charlie?" Lena called. "McClean from the Corporation Counsel's office, line three."

"Not on the phone. Tell him to get over here, ten minutes. *From a press conference?* Lena! Get Shapiro and Lowry, and tell Lowry to bring Montgomery. Here, one hour. And *Edgar?*" Charlie turned to Don. "That pious bastard. Who was it who fucked up my chances of doing anything about Montgomery? And now he's kissing *Walter's* ass?"

"Edgar's jumping ship," said Don. "He came to you to make sure the case against Glybenhall got made. Now he sees it can't be, he wants to be on the winning side. For something like this"—he pointed his cigarette at the TV—"Glybenhall will owe Edgar big."

"It's a fucking unholy alliance, Walter and Edgar. Jesus, it's sick."

"Glybenhall's drawing a line. Them on one side, you and Corrington on the other."

"Sick," the mayor said again. "*Walter's* friendship's been abused? Damage to his good name! He gets *off* on notoriety. His suit has no basis and he *at least* could have goddamn notified me!"

"Maybe he was afraid you'd talk him out of it. Based on your long and close friendship."

"Maybe he was afraid I'd kill him." The mayor threw the window open and leaned on the sill, breathing shakily. The air held a strange sweetness, from the blooms on one of the trees. Which the hell kind of tree was it, that blossomed as freely through last year's drought as this year's rain? Charlie wished he knew.

Harlem: Frederick Douglass Boulevard

When Ford walked into his office he found all hell had broken loose.

"Every TV station and newspaper in New York called." Yvonnia handed him a stack of phone messages.

Ford stopped and stared at the slips. "Why?"

"Didn't you hear Walter Glybenhall's press conference?"

"No. I was with a kid. Fill me in."

Before she could, the phone rang. She answered it looking fierce, but her face relaxed. She put the caller on hold. "It's Reverend Holdsclaw."

"You hear Glybenhall's press conference?" Ray demanded as soon as Ford picked up the phone.

"No, and apparently I've missed something big."

"It's the talk of the town, son. Everyone wants to know is it true you had a deal with the mayor and were you in on settin' up Glybenhall?"

"Setting him up?"

"Seems he's suing the city. That Montgomery woman, from DOI? He says she's been after him for twenty years."

"Lot of people must have had it in for him for longer than that."

"He's saying that's why the evidence was bad."

In his mind, Ford saw Ann Montgomery in the garden next door, wiping a little boy's mud from his hands. "What's he suing for? False arrest?"

"Oh, more than that. Where you come in is, he's suggesting the point of the whole thing was to get rid of him so 'another developer' could have the Block A site."

"He said that?"

"Of course not. He said he *couldn't* say that, not having the facts and all."

"Oh, Lord."

"In case you're interested, consensus around here seems to be, if you *were* in on it, you're a pretty smart fella and the fact that it blew up like this just proves you made two mistakes."

"What would those be?"

"One: getting into a conspiracy with white folks. They'll screw you every time. And two, going up against Walter Glybenhall. Even white folks can't win that."

Sutton Place

"Do I have to *tell* any of you how bad this is?"

Charlie Barr's red face and scalp radiated heat Ann could swear she felt.

"No, sir," said Mark Shapiro.

"I just came out of a meeting with McClean from the Corporation Counsel's office," the mayor said. "They're leaning toward settling."

"Settling?" Greg Lowry objected. "The suit's only a few hours old. They can't even have studied it yet."

"They've managed to pick out a few salient points," the mayor shot back caustically. "Basically we're accused of conspiracy to fuck Walter up. Our only possible defense, according to McClean, is that we were all too goddamn stupid to see what was going on."

"Mayor, nothing was 'going on,' " Lowry tried.

"Walter's saying we used a goddamn stalker to investigate him! That the evidence was distorted or downright *faked*—"

"I—" Ann tried, but Lowry cut her off.

"You'll get your chance, Ann. Mayor, we talked about this. We all felt it was important to do whatever we'd do if the suspect weren't a prominent citizen."

"Like use an investigator who's obsessed with him? You'd do that for anybody, is that what you're saying?"

"Ann's one of DOI's top people," Lowry answered. "We didn't know about her past with Glybenhall but frankly I don't see—"

"Oh, save the full-confidence bullshit for the press!" The mayor shifted his glare to Ann. "How much of what Walter's saying about you is true? And"—to Lowry—"why the hell didn't you know it?"

"There's nothing for him to know. It's not true," Ann said.

"Your mother—"

"My mother had an affair with Glybenhall twenty years ago. When I—when my father found out he went to confront them and skidded on an icy road."

"Walter says you've always blamed him."

"My father was driving too fast. He always drove too fast."

"And ever since—"

"Ever since, I went to college, and law school, and worked at Legal Aid, at the DA's office, and now here! Do you see anything that remotely looks like me stalking him?"

"Do *I* see? I haven't looked! I hope to God you have?" The mayor turned to Shapiro, who nodded.

"We're checking now."

Ann felt her face flame but kept quiet: of course they were, and if they were good they'd look under every rock she'd ever touched.

"Now? You never checked before?"

"A thorough background was done when she was hired, of course," Shapiro answered stiffly. "Under the previous Commissioner. I have that report, if you want to see it."

"And I told you, Mayor, I did a background check of my own on Ann when I came in," Lowry said. "There was no evidence of anything out of order."

"On me?" Ann said. "When you came in?"

"You were Joe Cole's partner," Lowry told her evenly. "You should have resigned, and you wouldn't."

"What you're doing now better turn up what she eats for breakfast," Charlie Barr told Shapiro. "I want to know every traffic ticket, jaywalking, every fucking dirty look she ever gave anybody. I'd say fire her but it's too soon, it would look like we're admitting something. Issue a full-confidence-in-my-staff statement. Like the one Sue Trowbridge is writing for me about *you* right now. Say she's on desk duty pending results of an internal investigation which you're sure will show what a saint she is. And find a way to explain how we bought that pile-of-crap evidence."

"It wasn't crap!" Ann exploded. "Every piece of it was good. Glybenhall got to the witnesses, that's what happened. He bought everyone off!"

The mayor turned to her, ice in his eyes. "You," he said, "clean out your desk. After a decent interval, you're gone. And I hope you have five million dollars you can spare. Because if the Corp Counsel settles with

Walter, the deal is, Walter gets a shitload of city money, he drops his action against me, and you're on your own."

"You can't—!"

"I goddamn can! You're lucky I'm not screaming for your hide. Don't push me." He looked at Shapiro and Lowry. "And you two may not have long, either. Even if she's guilty of nothing more than unbelievable stupidity, you never should have put her on this case. You should have known."

"What? That her mother had an affair with Glybenhall twenty years ago? How?" Lowry asked.

"Edgar Westermann knew! He sat in that chair and told me! I wish to hell he'd gone to you two instead. I wish to hell I'd fucking listened! Ah, shit," the mayor breathed. "Shit, shit, shit." He stood and stalked across the room. When he reached the door to his office he turned. "Dammit! You should have known."

chapter 70

Heart's Content

Joe stopped short and felt his smile fade. At first, turning into his drive-way to find the glossy Boxster parked on the raggedy gravel, he thought Ann had come up in victory. It had been four days since she'd headed back to the city to start tightening the noose on Walter Glybenhall: evidence-gathering, follow-ups with witnesses, and no doubt media in-terviews and pats on the back. He hadn't heard from her since, but he was a hard guy to get hold of. A couple of times he'd almost called her but he needed to pull the blackberries that wound around the holly-hocks, threatening to choke them. And near the house he had herbs to plant: rosemary, oregano, lavender, three kinds of thyme. A little use-less, because he didn't cook. But their traces in the air in the midday sun would be worth the effort. And though most herbs would probably not make it through the winter in this climate, some would. Those would flower next spring, filling this garden with butterflies and bees.

By the time he came in each evening, sweaty and exhausted, by the time he'd showered and had something to eat, it was late to call, and he hadn't.

So when he found Ann's car in the driveway he thought she'd come up to share her triumph. But then he saw her face.

"I've been sitting out here since noon." Ann's voice held no emo-tion.

Ann, in one spot for hours. "I did that when I first found this place," he said. "Sometimes all day."

"You can see the shadows move."

The mica veins sparkled in the boulder at the far end of the yard. A breeze passed over the grass like a single wave rolling to shore.

Joe sat beside her. "Tell me."

"It fell apart." She rubbed at something on her knee. "Walter got to everyone. All the witnesses, he bought them all off. They took back their statements, one after another. The DA dropped the charges, and Walter's suing for millions. The city. The mayor. And me." Her eyes were shining, but with tears. "Joe? You were right. He can't be stopped. He can get away with anything."

She took him through the past four days in a dull monotone. He listened, watching the sunlight slip from the grass. When she was finished he stood.

"I need to do this," he said. "You want to help?"

"Do what?"

"Transplant the rhododendron." He left the porch for the shed, brought a shovel to the stand of leggy shrubs. He drove the sharp edge in, rocking it forward and back, cutting a moat.

"Why can't they stay there?" Ann had come up behind him. She still spoke in that odd, dull voice.

"Too much sun, too much wind. They need a quieter spot."

"If it's a bad place for them, then why did they grow there?"

"They didn't; someone put them in. They must have figured anything this flamboyant belongs where the action is. But not these." He lifted the shovel, chopped into a tangle of grass.

"What do you want me to do?"

"I'll find you a shirt and some jeans first. You'll mess those clothes up."

She looked at herself. "Screw these. These are work clothes. I'm on desk duty."

Her words shivered with anger. He nodded. He'd been on desk duty all through his trial. When you were on desk duty no one wanted you anywhere near your desk. You were supposed to stay home and not contaminate the office with trouble germs.

"Grab hold there," he said. "Pull it, twist it, whatever you need to do to persuade it to come loose."

She did as he said, while he dug under the bush, cutting the smaller roots. "It doesn't want to come out," she said.

"It doesn't know how happy it's going to be."

By the time they were through, the sun had dropped deep into the trees and the wind carried a chill as though it had traveled across a distant ice field to reach them. Joe tamped damp earth around the shocked stems, dragged the hose over and soaked the roots. He rinsed his hands and offered the running water to Ann.

"You're a mess," he said as she splashed water on her face, her dirty hands leaving a wash of mud across her cheeks.

"And I stink, too."

"You can take a shower. I'll make dinner."

"You learned to cook?"

"Roast beef sandwiches."

When she came out of the bathroom she wore his Yankees sweatshirt and a pair of his jeans. The pants were six inches too long, the waist bunching up in a cinched leather belt.

"I want socks," she said. "It's cold up here."

He brought her a pair from his dresser drawer and watched her damp hair fall across her face as she bent to pull them on.

Seated at the table, he popped open a beer, poured half for her and half for himself.

"I'm betting this is the first time you've had beer in a glass since you've lived here," she said.

He nodded but didn't answer, hit by the oddness of "since you've lived here." He hadn't thought of himself as "living here." It was just where he was.

"I've been thinking," he said. "I have a question."

She looked up.

"Sonny O'Doul."

Her eyes darkened. "I thought this was there's-nothing-you-can-do-so-let's-work-in-the-garden therapy."

"How did he know to call you?"

She shrugged. "About the chain he found? Why wouldn't he? DOI had been all over that site for two weeks."

"Dennis Graham was all over that site. You hadn't been up there since Lowry transferred you guys around, had you?"

"No. But so what? Maybe he called Dennis and Dennis told him to call me. Maybe he called the office and reception told him."

"It was *after* Lowry told you to drop it and turn everything over to the NYPD. Standard procedure as soon as a case is transferred, reception's instructed where to direct people. So we don't—so DOI doesn't step on another agency's jurisdiction. Did Lowry change that procedure?"

"No. He'd already told them. He said so. But Joe, this was O'Doul. He'd have wanted to cover his butt with DOI, or lord it over us or something. Maybe he insisted."

"If reception couldn't shake him they'd have passed him to Lowry, not to you, so Lowry could blow him off personally."

"So maybe they did. Maybe Greg told him to call Luis Perez and O'Doul said no, I have something I want DOI to see."

"Then Lowry would have known O'Doul called. Either he'd have gone up to see O'Doul himself, or he'd have told you to. Either way, there wouldn't have been a message from O'Doul on your voice mail."

Ann sat for a silent moment. Then she hefted her bag onto her lap. She rummaged through it, pulled out her cell phone. "Dennis? It's Ann."

Joe drank his beer, listening to the one-sided conversation. "Thanks," Ann said. "No, I know. Yes, you're probably right. I just hope it blows over *soon*. I'll do that, thanks. Well, actually, there is something. I was wondering, Dennis, did Sonny O'Doul call you last week? I mean, did he not know you'd been transferred? No, of course not, there wasn't any reason you should have. But wouldn't that mean if he had something to say he'd have called you, not me? Did you give him my name?" Her brow furrowed as she leaned over the phone. "All right, Dennis, I appreciate it. Yes, I will. Thanks."

She clicked the phone off and looked up. "O'Doul never called him."

"So how did he know?" Joe asked. "To go to you?"

Sutton Place

Ann swung the Boxster alongside the guard booth on the Mott Haven site and flashed her badge. The guard shrugged; badge or not, there was no place to park, and he pointed her back to the street. *In your dreams, buster.* She wheeled around in the mud and pulled across the rear of a 4Runner. Let the s.o.b. who owned it wait until she was done.

With the guard's shout filling the early-morning air, she took the steps, threw open the cheap door, and stalked through the trailer. She palmed the badge to Sonny O'Doul and the three men in his office. "Beat it," she said to the others, and when they didn't move she said, "All right, stay. The more the better. I have an arrest quota to fill."

"What the fuck—" O'Doul began.

"Why did you call me, Sonny?"

"I didn't call you. Get the fuck out of here," he yelled to the other men. "Last week!"

"*Last* week?" O'Doul got up and slammed his door. "About the chain? I called you because I found that fucking chain. What the hell's your problem, lady?"

"Who told you to call me?"

"I called your fucking office and they told me you was on this case. I—"

"Bull, Sonny. You didn't call my office and you didn't call the guy from my office you'd already spoken to. Dennis Graham. Why didn't you call Graham?"

"He wasn't on the case anymore! Jesus, lady—"

"How did you know that?"

A heartbeat of hesitation, just enough. "I don't remember. Someone must've told me. Who the fuck cares? I seen in the news how Glybenhall's suing your ass. You fucked up bad, lady. So now you're looking to find someone to hang it on? Get out. I don't have time for this shit, I got work to do."

"All right. Whatever you want. I'll subpoena your phone records. Here, home, your cell phone. Maybe I'll find what I'm looking for. It'd be too bad if I also found a call to a bookie or something, though."

"What the fuck are you talking about?" Sweat beaded on O'Doul's lip as if her words had raised the temperature in the room.

"You used to play the horses, didn't you? That's right, I thought I remembered that. What does that hurt, a little action? Nothing that I can see, but it *is* a parole violation. What do you have left, Sonny? Three years?"

"You can't. You can't subpoena nothing. You're in the fucking dog-house: it's all over the news."

"My boss will do it. If it helps clear DOI's name, you bet he'll do it in a second." Actually, it was completely possible Greg Lowry wouldn't touch any of this with a stick. But Ann said it as though it were stone fact.

"You think you're so smart."

"No, I don't, but I'm way smarter than you. And I have smarter friends. One of my friends figured out that one of *your* friends is telling you things that maybe you didn't know."

"What, that this was your case? Since when is that some kind of secret? So what if someone did tell me?"

"Nice try, but forget it. Because the real question's why. First you tell me who, then you tell me why." She leaned forward, fists on his desk. *"Who?"*

"Fuck you."

Ann took out her cell phone. She'd punched three buttons before O'Doul growled, "Wait!"

She looked up.

"You're not near as smart as you think, lady. And your asshole friends, either."

She pointed at the phone.

"He's playing you." O'Doul's smile was a poisoned gleam. "And you know what? You're fucked. He got what he wanted. You think you're the cat but you're the mouse. No. You know what, lady? You're the mother-fucking *cheese*."

"You're not making sense, Sonny, and I have no time for it."

"He thinks I can't figure it out. 'Just do it, Sonny, do what I tell you.'

Well, fuck him. I see what's going on. And I'm not taking this fall for nobody. But you are, lady. Ask me, you were all along."

"For who, Sonny? Goddamn you, for who? Someone in my office? Some rat at DOI?"

"DOI?" O'Doul laughed. "I don't know squat about that. Maybe everyone at DOI is crooked as a dog's hind leg. But so what? Even if they was all straight, they couldn't save your ass. Not from Walter Glybenhall. No way in hell."

chapter 72

Heart's Content

"Cole! Break time! You want coffee?" Palmer's shout carried over the traffic.

"Black, large. I'll come with you. I have to make a call." Joe caught up with Palmer and they crossed the road to the diner.

"They got those mile-high pies," Palmer said. "Look at those things."

"Taste like cardboard, though." Joe stopped at the pay phone inside the door, fishing in his pocket for change.

"All that dust I been eating, I couldn't tell the difference." Palmer headed to the counter and Joe dropped quarters into the phone.

A ring and a half; then, "Ann Montgomery."

"It's Joe." He turned to the window, as though something were going on he didn't want Palmer to know about. As though Palmer, hitting on a gum-cracking waitress while he placed four men's orders, gave a damn.

"Joe? Where are you? Aren't you working?" He could hear a tension—not excitement, something darker—in Ann's voice.

"Coffee break. How'd it go? Were we right?"

"Something's going on, for sure. Listen to this: O'Doul swears he got my name from Walter."

"From Glybenhall himself?"

"He said I thought I was the cat but I'm the mouse. Then he said no, I'm the cheese."

"That's a lot of imagination for Sonny. What the hell does it mean?"

"I don't know. He suddenly clammed up, like he was sorry he told me that much."

"Why did he?"

"I threatened to bring Lowry down on him and put him back inside."

Joe felt something he'd never have expected: a pang of sympathy for Sonny O'Doul. "All right, but I don't get it. O'Doul's claiming Glybenhall personally talks to him? And how did Glybenhall know it was you?"

"Well, I'd been to Walter already, so that's how *he* knew. But it's way out of character for him to speak to anyone as low on the food chain as O'Doul. The only reason I can see for it, if it's true, is that Walter knew O'Doul *was* going to have something to say, and he wanted to make sure I heard it."

"So you're saying Glybenhall knew that chain was on the roof? That Kong told him he'd lost it?"

"That would put Walter and Kong knowing each other, just like Blowfish said they did. Before he retracted that."

"Why would Glybenhall want you to know about it?"

"To make the case for sabotage?"

Joe gazed out over the traffic, squeezed by the roadwork into two potholed lanes. "I don't know," he said. "That's not sitting right. Have you told Lowry?"

"Oh, Joe! Told him what? A guy's boss gave him the name of an investigator to cooperate with? And I learned that by visiting the guy while I'm supposed to be on desk duty?"

"What are you going to do?"

A pause. "Joe? What would you do?"

What would I do? I just spent three years in prison for doing what I do. "I guess," he said slowly, "I'd look at the discards."

"The what?"

"There are always ideas I start out with that I don't end up using, when things start to move. If I get stuck I go back and look at one of them."

Palmer appeared at Joe's elbow with a cluster of coffee cups in a cardboard box. He cast a significant glance at the clock.

"I have to go," Joe said. "Be careful."

"Of course."

"Call me later?"

A brief pause. "Of course."

CHAPTER

73

Sutton Place

Ann strode into the office carrying her usual Starbucks latte and a large shoulder bag. She'd barely gotten her coat off when Lowry materialized beside her.

"What the hell are you doing here?"

"The mayor told me to clean out my desk."

"You're crazy. Are you trying to scuttle whatever career you have left?"

"I have no career left." She faced him squarely. "No matter what happens. If Glybenhall fell on his knees and confessed today, I'd still be out of here. That's what happens to the messenger, Greg."

"You shouldn't have come in while this is ongoing."

"I have some personal things here. I didn't want to wait months." She picked up a silver-framed photo of her father, slipped it into a padded envelope, and placed it in her bag.

"It looks bad. It looks as though we've already told you you're through, without waiting for the results of our investigation."

"I hope you don't mind if what looks bad for DOI isn't my most pressing concern right now." From a drawer she started removing hand cream, breath mints, nail polish, and a brand-new paperback book. When she reached into a deeper drawer and lifted out a pair of slingback heels, Lowry threw in the towel.

"Finish up and clear out fast." He stalked toward his office.

She watched after him, but didn't answer. When he disappeared behind his door she turned back to her desk. From the deep drawer she lifted out a vase. Years ago, Joe used to bring in flowers from his garden.

He'd stand them on the windowsill, arranged in the spare coffeepot. The first time she'd seen that, she'd laughed. The next day she'd brought in the vase. The office hadn't had flowers since he'd been gone. But she'd never taken home the vase.

She found a padded envelope for it, too, and put it in her bag. She walked around the desk, shifting the bulky bag as though it were in her way. With both it and herself between her in-basket and Lowry's door, she slid a thick folder from under a pile of memos and mail.

When she left the office five minutes later, the bag heavy on her shoulder, she was grinning. She'd always liked to read, and she had lots of good reading ahead of her. The new Lisa Scottoline paperback, which she'd barely cracked when all this began. And three years' worth of Walter Glybenhall's subpoenaed financial statements, forgotten on her desk when things started to move.

Harlem: Frederick Douglass Boulevard

Yvonnia buzzed Ford. "Ann Montgomery's asking to speak to you."

"Tell her—no, wait. I'll tell her myself." Ford pressed the speaker-phone button. "Inspector? This is Ford Corrington. I don't think we have anything to talk about."

"I need your help."

"No. Those windmills turned out to be dragons."

"All the more reason to go after them."

"Or stay away from them."

"Walter Glybenhall will eat Harlem alive."

"He'll find us indigestible."

"If he can't devour you he'll destroy you. That's how dragons work. I have new information."

Ford had been about to cut the connection. He hesitated, finger above the button. "You were suspended."

"And you were smeared. I stand to lose my job and five million dollars. I think you have more to lose than that."

"Damn right I do. I don't know how I got between you and Walter Glybenhall, but it's not a position I like."

"I want to know how you got there, too. And a lot more. I can be at your office in fifteen minutes."

"Absolutely not. I don't want you seen anywhere near here."

"Meet me somewhere else, then."

"Inspector, I don't want to be seen with you at all."

"Well, I can't make myself invisible. And you're well known. How about somewhere neutral Sunset Park? Red bean buns on me."

Yellow cabs, illegally, refused to cruise Harlem, but car services, illegally, did. Ford flagged a car and gave the driver the Brooklyn address Montgomery had given him. Twenty minutes later they pulled up on a street lined with produce stands, restaurants, and check-cashing joints. He climbed from the cab in front of a fish market where two old ladies haggled with the fishmonger. Young men with dangling cigarettes gave passersby hard looks. Kids played tag and horns honked and the air smelled like fried food and the whole thing was a lot like Harlem, except the people all were Asian and the signs all in Chinese.

He spotted a pink neon teapot radiating neon steam. The Chinese characters above it read "Moon Garden Teahouse," according to Montgomery.

Already, he thought, he was back to taking her word for something.

Inside, it didn't look much like a garden, even one on the moon. Fluorescent lights buzzed above gray tile floors and white walls. Battered metal chairs edged gray Formica tables. Below a framed painting of a single pine branch, Ann Montgomery gestured from a table at the back.

"I appreciate your coming," she said as Ford pulled out a chair. A teapot and two cups sat before her, next to a lacquer tray of pastries.

"I'm still not sure meeting you is a smart idea. But if it had to be someplace, Sunset Park was a good call."

She smiled and didn't answer, not putting into words what Ford knew they were both thinking: the they-all-look-alike thing cut both ways. To the newly arrived immigrants in New York's newest Chinatown, they were a black man and a white woman — meaning not Chinese — sitting down to tea. As long as they didn't start throwing the crockery, no one would look at them closely.

"But frankly," Ford said, "that doesn't mean I'm comfortable with you. You've put me in a pretty deep hole."

"I want to get you out."

"Working from the hole you're in yourself?"

She poured tea for him. "I went to see Sonny O'Doul yesterday morning."

"Can you do that?"

"No. But it was worthwhile. He told me something interesting. He said it was Walter Glybenhall who personally told him if he needed to talk to DOI, call Ann Montgomery."

"I don't understand." The steam rising from his tea smelled sweet, but strangely sad.

"See, didn't I say it was interesting? And the other thing I did yesterday was study Glybenhall's financial records."

"How did you get those?"

"Technically, I'm on desk duty." She looked at him levelly and didn't expand. "Now try this: it's true Three Star took out additional insurance on Mott Haven four months ago, and the Three Star partnership is strapped for cash. But if you dig deeper, things change. A number of Walter's other businesses are doing quite well. He has available cash, not to mention credit lines, he could have applied to Mott Haven, with a little effort."

"So Walter Glybenhall's rich. Is that what you brought me to Brooklyn to tell me?"

"What I'm telling you is that he had no real reason for insurance fraud at Mott Haven. It only looked as though he did."

"Maybe it looked that way to him, too."

"I'm not being clear. It looked that way because he *made* it look that way. It took some fiddling to make Three Star seem as precarious as it does."

"What possible reason would he have for doing that?"

"I don't know yet. But it's obvious there's something going on."

"You said that last week. Now look at the mess we're all in."

"Mess notwithstanding, it was true then and it's still true."

"And it's still a mess. I have funders pulling donations, agencies talking about contracting with other nonprofits for programs we've always run. My board members are behind me 110 percent, of course. But if you listen hard you can hear words like 'for the good of the foundation' and 'resignation.' Tell me something: Why shouldn't I go to Walter Glybenhall on my hands and knees, telling him I'm sorry I got in his way? Asking him please to leave the Garden Project alone and let me minister to the innocent and needy children of Harlem, and promising never to cross him again?"

"Walter Glybenhall loves it when his enemies crawl. He'd probably send you a hefty donation."

"So why should I turn his donation down? What are you offering that's better?"

"A chance to find the truth."

The pastries on their lacquer tray had not been touched. Ford reached for a frothy white ball. "What's this?"

"Lamb's Tail, it's called. Because it looks like one."

"But it's not?"

"It's meringue filled with bean paste."

"I understand you're a wealthy woman."

"That's true."

"Why didn't you offer me a donation to replace what I'll lose if I don't go hat in hand to Glybenhall?"

"Because you'd have gotten up and walked out."

Ford bit into the pastry. The meringue was light and melting, the dark filling chewy and sweet. "What do you want?" he asked.

"First, to talk to T. D. Tilden's girlfriend."

"Why?"

"You never told anyone where she is."

"And I still won't."

"I'm not asking you to. But if you're really the only one who knows, chances are Walter hasn't gotten to her the way he did the other witnesses. She may be able to tell me something I can use."

"And then? You said that was first."

"That'll depend on what she says."

"What if there's nothing?"

"Then that boy Armand—A-Dogg. And the other gangbangers."

"If you're right, he's bought them off already."

"And they've already done what he paid them for. They have nothing to gain from long-term loyalty."

"Or from helping you out."

"I'll take my chances."

"This sounds like police work. Why don't you go to Detective Perez?"

"Perez won't take my calls."

"Can you blame him?"

"No."

Their eyes met in silence. Ford sipped his tea and looked past her to the brush-painted pine branch. Early autumn, that was the sadness in the fragrance: that first hint that the promise of spring would not come true and the glories of summer would, again this year as every year, wither and fade.

With a sigh, he pulled out his cell phone and dialed the number in Crawford County, Georgia.

The same guarded male voice answered, but this time when Ford identified himself he was told, "Yeah, just a minute," and Shamika came on the line.

"Hello? Mr. Corrington?"

"How are you, Shamika?"

"I'm good, real good. I told my mama, I'll be staying down here awhile."

"I know, she told me. I think that's great."

"My cousins could use a hand. And this farming, it's kind of interesting. My cousins got chickens and all. And three dogs!"

"I can hear them barking."

"Yeah, they're chasing the chickens." She giggled. "I ought to go out and stop them."

"Shamika, I have someone here with me who wants to ask you some questions."

"Umm . . . what kind of questions?"

"About T.D."

"Did y'all find what happen to him? My momma told me about Kong. She say someone kill him, too."

"No, we don't know any more than we did. That's why we want to talk to you."

"I don't know nothing I ain't already told you."

"Still, it might be important. Shamika, do you have a cell phone with you?"

"Yeah."

"Good. Can I have the number?" He wrote it on a napkin as she gave it to him. "This lady's going to call you. Her name's Ann Montgomery. It's okay to answer anything she asks. Except don't tell her where you are. All right?"

"Okay." Shamika sounded unconvinced.

"I'll be right here, sitting with her."

"Okay," Shamika said again. "If you think it's important."

"I do. I wish I didn't, but I do."

Sutton Place

Ann keyed into her cell phone the number Ford Corrington had given her. She heard two rings, then a girl's tentative voice saying, "Hello?"

"Shamika? I'm Ann Montgomery. I work for the city, for something called the Department of Investigation."

"You a cop?"

"A kind of cop, yes. What I want to do is ask you some questions about T.D."

"I already told Mr. Corrington everything about that."

"I know you did. But sometimes people know things they don't know they know. Can I just ask a few questions?"

"I guess."

"Thanks. First, tell me again just what T.D. told you he was doing."

"He say, he be going on up to the Bronx, make accidents where this rich white guy building a building."

"And he was working for someone?"

"Kong." She hesitated. "You know who that is?"

"Yes, thanks. But Kong was working for someone else, isn't that right?"

"Prob'ly. Kong don't stand up out his chair, he ain't being paid for it. I don't mean to disrespect no one, 'specially now he passed, but that's a fact."

"Do you have any idea who that might be?"

"Who Kong working for? T.D. didn't never say. I don't think he knew."

"Do you know where T.D. and Kong went, in the Bronx?"

"Uh-uh."

"Did T.D. say why they were doing it?"

"So it would cost the white guy money. I told Mr. Corrington."

"I know you did, Shamika. I just need you to tell me. When was the first time they went?"

"I don't know. Maybe a couple weeks ago."

"Did T.D. give you any details—time of day, tools they took with them, anything like that? Did he say how he and Kong got onto the site, like did they climb a fence, or break a lock?"

"First time, they climb over the fence. T.D. do that stuff all the time, but Kong, he have trouble getting his big-ass self over. Oh, sorry, miss!"

"That's okay, Shamika, I don't mind whatever you say. Go on."

"Well, T.D. say Kong cut his hand, then he trip when they was on the scaffold, bang his knee. T.D. tell me it just about crack him up, watching Kong fallin' all over hisself in the dark. When they get where they was going, Kong knock something over, make a lot of noise. An' something else happen when they was leaving, I don't remember what, but T.D. say he ain't going back to do the next job if Kong come along."

"He told you that?"

"Told Kong that, too. He say he can do it on his own just fine, don't need no helper."

"What did Kong say to that?"

"Well, he get all bent outta shape when T.D. say 'helper.' He all, like, T.D. *his* helper. But seem like he as happy as T.D. that he don't have to go up there no more."

"Wait. What do you mean?"

"To do the jobs, with T.D."

"Kong agreed?"

"Kong come like he ain't happy, but he don't fool nobody."

"Are you sure about that?"

"He just sit his fat ass down an' wait for T.D. to get back. Oh!" the girl said again. "Sorry!"

"Shamika, you have nothing to be sorry about. You've been a terrific help."

"I have?"

"Yes. Thank you. May I call you again if I need to?"

"I guess. You gonna find out what happen to T.D.?"

"I'm going to do everything I can to find that out, Shamika. Thank you again." Ann cut the connection.

"Did she help?" Corrington asked.

"I think she did."

"What did she say?"

"That T.D. and Kong didn't get along. Now there's someone else I want to talk to."

From his look she thought he might demand details, but all he said was "Who would that be?"

"Blowfish said he saw Walter Glybenhall and Kong down by the river, when he was 'getting next to' his girlfriend."

"And then he said no, it was someone else. I don't think there's much point in talking to Blowfish again."

"I don't want to. I want to talk to his girlfriend."

It took a call from Corrington to Armand Stubbs at his job at the bakery to locate Blowfish's girlfriend. She worked as a manicurist at the Beauty First Salon on Lenox near 122nd Street.

"Though A-Dogg isn't sure they're still together," Corrington said, as they walked to the lot where Ann had left the Boxster. "Blowfish doesn't seem to have a gift for long-term commitment."

"Even better. You sure I can't offer you a ride?"

"Being seen with you would be bad enough. Being seen in that?" He pointed. "I'll take the train."

Ann handed the ticket to the attendant and turned to face Corrington. "Thank you. If we have any chance of stopping Glybenhall—"

"I don't believe we do."

"Then why did you help me?"

"Because *you* believe we do."

By the time Ann entered the Beauty First Salon, it was nearing two. Five standing women in pink smocks and four seated ones draped in pink aprons from their chins to their knees turned to look when she walked in the door.

"Is the manicurist here?" she asked, a little breathlessly. Before the surprise on their faces had a chance to blossom into incredulity, she waggled her fingers in the air. "I'm going out tonight and I *cannot* go with my nails like this! I just started a job at the State Office Building and I'm on my lunch break. One of the girls says there's a manicurist here named Ra'shelle who's a total genius. Is that you?"

Mary Blige's "Slow Down" pounded so loudly from huge speakers hung off the sprinkler pipes that Ann wasn't sure her question had been heard. But a tall, thin young woman nodded. Under her pink smock she wore cropped jeans and high wedge sandals. Two magenta stripes flashed in her chin-length hair.

"Oh, good! Are you free, Ra'Shelle? Please say you're free!" Heads swiveled to follow as Ann maneuvered around the other women and plunked her bag in the corner beside a rolling cart arranged with emery boards, alcohol and cotton balls, and row after row of nail polish. All shades of red appeared, from palest pearl pink to crimson so deep it was near black, and so did some interesting blues, a few golden yellows, and a little rack of tiny glue-on gems and rainbows.

"Sure, I could take you," the young woman said, with an amused glance at her colleagues.

"But are you Ra'Shelle? Because Chandra said I had to see Ra'Shelle. I'm dating this new guy, and just look at these!"

"I'm Ra'Shelle." The thin woman examined the hands Ann thrust forward. "Man, that's nasty. How you mess them up so bad?"

With a nail file and a set of keys, Ann thought, but she said, "I've been digging in the garden. Can you do anything? I want a diamond, too, on this finger and a lightning bolt on that one."

"Go ahead, sit down." Ra'Shelle pointed Ann to a pink vinyl chair. She flipped her smock out as she sat on a rolling stool.

"Nice to have your own station in the corner like this," Ann prattled on as Ra'Shelle brushed the chipped scarlet polish off her nails with a damp cotton ball. "Much quieter."

"Kinda hard to be part of the conversation, though. With the music and all. Like, right now, they's all talkin' about how they was afraid they was gonna have to do your hair." She smiled and flicked a glance at the hairdressers and their clients. As far as Ann could see, all eight mouths were moving at once, and various pairs of eyes kept darting in her direction.

"I guess you don't get a lot of blondes here?"

"Not when they come in." Ra'Shelle's smile turned to a sly grin. "That your natural color?"

"Both sides of the family. Still, if I could get magenta streaks like yours, that might be cool. Not while this guy is so new, though. Does your boyfriend like them?"

"Don't make no difference to me. It's my hair." Ra'Shelle moved Ann's right hand to a dish of warm water and went to work on her left.

"Ra'Shelle," Ann said, "it's good no one can hear us over here. I want to talk to you."

The manicurist glanced up. "What you mean?"

"I work for the city. I want to ask you some questions."

Ra'Shelle froze, cotton ball in hand.

"You a cop."

"Yes. But no one needs to know that. You're not in trouble but I need your help."

"If I ain't in trouble what the fuck you want from me?"

"A great manicure, for one thing. I wasn't kidding about that. This new guy means a lot to me." She met Ra'Shelle's eyes. "For another, I want to ask you about Blowfish."

For a few moments, Ra'Shelle didn't move. Ann didn't either. With Ann's left hand still in hers, Ra'Shelle skimmed a look over to the other women. A nonstop conversation, none of it audible, was going on around the shampooing, snipping, and braiding.

Ra'Shelle flung the cotton ball into the trash. She dunked Ann's left hand in the bowl and lifted her right one out. "Blowfish." She patted Ann's hand with a towel, picked up a tool, and began work on her cuticles. This could hurt, even if the manicurist liked you. Ann steeled herself, but the process was expert and painless.

"Blowfish," Ra'Shelle said again. "You know what that is?"

"The fish itself? It's also called a puffer fish, I think."

"He call himself that 'cause you don't know what you doing when you try to eat it, that fish gonna kill you. Other thing about it, though, blowfish be puffing itself up real big, to scare all the other fish. But see"—she reached for a small scissor—"if that puffing thing really working for you, what you need the poison for?"

"You're not seeing him anymore, are you?"

"Shouldn't of never been seeing him. That don't mean I'm gonna rat him out."

"I'm not asking you to. I need you to corroborate his statement."

"Do what to it?"

"I'm sorry. Tell me whether it's true."

"Blowfish said it, chances is pretty good it ain't."

"He said you and he were down by the river a few weeks ago, and that you saw a white man get out of a limo and meet with Kong. Could you describe the man? Would you recognize him if I showed you a photo?"

Ra'Shelle gave her a scornful look. "Ain't no point. What color you want?"

Ann tapped a bottle of cherry red. "What do you mean, no point? You wouldn't recognize him, or you won't look at the photo?"

Ra'Shelle lifted the tiny brush from the bottle. "I mean, ain't no point because there ain't no man. I ain't never been to the river with Blowfish."

"He said he was 'getting next to his woman.'"

Ra'Shelle painted with deft strokes and didn't answer.

"I wonder," Ann said. "If you're not seeing him anymore, maybe it's another woman he was trying to get next to?"

"He try to get next to every woman he see. But don't make no difference. Latin Kings owns that park down by the river. Blowfish, oh, he such a big man, he have to go up in they face when they move in here. Now he got beef with the Latin Kings. He ain't been across that bridge in two years. Where you want the lightning bolt?"

"Here," said Ann, though it really didn't matter. The lightning bolt had already hit her.

CHAPTER 76

Sutton Place

"Mr. Morgenstern. So glad to find you here."

The jeweler, alone in his office, looked up at the sound of the buzzer. After a moment he stood and approached the door, but didn't open it. Instead he spoke through the intercom as Ann had, his words metallic when he said, "I'm leaving soon; Friday we have a short day. Everyone's gone already. What do you want? You don't have to show the badge around, I know who you are."

"I'd like to speak to you."

"I'm busy. I'm working."

"So am I. And I have to tell you, I'm in a really bad mood."

For a moment that was it, the two of them facing each other through the thick wire glass in the steel door. Like the prison, when she went to see Joe. Except here the lock, and the buzzer to call for help, were on the inside.

Morgenstern frowned, but he threw the bolt and let her in.

"I thought you were suspended or something like that." He pushed the door shut behind her. "I read it in the paper."

"Limited duty. Limited to this case," she said briskly. "I need you to confirm something."

"I made my statement already."

"You made more than one."

"The first one, I was wrong."

"No. Walter Glybenhall paid you to say you hadn't made that jewelry, the bling we found. But first—" holding up her hand to silence his protest, "first he paid you to say you did."

"What are you talking about? I saw the pieces, they looked like mine, so I said they were. Then I looked some more, and they weren't."

Ann surveyed the room, taking in the safe, the photos on the walls, the jeweler's tables with their mounted magnifiers and delicate tools. Steel mullions on the windows cut the sun into squares and laid it on the floor.

"I don't know much about jewelry." She turned back to the jeweler. "Especially things like this. But I'm told you're very good at what you do."

He replied with a cautious "My customers are satisfied."

"Don't be modest." She pointed to a photo, a gold-toothed hip-hop hopeful with what looked like fifteen chunky rings on his ten fingers. "I understand you're very hot."

"People are starting to come to me."

"That's what I've heard. They say when people can't afford Jacob the Jeweler, they go to Levi Morgenstern."

"Afford?" Morgenstern looked affronted. "Affording Jacob, this isn't the question. People like magpies, who see only glitter, who don't understand quality, these people go to Jacob, and welcome. Morgenstern's customers appreciate art."

"Or, if they don't appreciate art," Ann said, "I guess they can get imitations. I know lots of people walk around flashing bling they say is Jacob the Jeweler, and no one can tell the difference."

"Ha! The man doesn't have an artist bone in his body. Him, anyone can copy."

"Come on, Mr. Morgenstern. A few diamonds, a little platinum, I bet a lot of people can make something that looks like a Morgenstern, too."

"Looks like, maybe. From across the room! The kind of work I do, no one does it anymore, so precise, so fine. A lost art, I'm telling you. I learned from my father, he learned in Antwerp from his uncle. My customers, they recognize the kind of quality you only get from Morgenstern."

"Really? And yet you couldn't recognize your own pieces when I brought them here."

He frowned. "Please, don't insult me. You're setting me a trap. Those pieces—"

"Never mind. My forensic people can, I'm sure."

"You're sure what?"

"They can tell a real Morgenstern. Especially with all that precise, fine work to look for. Of course, once Forensics starts looking at those pieces, it'll be too late."

"What does this mean, too late?" His innocent delivery was contradicted by the faint sheen of sweat on his face.

"If they can prove those pieces are yours, and that you made them for Kong, I won't need your statement." *And if I'd thought of this back when Forensics was speaking to me, I wouldn't need it, either.* "This is a homicide investigation, and the city's been pretty embarrassed by what's happened so far. They might go after people they think are responsible." She left that vague, a cloud in the air. "If I don't need you, I can't protect you. Look, Mr. Morgenstern: you're not the only one. A lot of people lied about a lot of things. The ones who don't get in trouble will be the ones who cooperate now."

A pause. "I think you should leave."

When they were reduced to kicking you out, you had them. "However much Walter Glybenhall paid you," she persisted quietly, "it's not worth jail time."

His eyes searched the room again, all corners, the desks, the windows. Nothing had changed since Ann arrived. She waited, motionless, with an unaccustomed patience that was nevertheless unnervingly familiar. *Because it's Joe's,* she realized. *It's how Joe would do this.*

"No," Morgenstern said, gazing down, speaking to the floor, "it's not worth it. The guilt isn't worth it either. And to set the record straight, he didn't pay me. I don't want you should think I'd lie to the authorities for money."

"Then why?"

The jeweler shrugged his shoulders. "He owns this building."

"Glybenhall?"

"Who else?"

"He would have evicted you?"

"Not only. He was going to put it around, Levi Morgenstern is a deadbeat. Doesn't pay his rent, demands constant repairs on top of it, hires illegals and has them sleeping in the workroom, believe me you don't want him for a tenant."

"Put it around? He couldn't have gotten to every commercial landlord in New York."

"He doesn't have to. In my business, you don't have an address on Forty-seventh Street, you don't exist. This block, it's the whole show. These buildings, maybe eight men own them all."

"Friends of his?"

"Friends? Six of the eight are Jews. After they shake on a deal, Walter Glybenhall I'm sure washes his hands. But still."

"You think they would have believed him about you?"

"Believe, don't believe, so what? What he would want, it would be clear: Don't rent to Morgenstern. Why, they wouldn't care. Walter Glybenhall asks you a favor, you do it and he owes you. If you don't, he hates you. To be hated by Walter Glybenhall, this is something no one can afford."

"And that's why you did him the favor he asked you?"

Morgenstern nodded glumly.

Gently, Ann asked, "Can you tell me what happened?"

The jeweler sank onto the edge of his desk as though pressed there by a weight. "He called me. Walter Glybenhall calling Levi Morgenstern! I thought he'd seen maybe one of my pieces, not the bling-blings but a ring, a brooch, a refined piece like my father used to make. For his wife or, you know, one of his young ladies."

"But that wasn't it?"

"What he'd seen, he'd seen the chain and the ring for Mr. Kong. He asked, 'Morgenstern, did you make them?' 'Yes, Mr. Glybenhall, I did.' 'The police will be asking you about them,' he says. 'You can say you made them.' 'I can say?' I ask. 'What else would I say?' 'That you didn't make them,' says he. 'Which you will, when you hear from me.' I said I didn't understand, and he explained."

"He explained why?"

"No. He explained it would be a good idea for me to do like he was telling me."

"Did he give you a reason?"

"A reason to do it, he gave me. A reason he wanted it? Why would he have to? He's Walter Glybenhall."

"You didn't know there was a homicide involved?"

"Know? In my wildest dreams, I didn't guess! I thought, insurance fraud. Usually, when people ask a jeweler to lie, it's insurance fraud."

"That happens a lot?"

"It happens sometimes." Quickly, he added, "Never before did I agree."

"I believe you."

He nodded, sighing. "This, I didn't understand, this pretending my pieces are copies. But men like Walter Glybenhall, they live in a different world. Whatever scheme he was scheming, saving an insurance company money didn't seem worth risking my business to do."

"So when we brought you the pieces—"

"I told the truth. They're mine. Whether Glybenhall tells me to say it or doesn't, it's still true. So that was easy. Then I thought, maybe he won't call again, maybe it's a joke or a bad dream or whatever he's doing he can do it without Morgenstern. But in a couple of days he called. 'Morgenstern, tomorrow morning you'll get in touch with Inspector

Montgomery. You'll tell her those pieces are copies.' " He sighed again. "So I did."

"He used my name?"

"I had it anyway, you left me your card. But he gave it to me, to make sure. He didn't want I should call the wrong person."

"No, I'm sure he didn't."

Morgenstern shrugged. "I can get back to work now?"

"I want to thank you, Mr. Morgenstern. There's one more thing I'm going to need—a signed statement," Ann said.

"I can't come to your office now, it's almost Shabbos. Can it be Monday?"

"Well, we could type up something here, if you'd sign it."

"Now?"

"Please." *Since we'd get thrown out of my office if we showed up there anyway.* "Just something short. Saying Walter Glybenhall asked you to lie. That he threatened you. That you made all those pieces for Kong, and none of them are fakes. That will do until we get a formal statement."

For a moment she thought he hadn't heard her. Then he rose slowly and walked to a desk, where he clicked a computer screen on.

"Just to say what happened?" he asked.

"Yes, please."

"All right. But it's not exactly what you said."

"What's not?"

"I didn't make all those pieces for Mr. Kong."

"Wait—what have we just been talking about? You said they were your pieces."

"I made them, Inspector. And the first two you brought me, those were Mr. Kong's. But the chain with the big *K* on it, I made that for Mr. Glybenhall."

CHAPTER 77

Sutton Place

Ann walked slowly along Sixth Avenue in the purple light, cell phone in hand. Joe would be home by now. She pictured him in the garden, cutting blossoms, feeding roots. Tamping dirt around a three-leafed twig because in his mind he could see the tree it would become. He'd hear the phone, wipe his hands as he headed to the house to answer.

She didn't call.

In Bryant Park she slumped into a chair near the café. Perfect circles and shapeless blotches from a day's worth of coffee cups alternated across the tabletop, disparate expressions of the same mistake.

How could she call?

Now that she saw. Now that she knew the mistake, and whose it was.

Chairs rattled as an elderly couple shifted them to sit side by side. The woman brushed a flower petal from the man's jacket; the man pointed to something, someone, passing by on the sidewalk, and they both softly laughed.

Ann stood abruptly, cast around as though picking a direction—all directions were wrong, though—and without reason chose to wander through the park. It was that time of evening when pale colors, whites and faint blues, loomed like materializing ghosts. The ornate blossoms of peonies released an achingly sweet scent as she passed. Joe had peonies in the rear of his garden. The sound of the stream came back to her, the rumble and hiss she'd heard while she balanced on the rock she'd nearly fallen from. The stream and the garden: everything in the garden rooted and remaining, while the stream raced heedlessly ahead, cutting a gorge deeper and deeper with each rushing minute.

She still held the phone in her hand and she still didn't call.

What then? Nothing? Backed blindly into a corner by that bastard again, and again, do nothing?

But call Joe? Have him sympathize, see what it was she should have seen, understand what it was she should have understood? Have him know how she'd been played, this time—and the time before?

No.

Cheeks burning, she stared at the ghostly peonies. She couldn't call Joe.

But do nothing?

The peonies seemed to reach toward her, out of the dark. Friend or foe?

They're just flowers. Joe had said that years ago, spreading his slow smile, when she'd told him the daisies he'd brought in seemed to lean away from the lantana as though they didn't want to be in the same vase. *They don't have opinions about each other the way we do.* He'd moved the stems around, and everything was harmony again.

In the twilight Ann lifted the phone and dialed, but not Joe.

"Lowry."

"Greg, I'm glad I caught you. We need to talk."

Pause. "The hell we do."

"You're going to want to hear this."

"I don't want to hear anything from you."

"You're wrong. I'll come in. Fifteen minutes."

"Dammit, Ann, don't make it worse."

"Fifteen minutes. Greg, it's a bombshell."

"Like the last one?"

"I'm on my way in."

"Goddamm it!" He hissed out a breath. "All right, but not here. I don't want to be seen with you."

"A lot of that going around."

"What?"

"Nothing. Where do you want to meet?" Sunset Park, maybe?

"The Village. Dublin Six, on Hudson Street. You know it?"

"I'll find it. I'm not making it worse, Greg. I'm going to make it better." She clicked off and trotted down the steps to hail a cab.

Dublin Six turned out to be a bar where the action was going strong. Irish fiddle music and after-work drinkers flowed out the open front to the sidewalk. On the curb, Ann flinched. The jolly crowd, the noise and bustle: usually right up her alley, but now she felt like she was facing an icy stream when she was already freezing and exhausted.

But she waded in. Figuring Lowry wouldn't want to be planted with her where all the world could see, she bypassed the outdoor tables, found a secluded corner, ordered a pinot grigio. Greg Lowry arrived just after her wine did.

"Ann—" He pulled out a chair.

"Greg, just listen."

"No, *you* listen! Whatever you want, you can't have it. Just coffee," he snapped at the waitress, who raised an eyebrow and backed away.

"A couple of things have come up," Ann said.

"I don't want to hear them. I only came here to keep you away from the office. I have a career I'd like to salvage. And believe it or not I'm trying to do you a favor, too."

"How did Sonny O'Doul know to call me?"

"What the hell—what are you talking about?"

"O'Doul called me when he found the chain. Why me?"

Lowry looked at her as though she'd asked why the earth was flat. "You were the investigator on the case."

"He didn't know that. Someone had to tell him."

"So someone told him."

"It was Glybenhall—" Ann stopped, waited while the waitress set Lowry's coffee down. "Glybenhall told O'Doul that Dennis was off the case and I was on. He told him, if he had anything to say to DOI, to call me. He gave him my direct line."

"So what? And more important, how do you know?"

"O'Doul told me."

"When?"

"This morning."

"*Are you fucking nuts?*" Even in the swirling racket, heads turned. Lowry dropped his voice. "You went to see O'Doul? Are you crazy?"

"That chain? Morgenstern made it, like all the other pieces. None of them are fakes. The bling we found at Glybenhall's, it's Kong's. But that chain O'Doul claims he found isn't. Morgenstern made it for Glybenhall."

"*What* are you *talking* about?"

"Kong was never on that roof. He was only on the Mott Haven site once, before the first accident, the scaffold collapse. He never went back. And Blowfish hasn't been down to the river in two years. He never saw anyone down there, no white man with Kong. That was a lie. It was all a trap, Greg. And I fell right into it."

Lowry gave her a long, level stare. "It's loud as hell in here. I'm having trouble understanding you. It sounds as though you're saying you've been talking to witnesses in this case. I know you wouldn't do that when you're on desk duty. Must be the noise."

"Don't you get it? Why do you think he produced the gun so late, and it was the wrong gun? And the jeweler, and Blowfish, first one story and then another. It wasn't that he *got* to them *after*. He had them from the beginning. It was the whole point!"

"What was?"

"Setting me up." Her voice was steady but she had to swallow before she could go on. "Because of—because of the past. He *wanted* me to find huge amounts of evidence, because he knew I'd buy it. He *wanted* us to arrest him! Because he'd already set the case up to fall apart. So when it did, he could sue. It's all about the *money*, Greg. It always was."

"Jesus Christ," Lowry said, voice full of wonder. "You really are obsessed with Glybenhall, just like he says."

"No! No! He knew you'd all think that. That's why he did it this way. Goddammit, Greg, *he set us up!*"

Lowry, tight-jawed, picked up his coffee. He drank it as if it were medicine. When he put it down he said, "Ann, you have to help me out here. You have to back off."

"That's what he wants. That's what the lawsuit's for."

"No, the lawsuit's for fifty million dollars!" Lowry flared, then went on quietly, patiently. "Ann, you've shown incredibly bad judgment. Earlier, and especially now. But I'm sure that's all it is. I don't think you planted any evidence—"

"Of course I didn't!"

"I know that! I don't think you did anything at all that's actionable. Certainly nothing criminal."

"*Criminal?*"

"You must know Mark Shapiro's looking into making a case against you. Standard in situations like this, to cover the department's butt. They did it with Joe Cole, had a case ready to go, but the DA liked the NYPD's better."

"Both were garbage. And so's this. Mark Shapiro's worrying about covering the department's butt? Three people are dead—"

"One accident and two unrelated gang killings."

"You can't believe that. The sabotage—"

"Construction accidents."

"Oh, come on! You read Sandy Weiss's report."

"Expert witnesses can be wrong."

"Greg, you can't just sweep this under the rug!"

"Goddammit, Ann, get ahold of yourself!" Hands around his coffee mug as though to keep it from escaping, he dropped his voice. "What are you telling me? That Walter Glybenhall went to a huge, complicated amount of trouble to make Ann Montgomery look like an idiot?"

"No. He went to all this trouble for a multimillion-dollar settlement and a Teflon coating."

"What does that mean?"

"Look at it! No city agency will dare touch Glybenhall now! After a false arrest for homicide and a giant lawsuit? Building permits, licenses, variances, waivers, they'll fall all over themselves giving him what he wants. Any site in New York and anything he wants to build on it. Block A, in Harlem. Corrington was working with us—"

"With *you!*"

"Yes, yes, with me! And because of that he's disgraced. He'll never get that site, he may even have to resign from his foundation. You think that wasn't part of the point, too? A huge dollar settlement is nice. But look what else Glybenhall gets! Corrington's been put in his place, Glybenhall's shown Charlie Barr who's boss, I'm ruined—and Glybenhall's untouchable. Untouchable! Think of what that'll be worth over the years. Other developers will be coming to him, people who weren't giving him the time of day will be begging to be part of his projects. He'll be king! Greg, he engineered this from beginning to end."

Lowry sat unmoving. Quietly, he said, "The trouble with this theory of yours—besides the fact that it's insane—the *specific* trouble is that Glybenhall would have to have known Dennis would be moved off the case and you put on. Because when all this started you were still in Siberia. Where I wish to hell we'd left you."

"And why didn't you?"

"Because I wanted you back! Because you were good. I thought. Before I knew you were crazy."

"So you just hauled me in from the boonies?"

"Are you shitting me? I busted my ass lobbying Shapiro for you. Jesus, talk about digging my own grave."

"And he said, 'Sure'?"

"No, he's a lot smarter than me, obviously. He said maybe. He said let's wait until we have—" Lowry stopped abruptly.

Ann forced herself to say nothing, to not move, though she felt like a lava flow trying to keep from coursing down a mountain.

"No," Lowry said. Slowly, deliberately, he went on, "If you are assigning any part in your paranoid fantasy to Commissioner Shapiro, I'd suggest you reconsider."

"Greg." Ann heard the tremor in her own voice. "Just look at it. As a cop. As though you didn't know any of these people."

Lowry's gaze was stony. "You need to get help, Ann. You may be a danger to yourself. You're certainly a danger to my department and me."

"Why would Shapiro agree to put me on this case, this sensitive case? A loose cannon like me? He and Glybenhall had to know each other from the power-player tuxedo circuit, over the last twenty years. Glybenhall cooked this up and sold it to him!"

"The Commissioner," Lowry said, "agreed to put you on this case because I asked him to. Because, I can see now, I temporarily lost my mind."

"Are you sure it wasn't *his* idea?"

"Until a minute ago," Lowry said, shoving his coffee aside, "you were on desk duty. Now you're fired. You have no professional standing and you will stay away from everyone involved with this case. If you have a problem with this, your union rep can call me."

"Greg, please! At least talk to the people I've talked to. You'll see."

"I'm not talking to anyone! I will *not* be dragged into this insanity again."

"What about Sandy Weiss at Packer?"

"You will stay away."

"Weiss's report is still good. Glybenhall has no leverage with him."

Lowry, instead of answering that, studied her for a long moment. "Ann? When this started, you told me you thought you had something on the scaffold collapse, and that you were sending it to Weiss at Packer."

"What do—"

"If Weiss hadn't seen it yet, why did you think you had something?"

"The bolt holes—"

"You're not an engineer. What made you think you had something?"

This time it was Ann who said nothing.

Lowry's face purpled. "Jesus fucking Christ. That's what you were doing upstate, isn't it? You took those photos, you took our fucking evidence photos straight to the prison and you showed them to Joe Cole!"

"Joe's out," Ann said quietly. "Six months now."

"You did, didn't you?"

She didn't answer. She heard the fiddle music start up again; she hadn't realized it had stopped. The devil was reputed to play the fiddle, wasn't he?

When Lowry finally spoke his voice was hard. "I'm about one inch from arresting you. I swear to God, if I don't leave I'll do it right now. And if I so much as hear your name again, Ann, you are fucked. I promise you, completely fucked."

He stood, pushed through the crowd, and left.

Sutton Place

From the tone of Joe's messages, their content, and their number—three on her cell phone and three at home—Ann had known last night that he was worried. She'd gone to bed with that knowledge, tossed and turned with it, and, with it, reached for the shrilling phone as the morning sun stabbed through the window.

"Joe?"

"Are you all right? Why didn't you call last night?"

"I'm sorry. I'm fine. It got late."

He was silent, not contesting that, waiting for the answer to the question he'd called six times last night to ask.

"It's complicated, Joe."

"I have time."

"And it's bad."

"We were wrong?"

"We hadn't thought it through." *We hadn't thought about how people can be counted on to make the same mistake over and over again, like a night moth beating its wings against the glass.*

"There was more?" Joe asked. "So? That happens a lot. But we were on the right track?"

"I missed so much."

"But you see it now?"

"Yes. But I can't tell you about it. I have to go."

"Ann, what's wrong?"

"I have to go."

"Ann—"

"Jen's memorial service is this morning. I'll call you when it's over."

"I'll be at work."

"Tonight, then."

"I'll call you, when we take a break."

"If you want. Don't worry, Joe, please. I'll talk to you later."

She slipped out of bed and stood at the window. Sun glittered off the East River; it was glaringly bright but she wondered how far into the water it really penetrated. She hadn't meant, *when the service is over.* Though what it would mean for all this to be over she didn't know.

Ann showered quickly, did her makeup, dressed in charcoal gray. She phoned the garage and asked them to bring the Boxster out front. She locked up and slipped her earrings on as she hurried down the hall. Tapping her foot until the elevator doors opened, she flipped through a mental map, looking at the streets and the likely traffic so she could choose the best route. All this rushing, all this velocity; and in the back of her mind the barely acknowledged truth: it was counterfeit. She was on a treadmill, dashing madly forward to outrun the fact that she couldn't move.

She parked in a garage a block from the funeral home. As she rushed down the sidewalk she turned her phone off and dropped it in her bag. Someone's phone was bound to ring during the service; these days, during anything, someone's always did. But she didn't want it to be hers. Though Jen would have been the first to get a case of the cover-your-mouth giggles over that.

She entered the funeral home through a revolving door. Jen would have found that funny, too. The steamy June morning with its smells of diesel fuel and take-out coffee, its syncopated traffic and shards of conversations, vanished instantly, replaced by thick cream carpet and silent cool. A respectful young man asked whom she was "here for" and indicated the chapel, his charge to make sure loved ones didn't bow their heads in grieving reverence at the wrong funeral. Although, Ann thought, as a tribute to Jen, who'd always treated getting lost as an adventure and never could read a map, that was temptingly appropriate.

Dark-clothed mourners were scattered among the pews, clustering up front and thinning out toward the rear. Ann spotted Irene, Beth, and Shondi under a row of glowing stained-glass windows.

"Hey, girl," Irene whispered as Ann slid into the pew. "How's it going? Looking any better?"

Ann shook her head. *Looking a lot worse, actually,* she thought. But saying that would bring a new surge of sympathy, new offers to help. Her friends' loyalty made her feel like a thief.

Irene patted Ann's hand. Ann was saved from having to respond by the swelling of organ music. Ann had never liked the organ; it was cheap, she thought. Those deep-earth rumblings, those piping angels' reeds: the sounds themselves could stir the soul, whether the music was good or bad.

As the hymn went on, talk faded, fidgeting ended. Ann had the odd sense of having, after all, wandered into the wrong chapel. It seemed unreal, this gravity of music and stained glass, all these solemn people. What could they have to do with Jen, who exasperated her friends with her flakiness and made them love her for her laughing audacity and her refusal to judge?

The minister took the pulpit and Jen's family filed in from the side chapel. And Ann, so used to seeing in her mind the next step and the one after, so used to living as much where she was going as where she was, felt the life and movement around her recede without warning until she found herself still, directionless: becalmed on a wide, windless sea. Nothing moored her, but nothing suggested a direction to travel in; there was not even the haphazard help of a random breeze. The people, colors, lights, and music seemed both sharp and distant, as though she were observing them from afar. As though, now that she'd finally stopped moving, she was not here, not anywhere.

"Honey, are you okay?" Irene whispered. "You're white as a ghost."

There could be no way of explaining this alarming sensation to Irene, not even of describing it. Ann, at a loss for an answer and groping for one, was confused to hear Irene say, "Oh, my God! Now I get it. Oh, girl!" Irene put an arm around Ann's shoulder and gave a reassuring squeeze. Ann, bewildered, turned to look at her, but Irene's glare was fixed on something ahead. Ann followed her gaze, and suddenly the room snapped back into substance and the moment took on direction. Settling himself in the front pew next to Jen's mother and brothers, distinguished and respectful in a fine black suit, was Walter Glybenhall.

chapter 79

Sutton Place

Ann heard none of the sermon, hymns, or tributes. Not even Shondi's, though something Shondi said brought a soft laugh to the chapel; the sound scraped on Ann's nerves like a knife. Ann's cheeks, her scalp, the backs of her hands were flaming. She knew from the way Irene kept glancing at her that her white-water turbulence was visible but there was nothing she could do. As Jen's oldest friend she'd been expected to speak and she'd intended to, planning to say something about sunshine, but she shook her head when the minister sent her a questioning look. He nodded his sympathy and called one of Jen's brothers to lead a prayer.

Finally the service was over. The organ started up again, setting Ann's teeth on edge. Jen's mother, supported by her sons, made her way from the chapel. Cousins and uncles followed, and then everyone was freed. Ann sprang to her feet. "It was him!" she hissed to Irene. "That son of a bitch was the new boyfriend!"

Irene blinked. "Who?"

"*Who? Walter Glybenhall!* That hypocritical *bastard*! He killed her and now he sits there consoling her mother!"

"Honey, get a grip. What do you—"

"Don't tell me to get a grip! He's rich, he's famous, he's a horny old fossil. I don't know why I didn't see it before!"

"Ann! Damn, girl, chill. Even if he was Jen's boyfriend, that doesn't mean he killed her."

"He did."

"And he may not be," Irene argued. "They move in the same circles, don't they? Like you and her? Couldn't he just have known them for-ever?"

"That would make him want her more." She shook off Irene's grip.

On the sidewalk she waited near the row of black limos. She was sweating, her heart racing. When she saw Jen's mother come out of the funeral home, her back stiffened. When Walter came out moments later, she stepped into his path.

Eyeing her with distaste, he said, "What are you doing here, Ann?"

"Jen was a friend of mine."

"Well, I'm sorry to hear that. It's a sad thing to lose a friend."

"You killed her, Walter."

"What?"

"You were sleeping with her and you murdered her. And I'll prove it."

He shook his head. "Ann, my beautiful Ann. Had you not said so many enormously stupid things over the last few weeks, I'd be aston-ished by both your dementia and your boorish timing. While you focus on your own miserable obsession, people around you are grieving. Perhaps you might give a thought to them?"

"Walter," she said tightly, "you set me up. It took me forever but I have the pieces now. I don't know how Jen's death fits but I'll find out. When I do—"

"When you do it will be a cold day in hell. It amazes me that I'm even responding to your fantastic accusation, except to prevent the em-barrassment of this scene from growing. Please hear this: I had nothing whatever to do with Jennifer's death. I never had a relationship with the poor child, except as a dear friend of her mother's."

"If you were sleeping with her mother, you'd have wanted Jen too."

"My God," he breathed. He held up his hand to someone behind her, instructing them to wait. And they would. They'd do as Walter Glybenhall told them, the way everyone always did. "Ann," he said. "I'm going to assume the loss of a dear friend is causing this fresh bout of instability, and I will forgive you." He turned.

She lunged for him, seizing only his jacket, nothing of substance. "*Walter!* Don't think you can—"

A hand clamped her arm. "Honey, stop it now!" Irene whispered fiercely.

Walter's jacket slipped from Ann's grip. In a voice of gentle sympathy, he said, "Please accept my condolences on your loss." Smiling, he slipped into the waiting limo beside Jen's mother.

CHAPTER

80

City Hall

Louise's wineglass clouded up as her chardonnay was poured. That made the second frosty thing on her side of the table, Charlie thought. He held his hand over his own glass and shook his head. The waiter put the bottle on ice and discreetly retreated, leaving Charlie and Louise alone in the mayor's private dining room.

"You're not drinking?" Louise asked.

"I don't very much lately, in the middle of the day."

"Oh. That's a change. I suppose I hadn't noticed because until recently you haven't often been available for such an intimate little lunch."

"When people were willing to be seen with me, you mean."

She set her glass down. "That's exactly what I mean."

"This will pass."

"Darling, this will *not* 'pass.' You might improve the situation by taking action, though even that might not work. But certainly if you do nothing this will not pass. It will destroy you."

"I think you're exaggerating."

"Yes, you said that last week. When your approval rating was six points higher than it is now."

"The teachers' union—"

"This has nothing to do with the teachers' union!" Louise's eyes blazed. "Two months into your first term the sanitation workers struck and your ratings went *up*. Do you remember? People didn't like the piles of garbage but they liked you! You said you were sorry but the union's demands were unreasonable and it would take as long as it took. You led the news cameras to the garden and showed them Gracie Mansion's garbage bags. And everyone adored you. You can be pigheaded, wrong, and stupid and the voters will love you, darling, but you cannot appear conniving and petty. You just look nasty, and like a fool. Other mayors have been admired for their ability to flimflam but you never will be, Charlie, never."

"It's a dubious talent, anyway."

"Don't give me that. If you had it you'd use it." Louise attacked her Stilton-and-watercress salad.

Charlie bit into his crab cake, surprised to find himself wondering if that was true. He rarely questioned Louise's political assessments, of him or anyone else. And bullshitting people—flimflamming, in Louise's tasteful idiom—was an ability he'd never spent much effort to develop. But if he could? If he'd been born with the gift of humbug? Was he different from other politicians because he refused to lie to his constituents? Or only because he didn't know how?

"In any case, it's what we built your career on," Louise said, as though he'd spoken aloud. "People expect to see you acting straight with them."

To see me acting *straight.* An odd turn of phrase, Charlie thought.

"Now it looks like you and Ford Corrington conspired to screw Walter. And you just want to sit there and let it melt away. But it *won't.* Voters don't mind being lied to by a liar, but they won't put up with it from an honest man."

"What do you want me to do?"

"We already talked about it." She didn't bother to hide her annoyance. "You've got to cut Corrington loose. Make it look like that deal you had Sue leak—and I wish you hadn't done that, Charlie—was Corrington's idea, his end run around the public process."

"You wish we hadn't leaked it, or hadn't made it?"

"Both! I wish you'd stood behind Walter."

"Walter was about to be arrested for insurance fraud and murder."

Louise stabbed a forkful of salad and chewed as though it were her watercress she was furious with.

"Anyway," Charlie said, "Ford Corrington's in trouble with his own people already. It dirtied him up, to look like he was sneaking around with me."

"All the more reason. Maybe we could pick up some new supporters. People Ford's upset over the years."

"He could lose the Garden Project."

"You could lose the governorship."

"That foundation would fold without him."

"There are other charities. We'll choose one and make a big donation. If you want Walter and his friends back, you've got to offer up a sacrifice. This is the only message they'll understand."

Charlie looked at Louise, glossy black hair, shining blue eyes, anger adding a beautiful rose glow to her skin. Behind her, sunlight sparkled through deep green leaves. Louise, of course, could see none of this: nothing was in her line of sight but his tired face and the mayoral suite.

He said, "I'll never get Walter back."

"No, not publicly. His pride's too wounded."

"You're buying that?"

"But"—she gave him a cold look—"what you might get, if you work for it, is his quiet word in the ears of his friends. 'Fewer rules and regs' is still their best choice to protect their interests. They'll throw their weight your way for governor if they feel you understand where this all went wrong."

"If I crawl."

"If you admit your mistake!"

"My mistake was making a dirty deal with Walter. That's not what 'fewer rules and regs' was supposed to be about, and *that's* where this went wrong."

"Walter? Walter's the victim here."

"Only in terms of fact. Not moral intention."

"Oh, for God's sake, Charlie! Are you saying because no one *meant* to screw Walter except that insane DOI woman, he's not a victim?"

"No. I'm saying the least sorry person in New York that any of this happened is Walter."

"How can you say that? He was led through the streets in handcuffs!"

"And look at him now. He's got every last city department and regulatory agency by the balls *and* we're about to settle with him for millions. I'm beginning to think you could throw Walter off a cliff and it'd turn out to be the fastest way down to a gold mine."

"Walter's been a good friend to you, Charlie."

"Dammit, Louise!" Charlie clanked his fork to his plate. "Walter would've screwed me, you, the dog, and the cat any time in the last ten years if it would've gotten him something he wanted. And he'd kiss my ass in Macy's window this very afternoon if there were something in *that* for him."

Louise regarded him with that neutral, appraising look he knew so well, that look she fixed on strangers. "You're not going to do it, are you?"

"Do what? Hang Ford Corrington out to dry? No. I'm not."

"It's the only way, Charlie."

"The only way for what?"

Slowly and with the precise enunciation of the finishing schools she'd attended while he was at Stuyvesant, she said, "The only way you will ever be Governor of the State of New York."

"I hope that's not true."

"It is." Her blazing eyes gave him another familiar look, the one she used to finish people off. "And what's more, you know it is. I can see it on your face. Corrington, or Albany. You're as sure as I am."

Sutton Place

"Drink your latte and stop seething," Irene ordered Ann.

"I can't just sit here!"

"You can't get up and carry on like a crazy woman, either. Drink, calm down, and let's talk about it." The four of them were clustered around a tiny table in a crowded café.

"There's nothing to talk about. He killed Jen."

"Why? As part of this whole plot, this whole setup?"

"I'm sorry I ever told you guys about that. None of you believe me, do you?"

Shondi said gently, "I think we'd all like to. I know you wouldn't make up something like that. But it seems so . . . far-fetched."

"Forget about it. I don't give a damn. He probably got off on that from the beginning, knowing no one would believe me, if the light finally dawned. Bastard! He probably planned to *tell* me about it just to make sure I knew who won. But he's not going to win. I swear to God I'm going to destroy him."

"If you go anywhere near him now," Irene said, "he'll have you arrested."

"I don't care! He doesn't own the world, no matter what he thinks! Everyone says he can't be stopped, but I'm going to stop him."

"What you said to him," Irene said carefully, "about wanting Jen if he'd slept with her mother—"

"Forget it."

"Honey—"

"I said forget it. I don't want to talk about it. If you're going to help me, fine. If not, see you later."

Irene glanced at the others. "We're trying to help."

"No, you're trying to calm down your crazy friend. Helping would be lending me your phone."

"My phone?"

"Luis Perez isn't taking my calls," Ann said. "But he doesn't know your number."

Once more Irene exchanged a look with Shondi and Beth. Then she reached into her purse and handed over her phone.

"It's Ann. Don't hang up, Luis."

"*Madre de Dios!* Why the hell shouldn't I? What do you think you're doing?"

"I have new information—"

"I don't give a damn if you have a videotape! Leave me out of it. I have orders not to talk to you and believe me, I have no problem with that. I had IA all over my ass because of you, Princess."

"That evidence was planted, Luis."

"Oh, no shit!"

"Not by me. By Glybenhall."

"What the—"

"Because he knew I'd fall for it. He knew the investigator was me—was *going* to be me. It's a long story. Meet me, I'll tell you."

"No way in hell."

"That white woman they pulled from the river the day Kong and T.D. were killed? Tom Underhill's other case? Her name was Jennifer Eliot and she was sleeping with Walter Glybenhall."

A pause. Ann was aware of her friends' stares but didn't look up.

"Princess," Perez finally said, "you're nuts."

"No. But he wants everyone to think I am."

"Well, then, he's got what he wants."

"He was sleeping with her and he *killed* her, Luis."

"You have proof? A smoking gun? A confession? Two priests and a nun as witnesses?"

"No, I—"

"Call me back when you get them. But not from this phone. Now that I know this number." He clicked off.

Ann stared around the table. Irene's fierceness and Beth's discomfort she could take, but Shondi's kindly concern was too much. She handed

Irene her phone and abruptly said, "I have to go. I'll talk to you guys later."

"Honey—"

"Ann—"

"Come on—"

"Later."

She slung her bag over her shoulder and pushed out the door, refusing to slow down even when she realized she had no idea where to go or what to do. She made seven blocks uptown that way before she hit a red light and had to stop. A wave of exhaustion rose and crashed over her. When the green light came she could hardly move.

She felt a fatigue she'd never known before, a trembling hollowness. All she wanted was to go home. On the way she'd buy great armfuls of flowers. She'd lock the door behind her, sit on the sofa, and watch the East River flow. From there, surrounded by wild color and eddying scent, she'd call Joe.

A few blocks north she found a fruit stand. She bought crimson tulips and purple irises for their shades, stargazer lilies for their perfume, white peonies like the ones in Joe's garden. She retrieved the Boxster from the garage, dropped everything on the seat, and navigated across town. Pulling into the garage under her own building, she raised the top and steered into her space. She got out and walked around to the passenger side to pick everything up again.

The wrapping on the bouquets crinkled as she gathered them. She clutched everything close and reached for her purse, not sure how she was going to balance it all. When a hand clenched her arm and yanked her backwards, her first fear was for the flowers.

"Yo, bitch!" Clamping fingers spun her around to inhumanly mashed features: a stocking mask. A fist reared back and gold teeth glittered. Later she'd realize that his sneer was what saved her. The white-hot fury it sparked melted her frozen fear.

Smashing everything she held into his face, she ducked and kicked. A punch slammed her ear like a brick. Her head ringing, she clawed for the thumb of the hand squeezing her arm. He released his grip, but as she tried to straighten, another blow pounded her face, throwing her back against the car. Tulips and lilies littered the garage floor. As he grabbed her blouse and ripped it, she sliced at the mask with her keys, aiming for those horrible grinning lips. She heard a yelp and felt him let go.

"Give it up, bitch!" He backed just out of her reach, arms spread like a wrestler in a ring. The stocking mask was torn and peeling back, blood oozing from the slash. She felt hot bile rise, felt as sick as if the peeling nylon were flesh. "I got a message from the Boss. He say you ain't smart enough to give it up when you should, so you got to give it up now." He had her trapped against the Boxster's open passenger door and this was no standoff; he'd stopped his attack only long enough to deliver his message. Her keys, her only weapon, were a joke.

He lunged; she drilled the sharp toe of her slingback up into his crotch. Yowling, he folded over the pain. She drove her elbow into his face. Her arm went numb but he staggered and when he did she shoved him away and dove into the car. She yanked the door shut, squashed the lock button. The click came a second before the pounding thump of his fist on the windshield.

"Bitch!" he yelled. "Fuck you, bitch!" He pressed his bleeding face to the glass. "I kill you! I'm'a smoke you, bitch! Ain't being paid for that, fuck it, I do it *free!*"

But Ann was in the car. With a swift, icy calm she started up, shifted as though no one was clawing at her door handle, screaming curses. She held the clutch in while she gave the engine gas, let it up when it was revving high. The Boxster shot backwards out of the space, pulling her attacker with it. She blasted forward and spun left. Laying rubber up the ramp, she glanced in the mirror. She saw her attacker on one knee, howling and waving his fists, surrounded by shattered bouquets.

Heart's Content

Wild grapes threatened to strangle the young rudbeckia, and the rud-beckia, resourceful as always, had sent shoots to colonize every flower bed within ten feet of its homestead, just in case. The situation needed attention but Joe wasn't sure he'd hear the phone from that end of the garden. So he was retying the morning glories on the porch posts as though they weren't perfectly happy, and pulling the stems of the faded wood hyacinths though their leaves were still green.

He'd stopped pretending to himself that he was only angry at Ann for her silence, not worried about what it might mean, and had moved, in the hour since he'd gotten home, to trying to keep both feelings at bay. He'd give her until dark. And if he hadn't heard from her by then? What exactly, he asked himself, are you planning to do?

Weeding the herb bed by the door, where little had sprouted since he'd done this yesterday, he searched his memory for Ann's friends, people he could call, people who might say, *Oh, she's right here, sipping a Cosmo, hold on and I'll get her.* Then he could switch off the worry and focus on the anger.

Though for a while the only friend of Ann's whose name he could recall was Jen Eliot. Thinking of Jen only brought to mind the small, lost sound in Ann's voice.

He was holding in his mind the face of Ann's black law school room-mate, the one she'd gone into the DA's office with, hoping her name would swim into view, when he heard crunching gravel and an engine's purr.

Slapping his dirt-covered hands against his jeans, he jogged around the side of the cabin to the driveway. It was the red Boxster; it was Ann. He reached the car as she was climbing out and he started to say, "Where the—" but he stopped when he saw her ripped blouse, her tangled hair, her bare feet, and her bruises. She stood perfectly still for a moment, looking at him without expression. Then she started to cry.

Golden light warmed the yard, but when Ann emerged onto the porch she was wrapped in one of his turtlenecks and an old wool sweater. Her hands were lost in the fabric of their cuffs; his jeans bunched at her ankles. Her damp hair trailed around her shoulders, curling at the ends, and the whole effect was disquieting, as though she'd once been straighter, taller.

Moving gingerly to a chair, she avoided his gaze. A purple rim around her right eye and a split in her lip were the only visible damage; both would heal completely, from his experience, but they'd take time.

Joe went inside, poured coffee, fixed one with sugar and cream. She didn't turn when he came back out, didn't meet his eyes when he handed her the mug, but she took it.

He settled in the chair beside her, drank his own coffee, and watched with her as sunlight inched across the yard, illuminating some plants and leaving others in darkness. Ann's silence seemed to add richness to the birdsong, to the rush of the stream and rustle of leaves. He wondered what it would be like to be able to count on that silence.

"How badly are you hurt?" he asked when her coffee was almost gone and color had seeped back into her face. That had been his first question while they'd stood by her car, too, his arms enfolding her, her tears warm on his cheek.

"I'm all right," she'd said then, a patent lie.

"Should I call the cops?"

"No." After a time she'd pulled away and stumbled inside, toward the shower.

She didn't try to tell him she was all right now. For a while she didn't speak at all. At last: "I don't think anything's serious."

"Can you tell me what happened?"

"Walter sent—" Her voice cracked. She sipped some coffee and said again, "Walter sent somebody to scare me off. He was supposed to rape me."

"How—"

" 'Give it up!' " Her voice was suddenly savage. " 'The boss said you won't give it up so now you got to give it up!' That's what he said. He laughed. Pretty witty, huh?"

Joe wanted to reach for her hand, but he thought of her on precarious tiptoe on the boulder above the stream, and held himself back.

"Did you recognize him?" he asked instead.

"He had on a stocking mask. Black, taller than me, broader, too. Hooded blue sweatshirt, gray pants. Sneakers."

"Would you know him if you saw him again?"

"No. But I cut his face. Left cheek, I think his lip, too."

"Good for you," he said. "How?"

"My car keys."

"Where did it happen?"

"The garage under my building. He was waiting when I pulled in. If he'd been supposed to kill me he could have, easily. I kept thinking about that all the way here. Well, no." She gave a shake of her head. "I didn't even come to until somewhere past New Paltz. You should have seen me looking around, trying to figure out where I was."

"What happened to the guy?"

"I don't know. He smacked me around, ripped my blouse. I slashed his face with the keys and got in the car. He grabbed on but I shook him off. I don't think he was hurt badly. I wish I'd killed him. All those flowers." He saw a tear start in the corner of her eye, but she smeared it away.

"Flowers?" Joe said.

"What I was carrying. It doesn't matter."

A breeze wafted across the yard. "You want more coffee?" he asked.

"What you really want to ask is why I'm so sure it was Walter."

"Yes, I do."

"I'll tell you," she said. "If I can have a beer."

He brought out two beers and handed her one. He sat and waited.

"The short answer is, this morning I accused him of murder."

When she didn't go on, he said, "That's where this started. It's gotten him millions, the Harlem site, and a free ride forever through the city approvals process. Why would he send someone to attack you now?"

"It's a different murder."

"What do you mean?"

She stared across the garden, as though she were trying to make something out in the shadows. "My friend Jen," she said softly.

"Jen? Why would you think Glybenhall did that?"

"He was at the service this morning. Sitting with her family. You're about to tell me that they just know each other. Travel in the same circles. Irene tried to say that, too." She sipped her beer, still not looking at him. "Jen was seeing someone and she wouldn't tell me who. That means he was probably married and that I probably knew him."

"A lot of men fit that description."

"Jen's—*was*, she was big on inappropriate men. She never told us who they were if it would be bad for them if it came out. I think it made her feel powerful, to have this big secret that could ruin someone. To be so hot she could get a guy in that position."

"Powerful," Joe said. Barely thirty, dead in the garbage and reeds on the river's edge. "But all right. If it was Glybenhall, and they were having an affair, why would he murder her?"

"Lovers kill each other all the time. It could have nothing to do with this."

"Walter Glybenhall, in his sixties, has suddenly become a killing machine?"

"He always was."

"Ann?"

"Joe, wait."

She wiped angrily at her eyes again. This time he reached to take her hand, prepared for her to shake him off. Instead, she wrapped her fingers around his, held on tightly as though, together, they were preparing to jump.

"When I was fourteen, we lived in Switzerland. Zurich." Ann's voice was a quiet trickle. "My father found out Walter and my mother were having an affair. He went to confront them. It was a bad night, warm for winter, fog and rain. Dad spun out on a mountain road, and died."

"I know," Joe said. "You don't have to talk about that now."

"There are two parts of that story you don't know. And now is the only time."

She met his eyes. The mismatched blues in hers seemed to him to have intensified, and he realized that before today, he'd never seen her cry.

"My father was up in the mountains, skiing," she said. "I came up to join him. The way he knew about Walter and my mother was, I told him."

"You blame yourself?"

"I told him," she repeated, "because I'd caught them together. At Walter's place.

"He'd said he was having some people over for coffee, my mother included, and suggested I come around to say goodbye before my ski trip. A few days before *that* . . . a few days before, he'd made a pass at me. He'd come over for drinks, to our apartment. Some of my father's most important clients were there, too. Walter was . . . in those days he was rich, but not particularly anybody. Some of my father's clients were people he had his eye on."

"In what way?"

"He had projects he wanted them to invest in. Or attach their names to, at least. A word from my father would have gone a long way."

"But he didn't get it?"

"My father said Walter's schemes were all too big and not well thought through. My parents argued about it. It must have been my mother who invited him that afternoon. I'd never liked Walter, and I could tell my father didn't either, but he was a friend of my mother's so he'd always been around. I was so stupid then, I didn't even know what 'friend of my mother's' meant."

"That's the wrong word," Joe said. " 'Stupid.' "

She shrugged that off. "Anyway, he was there, and even I could see he was getting nowhere with the moneymen. I went to my room for something, I don't remember what, and when I came out, there was Walter. He cornered me. He said I'd better be quiet or I'd embarrass my father. I tried to push him away but . . . He touched me, kissed me . . . whispered things I'd never even heard. His breath was so hot. I kept twisting around, completely trapped. The only thing I could have done was yell. But I didn't. Because of the clients. Finally—it couldn't have been very long but it seemed like hours—someone called his name. He turned, and let go just enough for me to knee him in the crotch. One of the older girls at school had told us about that, to do it if a man got 'fresh.' I didn't know what 'fresh' meant and I didn't know if what Walter was doing was it, but the knee thing seemed like it might work. It did. He was the one who shouted. I squirmed away and ran to my room. I've always wondered what he told them about the shout." She paused again, but this time not for long. "I didn't tell my father about the hallway. When I told him about Walter and my mother I had some dumb idea he'd make Walter stay away from her, and that would keep him away from me, too. But what he got furious about wasn't the two of them so much—I think he must have known, somewhere, that that was going on—but that Walter had set me up to see it."

"Set you up?"

"Suggesting I come for coffee. There was no coffee. Just Walter and my mother, half naked and rolling all over each other on a bear rug. Have you ever heard such a cliché? My *mother* . . ."

A crow squawked and flapped in a pine, startled by something. Joe searched the branches but couldn't see it.

"He did it, Walter did it—he invited me, I mean—to get back at me. And because he knew I'd come. To show him I wasn't scared. Any sensible fourteen-year-old would have avoided him like a disease, after that scene in the hallway. But he knew I'd take it as a dare. And I fell right into it."

The deep shadows that covered the yard had settled into the trees now, too, though the sky was still light.

"He must have known I might tell my father," she said, "and he didn't care. More than didn't care. He wanted that. So my father could see who won."

CHAPTER

83

Sutton Place

Unable to stay still any longer, Ann plunged down the steps, strode across the yard until she reached the peonies backed onto the rocks and could go no farther. She stopped, looking around at the areas Joe had cleared and at the ones he hadn't gotten to, at the plants he'd brought here and the ones he'd uncovered and encouraged. Beside the peonies stood a patch of thin-leafed, knee-high stalks. Some kind of vine cork-screwed over them, weighing them down, but she could see more of them popping up here and there, even in the peonies. *Go ahead,* she could hear them say to the vines, *try to smash us down: we still have tricks up our sleeves.* Suddenly she wanted more than anything to be like Joe. She wanted to know what to do here, in this one place; to have a task she could accomplish and something cheering for her to succeed, even if it was only a patch of thin-leafed plants.

"Rudbeckia."

She hadn't heard Joe come up but she wasn't surprised to find him there.

"In a month they'll be almost as tall as you are," he said. "With yellow flowers."

"What do they need?"

"Just sun. They do everything else themselves."

"What about that?" She pointed at the vine.

"Grapes. I'll take it out but they won't really care. If they have to they'll grow right through it."

"They're coming up here, too, and over there."

"They're tough little bastards. They'd take over if you let them. Just the way the grapes would. In a way, they deserve each other. Except that it's not up to them."

"What do you mean?"

In the dusk she saw his old, slow smile. "It's up to me. Tell me why you told me that story. Why you said 'Now is the only time.' "

She wanted to keep talking about the flowers but she couldn't think of anything to ask. "Walter was responsible for those accidents. And the murders of those gangbangers, and Jen, too. Maybe he didn't kill anyone personally, I don't know. But he's responsible."

"All that evidence—"

"Was discredited. I know. And we thought that meant we were reading it wrong. But that's not what happened. We were reading it just the way we were meant to. It was all planted." She took a breath and told him the worst part. "And it was planted under *my* nose. Because Walter knew I'd fall for it." Now that she'd spoken it into reality she braced herself, expecting the weight of her stupidity, of the disgust and pity Joe would surely feel, to crush her into the ground.

Nothing happened. Joe didn't speak, the earth didn't open, and the sky stayed where it was.

Tentatively, as though stepping onto a log across a brook, she went on. "It was all so carefully planned. When everything was ready he had me called back from Siberia, gave me a stick to sniff, and turned me loose. And what a good little puppy I was! I dug it all out and brought it back just the way he knew I would. Just the way I found him with my mother, and told my father. Just the way he *knew* I would."

She gazed into the flower bed, then leaned forward and seized a handful of vine. She tugged; the entangled stalks bent but the grapevine didn't yield.

"Not that way," Joe said. "Its roots are back by the rock. Pull it gently in the direction it's growing from. It'll let go."

She waded into the rudbeckia, hesitantly at first, then with a rhythm, wrapping the vine around her hand as she tugged it loose. She followed it through the patch, to the boulder. "What do I do now?"

"If you can find where it comes out of the ground, pull it up. If it's between the rocks and you can't get at it, break it off."

"Won't it just come back if I do that?"

"It's better than nothing."

So she twisted and bent the vine until it broke, then plowed her way out of the rudbeckia, bearing her trophy.

"You think I'm crazy, don't you?"

"No. I think I need to hear what happened in the last two days that brought you to this conclusion."

"I told it all to Greg. *He* thinks I'm crazy."

"When did you do that?"

"Yesterday."

"Before you saw Walter at Jen's memorial."

"There was enough to tell."

"Then tell it to me."

Joe made scrambled eggs, toast, and bacon. "And Fig Newtons for dessert," he said.

"Don't you ever eat real food?"

"Canned beef stew?"

"I'll take the scrambled eggs. Are you going to put anything in them?"

"Canned beef stew?" He grinned when she smiled.

While they ate she told him everything: O'Doul, the jeweler, Shamika, Blowfish and the Latin Kings.

"I was wondering about the thunderbolt," Joe said.

She inspected her nails. "Only two got broken in the garage. I don't know what she uses but I think I'll go back to her. Joe? What am I going to do?"

"I don't know."

Those words might have brought despair but Ann felt a sudden wave of déjà vu. Not disorienting, as that sense usually was. Reassuring and familiar, instead. This was how they used to work, Chinese food containers or pizza boxes building a temporary landscape across his desk or hers. They'd lay out facts and look at them, talk about them, and decide what to do next. "I don't know" didn't mean Joe was at a loss. It just meant she'd asked too soon.

She cleared the table while Joe built a fire. He brought the box of Fig Newtons and sat beside her on the sofa.

"He's made you into the boy who cried wolf," Joe said. "If you're right about Glybenhall being the one who sent the guy after you today—"

"What do you mean 'if'?"

"—then it makes sense that the guy was supposed to hurt you but not kill you. You're still official, even if you're on desk duty, so killing you would bring down weight. But an attack in your own garage could be written off to just another mugging. You'd get the message without much risk to him. But . . ."

"But what?"

"But something doesn't feel right."

She stared into the night. "You said that before."

"I did?"

"When this started. You said it didn't feel right, and I said it felt like Christmas. It felt like that because it was. Walter was giving me gifts." A log crumbled in the fire. "Trojan horses. You were right."

"I just feel like there's something missing," Joe said.

"Like what?"

"The connections aren't clear. Even if Shapiro's working with Glybenhall—"

"For, not with. No one works *with* Walter."

"And why kill Jen? Why?"

"Like I said, lovers kill each other. Maybe it had nothing to do with this. Or maybe it did. Maybe she knew something."

"You think she helped set you up? Planted evidence, was a go-between?"

"God, no. No, not Jen. She'd do almost anything for a laugh but she wouldn't have thought that was funny."

"So it might be something she'd found out by accident?"

"Could be."

The fire was mesmerizing, beautiful to watch, but Ann found it wasn't warming her. "I need to go to sleep. But first I need to know what you're thinking, Joe."

"What I'm thinking is, if I were on the job, I'd want to do more digging before I set my trap."

"If you can think of how or where I could dig—"

"But you can't. It's not safe now. He'll be waiting to see whether you took his warning. If you did he'll leave you alone, but if he thinks you didn't there won't be a second one."

"So you do think it was him."

"It was somebody. Right now, he's most likely."

She smiled wryly. "You always were a belt-and-suspenders guy."

She expected that to make him smile, too, to find, after all this time, her eagerness still straining against his caution. But he shook his head. "Not always," he said, in a voice so soft she almost couldn't hear him. "Not when it counted most."

In the garden the moon cast a silvery glow and some flowers she hadn't noticed in the daylight seemed to gleam in answer.

"Move over." She settled against him and welcomed his warmth. She didn't speak. What could she have told him?

"We need a confession." He coiled his arm around her.

"I didn't do it," she said sleepily.

He looked down at her. "Not," he said, "from you."

"Oh. You want Walter to confess? Go ahead and call him, I have him on speed-dial. Though if this is your interrogation technique, I suggest you refine it."

"If we can't get a confession we need a smoking gun."

"I had a gun. It was the wrong damn gun."

"What about your friend Perez?"

"What about him?"

"Would he do some more digging?"

"He's been ordered off this. Told to keep away from me. If we had a map to the treasure with a big X on it, Perez might dig. Otherwise, I don't think so."

"But if we baited a trap, and it got sprung, could we count on Perez to come collect the rat?"

She sat up to look at him. "You have a trap?"

"I don't know. I'm thinking. But if no one's there except you and me to see it catch anything, it won't work."

"Perez got burned pretty badly. At this point I'm not sure what would make him join up with me again. But there is someone we could count on."

"Who?"

"Greg Lowry."

"*Lowry?* I thought he was ready to lock you up."

"He is. That's why. Look how upset he got when I told him Mark Shapiro had to be involved."

"You were dissing the honor of the agency. After me, that's got to be a sore point with Lowry." He smiled when he said that, but not with his eyes.

Ann kissed him and said, "I don't think that's it. Greg wanted the Commissioner's job and he's actually more qualified. It was political that Shapiro got it. Think of how frustrating it has to be for him to think that Shapiro's involved in this but that I screwed it up so badly that none of it can ever be investigated again."

"For that he'd have to believe you. You said he thinks you're crazy."

"I still could be right. The possibility must be driving *him* crazy."

"So how does that help us?"

"If whatever trap you've thought up—"

"I haven't thought up anything."

"But you will. And if it has the potential of handing him Shapiro if I'm right, and me if I'm wrong, I'll bet I could sell it to him."

"You? I'm not handing you to him."

"When did it get to be your choice? The chance of that is what'll close the deal. He has to see that he can't lose. Walter—and Shapiro—

for being as bad as I think they are, or me for stalking and harassing them, and Greg gets to save them. He's a hero either way."

"No." Softly, Joe said, "It's no joke, Ann. It's nothing to be brave about. You don't know what it's like."

"No, I don't. And I'm not very brave about it. But if Walter takes whatever bait you're thinking up, someone has to see it besides us, like you said. It's a risk worth taking."

"It's not worth taking. We'll think of someone else."

"*Who?* There's no one else, Joe. It has to be Greg. What's the name of those plants, the ones that get as tall as I am?"

"Rudbeckia."

"Think of me as them."

"You're much prettier."

"And Walter's the grapevine. Only this time, it's not up to you. I'm going to pull him up by the roots."

Joe stared, then burst out laughing.

She flushed. "That was a little grandiose, right?"

"Oh, maybe just around the edges."

"But you know what I mean. Walter can't do this to me twice. If there's any chance of nailing him, the risk *is* worth taking."

He gazed at her, his face shadowed. He pulled her to him and they didn't talk about the future again until morning.

Heart's Content

Over coffee and cornflakes Joe spelled out for Ann the idea that had come to him during the night, as she slept bruised and exhausted beside him and he watched the moon through the bedroom window.

He began by saying, "This may be crazy."

But she didn't think so. "It's perfect." Her eyes glowed. "Walter won't be able to stand it. He'll have to make a move."

"You'll have to convince Ford Corrington to go for it."

"That's the only part that might be hard. But he's in a bad situation. I'm hoping he's desperate enough."

"But it can't be Lowry. In case something goes wrong. Find a way to get Perez."

"He won't, Joe. No one will but Lowry."

He poured more coffee and that argument went on. They spent Sunday refining his plan, going over the angles. Planting the dicentra, weeding the herbs. And having that same argument. Until, finally, he gave in.

Monday there was one more argument before they left for New York.

"You're not coming," Ann said.

"It has to be me. No one will listen to you. I didn't want Lowry and it took you all day yesterday to convince me there's no one else. But you were right and I bought it."

"And now you're planning to argue over this all day today?"

"I don't have to. You know I'm right."

"If you get caught, Joe," she hesitated, "they could revoke your parole."

"Get caught doing what?" He spoke as though that thought hadn't haunted his night, hadn't forced him out of bed at dawn and sent him scrabbling up the boulder wall to inspect the cascading trumpet vine. He'd stood up there for a long time, astonished, as always, by the vast, unblocked view.

"Leaving the county," Ann said.

"I called my case officer," he told her. "I said I had a chance of a job in Manhattan, told him how I'd be going and that I'd be back Friday at the latest. He gave me his blessing."

"You did that already?"

"I was up early."

"It can't be you."

"It can't be anyone else."

"Irene could do it."

"Irene's a lawyer. She has too much to lose."

"And you don't?"

"She can get in trouble for acting unethically. I can't. Just illegally. Which this isn't. There's nothing I'll be doing that's against parole regs."

"You'll be lying."

He grinned. "You're kidding, right?"

"I can't ask you to do this."

"You're not. I said I wouldn't hand you to Lowry and you said it wasn't my choice. This isn't yours."

The argument they didn't have was over whose car to use. After they'd made the phone calls that got things rolling, Joe packed an overnight bag and locked up the cabin, but he didn't even take the pickup's keys.

With the top down they raced past farm fields and stands of pine, swooped up and over the Tappan Zee, and followed the Thruway until it became the FDR. Ann wove the little red car through traffic and out onto the Manhattan streets. Joe stayed silent as they stopped-and-started past buildings in whose shadows he was raised and others that had not been there when he went away. It was only as they neared Ann's place that he realized his palms were sweating.

When they turned into the driveway to her garage, Joe saw Ann's face harden.

"We don't have to go in here," he said. "We could put the car in another lot."

"I'm fine," she said tersely, and wheeled the Boxster down the ramp.

A few flattened flower petals lay on the oil-stained concrete. Ann didn't look at them. She parked in the most impassive and precise manner Joe had ever seen, locating the car in the exact center of her space. They crossed the garage to the elevator, Ann striding ahead with her jaw thrust out. Once in the elevator she visibly relaxed, and by the time she unlocked her door the color was back in her cheeks.

She dropped her bag on the foyer table. "Not bad, huh? I told you I bought it for the view."

Joe crossed to the wall of glass at the end of the living room. Sun gleamed on the East River and a summer haze obscured the horizon.

From behind him, Ann said, "I'm going to change. I couldn't talk anyone into anything looking like this."

When she was ready, he left with her.

"Where are you going to go?" she asked.

"Nowhere. But it's been a while," he said, in explanation.

She gave him a long look, then turned and peered critically at herself in the mirror.

"You look great," he said.

"Thanks. I kind of thought the shirt went well with the purple around my eye."

"What are you going to tell people about that?"

"The truth. That it's just one more example of why Walter's got to be stopped."

At a Cell Hut he bought a throwaway phone and gave her the number. Then she hailed a cab and he started to walk.

He headed uptown randomly, crossing at corners and stopping at lights. He fell right back into the rhythm as though he hadn't been gone for years. Rumbling traffic punctuated with horn honks and overlayed with passing sirens supplied the soundtrack. Hot dogs and bus exhaust provided the perfume. The visuals were ever-changing and exactly the same: distracted pedestrians, speeding bike messengers, tame city trees; towering straight-walled glass and steel, lower, older brick and stone.

He found himself noticing the changes: a construction site where four walk-ups had been, new windows going into a long-abandoned hotel. That these places had remained so lodged in his memory alarmed him; that he found himself passing judgment, thinking this change good and that one bad, was disconcerting. He no longer cared what happened here. He was gone, somewhere else, started over. Good changes and bad ones had meaning only if you had a vision for a place and they matched it or crossed it. New York was in his past, no vision now, just freeze-frame photos, fading, indistinct.

He jaywalked with a practiced skill, read headlines as he passed news-stands and noted an ailanthus tree reaching for the sunlight from a rubble-littered lot.

You could come back.

The tires' hiss, the sharp shadows of fire escapes, the scent of salt pretzels from a street cart all seemed to have one thing to say. The pulse of his blood answered the cadence around him. He'd been born here, raised in a walk-up like the one he was passing; he'd played stickball on asphalt streets like these, had his first kiss in a shadowed doorway like that one across the way.

It hasn't been that long. You could come back.

Sutton Place

"Joe? Corrington went for it."

"Hey, good work! Was it hard?"

"His board meets next Thursday and he thinks they're planning to ask him to resign. He called this a 'Hail Mary pass.' I said, 'Hallelujah,' and that was that. Where are you?"

"Madison and Eighty-third."

"What are you doing?"

"Walking around."

"Are you okay?"

"I'm fine. Why shouldn't I be?"

"I don't know. Being back, that's all."

"I'm fine, Ann. How about you?"

"Stiff and achey. Or I would be if I weren't on such an adrenaline high. I'll call you after I see Greg Lowry."

"Joe? Greg's in."

"Holy cow. How did you do that?"

"I told you he was bound to be."

"I didn't believe you."

"Because I'm blonde?"

"No doubt."

"Where are you?"

"Carl Schurz Park."

"Over by Gracie Mansion?"

"It has all new plantings."

"Joe?"

"Yes?"

"Nothing. Two down. I'll call you again."

"Joe? Don Zalensky said he'll think about it."

"Does it look likely?"

"Well, he didn't throw me out. It was harder than Corrington or Greg, but in the end I think he'll do it."

"If he can sell it."

"He's not going to try. He's going to handle it on his own. To keep Hizzoner clean."

"Can he manage that?"

"He wouldn't have to do much, just confirm that Charlie's about to do what we're saying he is, if anyone asks."

"You're amazing."

"No. I'm right. Where are you?"

"Harlem, 128th Street."

"What are you doing up there?"

"That jobsite. I thought I'd take a look."

"What do you think?"

"I think it's worth fighting for."

CHAPTER

86

City Hall

The mayor stared at the deputy mayor in disbelief. "You know," he said, "three weeks ago I was the Mayor of the City of New York. Now we're down the rabbit hole and I must be the goddamn Mad Hatter. Who are you and what have you done with Don Zalensky?"

"All right, it's extreme," Don said. "But if it works, you may get to Albany yet."

"If Albany's anything like this I'm not so sure I want to go there anymore. This is the craziest goddamn idea I ever heard."

"Could work."

"Only if Walter's guilty!"

"I hate to point out the obvious, but nothing ever said he wasn't. He just got too hot to handle."

"And this could make him radioactive! Setting him up for the murder of a girl we don't even know he knew—!"

"Of course he knew her. And we're not setting him up, Charlie. This is a trap only Jen's killer would fall into. If Glybenhall didn't do it, he won't fall for it."

"It's nuts. It can't work."

"I think it can. And it could prove we were right all along and make our people look really clever. I'll tell you what part won't work, though: Joe Cole going to Glybenhall. Glybenhall knows all about him and Ann Montgomery. He wouldn't let Cole through the door."

"There, see—"

"I'm going to suggest they go through Edgar Westermann."

"*Edgar?* Jesus, Don, what are you trying to do?"

"Whether or not Westermann believes Glybenhall killed Jen, the rest of it—the part about you and Corrington—will get him upset. He'll take it straight to Glybenhall."

Charlie ran his hand over his bald head. "What if this bright idea blows up in our faces?"

"No one will ever know you knew anything about it. I told Ann Montgomery I'd consider it, but that if I agreed, it would just be me. That I wouldn't tell you anything. This way if it comes back to bite us, it won't get any farther than me."

"Are you nuts? I don't work like that."

"If things keep going the way they are, I'll be out of a job soon anyway. You'll have to throw someone to the wolves."

"Not you, for chrissakes."

"Me, or six nonfranchise players. And that might not be enough to get you to the finals."

"That's a sports metaphor," Charlie objected.

"You didn't think I could do that? I've been practicing."

"In case you get traded to another team?"

"Something like that." Don eased a cigarette from the pack.

"Give me one of those."

"Really?"

"No. But give me something. This is insane. This could sink us." Charlie ran his hand over his head again. "Ah, what the hell. Go ahead. We're sunk already."

Heart's Content

"What can I do for you, Mr. Cole? Please, please, sit down."

Edgar Westermann reestablished himself behind his massive desk. The collar of his white-on-white shirt sat slightly askew, leading Joe to think he'd tightened his tie and shrugged back into his jacket when his visitor was announced.

Joe sat unhurriedly on a chair as substantial as the desk. Behind him, a wall of photographs showed the Borough President in three-piece-suited splendor performing various official functions. Heavy brocade drapes echoed the patterned Persian carpet. Joe wondered if all the furnishings in this office had been selected for the amount of light and air they were able to displace.

He waited a few extra seconds just to get Westermann off balance, then asked without preamble, "Do you remember me?"

Westermann made a show of frowning and searching his mental database. "Yes, I believe I do," he said tentatively. But Joe had seen calm familiarity in Westermann's eyes when he'd walked in the office.

Joe said nothing.

Like most politicians, Westermann was not on good terms with silence, so after a brief time the Borough President went on. "You used to work for the city. DOI, I believe. You were involved in that Dolan Construction disaster."

"Good," Joe said. "We don't have to go through the early chapters, then."

Westermann raised his eyebrows. "I don't take your meaning."

"I spent two and a half years in prison. I'm on parole for the next half-dozen. My wife divorced me and I dig ditches for a living. What happened in Dolan Construction wasn't my fault but the city needed a scapegoat and I got tagged. I'm pissed off, Mr. Westermann."

"Well, I can understand you might feel that way, but the law—and the community—saw it different. Now, if you're here to rehash all that, I'm not sure I see the good that can come of it."

"I'm not. I've come across some information that I think will be valuable to you. I want to make a deal."

"Deal? What sort of deal?"

"Money, of course."

Westermann grunted. "General run of things, people don't come to me much for money. I'm just a public servant."

"You do all right. And your friend Walter Glybenhall is loaded."

"This has to do with Mr. Glybenhall?"

"It does."

"So why come to me?"

"If you remember me, you remember that Ann Montgomery's a friend of mine. Glybenhall knows that, too. He wouldn't have let me through his door."

"No, I don't suppose he would."

"What I'm hoping is that you find what I have to say interesting enough to tell Glybenhall about. Because even though it came from Ann, it's something he'll want to know."

"Ann Montgomery is a troubled young woman."

"Troubled especially by the way the city's dealt with her."

"She didn't want to be heaped with scorn, could be she shouldn't have treated one of New York's leading citizens the way she did."

"I warned her. I told her, whether you're right or wrong, you can't go up against Walter Glybenhall, he'll crush you like a bug. But she had the same problem I had three years ago."

"What's that?"

"She believed in justice. Tell the truth, she thought, and it'll all work out."

"Might be that justice is what she got."

"Not even close. It still upsets her that it doesn't work that way. But I'm over it. All I want to do is score and get out. I told Ann, if we can't get justice we might as well get rich." Joe hurtled along, following an old engineering school motto: *If you can't blind 'em with brilliance, baffle 'em with bullshit.*

"Mr. Cole, I have to tell you, I don't like the sound of this. It's clear to me, you got some sort of scheme cooked up. If I'd known what your business was—"

"That's why I didn't say. Mr. Westermann, I've been watching the news lately. You've suddenly hitched your wagon to Walter Glybenhall's star."

"Walter Glybenhall and I have had our differences over the years. But I'll stand with anyone who's trying to hold this city accountable for its outrageous actions."

"Not for free, I'm sure."

"Now, look here, son! I resent the insinuation! If you're thinking this office can be bought—"

"I'm sorry, I mistook you for a politician."

"You've got no call—"

"Glybenhall's romance with Charlie Barr came to an abrupt end. I'm sure he's looking for a shoulder to cry on. You're a hell of an underdog for the mayoral nomination and your fundraising's off to a slow start. You need Glybenhall's money and his credibility in the white community. And he needs yours in Harlem."

"I'd put it a little different. I'd say Walter Glybenhall and I have discovered a mutual respect as we've found ourselves a common enemy—"

"Charlie Barr?"

"No, this city's disregard for justice!"

"And the silver lining on *that* cloud is how it threw you together with Glybenhall, just when you needed each other most."

"It's an ill wind, don't blow someone good."

"I'm not disagreeing. You'd be a fool to miss the chance to hook up with Glybenhall. And I've never heard anyone say Edgar Westermann's a fool."

"Through the years, I've had people calling me all sorts of hurtful things. And I've had many come sit in my office—right where you're sitting—and think they can con ol' Westermann, because he don't get but crumbs offered to him, so he's grateful for anything looks like a whole slice of bread. So Mr. Cole, come to your point. I'm—"

"A busy man. Yes, I'm sure you are. And I'm not. I have very little to do these days. Ann's not busy, either. She spends a lot of time having coffee with friends, now that she can't work anymore."

"My sympathy. Idle hands are the devil's playthings. Now, a bright person could take idleness as a chance to study on their shortcomings, to see how to improve them."

"Or how to improve their situation and to hell with their shortcomings. Mr. Westermann, sir, unless something's done about it, Walter Glybenhall is not going to end up with that Block A property in Harlem."

Westermann eyed Joe. "What do you mean by that?"

"By that I mean Glybenhall's not the only one who's mad and he's not the only one capable of pissing in the punch bowl before he leaves the party. Charlie Barr's approval ratings are at an all-time low. He'll never get to be governor."

"If that's true it's because he let Ann Montgomery lead him around by the nose. Or, considering her beauty, by his nether parts," Westermann retorted.

"Can't resist a cheap shot at him, can you?"

"Don't—"

"Go ahead, I'm not crazy about old Charlie myself. I'm not really fond of any of you. But, Mr. Borough President, you're my best shot. Over coffee with a friend who still works for the city, Ann found out that the mayor's planning to give that Block A building site to Ford Corrington."

"Say *what*?"

"Garden Walls, Garden Gate, Down the Garden Path, whatever they call it. Hizzoner's going to announce it at a press conference to-morrow."

"He wouldn't dare."

"He would dare. He's going to say the city's looked over Garden Walls' proposal, liked it a lot, bingo, Harlem's theirs. The mayor's calling in favors from Real Property and from Planning, for this."

"Favors? The man doesn't dare show his face in public these days. He's got no political currency to spend. He can't do this."

"Sure he can. It's his way of flipping Walter Glybenhall one last, giant bird. What does he have to lose? He's going down anyway. This way at least he goes down as Robin Hood. It'll redeem Ford Corrington in the eyes of the *community*, for sure. And once it's done, once a *community* group including men of the church and local banks and all sorts of popular people have their claws in that site, what are you going to do about it?"

"Me?" Westermann sat up, visibly regrouping. "Well, if this is true, it will be a fine day for Harlem and a new dawning for this community that—"

"Oh, turn it off," Joe said. "If Glybenhall gets beat out of Block A, you think he's going to give a rat's ass about Harlem? Or your campaign? You'll have lost him and his support, and Ford Corrington will have made you look like a fool. Mr. Borough President, sir, if you can't stop this from happening you can kiss your political future goodbye."

"My political future, *sir*, rides on the fortunes of the community I serve!"

"Oh. Not on Glybenhall's money? Oh, well, then, never mind. You don't need me, I guess."

"I can't imagine why you thought I ever did."

"But you haven't thrown me out, have you? You want to know. You want to know why I thought that."

He locked his eyes on Westermann's. Westermann glared but didn't look away.

Joe smiled. "There's a way out. I told you I had information you'd find valuable. That was only half of it. How about I tell you the rest, and you can do whatever you want with it. If it works out for you, I'll expect to be remembered. If I'm remembered, I'll forget we ever had this conversation. If I'm forgotten, you'll be sorry we did."

"I don't like to be threatened, Mr. Cole."

"I don't know anyone who does. Do you want to hear me out?"

"Well," Westermann said slowly, "you're here."

Harlem: State Office Building

"Walter Glybenhall was having an affair," Joe Cole said, sitting in front of Edgar's desk.

Edgar frowned. "Walter Glybenhall's love for the ladies ain't exactly news, son. And I can't see how it's supposed to help this situation."

"The woman's dead."

"Well, that's sad, but still . . . ?"

"She was murdered. Her body was fished from the river two weeks ago. Jennifer Eliot, her name was."

Edgar felt his heart skip. "I remember that," he said. "Poor child. But you can't be—you're not telling me you think Walter Glybenhall killed her?"

"Ann does. She told Glybenhall she did. Personally, I don't know or care. If it *was* Glybenhall, there's no way he'll go down for murder. But the situation offers an opportunity, if it's played right. Because Glybenhall wasn't the only man Jen Eliot was seeing."

"Really?" Edgar said slowly. "You don't say."

"As it happens, Jen Eliot played the field. Dated lots of men."

"How do you know that?"

"As it also happens, she was a friend of Ann's."

"Is that so? Small world, then."

"Small enough that Jen told Ann about another of her men. Not by name. She wouldn't tell her friends the names of her sugar daddies if it would make trouble for them."

"She kept quiet to protect them?"

"Or she got a kick out of having the power to destroy them. Though she didn't precisely keep quiet. Just kept their *names* under her hat. But Ann's been so distracted trying to corner Walter Glybenhall that the penny didn't drop on who Jen's other playmate must have been until yesterday."

"And when it did . . . ?"

"She told me. And I realized we had the goose that lays the golden eggs."

"And that goose, by name?"

"The goose is Walter Glybenhall. The name of the other playmate is Ford Corrington."

Edgar could only stare. "I *know* you're not serious."

"Oh, but I am. Jen Eliot bragged she was sleeping with two men who disliked each other, and she was getting a huge charge out of neither of them knowing where she'd been the night before."

"That doesn't mean—"

"She'd said other things, too."

"Why, that—" Edgar cleared his throat. "Why . . . You're telling me—you're saying this girl was carrying on with Walter Glybenhall and Ford Corrington under each other's noses?"

Cole nodded.

"And the police have no idea? Why hasn't Ann Montgomery gone to them with this information?"

"Who'd believe her? Two weeks late, tangled up with both those men in this other mess?"

"She could go to the press. Reporters feed on scandals like this."

"Oh, there's a great idea. 'Crazy Cop Makes Fresh Allegations.' Subhead, 'Further Desperate Attempts to Focus Spotlight on Developer Also Implicate Harlem Community Organizer.' Come on, Mr. Westermann. What paper would dare print anything unpleasant about Walter Glybenhall these days? He'd slap a lawsuit on anyone who looked at him sideways."

"Well, I can't say I don't think he's got the right."

"And I'm sure he doesn't give a shit what you think. If he murdered Jen Eliot it's just one more thing he'll never pay for. But Corrington's a different story."

"And what story would that be?"

"Walter Glybenhall had an intimate relationship with this young woman. He must have something in his possession that would amount to forensic evidence. An earring she left behind. Her mascara, her lipstick. A pair of nylons."

"If this relationship was like you say, I'm sure he does. So what?"

"Where's your imagination? Mr. Borough President, tell me, how would it look to the *community* if Ford Corrington's relationship with this dead woman were known? What would it do to Hizzoner's plan to give Block A to Corrington?" Cole sat back in his chair as the light began to dawn on Edgar. "And all it would take," Cole said, "would be for something Glybenhall digs out of his couch to find its way to the azaleas in Ford Corrington's garden."

Harlem: Frederick Douglass Boulevard

"I don't know whether to hope this works or hope it doesn't," Ford said into the dim quiet of the Garden Project's woodshop. "It won't make me happy to have it proved that people are willing to frame me for murder."

"If it works it won't prove that." Ann Montgomery sat on a workbench, staring through the window. "Just that they're willing to destroy your reputation."

From the shadows, Joe Cole added, "Given how Jen Eliot died, all they need to do is connect you up with her. That'll be enough to stop Charlie Barr from naming you his new best friend."

"It's not going to work." That sour remark came from Greg Lowry, who sat with his feet slung up on a table. "We're going to sit here like idiots until morning and then I'm going to arrest Montgomery on as many charges as I can think up. And you, too, Cole. Fucking extortion, making me let you in on this."

Montgomery had brought Cole with her in the hour after sunset as they'd arranged. "Greg Lowry's going to want to throw Joe out," she'd told Ford. "I'm asking you not to let him."

Joe Cole had extended his hand to Ford. "I want to thank you," he'd said. "For not jumping on the bandwagon three years ago. Dolan Construction."

Ford had taken the man's hand, but told him, "As I said to Inspector Montgomery, nothing I did back then was on your behalf. My concern was that the focus on you took the spotlight off the larger issue. I can't say I believed you were innocent."

Surprising Ford, Cole had said, "I wasn't. Just not guilty of what I was on trial for."

When Lowry came he found Montgomery and Cole already seated in Ford's office. Lowry's face had reddened and he'd demanded they leave.

"My office," Ford had said. "My garden. My guests."

The garden on this dark night was a jumble of odd shapes and strange shadows moving restlessly in a rising breeze. The sky had been clouding up all day, and by now it hung thick and low, obscuring the moon. A thin rain started. Cars plowed by on the avenue, their headlights sweeping the plants and pathways, changing the patterns.

Watching out the window, Ford noticed how big the abelia had become and how surprisingly well the crape myrtle against the wall had taken root. He found himself wondering how long it was since he'd sat in the garden. When was the last time he'd walked through just to see the new spring shoots, to admire the summer's abundance? When had he last pulled a weed or two? He visited to compliment the second graders on their vegetable patch, to attend a senior's meeting, to sit with a pregnant fifteen-year-old under the grape arbor and tell her somehow, someway, things would be all right. But he always had a meeting to get to, a proposal to write.

In his head he sorted through next week's calendar, and the week after, wondering—if this crazy scheme worked and he was still in charge here by the end of next week—whether he could cut back a little. Choose a plot near the back and turn over some earth himself. He was imagining the heft of the shovel when Lowry swung his feet to the floor.

Montgomery's back straightened. Cole didn't move but Ford felt him tighten.

A figure had appeared at the locked garden gate.

It stood a moment, working with the lock and chain; then it creaked the gate open and slipped through, re-draping the chain to look, from the street, as though it hadn't been cut.

"Son of a bitch," Lowry said softly. "What the hell?"

"It's not Glybenhall," Montgomery whispered.

"He was never going to come himself." Now Cole pushed off the wall. "Whoever this is, when he's trapped he'll talk."

In the rainy darkness the shadow was indistinct, but Ford saw that

Montgomery was right: it was shorter and wider than Glybenhall would have been. It seemed familiar, something about the way it moved, but in this light that played tricks it was impossible to be sure. They watched the shadow inch along a path and vanish behind shrubs.

"Fuck," said Lowry. "I do not fucking believe this." Another motionless moment, and then he started across the room. "You three! Do *not* come outside until I give you the all-clear. Do *not* fuck this up for me." Gun in hand, he eased open the door and stepped into the garden.

Ford stood at the window with Cole and Montgomery. They watched the shadow that was Lowry converge on the other shadow. As both moved deeper Ford lost them in the rustling foliage. He strained to see. Montgomery's hand squeezed Cole's arm. The darkness in the garden was hypnotic, hallucinatory: the rhythmic sweep of headlights, the bobbing of branches, the spattering of rain.

A gunshot broke the spell and sent them pounding out the door.

Heart's Content

The right-hand path seemed most likely. Rain slicked Joe's bare arms and soaked his shirt as he ran.

When the walkway lights sprang on everything changed. Bushes loomed or shrank, trees blocked his way or showed another.

"There," Ann shouted. Joe cast around, saw a leaf-draped shelter. Corrington reached it just after they did. Greg Lowry stood outside, gun in his hand, cell phone to his ear. A bulky form sprawled on the patterned brick.

"Blowfish," Corrington said.

"Eighth and 126th," Lowry was saying. "The Garden Project, in the garden. Yes. No. No. Fast. At least two. One down, the other over the fence in the back, probably down the alley to 127th. I'm going after him." He pocketed the phone. "Cops and ambulance on the way. There was someone else, someone waiting. The whole time we were in there! He shot this one as I got close, ran and jumped the fence. *Stay here!*" He took off running.

Blood seeped through the gangbanger's hooded sweatshirt. Joe knelt, felt for a pulse, and found one. He unzipped the sweatshirt, bunched up the cloth, and pressed it against the wound. Blowfish stirred and groaned. A .22 lay by his right hand. Ann, crouching beside Joe, wrapped a handkerchief around the gun and pocketed it. She asked, "Will he make it?"

Joe said, "If that ambulance gets here fast."

She leaned forward, face close to Blowfish. "Who sent you here?"

Blowfish didn't answer, Joe not sure if that was because he didn't want to or he couldn't. Rain pelted harder, spattering around them. Joe saw Ann reach toward something glittering on the bricks. She swept it into her hand and stared at it. "This is Jen's chain."

"Are you sure?"

"She wore it around her waist. It's been cut." She leaned toward Blowfish again. "Walter Glybenhall gave this to you to plant here, right?"

This time Blowfish managed a whisper: "Don't know shit about that."

"If that's true, Blowfish," Corrington said, "why are you breaking into my garden in the middle of the night?"

"Who was waiting for you?" Ann demanded. "Who shot you?"

"Wasn't no one . . ."

"Who're you protecting, Blowfish? Because he's sure as hell not protecting you."

"Wasn't no one." Blowfish's words were soft and his lids slowly closed.

"Where the hell's that ambulance?" Joe said.

Corrington took his cell phone out. He punched a number and spoke; Joe couldn't hear him over the rustling of the leaves in the rain until he lowered the phone and told them, "Nine-one-one dropped the call."

"What?"

"They have no record. Rainy night in Harlem, lots of calls for ambulances. It's on its way now."

"Dammit! That means they didn't send Greg any police backup, either!" Ann said.

"Hell!" Corrington pulled out his phone again.

They waited there like that, rain trying to push through the grape leaves, Joe trying to hold back Blowfish's blood. Finally, a siren wailed. Rain sparkled in powerful headlights. "I'll let them in," Ann said, running to the gate. In a few moments she came back with the EMTs. Another siren howled and a police car bounced onto the curb.

Ann flashed her badge at the cops who came quick-walking up the path. "This was a DOI operation," she told them briskly. "My boss chased another suspect over that fence. I'm going in the ambulance with this one in case he wakes up. Here's his gun. Mr. Corrington can tell you whatever else you need to know."

Well done, Joe thought. Someone had to stay with Blowfish, to catch anything he might say. With Greg Lowry out in the night chasing the shooter, Ann was the closest thing they had to law enforcement. Unless these cops were particularly sharp, they wouldn't know this was the infamous Ann Montgomery, wouldn't know that badge was no good, wouldn't know they were being set onto the well-respected Ford Corrington as a smoke screen. He met Ann's eyes and nodded as she left, gave her a small smile. Her eyes were shining.

CHAPTER

91

Sutton Place

"I'll take my own car," Ann told the EMTs.

"Harlem Hospital," one of them said.

Ann turned uptown. Her car was in a garage five blocks away. She'd have taken a cab, but she'd never get one in Harlem in the night, in the rain.

And she needed her car, because she wasn't going to the hospital.

If Blowfish talked, there was only one thing he could say: Glybenhall had sent him.

But if he said it to Ann Montgomery, who'd believe it?

Let him tell some cop. And when he did, the NYPD would find the situation so explosive they'd make endless calls up the food chain, before the full force and majesty of the law made its next reluctant move. By then the quarry would have taken flight.

Unless she prevented that.

The great thing was the rain. Splashing through puddles as she ran, she felt something like joy: a knife-edge balance, a dizzying, towering thrill. She leapt a tumbling gutter creek and half expected to keep soaring, rushing and weightless. She exulted in the elation of effort, her strides long, her breathing deep and even. The rain stayed with her, pushed, pulled, brought her along.

In the car, too, she flew, peeling up the ramp, cornering hard, beating lights and sailing down the avenue. It was impossible to be alone on the streets of New York, but as late as this with the rain this hard she came close. In the darkness and drum of the downpour, vision reduced to the wipers' arc and the headlights' reach, she felt herself to be solitary and almost unbearably lonely. But also singular, invincible.

Fifty blocks downtown, she slammed to a stop in front of Glybenhall's building, sprang from the car as the doorman came near.

"Ann Montgomery," she said briskly, striding past him. "Mr. Glybenhall's expecting me."

"Wait a second, miss, you can't leave that car there—"

"I'll only be a minute." She flashed her badge. "Walter Glybenhall," she told the concierge inside, not stopping. He frowned and as the elevator doors closed she saw him grabbing the phone to warn Walter. But so what? Walter certainly was not expecting her. But there was no way he'd be able to resist this, a visit from Ann Montgomery in the middle of the night.

When the elevator opened, Glybenhall was waiting, wearing a maroon dressing gown and an indulgent smile.

"My dear Ann. Always a pleasure. Even at this hour, and with you looking as . . . untidy . . . as you do."

"God, Walter, do you buy those cheesy robes by the case?" She pushed through the foyer and into the living room. The vast view, New York at Glybenhall's feet, was obscured by sheeting rain.

"Why, come in, my dear, please don't stand on ceremony," he drawled as he shut the door behind her. "Perhaps you'd like to get out of those wet clothes? I'd be happy to offer you a dressing gown."

"Don't be revolting. That kid you sent, Walter. He's going to live."

"Beg pardon? What are you talking about?"

"We have Jen's chain. However much you paid that kid, it won't be enough. He'll give you up."

"You're raving."

"Why did you kill her?"

"I assume you mean Jennifer? I didn't kill her."

"Did it have anything to do with the rest of this? Did she figure out your plot to screw the city out of millions?"

"*Plot? Screw?* You make it sound so—unsubtle. But even as a child you had no appreciation for nuance. Ann, darling, if it had only been the money I'm not sure I'd have taken the trouble. The idea's appeal was its complex structure and multifaceted rewards. With your hatred and your high-flying arrogance as my tools, I could see Corrington ruined, Charlie chastised, and Glybenhall—not Trump, not Ratner, and certainly not some visionless group of sanctimonious do-gooders, but *Glybenhall*—putting my stamp on Manhattan's last great building site! Do you realize my project would have set the tone for Harlem's future? That it would have become the benchmark against which *all* Manhattan development would have been measured?"

"You're breaking my heart."

"If there was a time when your heart interested me, it no longer does. Come, it's time to leave."

"I'm not leaving. I'm here to make sure *you* stay until Blowfish gives the cops a reason to get over their fear of offending you."

"Whatever this—Blowfish?—has to say will have nothing to do with me."

"Why don't we wait and see?"

"Because I don't like waiting."

"Screw you, Walter." From her pocket she pulled out her .38.

Glybenhall smiled like a tolerant uncle amused by a two-year-old. A surge of loathing, huge and hot, rocked Ann. She was surprised to find her gun hand still steady.

"Walter—"

He nodded, and she didn't know what that meant until she caught a movement from the corner of her eye. She spun around too late. The blow aimed at the back of her skull caught her forehead. Through the explosion of bright color she tried to lift out of her tumbling plunge and soar up again, but she just kept falling.

CHAPTER 92

Sutton Place

Motion.

She was in motion, and she liked that.

Not to stop was important, not to be afraid of moving and not to stop. You could trust the logic of speed. Hesitation broke the flow. *Lean* into *it, Annie.* Her father had taught her to ski, to drive. *Fear ruins your rhythm. Hesitation makes you fall.*

She was shivering, though. Pain in her head, queasy, so cold she was shivering; but the comfort of acceleration. Without that she'd be lost.

She lay on her side, back pressed into a yielding wall. When she opened her eyes they burned and watered. She shut them, forced them open again. Black and gray, splashes of silver, and everything moving. An attempt to sit brought a whirlpool of nausea. She moaned, sank down, and closed her eyes again.

"My dear?" A solicitous voice. Fury flared into a pummeling head-ache. Why angry? Walter's voice, it was Walter's voice.

Take inventory, she told herself. *Lean into it.* The weight of movement, a muted hum, the smell of leather: a car. She put out a tentative hand, felt cool steel where she expected to. Very slowly, she sat up, keeping her eyes shut until the queasiness eased.

"I hope you're not feeling too many ill effects?"

"I'm sick enough to throw up all over your expensive upholstery." She opened her eyes and saw black glass in front, beside, behind. Black leather, black carpet; silver door handles recessed into black steel. Beyond the windows, muted by tinted glass, mounded black forms of hills against gray sky.

"Don't be crude." A silver speaker stood in for Glybenhall; she could just make him out, ghostly through the glass.

"You're doing your own driving? Don't you have servants for these menial tasks?" Her voice sounded weak and ragged to her; she hoped he heard defiance, fury, recklessness.

"I didn't see any reason to summon the chauffeur. I always enjoy an opportunity to drive this car. It's powerful and quite well made."

He swerved left. Bile surged in her throat from the motion. The rectangular mass of a sixteen-wheeler slipped by her right-hand window as though reeled in from behind.

"Take it easy, Walter, or there'll be forensic evidence everywhere."

"I apologize. I'll attempt to make the journey as smooth as I can. I suppose it's fortunate I had the benefit of driving advice from your poor father."

"I'm going to kill you."

"No," he disagreed mildly, "I'm going to kill you."

He swung right again, leaving the passing lane. He was overdriving, pulling the wheel too hard for his speed. She leaned with the movement.

"It's goddamn cold in here." She reached out and fumbled with the door locks on either side. Useless, but it had to be tried.

"Again, I apologize. Here, this should improve matters."

"Who hit me?"

"An associate of mine."

"The guy from the garden, right? The one who shot Blowfish."

He chuckled. "In fact, yes."

"What's so damn funny, Walter?"

"You. No matter how dire the circumstances, you can be counted on to have something to prove."

He turned the car into a long, banked curve. Raindrops spotted the windows, leaving diagonal traces.

"Where are we going?"

"What difference can it possibly make if you know?"

"Well, wherever we are, someone will spot your license plate."

"At six in the morning, in the rain, at five miles below the speed limit? Poor Ann. You're beginning to sound desperate."

"Let me make my position clear." Ann spoke with a calm she didn't feel, a strength she didn't have. "I'd like to live and I intend to. Failing that, I'd like you to get what's coming to you; in fact, knowing you will would be almost as good. And you will. My car's still outside your building and your doorman and your concierge both saw me go up. Lots of people knew I was on my way there. And there are still the jeweler and all those other people. The cops will find them and talk to them if I disappear."

"I'm sorry to contradict you, but your car has been relocated to an obscure street in Queens. The doorman and the concierge saw you leave the building. They will say as much to anyone else who asks. Enough of 'those other people' can be taken care of that the rest will pose no problem, once you, who have become a rather large irritant, are gone. It's a shame, though. You'd been playing your part so nicely and I was enjoying myself. Until you took that extra step of trying to frame me for Jennifer's murder."

"Walter, you can't be framed for something you actually did. That's why you had me attacked, right? To back me off."

"In the garage? I had nothing to do with that. I wasn't told until afterward and I was quite cross; it was a stupid mistake. I thought everyone understood that throwing obstacles in your path only makes you more pigheaded. We'd counted on that from the start."

"That's why I thought it was you. Because it was a stupid mistake."

"I have to say, I'm becoming annoyed with your tone and your constant one-upsmanship. Let's pass some time in silence."

She heard a click. "Walter, damn you!" she shouted, but he'd broken her connection out of this cell of black glass, black leather, black steel, left her with nothing but silence and the sensation of movement.

Harlem: Frederick Douglass Boulevard

The rain had slacked to drizzle and the sky paled to gray by the time Joe Cole and Ford were free to go. Tom Underhill, roused and dragged to the scene by Ford's phone call, spoke briefly with the detectives who'd caught the shooting and then turned his glare on Ford and Cole.

"What the hell *was* this?" He listened, glowering, while Ford filled him in, and then snorted, "You are flat insane."

"It was a law enforcement operation," Ford reminded him.

"It was two DOI cops, one of them *on desk duty*! And she's out of control! You call that law enforcement?"

"Greg Lowry's a DOI Inspector General."

"Great! And where's he now?"

"All right, that's a good question. But we didn't tell him to go running off in the dark without backup."

"He thought he had backup," Cole put in. "He'd called it in."

Underhill snapped, "He should have waited until they showed!"

"And not chased a suspect?"

"You going to explain it to his Commissioner, Cole? He's on the way here."

Ford hesitated. "Tom, you understand there's some thought Commissioner Shapiro might be part of the problem?"

"Yes, Ford, I do understand that. What should I have done, told him we'd rather he stay home while his IG is lost in Harlem?"

"Just as long as you know."

"What I know is, this was a damn stupid idea!"

"It worked," Ford said.

Finally dismissed, Ford and Cole headed out the garden gate. "Wish I knew what was going on at the hospital," Cole said.

"Probably nothing, yet. Until they get Blowfish stabilized they won't let Montgomery talk to him."

"If they let her stay. I'm betting they'll have kicked her out already."

Ford found himself grinning. "Is she always like that?"

"Since I've known her."

"Must've been interesting, being her partner."

"Never dull."

Ford dug in his pocket, handed Cole his phone. "Her number's programmed."

"I already know it." Cole got Montgomery's voice mail and left a message. Giving the phone back, he said, "You tell me where we can get a good breakfast around here, I'm buying."

"In that case, follow me."

A few blocks up and over, Ford pulled open a glass door to a low stucco building. The scents of maple syrup and frying bacon floated down a flight of stairs.

"Where are we?" Cole asked.

"Church's."

Up on the second floor, at long tables set on a flowered carpet, mothers fed applesauce to babies while older kids munched sugar doughnuts. Three bus drivers in MTA blue sat eating waffles, trying to make time with a table of young women, maybe students from City College. Ford led Cole to the cafeteria line. "I recommend the hotcakes. Or you can get ham hocks and biscuits with gravy, if you're seriously hard-core."

Cole stuck to scrambled eggs. Ford got hotcakes and bacon and they took their trays to a window table.

"Popular place," Cole remarked, pulling out a folding chair. "I wouldn't have known it was here."

"What it really is, it's the United House of Prayer lunchroom. Sanctuary's through there." Ford pointed his fork. "Still where the flock does Sunday dinner, and in between, a nice moneymaker. Some of the best home cooking—" He stopped when his phone began to ring.

"Ann?" Cole asked.

Ford glanced at the readout—an unfamiliar number—and shook his head. He lifted the phone and said, "Corrington."

"Mr. Corrington? This A-Dogg. Sorry it so early—"

"No, no, no problem. You okay? Anything wrong?"

"I don't know. Could be. Something going down, thought maybe you should know. Because of what you said."

"About what?"

"Kong and T. D. Tilden, when you was askin' what they got going."

"You found out something?"

"Not, like, what it was or nothin'. Just, something happen last week, I ain't told you."

"And you want to tell me now?"

"Saw a guy. Talking to Blowfish."

"Blowfish? What guy, A-Dogg?"

"In the park, near all them big trees. I expect they think no one ain't seen them. But I was . . . sometimes I stay in one of them trees, you know?"

"You stay—you *sleep* there?"

"On this one branch. It's real wide and kind of curved. I got a super at the Hampton Houses lets me stay in the boiler room when it get cold, but he don't want me there in summertime. Thing about this guy," A-Dogg said firmly, switching subjects, "I seen him before. White guy. I seen him with Kong. Don't know his name or nothin', but I seen him."

"What does he look like?"

"Just, you know. Regular."

"Tall? Silver hair?"

"No way. Just regular."

Not Glybenhall himself, then: someone working for him.

"Kong just call him Boss. Kong always sayin' ain't no thing to him, dude paying him good, he call him any shit he want. Anyhow, Blowfish don't know I seen him with this guy, and I ain't said. But later, Blowfish tell me, keep my eyes open, if I help him out could be something in it. He say somebody be looking for Shamika."

"Did he say why?"

"Say Shamika got something belong to this guy, he want it back bad. So Blowfish, he go see her moms, tell her he a friend of hers, he worried, ain't seen her around. Her moms say Shamika get real scared when Kong come looking for her and she take off. Say she staying with her brother's baby mama in Jersey City."

Jersey City? Ford flashed on the Georgia area code and the antagonistic voice of cousin Ralphie.

"So Blowfish go over there. Baby mama say Shamika meet some Dominican, go off with him. José or Jesús or something, she don't know and she don't care. She say Shamika no fun, always tell her what to do, so she could go to hell, all she cared."

Well, I'll be, thought Ford. *A private witness relocation program. The underground railroad comes into the twenty-first century.*

"But dig," A-Dogg went on. "This guy? He just call me. Say he get my number from Blowfish. Say Blowfish got a little problem, so he wonder could he deal with me direct. Ask did I find Shamika yet. Mr. Corrington, yo, street say Blowfish get smoked this morning. In your garden."

"The street's fast but not quite right, A-Dogg. Blowfish was shot, but last I heard he's still alive. He's at the hospital."

"Damn! What go down?"

"I don't know." Not quite true, but not really a lie, either. "This man looking for Shamika—is that what he meant about 'Blowfish's problem'?"

"Don't know. But what I'm thinking, how do he get my number? Blowfish ain't about to give it to him, in case I be trying to cut Blowfish out. But if Blowfish ain't give it to him, only way I can think of he could get it, must be he got Blowfish's phone. Now how he gonna get *that?* How he gonna get it, he ain't the one shot him?"

Ford was wondering whether A-Dogg had too much of a juvenile record to get into the Police Academy when the boy said, "Mr. Corrington? Reason I ain't told you about this dude before, this the first time Blowfish ever ask would I help him. He always be laughing at me, like I'm some little kid, you know? And the crew, lot of them do like Blowfish do. You know?"

"Yes, I know."

"Probably I should've told you. But Blowfish, Carlo, the crew . . . yo, they got my back, you know?"

"I understand, A-Dogg. But now tell me, do you have a way to get in touch with this man?"

"That why I'm calling you," the boy said. "I mean, I don't know what the fuck's going down, but Blowfish getting popped, that's wack. My man Carlo, he buggin' out, first someone smoke Kong, now this. So I tell this dude, yeah I found Shamika, but you got to pay me. He say sure, bring her, I pay you. So we gonna meet in the park, that path under Noah's Ark. About a hour."

CHAPTER 94

Sutton Place

Don't sleep.
It seemed forever since she'd first told herself that, forever since it had become all she could say. She watched out the black glass of the left-hand window, then the right-hand one: she burned her stare through the privacy barrier and tried to make out the world beyond the windshield.

Normally (*you mean, if Walter weren't taking you somewhere to kill you?*) at this hour she'd be asleep and not near waking; under the circumstances (*you mean, no move possible back here, with Walter taking you somewhere to kill you?*) she might suggest sleep to herself as a way to conserve strength. But as matters stood (*you mean, a knock on the head, so that sleep could slip into an oblivion you might find it hard to wake up from, making it easier for Walter to kill you?*) she was doing everything she could to stay awake.

The sky lightened but the rain kept pounding. On either side, obscured by dark glass, rounded hills disappeared into low clouds. Headlights and taillights flowed toward them, and past.

She was grateful for the cold. It was unpleasant and uncomfortable, and comfort, right now, was the enemy. She concentrated on leaning with the car, on anticipating Glybenhall's driving, and his thinking, too. She worked on making a plan for their arrival, on making contingency plans for failures in the plan. That's how Joe would do it, and Joe clearly had the right approach to things because she was locked up in the back seat of Walter Glybenhall's car and he wasn't.

Finally, finally, she felt the weight of the car shift to the right and slow. They were pulling off the highway, onto a long, well-graded exit.

At a traffic light, they stopped. Glybenhall unfolded a map. *Too bad, Walter, a car this fancy must have GPS but you can't exactly call in for directions, can you?* The rain pelted the roof, sheeted the windows. Glybenhall spun the wheel and started up again. Left; a straightaway, and then up a hill.

She leaned back against the seat. It wouldn't be long now.

Harlem: Frederick Douglass Boulevard

Ford called Tom Underhill and gave the detective a recap of his conversation with A-Dogg. "It's the guy Kong was working for," he finished. "The guy his crew thinks killed him, and A-Dogg thinks he might be the one who shot Blowfish. He's meeting the kid in the park in an hour."

"Damn! This a new craze sweeping Harlem? Crazy setups by civilians?"

"After this one I'm out of business."

"You're out of business right now, Ford. And tell the kid to be a no-show, too."

"I already did. I told him I'd take it from here and to keep his head down. You'll be there?"

"Shit, sure we will. Citizen goes to all this trouble, least we can do is take advantage. But I don't want anyone cluttering up my sight lines."

"You planning on shooting this guy?"

"I'm not planning on anything. But he might not want to come down to the precinct for coffee and doughnuts."

"You should serve Church's doughnuts. Everyone would come." Ford clicked his phone off and looked at Joe Cole. "He doesn't want us there."

"I used to be in law enforcement," Cole said. "I see where he's coming from. But after all this? I'd sure like a look at this guy."

"Would you?" Ford regarded him. "I'm finding that I would, too. And I'd like to make sure we're the only ones."

"What do you mean?"

"I'm a little worried A-Dogg might show after all."

"To make a quick buck? Pretend he really does have the girl?"

"No, more like to see his clever idea work out." He stood. "Up for a walk in the park?"

Out on the avenue, jazzed on coffee, adrenaline, and exhaustion, Ford felt oddly saw-toothed in a soft-edged world. The mist had thickened to a warm fog. Buses and cars drifted by, pedestrians trudged, drunks snored in doorways. Here and there a streetlight still spread a dull gleam. Reaching the park, they found it dreamlike: arching trees, curving paths, gigantic boulders looming from the mist.

"You put us more than two feet from the action, we'll miss the whole show," Cole said.

"The meeting place is around that way. We'll be able to see from up there"—Ford pointed—"and stay out of Tom's way. And there's something there I think you'll enjoy."

He led the way to an uptilted slab of granite colossal enough to support trees growing out of its clefts. A steep path curved up a fissure, mud puddles everywhere and the stone slippery with rainwater. Ford scrambled up, stepped through a gap between two slabs of rock, and waited for Cole. Right behind him, the man slipped through and looked around. Slowly, he grinned. "Wow."

Ford smiled also. "Amen."

A series of stone slabs, the broken top of the boulder, formed a ragged circle fifteen feet across. But this hidden crater, though surprising enough, was just the beginning. All around them was painted, in great detail and vivid colors, a vast and violent ocean storm. Giant waves towered and crested on the slabs' jagged tops. Rain slanted and roiling clouds released explosions of lightning. Damp with the slickness of real rain, the mural was breathtaking: more powerful, Ford realized, than he'd ever seen it before.

"Over here." He tapped one of the stones. "Noah's Ark."

The hopelessly small ship, barely the size of his hand, keeled half over as it climbed a wave. Tiny, terrified horses and giraffes were tethered to the mast, while two monkeys clung to each other in the rigging above.

"I'd have missed that," Cole said. "In all this. Who painted it?"

"No one knows. Sometime in the early eighties, some kids came up here to party and found it, freshly done. Spray paint, mostly. Some graffiti painter who got tired of subway cars."

"And no one's tried to cover it, tag over it?"

"They don't tag stained-glass windows, either. Now we'd better get set." He stepped through a break in the stones to a wide granite shelf.

Crouching, he worked his way close to the edge. Cole joined him. From here, they could look down onto the path.

"That bum, sleeping over there?" Ford pointed to a form sprawled on a bench. "One of Tom's guys. They got here fast, huh?"

"You sure? He could be just a bum."

"No one comes back here. They know better."

He wrapped his arms around his knees and settled in to wait.

CHAPTER 96

Sutton Place

The car rolled to a stop. Ann didn't know how well Glybenhall could see her through the tinted glass barrier but she didn't want to take a chance so she didn't move. Glybenhall turned the car off; then he, too, just sat.

Fighting to keep herself immobile, a dammed-up stream waiting to crash and flood, she found herself seeing not black glass but the bright empty sky. It was her twelfth birthday. Beside her in the wind's roar stood her father, dressed as she was: flight suit and helmet, parachute with dangling cord. *When you jump out of a plane, you die*, she thought. *Unless your parachute works. Well, okay.* Her father, smiling, put out his hand. She clutched it, smiled back, and though he had done this many times and she never before, she jumped first.

Glybenhall pushed his door open and got out into the rain. She heard the electronic click as the locks released. The door was pulled open; rain splashed in.

"Come, Ann."

She didn't move.

"Ann, please don't be childish."

I'm not childish, you idiot, I'm unconscious. Your associate *slammed me on the head, remember?*

If she didn't leave the car, he'd have to reach in to get her. He had a gun; if she allowed herself to be kept at a distance she had no chance. Her only hope, her parachute, was contact.

"Ann!"

When she neither answered nor moved, he leaned in to pull her out.

chapter 97

Heart's Content

Noah's Ark. They might as well be on it, Joe thought, sitting beside Corrington, staring through the rain. Below, he could see in patches: a bench, a curve of asphalt. This hill was roughly the same height, twenty feet or so, as the one in his yard. If he were there he'd be looking down on the rudbeckia, free of grapevines since Ann's visit and reaching for the sun. Or did an early-morning rain blanket them, too, three counties away? It would be quiet there, a deep silence on whose surface the sweeping rain would dance but whose heart it couldn't penetrate. Unlike here, where, though muffled by rain and distance, the city's relentless sounds pierced far into the park. Tires, horns, a siren, a radio.

Footsteps.

A figure rounded a turn and stopped under the canopy of an oak. Joe strained to see his face but the high angle confounded his view. "Can you make him out?" he whispered to Corrington.

"No. Oh, hell!"

Another figure from the opposite direction: a thin young man, hunched shoulders, baseball cap.

"A-Dogg!" Corrington whispered. "Oh, Lord!" The young man spoke briefly with the figure under the tree. Then he turned as though searching out something in the fog, and he nodded.

"What's he—" Corrington began.

"*Yo! Boss man!*" A shout exploded and another shape burst from the fog. "This for my brother!"

"Carlo!" Corrington sprang to his feet. *"No!"* But Carlo's gun roared. Not once: twice. The first shot threw down the man by the tree. The second came when Carlo spun and yelled, *"What the fuck? This some fucking setup?"* and it caught Corrington right in the heart.

CHAPTER 98

Sutton Place

Glybenhall yanked Ann from the car. She moaned, stumbled, gasped when the rain swept her. In the hand not clenching her arm, he held a gun. She made herself heavy, gave him something to pull against. When he snapped her forward she dropped her charade, piled all her power onto his momentum, and pounded him in the stomach.

He doubled over, wheezing. She grabbed his slippery wrist, wrenched the gun from him, and stumbled back. Righting herself against the car, she wiped rain from her eyes. And was frozen by the sight of where she was.

Joe's cabin sat in the downpour, dark and closed, unaware.

She stared; and those moments she lost, they mattered. Glybenhall slammed against her, pinning her to the car. Desperately she twisted as he pressed his weight into her and tried to pull the pistol from her hand.

"Let it go!" he screamed, smashing her hand against the car, again and again. She tried to force her pain-seared fingers to keep gripping but he ripped the gun from her and pounded it into her face.

Sparks and an explosion of pain; Ann found herself on her knees in the mud. Walter stood above her, breathing hard.

"You son of a bitch!" she rasped. "Why here?"

"Use your brain! Think of the confusion! The authorities will spend endless hours working out what happened. Now move away from the car."

"Joe's in New York! They'll know he had nothing to do with it."

"I don't give a damn whether Cole's suspected. I just want to be sure that when your body is found—bloated, bullet-riddled, oh, such an ugly sight—no one will think of *me*."

"Like when they found Jen?"

"I had nothing to do with Jennifer, in life or in death."

"The chain that Blowfish tried to plant—"

"Ann, I don't know who or what you're talking about and I'm much too cold and wet to listen to you any longer. Get up!"

She slugged a handful of mud up into his face. Then she pushed herself up like a sprinter. Run, girl!

The car, and Walter, loomed between her and the road. Slipping on the slick grass, she raced around the house toward the woods.

Even in the pounding rain and roaring wind, the whine of a bullet seemed the loudest noise she'd ever heard.

She tripped and went flying, landing hard on her hip. Spring up: you're back in high school, running track. Another bullet screamed. Slipping and sliding, she reached the trees. Push through branches, brambles. Not left; that way leads down. In this rain the creek would be swollen, too powerful to cross and too high to follow. Right, then: up the hill, that massive granite boulder with vines trailing down its sides. If she could climb without Glybenhall spotting her, she might be able to make her way back through the woods on the ridge. Sooner or later she'd come to a road, a house.

Scrambling to the hill, she had to stop and rip away a tangling vine. She peered through the trees. Her heart stopped. Glybenhall stood in the center of the lawn. He towered, a nightmare giant.

He's forty feet away! she told herself desperately. *He doesn't even see you.*

She struggled onward, tripping on branches, sinking in puddles. Lightning bleached the sky; thunder crashed, so loud it was like a new sound. She reached the hill, found a foothold, started up. The rock was so slick it could have been oiled, but she clutched branches and vines and pulled herself along. She might have made it to the top if she hadn't glanced down to check on Walter.

At first she didn't see him. Then he called her name. She turned her head wildly and found him, a colossus trampling the rudbeckia directly beneath. "Ann!" he shouted again, and fired. His shot shattered rock six inches in front of her. Shards peppered her face. For a moment she thought she was all right, thought she'd kept her grip, but she felt her fingers scrabbling against stone and then she was skidding, sliding, tumbling backwards.

Heart's Content

The bum on the bench sprang to his feet, firing, and two other men erupted from the fog. Guns drawn, they charged after Carlo down the path.

"*Who the fuck's up there?*" Tom Underhill yelled.

"Corrington's been shot!" Joe shouted back.

The ambulance was fast and the EMTs efficient, scrabbling up the hill with their equipment, but Joe could have told them there was no point. When they reached the granite shelf and crouched beside Corrington, he said nothing, though. Maybe he was wrong.

But he wasn't. They brought Corrington down the hill with no haste at all.

"Cole?" Underhill was livid. "What the fuck was this?"

"He was worried A-Dogg would show up." Joe heard his own voice as dull, fog-wrapped.

"He knew about this? You knew?"

"About—you mean, that Carlo was going to shoot this guy?" Joe stared at the cop in disbelief. "Of course not. He was worried about A-Dogg."

"*Goddamn* it!" Underhill swung away. Joe could see him fighting for control. They'd been friends, the cop and Corrington, and Joe wanted to help. But help was impossible, as always.

"Do you know," Underhill asked, voice ragged, "what we have here?"

The question baffled Joe. Two deaths, one a good man, one a crook. What could be simpler? "I don't understand."

Underhill grasped his arm, pulled him along the path to the tree and the draped form beneath it. He stepped past the crime-scene tech and lifted the tarp to let Joe see the dead man's face.

It was Greg Lowry.

CHAPTER 100

Sutton Place

Ann grabbed branches, stone, anything. Pain scorched her arm as she scraped rough bark. Her wet hair covered her face; she rolled and slithered, bounced off a ridge. The thud that stopped her movement knocked her breathless.

Yellow blossoms glowed around her, hunched by the rain. Disoriented, dizzy, she struggled to her feet. The rain was sheeting so hard she couldn't see, but a bright day came back to her, the day she'd first seen this place and stood next to Joe by these lilies. At the wood's edge, wasn't that where they were? She had no air in her lungs but she took off anyway, headed again into the trees.

Bend, Montgomery! Low player wins! Her college basketball coach: she hadn't thought of him in years, never liked the game, but she dropped down now, stayed low, and it must be true, because Walter didn't fire. Crouching, she blundered forward. Up hadn't worked; try down, take your chances with the swollen creek. Any second now you'll hit the poison-ivy slope. But in one bone-jarring step the ground changed from slippery leaves to hard rock and she knew she'd picked the wrong path. This was the huge flat boulder, the one Joe had warned her against, that overhung the stream. This was a trap and she'd backed herself into it. From here there was no way down.

The shriek of a shot, a dark form in the trees. She dove onto her belly, lay in the soaking moss on the edge of the rock, still and silent, pounded by rain. *Well, it worked before. I'm dead, Walter. You did it. Now come see.* Slowly, footsteps neared. Panic gripped her when a figure loomed above, so huge; when he leaned over, so close. She wanted to scream, to dive from the rock, but forced herself frozen. She could see the gun in his hand, the water glimmering in his silver hair. He bent close and when he did she seized a tree root below the boulder's edge and swept her legs around. The rain-soaked moss was slick and slimy. Her flying legs tangled his and he stumbled, teetered, thrashed for something to grab onto. He clutched a sapling's branch, but he was too big, too heavy. It snapped in his hand. Pitching forward, he skidded over the moss, flailing his arms. For a second nothing moved; even the rain hung in the air. Then Walter Glybenhall dove over the cliff as though he wanted to fly.

Heart's Content

"I want A-Dogg! Wallace, take some uniforms, find him!" Underhill shouted to another detective. "Bring his ass in!"

"Don't need to do that," said a quiet voice, and Joe saw the hunched, skinny kid step from the rain.

Two cops swept out guns. The kid gave a scornful look. "That, neither. I ain't packin'." He spread his arms, waiting for the cops to pat him down. Instead, Underhill moved behind him, pulled his arms down and cuffed them. "You're under arrest as an accessory to murder. You have the right—"

"Yeah, I know that shit. You could skip it. How's Mr. Corrington?"

"He's dead."

For a moment, nothing moved in the boy's stony face. Then, "That ain't true," he whispered.

"It damn sure is!"

"Oh, fuck." The stone dissolved, melted into disbelief. And into something else, Joe thought, something that looked piercingly like loneliness. "Oh, man. Oh, no, oh, no."

"Did you know Carlo was planning this, A-Dogg?"

The boy shook his head. "You mean, that he was gonna shoot this fucker? No, man, he ain't said nothing about shooting no one."

"What *did* he say?"

"Tell me he just want a look at the Boss. Just see his face. He say it cool with him if five-oh take him up."

"You believed him? You had no idea about this?"

A-Dogg shrugged and looked away.

"Well," Underhill said harshly, "it happens the man Carlo shot—the man besides Ford Corrington—was a cop."

"Say *what?*" The boy snapped his startled eyes back to Underhill.

"You spoke to him. You must have seen he wasn't the man you were looking for."

"Oh, shit! Look, man, dig, I don't know nothing about him being no cop. That's fucked up. But that's why I went to talk to him, yo. To make sure."

"Of what?"

"That it him. The Boss. Maybe he a cop, but he for sure the white dude Kong working for. Carlo tell me, A-Dogg, he say, you gotta get close. Gotta go make sure, tell me is it him. Because Carlo and me, we couldn't see shit through the rain."

chapter 102

Heart's Content

An image Joe couldn't shake: the creek below his yard, rushing, churning. He didn't go down there much, and he'd told Ann that. All water was linked, always in motion and always part of something else, of everything else; he stayed in his garden, a finite, bounded place of rooted plants.

And this was why. This was why.

"That son of a bitch." He heard his own voice. "Lowry. *He* asked for Ann to be called in. She told him every move, every fact. He kept telling *her* what *not* to do because he knew she'd do it. Fucking son of a bitch."

"That's a hell of an assumption," Underhill said.

"You telling me I'm wrong?" Joe pulled out his phone, shook off Underhill's hand and his "Cole, what do you think you're—" but he only got Ann's voice mail anyway. He told her to call him and clicked off.

"Finished? Can you spare a minute?" Underhill asked caustically. "Because I don't give a shit about your theories about Lowry or Montgomery, or the man in the fucking moon! What were you and Ford *doing* up there?"

Joe's own surging anger receded at the look in the cop's eyes. "I told you that already," he said quietly. "If you want, I'll tell you something different, but it won't bring your friend back."

"*Goddamn!* I ought to arrest you, Cole."

"If you think that would help."

Underhill's hands rose and fell uselessly. He looked around him, and

Joe followed his eyes: rotating red and white lights, the ordered chaos of people with jobs to do, the impersonal rain. "I don't know," the cop muttered, "what would fucking help."

"Talking to Glybenhall," Joe said.

"Based on *what*?"

"Blowfish was planting that chain—"

"Oh, *Christ*! You tell Edgar Westermann a story, Blowfish shows up in Ford's garden, and you want me to talk to *Glybenhall*? Do you even have any proof that chain wasn't there when Blowfish got there? That he actually brought it with him?"

"You know he did."

"Can you prove it?"

"No," Joe admitted. "But—"

"Shut up! Just shut the fuck up." Underhill wiped rain from his face. "I never thought I'd hear myself say this, but I hope Blowfish didn't die." He dialed his precinct, asked them to reach the officer at the hospital and have him call. They waited, watching the EMTs zip Lowry's body into a rubber bag. When Underhill's phone finally rang he spoke briefly, then thumbed it off. "They think he'll pull through, but he's not conscious yet," he told Joe, his grudging tone a sort of apology. "Montgomery's not there, by the way."

"She's not? When did she leave?"

"She was never there."

"She went in the ambulance."

"Not according to the EMT. Montgomery told him she'd take her own car. But she never showed."

Looking at Underhill, Joe saw not the detective but Ann's shining eyes as she left the garden. *"Shit!"* He pulled his phone out, pressed the only number in it.

"What?"

"She went to Glybenhall's!"

"Don't say that."

"She doesn't answer. That's where she is. I'm sure of it. She'd have wanted to hold him until law enforcement came. I'm going up there."

"The hell you are."

"I'm a private citizen. You can't stop me."

"I can arrest you."

"Or you can come with me."

"To Walter Glybenhall's? Are you crazy?"

"Then get out of my way."

"Damn!" muttered Underhill.

The rain had stopped by the time they pulled up to Glybenhall's Park

Avenue building. They were in Underhill's unmarked car, but any Crown Victoria in New York that wasn't a taxi was NYPD and everyone knew it. The doorman's dismay was all over his face.

"Police." Underhill showed his badge. "We're looking for a woman who came to see Walter Glybenhall last night."

"I just came on."

"You, too?"

The concierge nodded.

"We need to talk to Mr. Glybenhall."

The concierge eyed him, then phoned upstairs. "Mr. Glybenhall is out," he reported.

"It's early to be out."

"I'm sorry, sir."

"Who did you talk to?"

"The housekeeper."

"Let me speak to her. What's her name?"

The concierge pursed his lips, but he handed Underhill the phone. "Mrs. Apfel," he said. "Gerda."

"This is the police, Mrs. Apfel," Underhill said. "I need to speak to Mr. Glybenhall. Where did he go? Then I'll need to see you. Yes, now." He handed the phone back to the concierge and waited pointedly.

"Penthouse," the man said.

Stocky and red-faced, the housekeeper was waiting at the door. She ran a glance over their wet clothes and muddy shoes and unenthusiastically let them in.

Underhill said, "Where's Mr. Glybenhall?"

"I don't know." She spoke with a hard German accent.

"We're looking for a young woman who might have come here last night."

"I saw no one."

"It was very late. You might have gone to bed."

"That is possible."

"You saw no one," Joe said. "Did you hear anything?"

She threw him a resentful look as though he'd caught her at something, but didn't answer.

"Mrs. Apfel," said Underhill, "Mr. Glybenhall may be in danger from this woman. If you know anything, I think you should tell us."

Glybenhall in danger from Ann? But Joe kept his face blank.

The housekeeper's eyes widened. "Is it that crazy woman? Who arrested Mr. Glybenhall?"

"Yes, ma'am."

After a brief silence, she said, "The concierge's buzzer woke me, but

Mr. Glybenhall answered it himself. If he let anyone in, I don't know. The doorbell didn't ring, but he might have been waiting. As I was for you."

"When was that?"

"Not quite five. But before that—"

"Yes?"

She paused, clearly uncertain whether to go on.

"Mrs. Apfel, your loyalty is commendable," Underhill said. "But—"

"Yes, of course. Someone came up in the service elevator. That is next to the kitchen and I hear it from my room. I thought it must be one of Mr. Glybenhall's young ladies. He often brings them up that way." She flushed. "It's private, you see. But this was a man. I heard his voice because they argued. Mr. Glybenhall was very angry. He called him 'Greg.' "

Joe's adrenaline surged. "Was he here, this Greg, when the doorbell rang?" Underhill could have silenced him, but he just nodded to the housekeeper: answer the question.

"Yes, sir."

"Did you see him?"

"No, sir. But later I heard his voice again. They went down that way. The service elevator."

"All of them? The woman, too?"

"I don't know if a woman was with them. But there's no one here now."

A quick pass through the penthouse's overfurnished rooms: all empty. Gerda Apfel opened Glybenhall's service elevator for them, took them down to the service yard, where they saw nothing; to the garage, where Glybenhall's Mercedes was parked but his town car gone. Underhill called Glybenhall's chauffeur to ask if he'd taken his boss somewhere during the night, then made other phone calls, looking for the night doorman, launching a hunt for Ann's car. Through all of it, Joe was beside him but felt as though he were drifting a long way off. The sights and sounds around him drowned in the roar of the creek in his head.

Until through the rush of water, a strange electronic beep.

Suddenly the creek was gone, everything clear and sharp. He yanked the new phone from his pocket.

No one but Ann had this number.

"Joe?" He'd never heard her voice so small, so still. "Joe? Can you come home?"

CHAPTER 103

City Hall

The mayor let his gaze rest on each person, one by one. Mark Shapiro, from DOI, here alone; the Police Commissioner, John Finn; Tom Underhill and Luis Perez, the detectives on the case; Underhill's captain, a guy named Freeman, and Perez's captain, Epstein or Einstein or something, here only because their men were here and it would have been hierarchically infeasible to exclude them. Hierarchically infeasible—Jesus, what a phrase. Charlie looked at Don, fidgeting at the end of the table, and at Lena, poised beside him with her pad. They were all waiting for something. Oh, right, it must be him: mayoral permission to get this meeting started.

Did they have to have this meeting? Couldn't they go straight to recess?

Don shifted in his chair. *Yes, yes, all right.* Charlie stifled a sigh and turned to Finn. "What've you got?"

Finn looked at Epstein, who nodded to Perez. *Christ!* said the mayor, but only to himself.

"We spent the last two days interviewing, reinterviewing witnesses," Perez began. "Picked up the gangbanger who attacked Montgomery. He confirmed it was Lowry that hired him. He also swears, by the way, he was only gonna scare her, he wasn't gonna hurt her."

"Glad to hear it," Charlie said. "What else?"

"Long story short: Montgomery seems to have been right."

Charlie could swear he saw Perez smile when he said that, but if so the smile vanished right away and the detective went on.

"Looks like Glybenhall, with Lowry's help, cooked up this scheme to get arrested, so he could turn right around and sue. The money was a draw, but the real point seems to have been to make Glybenhall pretty much unstoppable in New York."

"He was close to unstoppable already! What the hell did he need to do this for?"

"Seems he thought you were planning all along to double-cross him, hand the Block A site over to Corrington."

"He thought that? Why would he think that?"

"I don't know, sir. That's what his architect said."

But we had a deal, Charlie thought. *A fair-and-square under-the-table dirty deal. He thought I'd do that?*

"You can prove this?"

"With Glybenhall and Lowry both dead," Perez answered, "no, not a hundred percent. But when you put everything together, that's the picture that emerges."

Charlie's mind flashed to a picture emerging: a long-ago Polaroid of Louise on the deck of a cruise ship. Maybe that's where she was now, a cruise ship. Her note had only said she needed some time alone, and she was sure he felt the same. He didn't feel the same, and he was sure she knew it.

"All right," Charlie said, "take me over it. What do we have on Lowry?"

"He'd wanted my job," Shapiro said. "I'm sure you knew that, Mayor." His face was flushed as though he were confessing something. He slipped an envelope from his jacket. "I have my resignation here."

"What are you talking about?"

"He was my man. He did this on my watch."

"Oh, knock off the theatrics, Mark. That can't be anyone's motivation for shit like this: that he didn't get a damn job."

Shapiro's face darkened; his hand hovered over the envelope he'd pushed along the tabletop.

Take it back? Push it farther? Come on, Mark, make up your mind, I'm getting fed up with this meeting.

Shapiro lifted his hand, leaving the envelope lying there. "It wasn't," he said, tight-jawed.

"What wasn't what?"

"Lowry's whole motivation. His anger probably made him vulnerable to Glybenhall's proposition. But his motivation was money. He was a shareholder in Three Star."

"No kidding? On an IG's salary? Wait, don't tell me—he didn't buy the shares, Walter gave them to him."

"Yes, sir." *Yes, sir? Come on, that was worth a "Bingo."* "He appears to have

done that. The shares are worth a fair amount already, and they'd have
soared once the Block A development started."

"Walter, Walter, Walter." The mayor shook his head.

Shapiro eyed him oddly, then went on. "It was Lowry's gun that killed
Kong."

"What's our theory?"

"That they were prepared to go on having those gangbangers, Kong
and Tilden, create accidents at Mott Haven until Montgomery started
looking at Glybenhall like they wanted her to. But the Winston woman's death upped the stakes. Lowry and Glybenhall were afraid they'd
get ratted out now that it was homicide. They had Kong kill Tilden, and
then Lowry killed Kong."

"But Montgomery caught on?"

"They set her up to catch on. What they hadn't counted on was her
catching on to being set up."

"And her story checks out? The kidnapping? How Walter died?"

Perez looked at his boss again, who nodded. *Come on, knock off the bob-
blehead stuff!* Charlie wanted to shout. But that would have been hierarchically infeasible.

"Yes, sir," Perez said. "Bullets from his gun in the woods at Cole's
place, forensic evidence that she was in the back seat and never in front,
the crack on her head, Glybenhall's housekeeper's story. The night
doorman and concierge, once they got over the b.s. they started with."

"Great." Charlie sighed. "Just great. And we think Glybenhall killed
the Eliot woman, the way Montgomery says?"

Don sat up, sat back, said nothing. Charlie frowned. Usually he could
read Don; was it a sign of how sick he was of all this, that he had no idea
what Don meant?

"Well," Perez said, "we do, but it's a good thing we don't have to
prove it."

"Because?"

"Because it's all circumstantial. No one ever saw them together or
heard them talk about each other. And the gangbanger, Blowfish."

"What about him?"

"Well," Underhill said, "Lowry shot Blowfish. Meant to kill him, ob-
viously, but his bad luck, Blowfish was still breathing when Montgomery,
Cole, and Corrington got to them. So Lowry had to get clear, in case
Blowfish lived. He faked the nine-one-one call to give himself time. And
to give Blowfish time to die. But Blowfish didn't. He admits to breaking
into the garden to plant Jen Eliot's chain to frame Corrington, he says
Lowry shot him, but he also swears he got the chain from Edgar
Westermann. He won't budge on that."

"And Edgar denies that, of course."

"Yes, sir, he does."

"What's our theory?" the mayor said, aware that he was repeating himself.

"Well, it could be true," Underhill said. "Westermann could have gone to Glybenhall with the cock-and-bull story Cole told him. About you giving the Block A site to Corrington's group, and about Corrington having an affair with Jen Eliot."

"Was that true, by the way?"

"No."

"I didn't think so. Go on."

"So maybe Glybenhall gave Westermann the chain to pass on to someone who'd actually do the dirty work."

"I don't see Walter admitting to Edgar he'd killed anyone."

"To make the frame work, he wouldn't have to. Just that he'd slept with her."

Don was fidgeting again. Maybe he just needed a cigarette; after all, they were discussing the murder of a woman he used to date. "Open the window and light up if you want," Charlie said.

Don shook his head and shoved his hands in his pockets.

"Suit yourself," Charlie told him. To Underhill: "What does Edgar say?"

"That Blowfish's story is complete bushwah. That he was insulted by what Joe Cole was suggesting and he'd have thrown him out of his office except he thought the man was so unstable he'd better just hear him out. That he forgot the whole thing as soon as Cole left."

"He says he didn't call Walter about Cole's suggestion?"

"That's what he says."

"Do we believe him?"

"It's possible," the Police Commissioner said. "It certainly would be better if it were true."

"In other words," Charlie said, "we're going to assume Greg Lowry was the connection between Blowfish and Walter, hope to hell Edgar has nothing to do with it, and stop looking."

"Even if it were true that Westermann gave the Eliot woman's chain to Blowfish, there'd be no way to prove it," Finn said reasonably. "And *if* he did, that still wouldn't prove he knew anything about the Eliot homicide. Just that he was willing to do Glybenhall a favor and Ford Corrington a little dirt. We already have six bodies on this: Corrington, Lowry, Glybenhall, the Winston woman, the two gangbangers. Seven, if you count Jennifer Eliot. I'm not sure what's to be gained by pursuing Westermann."

"You mean, you're not sure how it would do what's left of my political career any good, or yours when you make your run for Attorney General. What, you thought that was a secret? No, let's not screw with Edgar Westermann just to clean up some mess in Harlem. Isn't that right, John? Yes, fine." He rode right over whatever the Police Commissioner had been about to say. "If proof Edgar's involved jumps up and bites you in the ass, go with it. Otherwise, drop it." Charlie snorted. "So when the smoke clears, the son of a bitch who ends up untouchable is Edgar Westermann."

No one answered.

Abruptly, Charlie stood. He had to get out of this room before the top of his head blew off. "Tomorrow too soon for a complete report?"

The room was silent with surprise. The Police Commissioner recovered first. "No, sir," he said, answering for the men who'd be putting in the overtime to produce it.

"Good. Thank you, gentlemen. And Lena, of course." The mayor strode through the door to his inner office and slammed it behind him.

City Hall

"You can't be telling me you're surprised." Hands in his pockets, leaning on the doorjamb the way he used to on the lampposts in Red Hook when he was young, the mayor watched the deputy mayor cross the room. "It's completely Edgar. Kicking me while I'm down."

"Surprised? No." Don threw the window open. "Pissed. In this whole shitstorm he's the only one who came out smelling like a rose. So why call a press conference and dredge it all up? What's the goddamn point?"

"To kick off his mayoral campaign with a bang."

"Why couldn't he just let it go? Consider himself lucky, focus on the future—"

"Put this behind us? Get some closure?"

Around the cigarette he was lighting, Don said, "You're fucking good-natured for a guy who was called the most corrupt New Yorker since Boss Tweed."

"Hey, it's politics."

"Edgar's gunning for you, Charlie! He said the rumor you and Corrington were double-crossing Glybenhall is true."

"He said he hadn't seen anything to prove it wasn't," Charlie corrected. "I'm not happy about him dissing a dead man like that, but that's between Edgar and his conscience."

"Edgar's conscience? Who are you kidding? And with all due respect to the dead, it's not Corrington I'm worried about. For God's sake, Edgar claims Shapiro would never have hired Lowry except that you insisted—"

"I did."

"—and that your refusal to take Ann Montgomery off the investigation proves your arrogance is out of control. Goddammit, he practically said you knew Glybenhall killed Jen!"

"If that were true," Charlie asked mildly, "wouldn't I have taken Ann Montgomery off the investigation?"

"What the hell is wrong with you? Edgar Westermann is skewering your ass!"

"Okay, so he's working it. I'd be surprised if he didn't. Doesn't that make it even more intriguing, that now he wants a meeting?"

"*Intriguing?* For shit's sake, Charlie! He's acting like keeping you out of Albany matters as much as landing his own fat butt in this chair!" Don kicked the leather armchair behind the mayor's desk. "And you're acting like you don't care!"

Because I don't. But this wasn't the time to say that to Don.

"Damn, Charlie, pull yourself together." Don shot a stream of smoke out the window. "We have a campaign to run. We can still win the state, but not if you're only half here."

Not here at all, Charlie thought, but said nothing.

"Look," Don said. "I know this is a hard time. You're—"

"No, I'm not. Pining for Louise, you were about to say. Of course I am, but that's not the problem."

"Glybenhall's death, Corrington's, the whole thing threw her. She just needs some time alone right now."

"That's the first thing Sue Trowbridge said that you ever believed."

Don hesitated. "She can't have . . . Because you're in political trouble? I don't buy it."

Charlie shrugged.

"She'll be back."

Charlie didn't answer, not because he thought Don was wrong, but because he really didn't know.

The outer door opened. In something very close to a whisper, Lena said, "Edgar Westermann's in the conference room."

Charlie nodded his thanks; softly, she closed the door. He sighed. For the last two weeks everyone around here had been walking and talking as though this were the house of the dead.

"I think it's a mistake to meet with him." Don tried one last time.

"Noted. Let's go."

Don smashed his cigarette out. He yanked open the conference room door, stepping exaggeratedly aside to let Charlie go first.

"Charlie! De-lighted!" Beaming, Edgar Westermann welcomed the mayor to his own conference room. "And Don."

"Edgar." Charlie poured himself coffee. Don took his usual chair at the end of the table with his usual scowl. No, Charlie thought: deeper than usual. "Wish I could return the sentiment," the mayor told the Borough President. "But I'm rarely delighted to see people who call me scum on the six o'clock news."

"Now, Charlie—"

"Don thinks I should have told you to suck eggs, and I did consider it." The mayor slipped into his chair. "On the other hand, people who call me scum usually don't ask for meetings. The floor's yours, Edgar."

"Now, Charlie." Westermann smiled again. "You know as well as anybody news conferences are mostly rhetoric. Got to give the people what they want! Don't make it colorful, who's going to listen?"

"I'm listening now. But skip the color. I don't have all day."

"Me, either. Lots to do, on this mayoral campaign. Though I got to say, I'm shaping up to be luckier than you, first time you ran. Terms of opposition, doesn't look like I have much to worry about."

"Congratulations."

"Yessir, I got Harlem behind me, Brooklyn and the Bronx. I got right-thinking New Yorkers behind me. Edgar Westermann's going to give the disenfranchised a voice, give the disrespected their day in the sun—"

"And give his campaign speech every chance he gets. But not here. Do you really want something? Or did you just come to gloat?"

"Gloat? Oh, Charlie, no, no!" Westermann's fingers circled above the cookies on his plate. "Charlie, you got yourself into a tight spot. You made a bunch of mistakes, I guess. But I know you're not a bad man, no matter what anybody says."

"Including you."

Munching, Westermann nodded. "Possible I did go overboard, way I spoke about you. I want to make amends. We've always been able to work together, Charlie, no matter our differences. No reason that should change now. I'm here to suggest we bury the hatchet."

"Really." Charlie sipped his coffee.

"Lots of acrimony, distrust of politicians going around New York right now, since this mess with Glybenhall and Lowry. Cynicism everywhere you look. Now, the signs all point to me getting elected, but I don't want to be mayor of a divided New York. And you, Charlie, you still got your eye on Albany, right? Well, then, seems to me we can help each other out."

"You're offering to rehabilitate my image. Make me look like a good guy again."

"Everybody makes mistakes. Voters'll understand that."

"And you'll tell them, because who better to hose off the shit than the guy who threw it? But damn, Edgar, I'm still the one getting hosed."

"Whoa, now, Charlie—"

"So in return for a little image-polishing, you want me to help *you* out with this 'divided New York' problem. You'll deliver the urban vote to get me to Albany. And I'll deliver . . . what?"

"Charlie, now don't underestimate yourself. You still got lots of supporters. Voters out in Queens, Staten Island—"

"Oh, come off it, Edgar! You don't give a damn about them. You're after money. You want me to smooth your way with the real estate and corporate people. You want access to the old boys' network and the heavy hitters. That's the only divide you want to erase. Well, you're welcome to them, but you'll have to do it without me. Not interested, Edgar."

Frowning, Don shifted in his chair. *Sorry, Don,* Charlie thought, *but you don't like that, wait until you hear the rest.*

The Borough President regarded the mayor through narrowed eyes. "Don't mind my saying so, you're making a mistake, Charlie."

"You, too, Edgar. The whole goddamn point of that press conference was to back me into a corner so I'd need your help getting out. Bury the hatchet? Bullshit. I've underestimated you, but I guess a lot of people do. That's what the damn-if-I-ain't-just-a-homeboy act's *for.* Like when you came here to 'warn' me about Ann Montgomery. Don and I shook our heads afterward and said, Shit, Edgar's done it again. Telling me about her history with Glybenhall just about ensured she'd have to stay on the case. Because how would it look if I took her off? Damn, we said to each other, Edgar wasn't thinking."

Don uncrossed and recrossed his legs, sat forward, sat back. He pulled his cigarette pack from his pocket but slapped it down without taking out a smoke.

"But we were wrong," Charlie went on to Westermann. "You *were* thinking. Or, Walter was thinking. Walter needed Montgomery to stay so he sent you to do his dirty work. Lowry wasn't Walter's only puppet. You were, too, weren't you? Blowfish said he got Jen Eliot's chain from you. That's true, isn't it? You went to Walter with Cole's story about Corrington and the Eliot girl, and Walter gave you the goddamn chain to plant! *Jesus Christ, Don, would you hold still?* Edgar, you're as dirty as anyone else in this. I can't prove it but I *can* tell you to take your help and shove it up your ass."

The silence was so complete Charlie could hear a bird tweet in the park.

"Charlie." Westermann spoke with cold control. "Talk like that could do our friendship some serious damage. But I'm going to do the Christian thing and forgive you. You've been under a lot of stress and I know you don't mean none of that. And as your friend, I suggest you reconsider my offer. You won't get to Albany without my help."

Oh, well, now's as good as any other time. "I'm not running."

It was a stop-motion moment: Westermann's sugar cookie hovering halfway to his mouth; and Don, frozen mid-fidget, immobile for what might be the first time in all the years Charlie had known him. Except for the color draining from his face.

"I'm sorry." Charlie addressed his deputy mayor. "This wasn't the greatest timing, Don, here in a meeting like this. But I've had it." He turned back to Westermann, as though the Borough President, soon to be mayor, deserved an explanation. "Walter was a greedy, pompous bastard, and Lowry was a dirty cop. Those gang bangers, well . . . And the Eliot girl? Anyone with the bad judgment to sleep with Walter, what could she expect? And the Winston woman was just collateral damage. See? I'm cynical and greedy enough myself, it seems, to be able to write all that off and keep going. But Ford Corrington—Corrington was something else. He wasn't like you, Edgar, and me, and every other son of a bitch in this city who claims to be the Second Coming. Corrington and the Garden Project actually did people some good."

Westermann gripped the table edge with fat fingers. Icily, he said, "The Garden Project's still there. Reverend Holdsclaw's taking it over."

"Not the point," the mayor said.

"What the hell is the point?"

Charlie turned in wonder. That outburst came not from Westermann, but from Don. "Did you—"

"What the hell do you mean, *you're not running?*"

Color had come back to Don's face; in fact Charlie had never seen him this red. Or heard him speak in a meeting, in eighteen years.

"I'm sorry," Charlie said again. "But I'm through. This is all on me. It all goes back to my deal with Walter."

"Oh, what *bullshit!* No mayor ever born wouldn't have made that deal!"

"Ah." Charlie smiled sadly. "But I was supposed to be different. You know, though, it's not even that I was willing to make the deal. It's that I'd convinced myself it was a *good* deal. The Bronx would get a nice project, Harlem would get a boost. Walter's help would make me governor and then I'd be able to do even more good. It was horseshit. And I sold it to myself and I bought it. I don't mind so much being a bad, bad man. What I mind is that I never noticed I was one."

Don stared. "This is why Louise left you."

The mayor nodded. "Not because I'm in trouble. Because I don't care. She'd be right here doing stand-by-your-man if I ran and lost. But choosing not to run—it was as though she found out I'd used a false name when I married her."

Westermann cleared his throat. "Now, Charlie—"

"Oh, shut up, Edgar. One of the great things about leaving politics is I won't have to listen to you anymore."

"You can't." Don's voice was rough. "You can't do this. After what I—"

"Don, I know how hard you've worked," Charlie told him. "I understand how you feel. But it's over."

"You have no fucking idea!" Don exploded from his chair and strode back and forth across the end of the room, as though lost in the woods, searching for the path.

"Don? It's not—"

"Fuck, Charlie!" Don whipped a folded paper from his pocket and slammed it onto the table.

"What's that?"

"The text of an e-mail," Don said tightly. "From Jen to me. A Dear John letter."

"I thought *you* broke up with *her.*"

"I did. But I felt guilty. This was her way of telling me not to worry."

Charlie glanced from Don to Edgar, reached for the paper, and started to read. He felt his skin grow cold. "Wait. I don't get it," he said, rereading, hoping that was true, that he wasn't getting it.

"She was seeing someone new. And to prove she wasn't mad, that she really wanted to stay friends, she told me who. So we'd share a secret. Like friends do."

"But . . ." the mayor breathed. "But Walter . . . we all thought it was *Walter.*"

"It wasn't Walter," Don said. "You bastard, Westermann. It was *you.*"

Another frozen moment.

"Don?" Charlie said. "You knew this? Why didn't you—"

"What? Tell the police? Think how that would've looked! Think what we were in the middle of!"

"How it would have *looked?* What the hell difference does that make? The girl was *dead!*"

"It would have sunk you! Us going after Westermann at that point!"

"You got this long before any 'point.' "

"But it didn't matter until she was dead. By then your connection with Glybenhall was sucking you under. It would've looked like us creating a diversion, playing the race card, deflecting attention to a controversial black leader—Jesus, Charlie, you'd have been history before the eleven o'clock news!"

Charlie stared at his deputy mayor. "You kept quiet to protect my career?"

Don jacked a cigarette. "When Cole came to me with the chain setup, I steered him to Edgar. I hoped that would get Edgar caught without you being involved. When that didn't work out . . ." He shrugged, didn't meet Charlie's eye.

"Oh, my God. You bought it, too," Charlie said. "The horseshit I was selling. All the good I could do. You bought it." He shook his head, told Don, "I'm sorry."

"*You're* sorry? Don't you get it?"

"Get what?"

"If I'd dropped the dime, Montgomery wouldn't have focused on Glybenhall for Jen's murder. This bullshit with the chain in Corrington's garden wouldn't have happened. Corrington would be alive, probably Glybenhall and Lowry, too. Louise wouldn't . . . This all would have been over weeks ago when it *looked* like it was over."

"And Walter and Lowry would have gotten away with their whole goddamn scheme!"

"And you'd be on your way to Albany! You'd have stayed on top!"

On top, Charlie thought. His whole political life, he'd been on top. You'd think from on top you'd have the broadest view, but it didn't turn out like that.

"*I'm* sorry," Don said.

"It doesn't matter."

"It—"

"No. It really doesn't."

Westermann shifted his bulk like an earthquake, and stood. "Well, this here's a touching scene, y'all apologizing to each other and talking about me like I wasn't here, but I got to be running along. That thing"— he pointed to the paper in Charlie's hand—"ain't but the purest bull. I got no idea why this girl wanted to scandalize my name like that, but I never even met her. I do feel sorry for her, though. Sounds like she was a disturbed little thing. Don, I know you got no intention of making more trouble for Charlie, or yourself, by spreading groundless gossip. I know you're planning on feeding that into the shredder directly."

"I just want to know why you killed her," Don said.

"I did not even know her."

"Well, good," Don said. "Then you have nothing to worry about. No forensic evidence in your house, your car. No credit card bills for romantic hideaways where someone will remember you and your little blonde girlfriend. No jewelry, no perfume. Shalimar, that's what she wore. No calls to you in her phone records. What a relief."

"Ridiculous," Westermann sputtered. "And insulting as all get-out. You're—"

"That's why you had the chain. That was the one thing Glybenhall said that was true: he had nothing to do with Jen's death."

Westermann's eyes flicked from Charlie to Don. "Okay. Maybe I knew her. Maybe I even had a fling with her. Hard for any red-blooded man to resist a cute piece like that throwing herself at him. Surprised *you* was able to turn her down, Don. But it didn't last long, me and her. And that chain, she gave it to me. As a going-away present, when she quit me."

"Bullshit! She got that from her college sweetheart and never took it off for any man since. There's—"

"They were friends." Charlie was shocked to hear his own voice, but it seemed to have something to say. "Ann Montgomery and Jen Eliot. Jen must have figured out Walter's scheme to set Montgomery up. So Walter and Lowry needed her dead. Walter *did* have something to do with her death, Don. He told Edgar to kill her."

"You think?" Don said. He turned back to Westermann. "Makes sense. And after that, Glybenhall blackmailed you into being part of his scheme."

"I'm telling you, I didn't—"

"Oh, screw it. Let the cops and the DA figure it out." Don ground out his cigarette. He headed for the phone on the sideboard, but Westermann stepped into his way. Charlie felt a sudden pressure drop like the one that stills birds and grasses before a storm.

"Don." Westermann finally spoke, quietly, shaking his head. "Don, Don. And Charlie. I had no idea you were both so dumb." Rocking on his heels, slipping his hands into his pockets, he looked for all the world like he was about to offer them some gem of down-home country wisdom. "Walter Glybenhall, criminal mastermind, forcing that buffoon Edgar Westermann into doing his dirty. That's how you got this figured, right? You're as big a pair of fools as they were. Glybenhall and Lowry? They didn't dream that scheme up. They didn't neither of 'em have the brains. I did."

Charlie stared at the Borough President and marveled: *Nothing sane ever happens in this room anymore.*

"Yeah, me. Sorry-ass ol' Edgar Westermann. See, Charlie, there you was, fixing to run for governor. Now, long as you was in the picture in the state of New York, doin' the nasty with Walter Glybenhall and his high-rolling homeboys, Borough President was as far as Edgar Westermann was about to get. After all, last and only black mayor New York had was all Brooks Brothers and tennis racket. To lots of folks up in Harlem, he was a white man passing.

"So I said to myself, so what? Maybe politics ain't all that. Maybe it's time to retire. But how I'm gonna do that, on what I been paid, all my years as a dedicated public servant?"

Westermann, Charlie noted, had the street-talk valves wide open.

"Well, I ain't got your connections, Charlie, but I got some eyes and ears. It came to my attention Walter Glybenhall was spending time in Harlem, staring through a ripped-up fence. Why? I wondered. So I did some snooping. Who owned that site, what they had in mind. Turned out the city owned it! Well, I thought, ain't that the damndest thing?

"Whole thing you and Glybenhall was scheming wasn't hard to figure out, Charlie. Him building up in the Bronx and all. Big question was, how was I gonna turn what you got goin' to Edgar Westermann's advantage?

"As I'm studying on this, damned if Ford Corrington don't come to me with *his* plan for the site, see if he could drum up support. Now there was a boy who really *did* want to bury the hatchet, so we could show the world Harlem united." He smiled and shook his head. "Well, I thought, this is tasty. Next step, a couple of glasses of gin with Glybenhall, and I got him believing Corrington's in bed with you, Charlie. Good work, Westermann, I thought, and now what?

"And then one evening I'm drinking champagne with Glybenhall at some fundraiser, and he points out a tall blonde. 'Drop-dead gorgeous,' I say, and Glybenhall says he's the one she wants to drop dead. Tells me a little about her, how they go way back, and I get a vision. An inspiration, Charlie. By God, it's genius.

"Next morning I put in a call to Greg Lowry. I knew how pissed he was when you gave Shapiro his job—oh, come on, Charlie, you know it should've been his. All I did, I helped that seed grow. Fertilized it with some prime manure, if I do say so myself. But see how beautiful it was? I hit my ceiling because of blackness. Lowry hit his because of whiteness.

"I worked the whole thing out and explained it to them, because they wasn't either of 'em too swift. How we was all gonna get rich in spite of the double-cross you was pulling on Glybenhall. As a matter of fact, *because* of it. Say what? You wasn't? That made it even sweeter, Charlie, take my word."

Westermann had been resting a cordial, professorial gaze on the mayor. Now he turned to Don Zalensky and sighed. "But it's always a woman gets you in the end, ain't it? We didn't plan on no one getting killed, just enough accidents up in the Bronx that DOI would have to look into it. Hired Sonny O'Doul because we knew that would get Montgomery's goat. All we wanted was for Montgomery to smear Glybenhall bad enough so he could turn around and sue. But when them bricks bashed poor Harriet Winston's head in, Lowry panicked. Stupid s.o.b. called me at home, middle of the night. I told him to calm his ass down, move the schedule, bring Montgomery in right away.

"And damn if Jen didn't hear me."

He shook his head sadly.

"I did everything else right. Every screwup, everything we didn't foresee, I came up with something, make the plan work even better. That shit with Glybenhall's gun, after it got to be obvious we had to get rid of Kong . . . That was Lowry who did him, by the way. Lowry was our hands-on guy. Glybenhall, he used some of them germ-killing wipes every time he went to Harlem, even if he never got out of the car. I can't truly say, Charlie, that it grieves me to see him dead." Westermann sighed again. "No, I was damn good. Just that one mistake."

"Killing Jen," Don whispered.

Charlie was impressed that Don could talk at all; he felt completely paralyzed, himself.

Westermann's eyebrows rose. "What? No, definitely not. That, I was just doing what I had to do. No, my only bad was, I kept the chain. But damn! She was so beautiful."

A tree branch outside the window bounced as a bird landed on it. So apparently some things could move. It seemed Don could, too: after a long stare at Westermann, he headed once again for the phone. Once again, Westermann stepped in front of him, and from his pocket he pulled a small silver pistol.

Suddenly, Charlie was loose, free. "How the hell did you get that up here? The metal detector—my policy—"

"Oh, Charlie! Of course I went through the damn thing, offensive as it is. The guards know I carry this. I'm President of the Borough of Manhattan, Charlie. It's a dangerous job."

Westermann didn't move, Don didn't move. Westermann's pistol, pointed midway between Charlie and Don as though ready for either one, didn't move.

Charlie did. He pushed back his chair and stood, starting toward Westermann. "Edgar, you can't be planning to use that. Shooting the mayor and the deputy mayor in City Hall? You'd never make it to the door."

"Wish I'd known how slow on the uptake you was all along, Charlie,"

Westermann said. "Would've made my life a lot easier. Damn right I'm planning to use it." He lifted the gun. Charlie was never sure he actually heard the shot. But for the rest of his life he remembered Westermann's blood splashing crimson on the window, blocking out the green leaves beyond.

Heart's Content

Joe walked onto the porch, watched the late-day breeze play with Ann's golden hair. Watched her permit this, make no effort to smooth and order.

"You're looking better," he said as he sat.

"Than this morning?"

"Than ever." When he kissed her, she tasted of spice, a promise of sweetness.

As they settled back in their chairs she scowled. "You brought the New York papers."

"I'm afraid you need to see this."

"No, I don't."

Amazing, what had happened. In the weeks since Corrington, Lowry, and Glybenhall died (upstate cops crushing his lilies as ruthlessly as the NYPD trampled Corrington's tomato patch), Ann had not left his cabin and yard, except one early morning when, alone, she'd driven to Skidmore to see the pear trees and the theater. She woke with him as the sun rose, sat on the porch with him drinking coffee; after he left she read, sat by the stream, listened to the radio but always turned it off when Joe came home because she understood about the silence. Her black eye, the gash on her arm, all her scrapes and bruises were fading. She'd made herself available to any cop who wanted to question her— local cops, and cops who came up from New York: her friend Perez, who called her "Princess"; Dennis Graham, the DOI wunderkind; Tom Underhill; three or four or a dozen others. She'd also made it clear she would not be going back to New York for some time.

"You're a material witness," one of the cops, not a friend, had started. "If we need you to testify—"

She'd cut him off: "At what trial? Everyone's dead."

So while Joe went out and spread gravel and asphalt, Ann sat at anchor on his porch.

She had not wanted the news from New York. He, though, found he couldn't get enough of it.

He was fascinated every time a pebble from this case rippled the water. A fiery first-term Councilmember, strikingly reminiscent of the young Charlie Barr, was demanding an overhaul of the city's real estate procedures. Calls had gone out for more stringent security rules for building sites. A museum in St. Louis had fired its architect, Henry M. Martin, with a terse statement citing "philosophical disagreements." To make sure he missed nothing, Joe had taken to buying the New York dailies. And to his own surprise he'd found this wasn't the only story that interested him. He'd page through the papers, following threads, having opinions, formulating arguments pro and con. None of which he shared with Ann; what he shared was his surprise to find it happening at all. And he always tossed the papers away before he went home because he, too, understood about the silence.

But what had happened today, she needed to see.

Sutton Place

"Oh, my God." Ann felt her blood freeze as she read the paper Joe had handed her. "Oh, God, Joe. Westermann?"

"Seems that way."

"But Walter . . ."

She felt Joe's eyes on her but couldn't meet them. She ran through the article again, as though it might change.

"I could have—"

"Nothing. You couldn't have done anything."

"If I hadn't been so idiotically fixated on Walter—"

"Jen's murder wasn't your job. Everything else you thought about Glybenhall was true."

"But if I'd . . ."

"You didn't."

"What?"

"Whatever you were going to say you should have done, might have done, wish you'd done. Whatever it is, you didn't, and you can't, and this is where we are now."

She looked up at him. "Where we are?"

"Here." He spread his arms, showed her the garden. "Come with me."

She followed him across the yard to the hill, where the rudbeckia was now as high as her waist. "They need to be weeded," Joe said.

Ann stood, unsure, no direction to go.

"It's going to rain." Joe crouched by the flower bed, started to work, separating the things he didn't want to keep from the things he did.

Ann looked up. Opulent clouds floated in the sapphire sky. *Rain?* She didn't know how he knew that, didn't know if it was true. *Well,* she thought, *I guess I'll have to wait and see.*

She knelt and joined him.